Trailblazing

TEE

Fulton Books, Inc.
Meadville, PA

Published by Fulton Books 2020

ISBN 978-1-64654-396-0 (paperback)
ISBN 978-1-64654-397-7 (digital)

Printed in the United States of America

This novel is dedicated to the Urban struggle and the solution We are responsible to bring about. Be sure to enjoy the action, all while recognizing the lessons.

Contents

Prologue

❖❖❖❖❖

January 24, 2001

"Manny, I miss all the little things we used ta do together." Trina pouted in the middle of their conversation. "Remember when—"

Her words were cut short as Manny began to back up and seemed to fade away.

Manny spoke with a chuckle. "You aight, yo. Trust me, you good."

"No! Wait!" Trina was hysterical. "Don't go!"

It was too late. Manny was gone.

Trina was sitting upright in her bed, in a shallow sweat. Her heart raced for a moment, then she lay back down, to close her eyes and see Manny again, even if it was just a dream.

Something was terribly wrong in Trina's bedroom. What was wrong wasn't inside of her home, though; it was housed in the mind of her man. He didn't even budge when she jolted from her dream. She wanted badly to know what was wrong but knew that finding out would be next to impossible. Troy wasn't exactly secretive when it came to her, but he unapologetically protected her from information and situations he felt could be disheartening or harmful. She truly appreciated his guard but often felt overprotected.

The entire apartment was still. The only prominent sound was the ventilation system's soft purr as it pushed out a comfortable, warm current. Trina hardly made additional noise when she rolled over in the soft king-size bed and rested her head on Troy's chest. The off-white satin sheets titillated the hairs on her nakedness, allowing for a discreet appreciation of the self-gratifying pleasure. The familiar musk of Dial soap, along with the natural masculine scent of his body, was both pleasing and suspect but placed her in a state of complacent security.

His chest moved up and down with an even thump and rhythm that interrupted the ventilation system's purr. It drew her attention completely to her man. He was awake, his hard brown eyes burning a hole in a single spot on the ceiling. Both hands were clasped behind his head. The steam emitting from his nose and ears was merely a figment of her imagination, but his mood was evident.

She peeked over at the black marble nightstand. The large red numbers read 6:33 a.m. on the digital clock.

Troy never liked to be up in the mornings, but instead of immediately voicing her concern, she lay in silence, consumed in her own thoughts.

She adored the diverse array of memorabilia around the room. Some reflected the times they shared together; most illustrated who Troy, the person, was.

Two large framed pictures of his favorite rap and R&B artists, R. Kelly and Scarface, dominated one wall. The Boston Celtics All-Star Paul Pierce had nearly a wall of his own. Troy's most personal wall was filled with strong, influential leaders from the past and present.

Trina smiled at the picture of her with R. Kelly and LL Cool J on top of the large dresser. She looked so young with her short dreads and most cherished Cuban link necklace. That was a very special memory. That was a day she would never forget.

Three-foot-tall African sculptures stood in two corners. Smaller warrior-like ones guarded the bureau and large dresser. Troy's recent interest in this form of art was a mystery to her, but she found it very exquisite and tasteful.

It was no mystery that his love of plants, not flowers, came from Joyce. In fact, the large spider plant that he had had since it was a baby was now full-grown and crawled along the white walls and ceiling, enclosing the entire room in its web, as did Troy's presence wherever he was.

Troy was Trina's ideal mate—intelligent, handsome, business savvy, and thugged out. He reminded her of Manny in so many ways, which drew her even closer to him. Her mind often wandered to Manny while she was around him. She was proud to represent Troy and reflect his light, whether in his presence or absence. Troy Newton was Trina's everything!

There was absolutely nothing she would not do for him, and there wasn't a shadow of a doubt in her mind that the feeling was mutual. Without Troy, Trina would be a mere fraction of the woman she was.

Trina instinctively grazed her nails across Troy's chest. She asked, "What's wrong, baby?"

They had been together for four years, and for the past eleven months, they had lived together in a downtown Boston luxury pad. There wasn't much that he could keep from her. She had a gift of reading him since the first day they met.

"Ain't nothing," he lied. "I just woke up and couldn't get back ta sleep."

Troy had an unnerving confrontation with his brother the night before, which was stirring up a mixture of concern and anger. That was really why he'd been awake and staring at the ceiling for nearly an hour.

Rather than prying, Trina figured she'd interrupt his troubling thoughts. "If it ain't nothing, then come give me some good morning loving," she said while rubbing her lips around his nipples, sliding her hand down to grip his dick.

The tension released from his face. "You know I can't deny you that."

He parted his legs wider as she traced his six-pack with her tongue, through his pubic hairs, and landed her warm mouth on the head of his shaft. He sighed, lay back, and enjoyed her work. She was always more than a pretty face and fuck to him. She always did the right things at the right time in their relationship.

Trina squeezed his nipple with her free hand while humming, slobbering, and bobbing down low. She let his polished pole lie on her cheek, while she skillfully used her tongue to circle and lift his balls into her mouth. A mischievous smirk materialized as she commended herself for her desire and ability to be the freak her man desired.

He gyrated his hips and gripped a fistful of her shoulder-length dreads, all to her satisfaction. His dick wanted to explode, but Trina was just getting started.

She pulled her mouth away and continued an expert tongue motion between his thighs all the way back up to his neck.

"You want ya pussy, Daddy?" she asked while straddling him. Her soft, light eyes stared deep into his. "I need that thick chocolate, baby. You wit it or what?" She wore a naughty smirk on her round face, showing off deep cheeks and chin dimples.

Troy admired all her attributes but mainly focused on the large melons with Hershey Kiss nipples she was shaking in front of his face. It took her no effort to keep a flat stomach, nice hips, and firm ass. He had to put in work to maintain his solid two-twenty on a six-four frame.

"If you woman enough, go head and take it," he challenged. "See if you can handle all this meat."

Troy matching her wit made Trina even hotter. She palmed his dick, rubbed his mushroom around on her tender clit, and clenched her teeth. Seconds later, she began panting until she released a small but satisfying orgasm. She gave a quenching, lip-licking grin, then worked her hips 'round and 'round, up and down, until her walls swallowed him inside of her. He shocked her body, quickly taking away the control she had when he gripped her small waist. He began to roughly push in and out of her. His ass left the mattress with each powerful lunge. He controlled her movement, bouncing her up and down on top of him like a pogo stick.

"Owwe! T-Troy…baby! Ahh!"

"This what you asked for, girl, ain't it? Huh?" He thrust upward, hard. "Huh?" he repeated.

She understood. He was taking out his built-up frustration on her innocent vagina. It felt good but hurt like hell too. Her goal was being accomplished. She disregarded the pain. "Yes, baby! I asked for it!" Her titties bounced wildly. "Tear this pussy up! Oooh...tear it up!"

Troy gave his woman all she could handle. She clawed his chest, sucked hickeys into his neck, all while begging, pleading, and enjoying the pain that brought so much pleasure to her soul.

When he ejaculated, her egg readily accepted his seed of life for the first time.

Trina collapsed on top of him, and with no confirmation from him being necessary, she assured him, "You and ya brother will get through this. Just stay strong for both of ya'll."

They fell back to sleep in each other's arms. Mission accomplished. Her man's mind was at ease.

Chapter 1

Four and a half years earlier

Orchard Park (OP) was one of the larger housing projects in the city of Boston (the Bean). A mixture of preteens to senior citizens, hustlers to addicts, criminals to law abiders moved in unison inside its perimeters from sunup to sundown. Hardship was commonplace. The lower-class working family seemed like they could be counted on one pair of hands.

Forty to fifty three-story redbrick buildings, with four congested apartments on each floor, were the primary structures. Hallways were graffiti filled, cement walls with trash, and urine-stained stairwells at given times throughout the year. Broken glass, used syringes and dilapidated concrete made a hazardous environment for children, but were the norm in the projects. Those conditions went ignored by residents and authorities the same.

OP was the poster child of poverty, problems, and pride. Some wondered if Dorothy would've clicked her heels three times to get back there.

Assorted apartments and neighborhood businesses were effortlessly scattered around the outskirts of the projects' bricks. The neighborhood was Dudley Square. The sizable Dudley Station sat in the center of it all with a constant flow of mainly minorities, buses, and trains through its subway system.

Roxbury (the Bury, as residents affectionately called it) was one of Boston's poorest ghettos. Dudley Square was well-known as the heart of the Bury.

Neighborhood gangs made up the streets and projects of the Bury and the Bean on a whole. Gang members were often identified by sports logo, worn mostly on hats, but on other apparel as well. OP was recognized by their red and black colors and Portland Trailblazers logo, known around the Bean as the OP Trailblazers.

"Yo, Rick! I got next!" Troy yelled as he walked into the projects park.

Troy's broad nose crinkled from the smell coming off the three-day-old corpse of a cat on the side of a building. The harmless animal was tortured by a group of children. The smell wasn't foreign in the projects. Troy knew that it would simply blend with the normal air after a few moments.

It was a beautiful June afternoon two days after school let out for the summer, a perfect day for a game of basketball.

OP's park was large. On the side that Troy entered, there was one full-length basketball court. It was fenced in from a side street on one end and from a cement walk on the other.

A smaller quarter court, with an eight-foot rim, was on the side of the larger one. It was usually used for one-on-one and two-on-two grudge matches. A few run-down picnic tables were built into a dirt area between the two ball courts. When the quarter-court's hoop got torn down, as it often did, a crate was nailed to a lone leafless tree in the dirt area.

The grudge matches continued.

The other side of the park had the main entrance to a large baseball field. The field was rarely, if ever, used by project kids to play baseball. The whole field was so polluted that it was primarily used as a hangout and shortcut across the projects.

Two wood-surrounded sandboxes, with swings and jungle gyms, bordered two more full-length basketball courts. These courts were often the ones used when it came to inner-city league games.

Rick yelled back to Troy as soon as they stopped play for a moment on the court. "Damn, dogg! Why you ain't get here ten minutes earlier, so you could've been my second-in-command, knocking these scrubs off?" He pointed at his brother, who was teamed up with Ace, Terell, and the twins, Eric and Derrick.

"I had ta get my hair braided, but I'm here now, and I already got my five, so you better win." Troy tied his do-rag over his fresh corn braids as he spoke and prepared to play.

"Whatever, dogg," Rick said confidently. "I just gotta step my game up." He shot a long-range jumper through the netless rim. Besides Troy, Rick was the best thing happening on a ball court in OP.

Troy scanned the crowded park, acknowledging all his people with nods and hand gestures while he stretched out. The park was full.

Orchard Park was its own tight-knit community. The majority of its occupants were second- through fourth-generation residents. Sometimes, friends wouldn't find out until their teenaged years that they were actually more than just friends. Their bloodlines ran secretly through the teenaged years of their parents, uncles, and aunts.

There was no shame in hanging clothes out to dry on long clotheslines used by the entire projects. Neighbors knocked on one another's doors, requesting to borrow food, money, and even more personal things. The village, or in this case, the projects, truly did raise the child.

Troy laughed to himself as he watched Jimmy tossing his two-year-old, Junior, high in the air, scaring little Jimmy's mother with each toss and landing. Crystal slapped Jimmy's arms and tried to take her son from him every time he landed safely. Jimmy bobbed, weaved, and blocked with his shoulders, preventing all her rescue attempts. Even Jimmy Jr. seemed to be enjoying his mother's concern. He just laughed and drooled as she fought for his safety.

Jimmy had three years on Troy. He was a well-respected enforcer in the projects. He had a dangerously serious aura too. All his peers were from OP. There was never a question where his loyalty began and ended. He loved his projects and despised his enemies.

Jimmy Jr. was the best thing that could've happened to Jimmy—it was a literal life changer. He brought out a warmth in his father that even Crystal didn't know existed. Jimmy unashamedly accepted that he was only a role model to an upcoming Blazer. He made it a point to show Junior a better way, even if that meant trusting pieces of his son's development with men on a straighter path than he was.

"Damn, dogg! I was looking for ya charcoal-face ass all day! On, doggs!" Jermel barked as he approached with a stretched-out, open hand for some dap.

Troy reached out and met his embrace. "Why you looking for me? You tryna ball too?" Troy joked, knowing that Jermel didn't know anything about sports and definitely didn't play any.

Whenever Troy was around a ball court, he was one of the first picks. His reputation was one of the best ballplayers in the city, a born winner.

At six-four, two-ten, he was known to leap taller buildings than a superhero. As an all-scholastic, highly recruited shooting guard entering his senior year at Madison Park High School (MP), he was well-known throughout the city's sports circles.

Jermel was the opposite of Troy in many ways, yet still a perfect match. They were both players, hustlers, and though Troy didn't revel in violence like Jermel did, violence was a part of them.

Jermel couldn't care less about sports but loved to watch Troy play. Troy loved all sports. Jermel was only streetwise, but Troy was even wiser than him in the streets, as well as formally gifted in a classroom. Jermel dropped out of MP when he and Troy were just beginning their sophomore year. As they started making a little money in the streets, he saw no need to keep struggling inside of a worthless classroom. Where Troy was cordial at times, Jermel was almost always hostile.

They were both young and fly, but with completely different physical makeups. Jermel was six-foot even, a pudgy two-thirty, a teddy bear who easily morphed into a grizzly. Confidence was never one of his lows. He had smooth, peanut butter skin, silky curly black hair, with hazel eyes as hard as rocks. The hard stare from Jermel's hazels usually put a chill in others. It was mainly the result of a rough, painful childhood at the hands of an abusive father and crack-addicted, prostituting mother. When his father's mangled body was found decapitated by a train in the middle of Dudley Station's train tracks, Jermel was only eight years old. The death didn't pain him like the loss of a parent would the average child. Though his young mind couldn't actually comprehend it at that time, that was the first experience that allowed him to see how cold he was inside, cold as ice.

Troy and Jermel lived in the same 890 Albany Street building, Troy on the first floor, Jermel on the second. They were best friends since the womb. The entire projects referred to both only children to their parents as brothers. They saw themselves as nothing less than actual siblings.

Everything they knew in their young lives, they learned together the hard way. They looted corner stores and malls, fought side by side, kissed and humped girls when they were as young as seven, got ass whoopings from just about every parent in the projects, their village. Eventually, out of necessity, they got into robbing and selling crack as early as eleven years old.

When Troy grabbed Jermel's extended hand, he added a strong left-armed hug to go with their dap. "What up, dogg? What you looking for me for? I told you I was getting my hair braided in Kiki's building."

"You hit it?" That was always Jermel's question whenever it came to females. "I need ta let her sexy ass play in my hair so I can play in that coochie."

"Me and Kiki's just cool, yo. I ain't tryna tap that."

Jermel swatted the air, ignoring Troy's reply. "Whatever, dogg." Troy always had a secret dime piece in the cut, so Jermel assumed he hit it regardless. "Check this out, though, dogg. Even though Ella mad at me, you know her ass ain't going nowhere, right?"

"Of course, dogg. Ya'll should've been married by now. What up with my sis? I knew you had ta be fuckin' up again, 'cause I ain't seen her around in a couple weeks."

"Why I gotta be the one fuckin' up?"

It was Troy's turn to swat the air. "Whatever, dogg."

"Anyway!" Jermel turned his lip up. "She just be acting sometimes. She be on some bullshit! Fuck that, though. I finished tearing that ass up earlier, and as I was creeping out her crib, I caught some of them kids slippin', shooting dice in her building. Them clowns never even saw me coming till I had my fever pointed at they ass, laying 'em down and runnin' they pockets. I came up on twenty-three hundred and some jewels. I'm pawning the jewels. Here, take this stack," he finished with a smirk while tossing Troy some rubber band-wrapped bills.

Troy put the money in his sweatpants pocket while eyeing Jermel suspiciously.

"What?" Jermel asked, uncomfortable under the obvious scrutiny.

"I hope you was masked up."

"Nah, I ain't have time. I—"

Troy cut him off forcefully. "Man, I told you about that dumb shit! You gonna make us and the whole damn projects catch unnecessary beef behind that shit! On, doggs! Why the heck you think we keep masks on us? They ain't for show! Did you even have one with you?" When Troy vented, he was a force. His swarthy, dark skin seemed to turn purple. A large vein popped out of his neck. His warm, welcoming gaze turned chilled and uninviting. His baseball glove-sized hands swung all over the place as he went off on Jermel.

Troy and Jermel clashing was the equivalent of a silverback meeting head-on with a grizzly. Jermel was one of not many who knew Troy's tendencies but would still disregard his tirades at times.

Now was one of those times.

"Dogg, go 'head with that bullshit, 'cause I ain't tryna hear it!" he snapped back. "Fuck them chumps! We already beefin', so muthafuckas better stay on point, anyway! I caught them slippin', so I—"

As if on cue with his statement, a shout came from a slow-rolling maroon Nissan Maxima outside of the park's fence. "There that sucka go right there!" Familiar evil eyes locked in with Jermel's from the back seat.

The ten players on the basketball court were at the opposite end, arguing a call. They never even noticed the death on wheels or heard the shout. Most of the bystanders recognized the imminent danger, but their reactions widely varied.

Almost simultaneously with the shout came the sound of endless thunder as bullets filled the air like a swarm of killer bees.

Hocka hocka hocka hocka hocka!

Everyone in the park either hit the deck or scurried for cover.

The cement basketball court sent debris in all directions. Sparks jumped off the fences and metal poles that held the hoops as bullets struck them. Fleeing bodies crashed into one another and hit the ground, some getting trampled on in the melee.

To some, the park-turned-war-zone became a slow-motion picture of destruction, while others saw a scene of inescapable death that crept up and played out entirely too fast.

Jimmy tackled Crystal in the dirt, secured her and Jimmy Jr. under a picnic table, then came up firing.

Boom boom!

The slide of his .45 continuously clanked back, hard and fast, but it wasn't much of a match against their assailants' high-powered fully automatics. It served its purpose, though. It caused a faster retreat than the enemy intended.

It saved lives.

He knocked ten-year-old Kendra to the safety of the ground and never stopped squeezing his trigger in the process. There was no shock or hesitation in Jimmy's action. This was how he got down. This was what he did. These were the people he loved.

Troy and Jermel hit the ground when the shots rang out, fumbled with their waistlines, then began busting as soon as their guns were free. The majority of the assault from the car came in their direction, so they had to stay grounded for cover. Their defensive positions didn't allow them to get off good shots.

Other Blazers shot back also, but the return fire was too late. The element of surprise allowed the Maxima to cause maximum damage and flee.

The entire area smelled of gunpowder. Smoke hovered over the park like a storm cloud, ensuring disaster. When the panic-stricken crowd began to rise, people began to notice Chris and Jimmy remained down. Some rushed to their aid, but the outcome was visibly grave.

Jimmy was a deformed frame, bullet riddled and leaking a puddle. His eyes remained wide-open. One could only pray that his soul was headed in the direction of the heavens they appeared to gaze into.

Chris was choking on his own blood, clutching an area near his heart where a thick crimson blob protruded and oozed through his fingers.

"Daddy! Daddy!" Jimmy Jr. called out as he tried to pry himself away from his mother's grasp to run to his father.

Crystal held him tight to her bosom. Her body was in a trance, though she somehow managed to slowly move toward her childhood love, the only man she ever loved. When she was close enough to actually see the reality of Jimmy's demise, she dropped to her knees and lost it.

"No! Noooo! No! No! No! Jimmy, please! Please don't do this ta us! Please don't leave us!" Tears streamed down her cheeks.

A needle stabbed at her heart.

Jimmy Jr. cried with his mother. She rocked with him in her arms, never loosening her grip on the only continuation of Jimmy's life left in this world.

Ten-year-old Kendra stared back and forth between Jimmy, Chris, and the corpse of the cat. Tears welled in her eyes.

What was the difference?

It was her first time witnessing the death of a human being. She watched as a boy removed his shirt and applied pressure to Chris's wound, but the pain in his eyes said he wouldn't make it.

She knew Jimmy and Chris all ten years of her life. She complained for days about the smelly dead cat, but nobody listened and got rid of it. Now she saw it as a bad omen. Death was already a part of her life.

Everyone with drugs and guns scattered as police sirens neared the park. The ones who weren't dirty ran in the streets to flag them down, urging them to call an ambulance. By time the ambulance arrived, nearly fifteen critical minutes had passed. Chris's chances at life were next to none.

Troy and Jermel crashed through the door to their building and hopped two steps at a time up to Jermel's apartment. Fewer questions had to be answered at Jermel's crib, so it was always the understood crisis spot. Actually, no questions had to be answered at Jermel's crib; it was basically a parentless home.

When they got upstairs to the apartment, Troy went right back to blitzing on him. "I told ya stupid ass! Now you see? Damn! You never listen, dogg! I'm tired of answering ta these dudes about your shit! We gotta—"

He stopped midsentence. His body deflated.

"Damn, dogg…Jimmy and Chris looked bad." His head was shaking. "They ain't look good at all." His voice trailed off.

Chris was only fourteen, just getting his feet wet in the streets. He was nothing more than five six, a buck forty in full hockey pads. Though a slight stutter impeded his speech, he entertained crowds with a flawless flow when he rapped. His father, Reverend Childs, was a well-known and well-respected clergyman in the community, which meant a big deal would be made about the shooting.

"Damn, dogg. Damn…I ain't think them cats would come right back through like that. Damn." Jermel had his head in his hands as he slumped in the beat-up sofa. He was in obvious anguish.

Troy felt like telling him that he never thought, but instead he said, "You gotta be more mindful, dogg. I'll tell you what, though."

"What up?" Jermel's head popped up from his hands. His hazels told the violent story that they told so well.

"Them chumps ain't 'bout ta get that off on us!" Troy finished with deadly finality.

"That's my dogg!" Jermel got up and dapped him up. He got frustrated at times when Troy chastised him, but he knew that he was usually right. More importantly, he knew that his brother was with him 100 percent.

After Jermel rekindled the beef with OP's sworn enemy, Academy Homes (the A), it was evident that it was going to be a drama-filled summer.

Jimmy died, but Chris fortunately survived. Besides them, three more Blazers were wounded in the weeks following.

Both sides assailed on a weekly, sometimes daily, basis. Retaliation on the A was deadly and unprincipled.

When a young football star who graduated from West Roxbury High School and was on his way to Ohio State University was gunned down in the A, the Boston Police Department (BPD) came out in force. The victim, Manny Goslin, was shot at point-blank range by a single .357 bullet to the head. Manny Goslin wasn't gang affiliated or in the streets at all. Manny Goslin, like so many others in the ghetto, just happened to be in the wrong place at a fatally wrong time.

Though others from the A and OP were violently assaulted, it was Manny's high-profiled homicide that moved law enforcement to act. Most of the Blazers and A Team directly involved in the constant back-and-forth battle were juveniles. The BPD called on the Department of Youth Services (DYS) and juvenile probation officers to round up as many teens as they could who were under their supervision. This strategy had a positive effect on the immediate problem but by no means served as a permanent solution.

Loads of "at-risk" and "troubled" youth were scooped up and put behind bars for the summer. DYS tried to keep both sides separated in different facilities, but affiliates were sprinkled all through the system.

The attacks continued.

After six weeks of uncontrollable bloodshed, respected OGs from both sides had to step in and restore some sense of order. The situation was out of control, too dangerous for even the rough streets of the Bury. Parents and innocent residents lived in fear. Businesses closed early and refused some customers even when they were open. The media added unnecessary hype, further fueling the fire to the feud.

Pain.

Fear.

Mourning.

Anger.

These were all hazardous emotions mixed up with teenaged gang members with weapons.

Fortunately, the OGs were able to negotiate a temporary ceasefire. It was "temporary" because the tension was so tight it was understood that the slightest resistance could cause it to pop at any time. It was a given that some were just hotheaded, while others held different levels of hate. So when, not *if*, it would start up again was totally unpredictable.

Academy Homes was about two miles up the road from Orchard Park. The housing development was split in two sections.

One side consisted of a small number of brick buildings, similar to OP's, along with brownstone apartments and two-family duplex houses.

The other side was mostly duplexes and primarily too small two-story apartments that were built dangerously close together.

The split complex, in its entirety, occupied sections of two of the city's largest roads, Washington Street and Columbus Avenue, the former being labeled the Light Side, the latter the Dark Side.

Gang members from the A sported Atlanta Braves attire. Their closest allies, a stone's throw up the street in Egleston Square, wore Minnesota Timberwolves gear.

The Bean was definitely not the city for a person to be in if they didn't respect the dress code. A favorite baseball team worn in good sportsmanship could easily cost a person their life.

OP and the A were at odds with each other since the late eighties. Residents from both hoods had friends and even family in the opposing hood. Those who weren't gang affiliated had close relationships with one another. Respect existed despite the on-and-off beef.

There were times when groups or individuals from each hood encountered one another, and there were no problems. At other times, the hoods would bump heads and the gates of hell were opened. It was an unbalanced, unstable existence between the two, and the scale would continue to tip.

Chapter 2

✦ ✦ ✦ ✦ ✦

"Yo, dogg, I'm tired of pushing this bullshit ass-whip and dealing with all this comp out here," Troy vented to Jermel. "We need a real come-up before my last year kicks off. I'm tryna shine, dogg. On, doggs."

Troy was in an obvious foul mood. Money was slow on the hustle, the projects was hot due to the month and a half of heavy feuding with the A, and his mother had been chewing him out about all the shit he was getting into. His mother was the problem that was really getting to him. Jermel sat on a crate in front of their building, while Troy leaned against the doorway, almost seriously wondering if he could get away with strangling her.

Joyce Newton, Troy's mother, was a Kingdom Hall-going, *The Watchtower-* and *Awake!*-reading, door-knocking Jehovah's Witness. She tried to raise him so strict that it assisted in his rebellion against rules, religion, and many other areas of common civilization. Overall, they had a good bond, but she worked his nerves and he caused her many sleepless nights. His thoughts of strangling Joyce were easier imagined, so it let him know that his calm came from him. It also let him know that his rough side was 100 percent the genetic makeup of Joyce. Before being humbled by religion, Joyce was a tough physical force to be reckoned with. She was always a heavy girl with a heavy hand to match her pounds. She had enough victories to make most females and some men back down from a squabble.

Joyce was a daughter of Orchard Park since the fifties. No doors were ever closed in her face when she knocked to deliver the Word from Jehovah, lest the plagues inflicted on the pharaoh in Egypt come upon the violator tenfold in OP—Joyce!

Troy and Jermel were in and out of DYS throughout their young years, Jermel more than Troy, but it never deterred them from robbing and selling drugs. Joyce accompanied them to all their court hearings, dealt with their probation officers, and visited them at the DYS facilities. Liona, Jermel's mother, was usually caught up turning tricks on a corner and chasing her next hit.

Joyce did her best to make ends meet, but her check-to-check manager's position at Filene's clothing store did little to support her and her son. Troy hated watching her struggle his whole life. He was tired of his stomach growling and touching his back at night while trying to sleep. He was tired of wearing worn-down clothes. He was tired of being broke. These same circumstances were primarily what caused both Troy and Jermel to begin robbing and ultimately jumping into the crack game preadolescence. Joyce tried to reject the money he would leave in her bedroom or on the kitchen counter, but necessity usually outweighed morality.

Jermel studied Troy's scowl and read his thoughts like they did so well with each other. "Ma at you again, yo?" He chuckled as he rose from the crate and walked past Troy into the large metal door of their building. He pulled a black marker from his jeans pocket and tagged his name next to a large O and P on the wall in graffiti.

Troy's grimace didn't change as he stepped in behind him. "Ma, po-po, dudes around here…every fuckin' thing! I know you ain't satisfied with this chump change we making or that bullshit Volvo you pushing. And you know we still gotta lay low after all this shooting and shit we been into. I'm surprised DYS ain't scoop us up with everyone else."

"Shit, they ain't scoop us 'cause we ain't been sleeping at the crib every night. Them muthafuckas been lurking, though. I ain't call my PO in over three months! I see you stressing and shit, but what else can we do? Our clientele's tight. It's just a little slow 'cause shit been on fire out here. We got this fake-ass peace treaty going on, so the flow's gonna pick back up."

Jermel studied Troy and saw that he was still agitated. He threw some light humor at him to get his thoughts out of his head, into the air. "All you wanna do is bounce that ball and floss for those MP hos anyway."

Troy said, "That's part of it, dogg, but believe me, that ain't all. We seventeen years old now, not fourteen! It's time ta shine! We put in mad work in these streets but ain't got shit ta show for it." His eyes wandered, and his thoughts traveled beyond the Milky Way. His peripheral caught Jermel nodding, indicating for him to continue, so he came back to this galaxy to relate. He climbed up on the waist-high part of the metal stairwell railing and sat. "My man Jack from Mission Hill that go ta Madison with me always kick it about hittin' them banks downtown and around Cambridge. I thought he was just buggin', but he's eatin' and his whole game's on the low. It's about time we step our game up!"

"I know you dun bumped ya head now!" Jermel stood straight up from his lean on the wall and paced the short distance to the skinny window that faced the back of their building. "This mutha-fucka buggin'," Jermel whispered to himself in disbelief. His mind momentarily drifted as he watched a group of kids rock fighting. He chuckled. They use to do the same thing when they were young. It seemed crazy now how kids in the hood found something that was so dangerous to be so fun. His mind came back to Troy. "I never even been inside a bank!"

The whole thought was crazy to Jermel, even though he was down for just about anything when it came to crime. "Plus," he continued, "you fuckin' with the feds with them banks. They'll give our black asses a thousand years!" He was animated and emphatically disagreed. He felt that his caution was enough to deter Troy, if in fact he was serious.

Jermel figured Troy was just fantasizing anyway. He started to dismiss the conversation but saw that otherworldly glare in his brother's eyes. That meant business. He knew that glare all too well. It appeared when Troy was ready to dominate a basketball game, got into a fight, was on a homicidal mission, or was simply determined to succeed at something.

"Yo, dogg. Feel me on this," Troy said. "The feds is roping dudes off for this crack game way harder than them banks. The hood's getting hit with football numbers for crack, and we ain't even really eatin' off it. Trust me, dogg, I been checking out all that federal sentencing guidelines shit. Look at them white boys in Charlestown, Southie, and Brighton! They getting slapped on the wrist for them banks, and they coming home to money from the lick."

"You just said the key words," Jermel countered. "*White* boys! We black!"

"I ain't tryna hear that shit! You think I came up with this shit overnight? When I'm on my job, I'm on my job!"

"Oh, so now you just putting all types of plans together on ya own?" Jermel wasn't really surprised; he just got lost for words and needed to lash out. The majority of their best moves came from Troy planning alone then bringing him into the picture. Jermel was never much of a thinker.

"Dogg, I went in and out a few of them ta see if the scene's as sweet as Jack said. It most definitely was. I been on this shit for some months now."

Jermel got even more upset. "How you just gonna trust this Mission Hill-ass muthafucka like that?" He wasn't really upset about Jack; he just used him to vent. He was really upset because Troy had never even mentioned anything remotely close to this type of thought before. He couldn't believe he was serious about the nonsense.

"I ain't gotta trust Jack or nobody else but you, 'cause nobody's gonna know but you! I just got the idea from Jack. How me and you handle it is on me and you."

Troy's last statement did wonders for Jermel's ego, but he pretended he didn't catch the confidence in it. "What you mean 'how me and you handle it'? You act like I'm supposed ta just roll with this Wyatt-Earp-and-Doc-Holliday-ass fantasy."

"Of course you gonna roll with it. You my brother, and you know I don't half-ass nothing. And it's *Butch Cassidy and the Sundance Kid*, not Wyatt and Doc."

Jermel looked confused. "Huh?"

"Never mind," Troy said. He locked eyes with Jermel to be sure he had his full attention. "Dig the whole jump off before you start buggin'. We ain't running up in there on no movie-type bandit shit, with masks on and guns out. We gonna be strapped, best believe that, but I seriously doubt muthafuckas gonna get froggy. All we gotta do is walk in, slide the teller a note, collect our cream, and step off." He made the plan sound like A-B-C.

Jermel's body tensed. He looked to be doing all that he could to control himself. "Man…this muthafucka dun lost his mind for real this time!" he said to himself, as if Troy weren't even there. The plan sounded so out of whack Jermel couldn't believe it was actually coming out of Troy's mouth. Shit, it sounded like some shit he would've come up with and Troy would be doing the scolding. Jermel looked at Troy like he was wearing a clown suit. "Who the fuck gonna give us some cream 'cause we give 'em a love letter? You lost ya fuckin' mind or something?"

"Whoever the fuck is behind the counter is gonna give up that cream!" Troy roared back. He was insulted that he wasn't even being taken seriously. It was times like this that he wished he could stay in some of the places his universal mind allowed him to travel. This realm was always light-years behind him. "Listen, dogg, bank tellers ain't the muthafuckas in the hood we be hittin'. They squares who follow the protocol of their job description, which is ta give up that paper and don't risk lives." He tried to drill his limited knowledge into Jermel's head as if it were expert, then finished in frustration, "I'm handling the shit anyway. All you gotta do is watch my back."

Seeing Troy's determination caused Jermel to really tune in. He was also starting to see the vision a little. "Aight, dogg. Break it down."

Troy noticeably relaxed, then began breaking down his plan. He told him the location and type of bank he had lined up.

Jermel's eyebrows rose slightly.

Their disguises would be simple—construction gear and contact lenses. They needed to blend in with the afternoon crowd, so masks were definitely a no-no. Their faces would be lathered in Vaseline to hopefully give a slightly distorted feature in case the cameras got a good shot.

Jermel didn't like the thought of leaving a stolen car running in the middle of the area they would be in. It would look too suspicious, and they would be at least five blocks away from it. He suggested they let Ella drive and keep her in the blind. "She ain't gonna ask no questions," he told Troy.

Ella was thorough and had been around on more than a few occasions when Troy and Jermel put in work. Jermel figured Troy would be comfortable with her in their presence. He could tell that Troy was silently running the suggestion through his always-active mind. He was pleased when Troy seemed to approvingly agree. Being able to contribute to the plan boosted his sense of value to it.

Troy was iffy about this part of the plan, but Ella had proved to be thorough in the past. Plus, a female driver would probably draw less heat if shit hit the fan. He also felt obligated to let Jermel contribute to the plan since he dropped it in his lap with no warning.

Three days after their way out of the ordinary hallway conversation, Ella was driving down the Bumpy Roads side of Orchard Park, with Jermel riding shotgun. She pulled in front of a building in Batan Court, and Jermel reached across the seat and mashed the horn.

Troy occasionally hustled out of a second-floor apartment in the building. He chose to hang around there instead of his crib while waiting for Jermel to scoop him. He wanted to avoid all possibilities of having another fallout with Joyce. It was his big day. He saw it like him being a rookie in his first game. Everything had to be perfect, and so far, so good.

Troy heard the horn, looked outside, and saw Jermel leaning out the window of a clean money-green Audi. Good choice, he thought as he grabbed his Carhartt vest, ran out of the apartment, and leaped down nearly the full flight of steps. He knew Ella didn't know the car was stolen, so he couldn't commend Jermel on his hotbox skills.

"What up, y'all?" he said as he hopped in the back seat. He gave Jermel dap and playfully mushed Ella in the back of her head.

"You better stop playing, Troy!" she yelled with artificial anger.

He ignored her act, sat back, and laughed.

She switched her act off quick. "When you gonna bring ya fine chocolate ass around my way? I been telling you ta come through so I can hook you up with one of my girls."

"I ain't never coming around there. I don't wanna have ta fuck none of them chumps up." He didn't speak with malice, but he was dead serious.

"Ain't nobody gonna mess with ya'll!" She had genuine anger now. "Y'all need ta get off that bullshit ya'll be on!"

Ella hated that their hoods couldn't get along. Jermel was her heart. Troy was her brother. They were all truly the best of friends. They loved being in one another's company.

A very lively freshman year at MP began their unconventional bond. Ella and Jermel were in the same homeroom. She met him first and was immediately caught up in his thugged-out swagger. Ever since Jermel introduced her to his brother Troy, she never shied away from letting him know how fine he was. She never bit her tongue about much, really. She never regretted her choice of the two. She would never violate Jermel, so she constantly tried to hook Troy up with one of her girls. She at least wanted to get some details of his sex game. The mind of a young lady…

"What, ya'll 'bout ta go work on houses or something?" she joked, in reference to their clothes.

"Nah. We just on some other shit today," Jermel retorted, knowing Ella was sharp. He wanted to avoid her line of questioning.

She rolled her eyes. "Whatever! I know when ta mind my business."

Ella was the closest thing Jermel ever had to a girlfriend; they just didn't have the label. She would ride to the end of the Earth with him, even when it was believed to be flat. They kicked it intimately for three years, and throughout those interesting years of her life, she grew to accept his reckless ways and fear of commitment. He was her man, and the whole city knew he was her man, even if he wouldn't admit it. She understood him and loved him for exactly who he was.

Ella was an all-around winner. All three of them were seventeen, but even when they were fourteen-year-old freshmen, she was built beyond her years.

At five-five, one-thirty, she had the sculpted body of an Olympic sprinter. Her bright smile was both sweet and sexy. It was a near-permanent fixture on her face, especially after her braces were removed her junior year. She was big on all the latest fashion and switched hairstyles like she lived in a salon. Her dark-almond skin was smoothly feminine, with a few scars that were a testament to her tomboy early years.

Troy cut out the small talk they were all engaged in and became all business as they neared their destination. The bank they were hitting was on Boston's popular Boylston Street, which was overwhelmingly packed on this desert-hot summer afternoon, so being fully focused was a must.

Boylston Street traveled about five miles through the historic downtown and Fenway area of Boston. From end to end it was brimming with landmarks, entertainment, institutions, and businesses. It was home to the country's second largest library, the Boston Public Library, which sat almost directly across the street from their mark.

There was no room for error in this environment. The familiarity and cover of hallways, alleys, and a code of silence was nonexistent. What was only a separation of a few miles from the hood to downtown suddenly seemed like whole worlds apart.

They neared a Burger King about five blocks from the bank. Troy told Ella to pull beside its parking lot, not inside of it.

"You want something out of here?" Jermel asked Ella.

"Hell no! You greedy as shit, chubby. We just ate at Boston Chicken a few hours ago. That's why you so chubby now."

"Yeah, you love this chubby, though." He smiled. He knew she would reject his offer. It was just to throw her off. He squeezed the inside of her thigh. "We'll be right back."

Troy ducked his head in the seat and slid his contacts in before stepping out of the car. The two of them strolled Boylston Street, clipboard in hand, hard hat and gear on, looking the part of construction workers on their lunch break. Troy's poker face was blank. His tongue traced the inside of every tooth as it often did when he was anxious, angry, or nervous. His heart raced. His mind ran wild as it methodically sorted through every detail of the task at hand. His senses were heightened to foreign levels. Surrounding conversations were clear whispers in his ears. His sense of smell was of the wild. The sun became his antagonist, challenging him with its scorching, universal idea versus his own scrambled thoughts. Murderous missions never even affected him so awkwardly. Being so far out of his comfort zone added unexpected pressure.

Jermel moved through the crowd with ease. His nerves were also working against him, but nothing too out of the ordinary like Troy. His outlook on life didn't allow much room for caution. He was a ready-shoot-aim type of person. No thought, just action, which was usually followed by trouble and regret. His job was to watch his brother's back. That was his number one objective, making the actual bank job a distant second. His blood ran as cold as his gaze. He was unconcerned with all things surrounding him except Troy.

Troy had taken Jermel to case the area two times in the past forty-eight hours. He detailed their plans A, B, and C to be sure that they were on the same page and well prepared. He didn't have to do any extra persuading; once Jermel realized that he was serious, he was all in.

They casually turned from the street, walked through one of the bank's large glass doors with butterflies in their bellies and money on their minds. As they entered, they rolled their heads to the left, being sure to avoid the camera above the row of ATMs on the right. Once inside, they kept their heads and hard hats low as they positioned themselves.

Jermel quickly located the lone security guard. The man was seated in a corner as if it were the privacy of his own living room. Jermel made his way over to an information stand nearest the guard's post and pretended to fill out a money slip. He never took his eyes off the comfortable old man for too long. He was careful not to touch anything he didn't have to. His instructions were to pocket the lone money slip he toyed with when he made his exit.

No unnecessary evidence.

Jermel figured he'd have no problem disarming Archie Bunker if anything went wrong. Archie Bunker—that was exactly who the security guard reminded him of. His whole demeanor reminded Jermel of a scene right off the *All in the Family* sitcom. He watched the show often and actually liked Archie despite disagreeing with just about his entire belief system. If Archie acted up today, though,

Edith would be a widow. Troy advised him to disarm and subdue, but if it really got hectic, he would enjoy dumping his .45 in Archie's head.

Ready, shoot, aim.

Troy chose line 1 mainly because it was the closest to the door that he would need to get out of. He stood behind a short frail man that he believed to be a young bootlicker. He appeared to be about seven years older, already balding, probably from a lot of ass-kissing at whatever type of job he slaved at daily. That would never be him, he thought. Troy despised the thought of inferiority. Even average didn't sit well with him.

After his totally baseless assessment, he didn't pay the insignificant man another thought. Instead, his eyes surveyed the bank's forty-foot-high ceiling, emergency exits, and ten thick-glassed window booths, three with "No Service" signs in them. Most of all, he studied the people.

When he had first cased the inside of the bank, it was a chilly Tuesday in April. It proved to be a much different environment than this hot Thursday afternoon in August. He didn't account for the many extra bodies who were cashing checks, making withdrawals and deposits. He wasn't in tune with the life of average citizens planning trips, school shopping, and whatever else it was that they did that involved being in a bank at this time.

There were old and young people of all ethnicities in the seven open lines. Troy didn't like it. He didn't like it, but he didn't sweat it too much.

The overwhelming list of distractions that clouded his mind while he made the transition from the hotbox Audi to the bank were now gone. Upon his full acceptance that his plan was really in activation, his fear shifted to focus. Butterflies flew away. Thoughts of obliterating the solar system faded.

He coolly took in his surroundings and used it all to his criminal-minded advantage. He zeroed in on a young girl, maybe eight years old, with green eyes and pink cheeks who was in line 4. A wrinkled seventy-something Hispanic woman in a futuristic wheelchair was in line 2. Tubes ran from her nose to a small green oxygen tank. A five-foot-one middle-aged Asian woman was in line 6. She had an infant in her arms and wore glasses as big as the safety goggles strapped to his hard hat. These were the people who he promised would be harmed as he stood in line and rewrote his letter to the teller on his clipboard. The original one no longer suited the circumstances.

He also volunteered the services of a tough-looking Wesley Snipes clone in line 3, wearing dark shades and a jacket too heavy for the weather. If the teller disobeyed, according to Troy's letter, Wesley Snipes would go Demolition Man in the bank. The working man, who Troy baselessly labeled a sucker, stepped to the teller, leaving Troy next in line.

Troy was even more on point now and highly alert. He noticed that the man seemed to have a good rapport with the bank teller. They smiled and shared a few words as the man placed a midsize company-labeled duffel bag on the counter. He began pulling out stacks of money.

Oh, shit! Troy's eyes widened. He had to fight with conflicted thoughts of aborting the original plan. He could rob the man, the teller, and whoever else had something of value. His poise won against his impulse, though. He simply understood that his pay on this payday just significantly increased.

When the man was finished taking care of his large company deposit, he and the teller exchanged more pleasantries, then he walked away. The teller held up one finger to Troy, signaling for him to give her a second, but he wasn't hearing it. There was no way he was allowing her to get up and put that money in a vault or whatever she thought she was going to do with it.

As she started to get up, Troy stepped up to the window. The smiling borderline-obese middle-aged redhead teller's welcoming smile turned upside down within seconds of Troy sliding her his note. Besides the threats of violence, it demanded fifties and hundred-dollar bills, no dye packs, and instructed her to keep one hand visible while she filled the bag. The most important instruction was for her to slide the note back.

No unnecessary evidence.

The butterflies that flew from his belly were replaced with a wildfire that rose up his body and shot through the gray contacts he wore. The teller's balloon of a body began to deflate. It was evident that she had no resistance in her. She hesitated momentarily to figure out if she was awake or in a nightmare. When she semiregained her consciousness, she began reluctantly putting stacks of money from the top, inside, and underneath the drawer into the duffel bag Troy handed her.

Archie Bunker rose from the comfort of his wooden chair. He seemed to be bothered by something. His forehead wrinkled. He squinted hard as he rubbed his chest, probably reflexively, in slow circles. He looked like a man well-seasoned in his usually boring job.

For a moment, Jermel thought he might have underestimated the senior citizen. He followed the man's eyes, and as he suspected, almost feared, they led to line number 1. A rage began to build inside of him that took up too much space to even allow fear to fully set in.

As Archie Bunker began to move in that direction, Jermel eased his hand down to his .45. He dropped the money slip and fell in step a few paces behind Archie. The need to come out of the lick with a come-up, messy or clean, caused him to actually think for a second, but the killer in him threw caution to the wind.

Archie reached for his service revolver as Jermel gripped his murder weapon tighter.

Instead of Archie taking his pistol out of the holster, he just adjusted his belt. He approached a wandering young boy and squatted down to see if he was lost. After a brief exchange, he took the boy by the hand and led him in search for his parents.

Jermel wasn't even aware that he had begun to sweat or that his heart was racing at a violent pace. Close call. Too close. With his eyes still on Archie, he went back to his original position and grabbed a new money slip.

The teller did as she was told, then pushed the bag back to Troy. *Nah,* he thought. He was extra bold at this point, Trailblazing.

"More, bitch," he snarled at her and pushed the bag back. He had to refrain from showing the victorious smirk as he watched her reach below the counter and put extra stacks in the bag. He took the bag when she slid it the second time, slung it over his shoulder, and slid away from the counter.

The traumatized woman glanced over at Demolition Man with pleading eyes, praying that he knew she did exactly as she was told.

Jermel couldn't believe it when he saw Troy and the full bag head toward the doors. He wanted to jump for joy but remained diligent, pocketed the money slip, and slid in behind him.

They rolled their heads to the right as they approached the glass doors, then fought the urge to run for their lives once outside.

As they covered the first couple of blocks, Troy prayed that the teller continued to believe that Wesley Snipes was part of his lick. They just needed to make it to the safety of the hotbox.

A siren sounded. It stopped Troy's thoughts and his heart.

Troy and Jermel were doing their best to blend in and flow with the crowd, but an easy getaway seemed to be too good to be true. Troy's excessive sweat wasn't from the sun this time. His mind immediately went into attack mode.

Jermel's eyes got murderously wide. He instinctively reached for his gun. Fortunately, the BPD patrol car was across the street from them. It sped off toward the bank without paying them any mind.

They quickened their pace to clear the last blocks.

Troy started to wonder about Ella's ability to remain calm under this type of pressure.

Jermel was the exact opposite of Troy's concern. The closer they got to the Burger King, the safer and more confident he felt. He had no worries on Ella's end.

They were both relieved when they entered the lot and saw Ella singing behind the wheel. They rushed to the car in a short sprint. Troy lay down in the back seat, while Jermel reclined all the way out of sight as soon as he got in.

"What the heck is wrong with ya'll?" Ella's face was accusing Jermel without him even saying a word.

"Troy just knocked out this Chinese dude. Pull off before five-O come."

"Ya'll can't go nowhere without acting up!" she complained while pulling off like she was told.

She turned the music up louder and continued singing out the window. The police car that came flying up the wrong direction of the one-way street that she turned onto was either thrown off by her antics or simply ignored her. It sped right by.

"Y'all ducked just in time, 'cause five-Os all over the place."

"Just be easy and get away from this shit," Troy said in a hard whisper.

"Shut up!" Ella snapped. "I got this. Ya'll just stay the heck down!"

Neither of them had a breath of argument for her. Ella was in control. Their lives were literally in her hands now.

She saw how wild the police were going and knew that her passengers were up to more than just a fight. Whatever it was, she didn't care to know at the time. Her only concern was getting her man and her brother out of the immediate danger around them.

She kept it cool and got them to the highway instead of riding through the downtown streets. Police cars were even on the highway, on high alert. What the fuck did these dudes do? she wondered.

The Roxbury exit off I-93 was only six or seven miles from the downtown exit. They were safely descending it after fifteen long minutes of hell. Ella narrated the scene the entire way back. Even when she said it was safe, none of them dared to sit up until she let them know that they were officially entering the Bury.

When they poked their heads up and saw Suffolk County House of Corrections (South Bay) to their left, they had to laugh at the irony of it being their first sight after a heist. Their shared laugh wasn't lost on Ella. Neither of them had been behind the gates and walls of South Bay, but many of their associates had been, and were currently, captives in the prison.

At seventeen, Troy and Jermel were now South Bay eligible. Any new arrest could land them there even though they were still the custody of DYS until their eighteenth birthday.

They were all back in their element as Ella made her way through the ghetto streets. Troy and Jermel stripped off their construction gear down to the white T-shirts and the jeans they wore under them. The colored contacts were popped out and tossed. Jermel had Ella pull over near a dumpster so he could dump their clothes and their description with it.

When Ella pulled into her parking lot, instead of getting out, she sat defiantly, eyeing both of them. They pretended not to notice. She sucked her teeth extra loud.

Jermel leaned across the seat, kissed her on the cheek, then indicated for her to get out. She sucked her teeth again as she climbed out. He smacked her on the ass and slid over to the driver's seat.

Troy got low again in the back, gun out, just in case any of the A Team was around.

Jermel drove a few blocks to MLK Boulevard and pulled over on a side street near Washington Park.

Malcolm X Park, more so known as Washington Park, was usually packed on summer afternoons. Its recreation center and fields were used for unstructured recreation, cookouts, and summer youth camp activities. Its three concrete basketball courts saw some of the best action from the best ballplayers in the city. Vendors, in carts and vehicles, made money off the large crowds. Hustlers showed off big trucks and big cars. Females "hood-modeled" like it was a video shoot.

Troy was a Washington Park star already, but he wasn't about no games on this day.

They did their best to avoid the crowd, thoroughly wiped down the Audi, then jumped in Jermel's Volvo. The short drive back to OP was in unfamiliar silence. For the first time since diapers, neither brother made a sound to the other.

Large crowds of people were out when Troy and Jermel pulled into the parking lot behind their building. Blazers posted up on cars, against buildings, and on top of small wooden fences. They hustled and kicked it while project kids played in the run-down excuse for a play area.

Jermel and Troy tried to act as normal as possible as they moved through the crowd, but it was a tough emotional task. Some of their closest associates were out. If they looked suspicious and questions were asked by certain people, they would be hard-pressed to put the right spin on things.

Luckily, they were able to pass by everyone with quick greetings and daps. Troy was regularly coming from a gym or a ball court, so a duffel bag slung over his shoulder was ordinary. They walked fast like they were on something serious. That type of body language was understood in the hood. Nobody slowed them down with small talk.

Once inside Jermel's crib, Troy nearly ripped the bag open and emptied it on the bed.

Jermel's eyes were wide as dinner plates. "Damn, yo!" was all he could get out.

"I told yo ass we was gonna be straight." Troy put on a good laid-back act but was really still in awe of his own work. He couldn't believe that all the money laid out on the unmade full-size bed was theirs. It looked like a stack of green project bricks.

They dapped each other up in brief celebration, then got right down to counting. Troy dragged a beat-up cotton armchair over, cleared a section out, and dug into the stacks. The creek from the worn bed and the shuffling of fresh paper were the only sounds heard over their heavy breathing. Shouts, sirens, and other common racket outside of the second-floor window were unconsciously blocked out.

Controlling the excitement they felt after totaling their take was impossible. Even though Troy explained that they had a lot more, due to the sizable company deposit that was made in his face, the money was still unbelievable.

The fresh scent of money was unfamiliar to two young ghetto boys trying to survive. They estimated about forty grand from the piles' initial appearance, but it ended up being a far-greater six-ty-eight. They never even handled a quarter of that amount before.

"Yo, dogg," Jermel said, "we just stacked more bread in a hour than we did all our damn lives." He was excited and disappointed all at once. The excitement was self-explanatory; the disappointment came from feeling foolish for struggling for so long.

Troy showed similar emotion. "I know, dogg." He sat and stared at the stacks. "Now we gonna step our shit up like we suppose to. This lick came off sweet, but it was tougher than I expected. We gotta be easy and make sure ain't no heat on us."

Troy was fearless in plotting and carrying out a mission but usually extra cautious after the mission was accomplished.

"Man, cut all that spooky shit out!" Jermel teased while thumbing through a stack of fresh bills. "Nobody gonna think we did no crazy shit like this. Shit, I still don't believe we did it." His voice trailed off as he tried to grasp the reality of the situation. They were in position now. Just like that. "We 'bout ta grab that bomb-ass Flave and flood the hood, I know that!"

A mischievous smirk crossed Jermel's face as he thought about stepping into the big leagues. All the ones with the big weight in the hood always tried to act like they were better than them. He couldn't stand that shit! Most of the chumps only wanted to deal with Troy because they were scared of him. They figured Troy would play fair but that he would be plotting to rob them. They actually knew more than figured, because that was exactly how it would've gone down.

Little did those heavy, drug-pushing suckers know, whenever they did get robbed, Troy was the mastermind behind it. Jermel would always vent about how the connects were all suckers with money who looked down on them. Eventually, he and Troy would be masked up outside of one of their spots.

Jermel was already envisioning buying big weight and looking down on them for the suckers they were. He knew the streets would be better if he and Troy had them. He wanted—no, he needed—that power. He smiled wide, then came out of his daydream and was back in his bedroom. As if he had an epiphany, he said, "Let's go get fly tomorrow, dogg! Fuck all that lay-low shit."

"I'm cool with getting fly," Troy said, "but we still gotta be easy."

The next morning, thirty-four stacks apiece stronger, Jermel and Troy were ready to shine. They tried to buy out the entire mall and downtown strips, then went shopping for new whips. Troy kept his spending fairly modest, while Jermel went all out.

Jermel dropped six stacks in the malls and strips. He swapped his Volvo, added sixteen stacks, and bought a '93 cherry-red 5 Series BMW. He gave Troy ten stacks for their re-up and tucked two under his mattress to splurge on Ella with.

Troy put fifteen with Jermel's ten to re-up with his connect. Eleven stacks plus trading in his Altima got him an all-black match to Jermel's Beamer. He spent four in the malls and strips, put twenty-five hundred on Joyce's dresser, and stashed the remaining fifteen hundred in his closet.

From one August week to the next, they nearly did a complete financial transformation. They were, without a doubt, on another level. The projects noticed immediately. Many were trying to figure out their formula, but the two were so well-known for their personal mischief that nobody had a clue.

Speculation of upcoming drama was in the air. The mischievous brothers could've robbed some major players in the game. The projects' collective was on their toes. They spread a little love within the bricks, so it wasn't much to be complained about. Some people hated regardless. Some congratulated. Some got on board.

A week and a half after Boylston Street, they hit another downtown bank for a lot less than the first, but still a decent amount. The act was like sex. The climax was getting away so clean and easy. The banks were their secret whores, but Troy had to make his undisciplined brother promise to never fuck one alone or have an orgy without him. Jermel promised, and the robberies were added to their long list of sibling secrets.

Chapter 3

◆◆◆◆◆◆

Madison Park High School (MP) was full of gang members, hustlers, and some of the flyest young females in the city. There was also the polar opposite: squares, nerds, and mud ducks. Orchard Park and neighborhoods affiliated with them made up a large part of the troublesome student body. The A and their allies were around, but scarce. Their stronghold was West Roxbury High.

Nicknamed Fashion Show High, MP lived up to its hype. Big jewelry, fresh gear, and salon swagger were everywhere. At a few hundred meters in length and more than half that in width, the rugged cement structure was one of the largest schools in Massachusetts. Not many of the students from the hood-crazed crowd put much emphasis on academics. For them, MP was more of a social establishment than a place of formal education.

There were many good times inside its walls, which was what kept many students who couldn't care less about a diploma coming back. Even dropouts, like Jermel, often popped up to peep the scene.

Once MP fam, always MP fam.

Ella yelled, "Troy! Troy! I know you hear me! Bring ya black ass over here and meet my girl! And stop acting like you too good for us!"

The hallways of MP were jam-packed with loud and live students. Ella stood in the long corridor of the science building, with her hands on her hips, impatiently waiting for Troy to fully acknowledge her. As she waited for him to stop talking to the pretty, dark girl he was caught up with, she whispered to her girl, "All these bitches be sweatin' him, but none of them got nothing on you."

Her girl stood next to her, kind of embarrassed and feeling like a groupie. "Ella, I ain't really tryna meet nobody. I know ya ass, you tryna hook a bitch up, and you know I ain't with that right now."

"Shhhit! You just ain't met Troy's fine ass yet. Trust me, that's the only reason you saying that," Ella countered with the dramatics of an Oscar-nominated actress.

"What up, sis?" Troy had a high-spirited smile on his face and was full of energy as he approached and hugged Ella.

"What's up is you got me and my girl over here waiting while you all up in that hoochie's face," Ella barked while rolling her eyes, neck, and shoulders.

"Chill out, yo. You know you my priority. I just had ta take care of something important with Renee," he responded, trying to lighten his scolding.

"Well…," she continued with her natural extras, "Troy, this is my best friend, Trina. Since you never come through the A, you can finally meet my girl here. Now you know she's with me, so nobody better disrespect her! She transferred from Westie 'cause she ain't tryna be all up under them dudes from around our way all damn day and night. She—"

"Damn, Ella! I know how ta speak!" Trina shot her a look that said she was embarrassing her.

Troy hadn't paid much attention to Trina until she spoke, but when he did, he was more than impressed. He had a movie moment, where his surroundings became a blur and she was the only part of the picture that was clear. Her humongous cat eyes batted in slow motion as he danced to her rhythm, seeking. Asking? She had Werther's candy caramel skin. Her nose was broad, lips thick and brown. Her frame was a voluptuous five three, one-thirty pounds. She looked fresh off a magazine spread, with short dreads, fresh manicure, and pedicured toes in two-inch heels. A perfect 10!

The more he studied her, the more he was almost sure that he knew her.

He had met her before, he thought. But no, there was no way he would've let the type of beauty in front of him get away. There was no look of recognition in her eyes, so he dismissed the thought as a wonderful dream he must've had.

"How you, Trina? I'm Troy." He politely extended his hand. "Nice ta meet you."

She took his hand into hers and nearly melted. This was the most handsome man she had ever seen off or on screen. Ella exaggerated a lot, so Trina thought that it might be the case with this Troy she always spoke about. But the magic of the man in front of her was no hocus pocus. Ella couldn't properly give this man justice through a mere description.

Trina did her best to appear unfazed by his force. "I know who you are. Ella never stops talking about you and your brother. It's nice to finally meet you."

Her smile softened him like none other before it. This girl was special. It was much more than her physical beauty attracting him. The attraction was so unordinary he couldn't begin to identify it. He composed himself as they all kicked it for a bit.

When the bell sounded for the first homeroom period of the '96–'97 school year, the girls turned to go their way, while Troy just stood and watched. Trina's perfect apple did something special in her jeans as he watched it bounce and sway away.

Ella looked over her shoulder, peeped him ogling, and gave a knowing grin.

Troy nodded in agreement. He couldn't deny the obvious.

After the final bell of the first day sounded, Troy pulled his Beamer out of the lower parking lot, double-parked among the many illegally parked cars, and waited for Jermel. He kicked it with some associates he hadn't seen over the summer, answered questions about his whip, and got the 4-1-1 on things he missed.

Shiz and Will from the Mission Hill projects, crushed him when they told him that Jack got locked up for a hotbox. They may not have known, but Troy knew for sure why Jack was in that hotbox and where he was headed in it. Even though he wouldn't have admitted it, he knew that Jack would recognize that he hit some banks. He wanted to repay him for the blueprint and wouldn't let him being locked up stop him from showing love.

When school let out at MP, it sometimes resembled the atmosphere of a club letting out for the night—it was an event in itself.

Students and nonstudents hung out along the side walls, in the street, or in front of the entrance for over an hour. Age never seemed to matter. The gatherings ranged in age from fourteen-year-old freshmen to forty-year-olds. Ballers flossed in big whips and big jewelry while waiting on their PYT, whether she was a freshman or a senior. There was no shame in the game.

Ella and Trina posted up under the flagpole with a few friends as they waited for Jermel. Trina was the main attraction, new meat. And Ella was waving pursuers off left and right.

Troy slid through the crowd and crept up on Trina. "Why you wait till ya senior year ta transfer?"

Trina jumped. She didn't see him step to her; she just heard his voice in her ear. "Boy! You scared me." She wore a slight smile when she saw it was him. She shrugged off his question. "I just wanted ta be in a different environment."

"Uhnuhn!" Ella butted in. "She ain't wanna be around all them dudes from around our way!"

"I wouldn't either," Troy joked, then focused back on Trina. "But you gotta live around 'em, so you can't escape."

"Yeah, I know, but the less, the better," she reasoned, seeming to be in a thought way heavier than the light conversation he tried to spark.

Ella jumped back in. "Them dudes started showing they true colors after Manny was gone! They went from looking out for her ta all tryna fuck and everything else!"

"Who's Manny? He ya man or something? He locked up?" Troy asked as if it were unimportant.

Trina's head dropped and shook a little. "Nah, he was my brother. He got killed a couple months ago."

Troy's whole demeanor changed. He felt stupid. Surprise and embarrassment filled his eyes. He couldn't believe how insensitive he spoke without thinking. "Damn, I'm sorry ta hear that, Trina," he managed to get out genuinely. "I ain't mean ta come across the wrong way. I—"

"Yes, you did." She brushed off his apology in a controlled, even cadence. She wasn't letting him off the hook that easily. "I understand…I understand, and I ain't mad at you for it. You're from OP. I don't expect you ta feel bad about my brother. I expect that from y'all. I just didn't expect it from his so-called friends he grew up with." Trina went from sad and vulnerable to angry and aggressive in the blink of an eye. "That beef shit y'all be on is so childish!" Her nose flared. Her eyes screamed louder than her voice. "Y'all must think fighting and killing each other makes y'all look tough or some-thing. All it does is make y'all look ignorant and ugly." As quickly as she blew up, she calmed back down. "I'm sorry, Troy. I don't mean ta direct my anger toward you. You ain't the cause of my problems."

Troy was still ashamed of himself and was at a loss for mean-ingful words. "You don't have ta apologize. I feel where you coming from."

Jermel beeped his horn and relieved the uncomfortable moment. They all walked over to the cherry-red Beamer. As the girls got in, Jermel hopped out to greet Troy. He saw the disturbance in Troy's face. "What up, yo?"

"Man, I just bugged out kickin' it ta Ella's girl. You know her?"

"Yeah. That's Trina. I don't know her all like that, but I been told you she was a dime. You just don't pay attention. Why? What up?"

"Dogg, she's that dude Manny's sister," Troy said uneasily.

"Who's Manny? Oh, dude from the A?" Jermel asked, surprised. "Yeah."

"That's crazy! Colleges, congressmen, the mayor, and all types of muthafuckas been talking about dude ever since he got hit up. He still in the news, and that was a minute ago." Jermel chuckled a bit. "They say he was the next Jerry Rice or Irving Fryar. Ella was fucked up about that for a while too. She probably did tell me dude was Trina's brother." Jermel stopped to study Troy's face. Troy was one of the hardest dudes he ever knew but was uncommonly sensitive to certain situations. Jermel couldn't figure out why that was for the life of him. He could tell that this was one of these situations.

Troy always showed sympathy toward Manny's death. He said that his own athletic life, and life in general, could easily end the same way. So he felt some type of fake-ass athlete-to-athlete compassion. Jermel couldn't stand hearing it at times. When they first saw the story of his death on the news, Jermel laughed, simply because he was from the A. The fact that he wasn't gang affiliated meant nothing to him. Troy, on the other hand, immediately felt bad for the young NFL prospect. Trina was the beautiful damsel in distress. She would love Troy's strong shoulder to lean on. But hell no! Jermel wasn't hearing that!

"Dogg, don't go stressing yaself out about that hoe's problems. Her grief is her grief. She fly and all that, but she ain't worth no unnecessary headaches. If you can't fuck her, then flee. Don't fuck with her at all. It's too many hos with no problems for you ta be playing Captain Save-a-Hoe with this one chick."

That was Jermel's brotherly advice. He ended it on that note, dapped him up, then got back in his whip. He pulled off with a silent disdain for Trina in his back seat. She felt it but thought she might have been reading him wrong.

By the time January rolled around, high school basketball was in full swing, and Jermel and Troy were ballin' like crazy in the streets. They hit five more banks, all squeaky-clean licks. The brothers were the subject of many circles' conversations. Females pursued them even harder; fake friends tried to cut in from all angles.

They both gloated in their newfound status, to some degree, but Jermel's degree was a lot hotter than Troy's cool temperature.

The streets speculated, but none of their guesses were even close to the source of their initial come-up. It was accepted that they were eating off heavy plates, strictly due to the weight they pushed around the city and the rocks they pitched in the projects. Only the two of them knew their worth, but the guessing went on, and along with the guessing came the scheming.

Not many were brave enough to try the two of them. To try them would most likely mean to be ready to kill them. Contrary to popular belief, premeditated robbery and murder weren't many people's cup of tea. Accident murderers lived off false personas, but those were the ones who weren't willing to try Troy and Jermel. Being that they were verifiably dangerous, they had to be tried by ones who were cut from the same cloth. Their violence was respected before the money. Nothing changed in that department. Most schemers merely had pipe dreams about robbing them, but some really felt froggy enough to leap.

Whenever and wherever MP had a basketball game, the projects and most people who were followers of the sport showed up to see Troy play in person. The first game of the season was against Dorchester High.

Troy put the Madison Park Cardinals on his back. He loved performing for large crowds and rarely disappointed. He wasn't much of a showboat on the court, but he played the game at such a highly skilled level that it was always an awesome display.

Against Dorchester High, Troy gave the heavy crowd a triple double (26 points, 13 rebounds, 10 assists). Madison won by fourteen on Dorchester's floor. He was a man among boys but was usually a gentleman. He understood that he was head and shoulders above most of his high school competition, so he moved with humility and good sportsmanship. He shook hands at the end of games and gave encouraging words to teammates and opponents.

Even though Troy fell back from Trina after that first day of school, she persistently pursued him. He was polite and acknowledged her presence when she was in unavoidable space, but other than that, he took Jermel's advice and avoided the unnecessary headache she could be.

Troy dealt with a traumatized girl in the past. It drained him with the constant mood swings he had to deal with and the all-too-necessary consoling. Jermel hated that he even put up with the girl and was glad when he finally kicked her to the curb. Dealing with Trina would be like déjà vu, Jermel convinced him.

Trina didn't chase after Troy with lust or greed, like most girls did; her pursuit was more personal. She wanted to be friends, to bond. Ella was Troy and Jermel's family. Trina thought that was a beautiful place.

Besides simple greetings and very short conversations, Troy paid very little attention to her through their first couple of months of school. However, she eventually won over his companionable side with the natural beauty of her being. She was comfortable in her own skin and made it nearly impossible to disregard her.

When Ella first introduced them, an unearthly captivation came over her, as if she had known him all her life. The magnetic pull was undeniable, though she couldn't understand it. His strong yet sensitive brown eyes, his thick dark lips, his demeanor were irresistible. Visualizing being with him sexually was done unconsciously, but her attraction dived much deeper than lust. She recognized his true strength, intellect, and a caring interior that existed below the rugged exterior.

Trina began easing her way into Troy's and Jermel's whips with Ella and hanging out with them whenever the opportunity presented itself. When a chance popped up, she drew Troy into intelligent conversations. Though he was smart, the conversations made him uncomfortable at first, simply because he wasn't used to having them.

Troy wasn't really comfortable dealing with his sensitive or intellectual sides, but Trina had a way of bringing them out without making him feel insecure about it. They rarely dwelled in discussions about the streets or their hoods; Trina's interests were in his dreams and what he planned to do about them.

Jermel teased Troy that he was falling in love with Trina and that he was going to go through the same problems he went through with the last psycho, mourning girlfriend. Troy made weak attempts to weave in and out of the verbal jabs. He tried to convince him that it was just a friendly relationship, but Jermel wasn't hearing it.

Ella teased them both, but in a more good-natured spirit than Jermel did. She praised Trina for being able to captivate him like she'd never seen a girl do before.

Neither Troy nor Trina needed any extra prompting. After a little time, feelings began to form naturally. When she finally cracked his hard shell, they became very close friends, which was why she was right next to Ella in the bleachers at Dorchester High, cheering him on as he hit jumper after jumper on the court.

After the opening-night basketball victory, the projects and associates celebrated at the Beritz, a popular hole-in-the-wall bar that bordered OP.

Jamesie, who was of age, bought the bar out, allowing everyone to enjoy the homely vibe. It didn't matter that Troy and Jermel were only seventeen and that most in their circle were under twenty-one; the Beritz was home, so a blind eye was turned.

Last call for alcohol was at one o'clock, and the Beritz closed at its usual 2:00 a.m. All the tipsy attendants poured out onto Dudley Street, gave final daps and hugs, then went their ways. Troy, Jermel, Amin, and Peanut left together.

Amin and Peanut were the other two corners that completed the square of their four-man crew. They were like the two older brothers since they were all young. They were two years older than Troy and Jermel.

Amin was a rational thinker and plotter. Troy, more so than Jermel, learned valuable lessons through his rational outlook on life. His voice held weight in and outside of their circle. He was good-looking, cocoa-complexioned, stocky, and five foot ten. He was known for his fighting skills and his skills with the females. The back of his head was egg-shaped, which was why it was the focus of many of Peanut's jokes.

Peanut was a natural-born comedian. He found ways to implement humor in just about any situation, regardless of its degree of seriousness. He could easily pass for the youngest of the four. His youthful appearance often worked in favor of his violent tendencies. His baby face was sometimes taken as soft, which was always a very bad mistake by foes. He was tall, five eleven, weighed one-seventy, light brown, with pointy features and slanted eyes. He kept a low cut on top of his peanut head, with pencil-thin, chin-strap sideburns and goatee. Like his other three main men, he was a ladies' man too.

Before Jermel and Troy attended Madison, Peanut had already dropped out after his freshman year. Though classrooms and schoolbooks weren't his thing, Peanut was highly intelligent. His intelligence was a blessing from birth. He excelled in analytical studies rather than formal ones. He had an incredible ability to analyze situations—history, war, religion, relationships. He gave in-depth analyses on just about everything. He was called the philosopher by some of his close peers.

Troy got in Amin's whip when they left the Beritz. Peanut walked around the corner with Jermel to ride shotgun with him.

When Jermel pulled up on the side of Amin's whip, Peanut leaned out the window and told Amin, "I'm hungry, dogg. Let's grab some grub at Food Court."

"That's what's up," Troy slurred from the other side of the car. "I gotta get some Plane from the spot first!" Jermel yelled across Peanut. "I gotta handle this light shit before I take it down for the night. We'll catch y'all down there in about twenty minutes. Order me some wingdings and fries."

"Get me a steak and cheese with mayonnaise, onions, and peppers!" Peanut yelled as Jermel pulled away.

"I got y'all," Amin assured from the back of Jermel's Beamer, then bust a U-turn and headed to Food Court.

None of them noticed Beam and Q sitting low in a maroon Dodge Stratus across the street from the Beritz. When Amin busted the U-turn, Beam pulled out and tailed Jermel and Peanut from a safe distance.

Beam and Q were from the A. They were lifelong stickup kids and in their midtwenties. They were ruthless. Known to harm and kill if their victims resisted even slightly. Many hustlers secretly paid them just to keep from possibly being targets. They were death on foot, death on wheels, or death on horseback, if that was their means of transportation to their victim. Gun, knife, razor, or bat, it didn't matter; all these tools were instruments they used to maim and murder.

Beam was the unquestioned leader of the duo. *Ugly* was an understatement when describing him. At six two, two-fifty, he was an imposing force. And he always abused his physical attributes. His hands were big as frying pans and strong as vise grips. His head was a large shiny bowling ball, not a shade lighter or size smaller. His face was a forever-menacing scowl. Puffy black buck-fifty razor scars were carved from eye to lip on the left and ear to chin on the right. Both scars told the gruesome tale of a deadly riot that broke out on the prison yard in Concord. Beam was only eighteen at the time of the Concord riot. He was doing a three-year bid for assault and was still too new to the signs of the system to recognize the riot coming before it came. The attack came and went before he even knew that

Jonathan cut him. He didn't even know Jonathan could use his legs to get up out of his wheelchair. He never viewed him as a threat. It looked like red teardrops dripping down his face.

Beam always hated OP, but the scars Jonathan put on him multiplied that hate times ten. The scars were unwelcome tattoos that stole the minimal sanity he had. They assisted in his path to alcohol and heroine abuse. If your name wasn't Q, then Beam couldn't be trusted. Period.

"Arthur just called Jermel's punk ass. He should be going ta get the Flave right now. I doubt he got that much work on him," Q said from the passenger seat, with his good eye focused on Jermel's Beamer. "Wherever he pull over at, I'm on his ass."

Q was far less physically imposing, with his short frail frame, but probably even more dangerous than his violent comrade. He existed in complete darkness, with no signs of light at the end of the cold tunnel. Life or death was a choice that meant nothing sentimental to him; it just was. Morals and principles left him as early as his parents did when he was eleven. They were victims of a syringe. His entire left eye was missing, causing the lid to stay shut. He turned his head for a second too long as he raped the thirteen-year-old daughter of one of his victims. The young girl took the opportunity to grab a sharp paper weight next to the bed and stuck it deep into his eye. Needless to say, she and her father were killed during that robbery.

Q was short-tempered, with zero tolerance for those who opposed his will. This was the cause of the majority of the violence during their capers. Beam attempted to tame him at times but usually fell in line with the savagery of his sadistic sidekick. Outside of their robberies, Q looked to Beam for strength and guidance, but once they were on a job, he was nearly impossible to keep in check.

No matter how many jobs they pulled off, their addiction to drugs, alcohol, and women kept them on the hunt for their next fix. Troy and Jermel's reputation meant nothing to them. OP meant nothing to them. Beam and Q were cut from the same thorough cloth, and they were before the two brothers' era.

"You ain't bout ta have all the fun, dogg," Beam gritted in response to Q's selfish anticipation of attacking Jermel. "I been waiting ta get this bitch muthafucka forever! I wish that muthafucka Jonathan was with him. I'll be right behind you."

*****

"Let me get four Pepsis with that too," Amin told the old Puerto Rican cashier at Food Court.

"Okay, sir," the cashier replied. "That will be twenty-seven dollars and ninety-five cents."

Troy said, "I got it," as he approached the counter and placed a hand on Amin's arm. "Y'all already spoiled me at the Beritz. The least I can do is pay for some grub."

"Dogg, you know that ain't shit. Just take ya ass ta the NBA and let us finish shit up in these streets."

"Never that! The NBA can't even stop me from running the streets. I am the streets!" He chuckled.

Amin always encouraged Troy to go as far as he could with school and sports. Troy loved sports, but he loved the streets more. He wanted to take his game to the next level, but he balled more off natural ability than hard work. His heart was definitely more in the streets than on the ball court. His lack of effort got him by, even kept him dominant, but it wasn't a good formula for the next level of competition.

Amin even traveled to a few campuses with him. They stayed weekends at some, mingled and got a feel for the life. The environments at Boston College and UMass were the best feels for them.

Amin graduated from MP but had no personal interest in college. All his passions were in the streets. He was content with what he was into. Troy and Jermel were his younger brothers, and Peanut his rowdy twin. If it wasn't about their circle and Orchard Park, it wasn't about anything in his eyes.

They all did so much together, good and bad, and if he were to lose any piece to their puzzle, finding peace after that would be nearly impossible. He had a large biological family, with three sisters and lots of cousins, but Peanut, Troy, and Jermel were his only brothers.

*****

Jermel stopped his car, double-parked, hit his hazard lights, and hopped out too fast for Q to jump out behind him. He almost fell when his Timberland boot landed on a sheet of black ice near the curb. He recovered quickly, though. He knew that Peanut was laughing, so he didn't bother to look back. Peanut was going to get a lot of laughs off him about that slip when they got around Troy and Amin at Food Court.

Shit. Jermel was more cautious with his steps up the stairs of the brownstone building he entered.

The night was cold and still. It hadn't snowed in a few days, but the temperature was in the teens, which froze mounds of snow and dirt together to form small muddy white hills all over the streets. Movement was minimal in the area.

The liquor ran through Peanut's blood, causing him to ignore the bite of winter. He rolled down the window, turned up "Ain't No N***a" from Jay Z's *Reasonable Doubt* album in the tape deck, and blew out a cloud of hydro weed smoke. His seat was leaned all the way back. He was in deep thought, totally unaware that he was being stalked. He was usually overly aware of his surroundings but was all the way off point at the moment. His mind was on the night he was about to spend with his daughter's mother when he got back to his crib. He hadn't spent any intimate time with her in a few months, which was way too long. He was looking forward to it. She wanted that dreadful word out of him, *commitment*. He wasn't ready to settle down, so they stayed in and out of riffs with each other.

He was a good father, and she loved him, so she stuck by him. But lately he'd been sensing that he was letting her slip too far away. She had her needs, her life, and he respected that, but he never wanted her to drift so far away that she forgot where home was. Tonight he planned to seriously remind her who home was and why.

Beam parked a safe distance back from Jermel's car, killed the lights, and left the engine running. He rolled his ski mask over his face. Q pulled a dark stocking over his face. They didn't perform any superstitious rituals before a job; they simply trusted each other and moved on instincts.

The weather didn't matter. The adrenaline rush from hunting a longtime enemy, with a major profit in the end, generated enough heat to melt the snow and ice beneath their feet. They stepped out, stayed low, and crept along the side of the parked cars on the street until they got within one vehicle of Jermel's. No verbal communication was necessary; everything was understood.

Beam had his sights locked onto the brownstone's entrance, his hand on his burner. He knew he couldn't hesitate or misstep in any way with Jermel; that was the only reason he didn't sniff a few bags before the hit, nor did he allow Q to. Their victims were thorough. Even his hate wouldn't let him deny that. The spoils of this one-sided battle would be enough drugs and money to set them straight for real.

Q smelled the weed and saw the smoke coming from the window. Peanut was really slipping. He wanted to rush him right then to be sure the blunt kept him off point, but the timing wasn't right. Watching Peanut flick the ash off the tip, Q pictured his other hand lying dormant or clutching a pistol. He chose to assume the latter, for safety's sake. He heard Foxy Brown's verse clearly, so he knew that Peanut was still in Beritz mode. That would work in his favor.

These clowns think they untouchable! he thought.

When Jermel came carelessly trotting out of the building, Beam went right at him, .45 pointed center mass.

Q rushed the passenger door of the Beamer at the same time and put his Glock 9 in Peanut's face. He focused on his free hand as he pulled the door open and yanked him out. Q patted him down thoroughly, confiscating every item he touched, including a .357 snub nose in the pocket of his leather jacket.

Beam was doing the exact same thing, relieving Jermel of jewelry, money, the drugs he just got out the stash house, and a pistol.

Surprise. One of the deadliest weapons.

Beam and Q weren't wasting this golden opportunity on a small profit; they wanted it all. After their pat-downs, they ordered both of them into the hallway. The robbers saw disdain instead of fear in their victims. They moved extra cautious because of it. Beam and Q had the obvious advantage but took nothing for granted.

Q held Peanut hostage at the bottom of the five cement steps leading to the entrance of the building. Beam held his gun on Jermel at the top. Q kept Peanut facing away from him to be sure he didn't try to see into his mask and notice his one evil eye staring back. Beam told Jermel to open the door.

And that was when all hell broke loose!

Jermel, being a seasoned stickup kid himself, could tell that these were experienced robbers. He figured that once they got them inside, they would take everything, then kill them. He couldn't go out like that.

He faked like he fumbled for his keys, then looked for an opportunity to attack. He knew Peanut would be on point once he moved, but when the keys hit the steps, the masked man stepped back and shook his head, making it clear that he was not falling for it.

Jermel felt foolish for even attempting the move. Its failure caused his anger to grow out of control. He decided to determine his own fate. He bent to pick up the keys, then acted so fast nobody knew what he was doing. "Fuck y'all suckers!" he yelled as he turned and threw the keys as far as he could into the unforgiving night.

Beam was startled by the sudden move. He instinctively pumped three shots in Jermel's body.

Peanut leaped at the man with the stocking on his face but was spun 180 degrees by a shot from his attacker. Peanut took off down Dudley Street, running in a zigzag on a long sheet of ice but popped up like a professional hockey player.

Beam and Q quickly retreated back to their hotbox, while Jermel was left lying at the bottom of the steps, facedown, in a pool of his own blood.

Chapter 4

"I gotta get up ta the Bay and drop Jack off some more dough tomorrow," Troy said while staring across the road at the jail's eleven-story tower building.

"You really fuck with dude, huh?" Amin's question was more of a statement. "How much time he got left? I gotta meet him when he touch down."

"He got, like, eight months left. He good peoples, yo. Y'all gonna vibe."

Boston Food Court was less than three miles from the stash house where Jermel and Peanut were ambushed. It was a small wooden hut-like structure that was popular after the club and bar let out. A few welded-down, booth-like tables were placed around but were rarely used due to Food Court's usually rowdy crowds.

Troy and Amin stood outside in front of the hut while waiting for their orders. They wanted to avoid the thick crowd, plus Amin needed to smoke a cigarette.

Vehicles were double-parked and on top of the curb. Tipsy partiers disregarded the cold as they hung outside and inside of whips. As Troy traced his Adidas in the light remainder of snow and complained about the cold, a bunch of police cruisers flew by with their sirens blaring. The two cruisers that were assigned a detail at Food Court took off too.

"Muthafuckas acting up somewhere tonight," Amin said. He puffed his Newport. "Let me hit up Peanut and make sure it ain't them two acting crazy." Though sarcastic, the truth of his comment was all too serious.

After a minute, Amin complained, "I hit both their horns, and none of them answered, dogg." He tried to disguise his concern, but the combination of no answers and the proximity of sirens disturbed him. It wasn't common for teenagers to have cell phones at that time, so since they had them, they always kept them on.

Troy's beeper went off. He checked the number, then began to call back. "They aight, dogg. This Peanut's crib right here," he said while pulling out his phone.

"Yo, dogg!" Peanut yelled. He was out of breath and wheezing, like he was on the verge of an asthma attack. "I got shot in my back." He continued through gritted teeth, "And bruh got hit bad in front of the stash house."

"What?" Troy's reaction froze Amin in a way that the weather couldn't.

"Dogg...bruh got touched bad. He took at least three point-blank. I had ta get ghost, but they was tryna air me out too." He sounded like he was on the verge of breaking down.

Amin saw Troy's body language get weaker. He spoke up. "What the fuck happened, dogg?"

Troy held up a finger and silently analyzed the situation before speaking again.

"Man, two cats rolled up on some stickup shit. It was a stick... but they was gonna body us, yo." His voice was low and distant.

Troy knew that Peanut was running the scene through his mind. He didn't interrupt.

"Masked up..." Peanut's voice continued to wander, then suddenly snapped back. "They tried ta make bruh open the door ta the building, but you know his wild ass wasn't going for that. He threw the keys in the street somewhere, and dudes started bussin'. Awe, shit!" he yelled in physical pain this time.

"Wasn't y'all strapped?" Troy asked.

"Shit happened too fast, dogg...straight up...too fast."

"You gotta get ta the hospital," Troy said. "We on our way over ta the stash house. We saw all the Jake headed y'all way, so..." Troy was trying to play his usual calm, in-control self, but Peanut heard the panic in him and cut him off.

"Slow ya smart, dumb ass down," he said. Even in mental and physical anguish, Peanut was still able to see straight and in advance. "Five-O gonna be all around the stash house. I wasn't gonna fuck with no hospital, but this shit's bad…shit! Y'all get over to City and wait for bruh ta get there. The ambulance will get him there. Ain't nothing y'all can do for him at the spot but go ta jail. I got Nish tryna get me out the door ta the hospital now. Ahh!"

Troy wanted to lash out at Peanut for how he came at him and made an attempt at verbal retaliation. "Hurry the fuck up, then!" He hung up and hung his head. He focused on the O and P he traced in the snow with his sneaker.

Amin braced himself for the horrible news.

"Somebody ran down on them, dogg," Troy mumbled. "They both got hit up. Jermel got hit bad."

"I heard enough ta figure that out. What's up?"

"Come on. We gotta get ta City," Troy said while heading to Amin's whip.

Boston City Hospital sat right around the corner from Boston Food Court. Troy and Amin could've run there just as fast as driving, if not faster. It was a large complex building that handled probably 70 percent of the city's emergencies. People complained of inadequate treatment at times, but in actuality, the hospital was literally a life saver.

Albany Street ran from Troy and Jermel's building in OP, past City's emergency entrance and the connecting morgue. The beginning and the end.

Amin pulled into the small U-shaped emergency room parking lot, and Troy hopped out as he went to get a parking spot.

Troy entered the hospital through a set of electric sliding doors, into a long hallway with a waiting area to his right. The building was quiet. A pint-size grandmotherly woman looked tired behind the long reception desk.

Amin quickly found a parking space and was through the electric sliding doors within two minutes behind Troy. As soon as he entered, he saw Troy raising hell with a startled older woman. He hurried over to intervene. "Whoa, whoa, whoa. Calm down, dogg," he demanded. "What's up?"

Troy pointed disrespectfully at her. "This lady ain't tryna do her damn job! That's what's up!"

"S-s-sir," the silver-haired receptionist addressed Amin. She hoped that he was more reasonable. "All I told this young man is that we haven't received any patients with gunshot wounds in here tonight."

Amin looked apologetically at the woman. "I understand, ma'am. Let me speak ta him." He led Troy over to a corner near a set of pay phones to calm him down. Fortunately, there were only a few women and children in the waiting area. Amin didn't really have to worry about Troy taking his anger out on them. However, he did wish they would stop staring at them, just in case.

As he was calming Troy, Amin saw the receptionist pick up the phone and hoped she wasn't calling the police. After a moment, she waved them over to the desk and explained that they just received a patient but she wasn't authorized to give them any information. They pleaded, but she put her foot down, displaying strength that they didn't know existed in her little body.

Amin laid all his cards on the table. He told her that the patient's name was Jermel Gilliard, a seventeen-year-old from 890 Albany Street. He even gave her the address to the building he was shot in front of. "He's our brother," he pleaded with the lady.

The receptionist was a twenty-year-experienced worker at City Hospital. She was also a mother and grandmother to boys just like Troy and Amin and recognized that they were simply concerned about their friend or family member. She'd dealt with thousands of situations where family and friends stormed through the emergency room doors, frantic over their loved ones. She had a front-row seat to the escalating violence in the city. She even lost two of her own grandchildren to the epidemic. She contemplated leaving her job on many occasions, but the notion that she was able to comfort people in their weakest state allowed her to stay on and stand strong.

She decided to slightly bend the rules by confirming that it was Jermel who was just brought in and that he was shot multiple times. She then assured them that if they were not immediate family, neither she nor the doctors would be able to release any further information to them.

Jermel's mother, Liona, was useless in these types of situations. Troy knew that even finding Liona at that time of night would be extremely hard.

"Listen…" Troy tried to reason now. "First, I apologize for disrespecting you."

She gave him a defiant look, as if she wasn't impressed.

Troy continued, "He's my best friend, my brother. My mother been handling our health issues all our lives. Will the doctors talk ta her?"

"I'm afraid not." She shrugged.

Troy's temperature flared up again. He stormed out the door, unfazed by the weather, and pulled out his cell phone. After six rings, he heard Joyce on the other end. "Ma!" he almost screamed into the phone.

"What's up, baby?" she asked, sensing that something was wrong. She was still more asleep than awake.

"Listen, Jermel got shot. It's bad too. I need you ta see if Liona's upstairs and get her down here, 'cause these people won't tell me no nothing!"

"What time is it?" she asked, more to herself than her son. The springs on her old bed squeaked as she rolled over. She had to hold an arm across her large, heavy breast to prevent them from flopping. Her eyes widened when she saw that her alarm clock read 2:48 a.m. "Okay, baby, I'm getting up now. I hope this little girl's home." She referred to Liona as "little girl" whenever she was upset with her. "I'll be down there regardless. You all right?" she asked.

"I'm cool. Just get here. Love you."

"Y'all at City, right?"

"Yeah."

"Okay. Love you too, baby."

Joyce hung up and rolled out of her bed. Her back ached, mainly from years of carrying her large bosom, also from constantly being on her feet at work. The stone floor was cold under her bare feet as she dragged them to the tiny bathroom in her thin robe. She stared at herself in the medicine cabinet mirror above the sink and silently cursed Troy and Jermel for the heavy bags under her eyes and extra creases in her face. She was only thirty-nine but felt closer to fifty.

After getting herself together, she walked back to her bed, knelt down, and said a prayer.

After Troy hung up with Joyce, he went back inside and saw Amin at the desk, chatting with Grandma. He peeped a woman in the waiting room peeking at him but ignored her questioning gaze. He was mad at himself for causing a scene. He called Amin over, hoping to hear some new news.

No luck. Grandma was back to going by the book.

As Troy and Amin spoke, Peanut stumbled through the door with Danisha and his mother, Ms. Goode, supporting him. His shoulder was sloppily wrapped in a sheet, and he was bloody and on the verge of collapse.

Troy and Amin rushed to his side while Grandma got on the phone to call for help.

"Who did this, dogg?" Amin asked in an angry whisper.

"I don t know, but this shit got worse," Peanut said, squeezing his eyes tight and scrunching his face up. "Where's the fuckin' doctors?"

On cue, nurses rushed from the back doors into the hallway, put Peanut on a stretcher, and rolled him back through the large white doors they appeared from.

Grandma eyed Amin, Troy, and Danisha suspiciously as they huddled up. She knew that victim number 2 was in some way related to number 1.

Danisha and Peanut had their daughter, Angel, when they were fifteen. Both girls were his heart. He just had a hard time giving in to Danisha's full desires. They were lifelong companions, going back to the projects' days of seven minutes to heaven, a game played mostly by preteens, where the girls had a chance at a head start to run and the boys would chase them. If a girl was caught, the boy got his seven minutes alone with her in a hallway, abandoned apartment, or any other available secluded place. Ever since they were nine, Danisha always let Peanut catch her. Their seven minutes eventually turned into nine months and Angel.

Joyce looked up to Danisha's grandmother, and Troy grew up tight with her family. Troy still hustled out of a second-floor apartment in her Batan Court building.

Amin had no more patience. Being in the blind was killing him. Peanut's mother went to talk to Grandma at the reception desk, so he went right in on Danisha. "What he tell you, Nish?"

Danisha was calm, but her eyes were worried. They were ready to drip. "He just kept talking like he was crazy or something. It was like he wasn't even talking ta me or Ms. Goode. When we was in the car on the way here, he kept saying…he thinks bruh's gone." As soon as the words came out, the tears poured down.

Amin hugged her tight.

Troy began to pace in a short line, irate, with homicidal thoughts playing out in his mind. His phone rang. He pulled it out and answered on the first ring, anticipating Joyce. "What's up?"

"Troy! What happened? Are y'all okay? Why ain't Chubby answering his phone or beeper?" Ella sounded hysterical.

Troy was surprised to hear her voice. He tried, unsuccessfully, to be the in-control person she knew him to be. "I don't know what the fuck's up yet, yo! Jermel and Peanut got hit up, and I'm stuck in this emergency room, not knowing shit!"

Her silence said she wanted more information.

"It don't sound good with Jermel, sis," he finished.

"I'm on the way down there. I'm pulling out my parking lot right now. I'll be there in, like, ten minutes."

"Let me talk ta him!" Troy heard Trina in the background. She got on the phone. "Are you okay, boo?"

Even in this rough situation, her voice seemed to smooth things out a bit for him. "I don't know, baby girl. I'll see y'all when y'all get here." He hung up and went back to Danisha and Peanut's conversation.

Within fifteen minutes of their call, Trina and Ella scurried through the electric doors of the emergency room. They hugged Troy, Amin, and Danisha.

"How y'all know something happened?" Troy asked.

"My girl Tanyah was on Dudley Street and saw Chubby's car with a bunch of police and an ambulance around it. She got out and called me from the pay phone right there, but she couldn't tell if anyone was in the ambulance, police cars, or nothing." Ella had tears streaming down her high cheekbones. "I kept beeping and calling him, but he wouldn't call back. He was supposed ta come over after y'all left the Beritz."

Troy pulled Trina and Ella to the side to explain the little that he knew. Trina was overwhelmed with the whole situation, the tragedy of Jermel and safety of Troy. She unconsciously hugged his waist as he spoke, showing a surprising display of emotion to all of them. She wanted to personally assure Troy's safety.

Trina felt so natural on his hip that he casually wrapped a strong arm around her and squeezed her close to him.

Within an hour and a half of Troy and Amin getting to Boston City Hospital, nearly twenty people from OP walked through the emergency room door, inquiring about Jermel and Peanut. Word was traveling fast through the projects. It was 4:00 a.m., and City's emergency room lobby resembled the Orchard Park Neighborhood Center building.

Just after 4:00 a.m., Joyce stormed through the door, with Liona behind her. Joyce appeared to be her usual calm self. Liona looked like she just climbed out of a trash can.

"Hi, Ms. Newton," a few people said as she entered.

"I told y'all stop calling me Ms. Newton. My name's Joyce!" she snapped.

Troy went over, hugged his mother, and greeted Liona. Besides looking like a wreck, Liona appeared alert and concerned.

"How's my baby, Troy?" Liona was looking for him to give her an answer that only a doctor could at that time. "Is ya brother okay?" She studied his face for something positive.

Troy stared into her hazel eyes and saw Jermel staring back at him through them. They could pass for twins. "I hope so. Come with me." He turned and led them toward the reception desk.

"It took me so long 'cause I had ta ride all over Roxbury ta find this little girl." Joyce was clearly upset. "Then I had ta take her home and search the whole apartment just ta find her ID."

Ever since they were young girls in the projects, Joyce had looked out for Liona. She was always like a younger sister, a pain-in-the-ass sibling. Liona looked up at Joyce and only got her act together under Joyce's scrutiny. The problem was, she never kept it together for long.

Their parents were close, as was the majority in Orchard Park in the fifties and sixties. While Joyce's father made her life harder by abandoning her and her mother, Liona's stayed around to make hers harder through mental and physical abuse. It was Liona's abusive father who ran her into the arms of an equally abusive older lover who got her hooked on drugs and pregnant at just fifteen years old.

They both conceived within weeks of each other, but Joyce was twenty-one and in a more stable situation. During their pregnancies, she made sure Liona made it to doctor's appointments, fed her, and kept her out of the streets as much as possible.

"This is Jermel Gilliard's mother," Troy told Grandma when they got to the desk. He pointed at Liona when he told her. "Can you get someone out here ta let us know something now?"

Grandma looked at Liona and understood Troy's concern from earlier. She picked up the phone, conversed for a little over a minute, then hung up. "Someone will be out as soon as they're available." She opted for a polite smile. "Just take a seat and try to relax."

Both women understood that the smile was meant to comfort them, but they saw through the gesture to its core. It was sadness and concern.

Grandma must've felt the women's intuition. She wasn't able to look them in their eyes for long.

After three more hours, which felt like three days, a doctor finally appeared from the back. He was taken aback by the determined crowd that swarmed him. His pale skin flushed. His big hairy ears turned bright red. He rubbed his neat beard, peered over the top of his thin-rimmed glasses, and nervously surveyed the crowd. "I...need to speak with immediate family members only, please." His strong baritone deceived his weak appearance.

The crowd fell back to let the doctor speak to the mothers, Troy, Amin, and Danisha. He wasn't graceful or unrealistic in detailing the severity of Jermel's condition. Jermel was hit twice in the abdomen and once near the heart. His condition was bad, but his life was in his own hands now. The medical staff did all that they could, removing two bullets, but they couldn't remove the one near his heart. The rest was up to Jermel's will to live.

Peanut's update was a lot lighter. He was being disinfected, patched up, and would be free to leave in a few hours. He was hit on the right side of his upper back and would require a sling on his arm while the wound healed.

The mothers went down the hall to the hospital's main lobby to get a clear head away from the crowd. Troy, Amin, and Danisha spoke to separate groups in the crowd, explaining the situation to many mixed reactions.

Trina went back to Troy's side, where she had been for most of the night. She and Ella got a few angry stares from the project crowd.

Neesie, a pretty, light-skinned, tough girl, was staring the hardest. She eventually said what was on some of the crowd's mind. "Troy, why them A bitches in here? If I find out they had something ta do with this, I'mma whoop they ass!"

Troy was caught off guard by Neesie. Trina and Ella were so tight with him and Jermel he disregarded where they were from. For a second, he questioned his own judgment. Then, without showing any signs of indecision, he said, "I feel you, Neesie, but chill out. Not now. These are our peoples." He figured his simple assurance would be enough.

Along with Neesie, Cheryl, Nut, Dolly, and Penny wore serious scowls. Troy completely understood their skepticism. They were ticking time bombs. He needed to hurry up and cut the right wire to defuse them.

Neesie didn't back down from Troy as easily as he expected. "I just hope that pussy ain't got you fooled, 'cause I will whoop they ass!" She wasn't letting up and was now getting supporting nods from around her.

Shit. Troy knew he had to dead this quick. Normally, he would've checked Neesie or anyone else who questioned him, hard enough to put an immediate end to it, but his mind was off and the situation was sensitive for everybody.

"Listen!" He stared Neesie down, then searched the room for every dissenting eye. "My brother's in ICU, fighting for his fuckin' life! Nobody in here got time for this bullshit right now! Y'all know damn well I'mma find out what the fuck happened and deal with it! Leave that shit ta me!"

The females knew better than to push Troy any further, but they still shot daggers at Ella and Trina, daring them to hold their gazes too long.

Ella was a prideful girl. Though she knew she had no wins in the emergency room, she couldn't stand by and be insulted like she was being. She knew Neesie and some of the others in the crowd on a usually cordial basis. She felt compelled to speak up.

"I know y'all hurting, but damn, I am too," she said. "Jermel's my man. I love him just like y'all do. I ain't never been no trifling, setup bitch, and you know that, Neesie."

Ella's words were sincere and good-natured but delivered with a little too much attitude for this hostile crowd.

"Bitch! Who you rolling ya eyes at?" Cheryl stood up, ready to fight.

Troy held Trina with one arm. He positioned himself between her and the crowd.

Keywon, Ace, and Moe stepped in to help Troy.

Terell yelled, "Y'all chill out, yo! On, doggs! That's they peoples...respect that!"

It was now understood that everyone better stand down, but Crystal couldn't resist one last shot. She was, and would always be, bitter with the A for taking Jimmy away from her and their son. "That bitch is probably tryna set all y'all up 'cause her brother got killed in the summer." She looked Trina in the eyes. "Yeah...I'm hip ta you, bitch."

Trina almost broke free from Troy's grip, but he had her in a vise grip.

"Let that bitch go!" Penny yelled.

Amin gripped Ella tight. She was ready to throw down and get beaten down with her girl. He dragged her toward the electric doors and signaled for Troy to do the same with Trina.

The three mothers heard the commotion and ran to the waiting area, led by Joyce, who restored order.

It was now morning. The school and work crowd was moving with a purpose.

Once outside, Amin took a deep breath. "Let's just cool off in this air." He sparked a Newport.

"Troy, you know I would never try ta hurt you, right?" Trina's big brown eyes were staring up into his.

He truly believed her words. He held on to the moment, then looked at Ella to be sure he had her attention too. "Y'all my peoples, yo. Everyone's just scared and upset right now. I know y'all wouldn't cross us." He squeezed Trina tight, and she squeezed him back.

Chapter 5

The two weeks following Peanut's and Jermel's shooting were chaotic. Amin and Troy grilled Peanut on as much detail as he could remember from that night. They also scolded him for not being on point while conducting business.

Peanut's recollection of what happened wasn't all that helpful. Though he laid out a clear picture, motive, and intent, it was still nearly impossible to figure out who did it.

Amin and Troy handled all the business in the streets. They forced Peanut to stay in the house and be cared for by Danisha and his mother.

Ms. Goode was still a bit distraught about waking up in the middle of the night, seeing her son drenched in blood. She was thankful that she was even able to care for him over his recovery period.

Amin took on the bulk of the business, refusing to let Troy miss any school or practice time because of it.

The one game Troy played was against West Roxbury High, home to much of the A-Team. The murderous performance he put on was a message. He had no idea who tried to kill his peoples, but it was always a good chance that the culprits were from the A. He scored forty-seven points, twenty-nine of them the hard way, with dunks and layups, and grabbed twenty-two rebounds.

His animalistic aggressiveness at both ends of the floor was uncoachable, so Coach Wilson just sat back and watched his star perform.

The fans recognized the lunatic aggression and, though entertained, were left bewildered. The players on the court, as well as the players in the streets, received the intended message. Trina and Ella were reduced to worried spectators rather than the cheerful fans they were at his opening game against Dorchester High.

Two days after the abuse he put on West Roxbury High, Troy got the best news he could ever hear. Peanut called him from the hospital and told him that Jermel was asking for him. He was in his last period when he got the call, so he waited until the final bell rang, then met up with Trina and Ella in front of the school.

It was routine for them to visit Jermel for a few hours after school and talk to him in his comatose state. He had been unresponsive, but that never broke their will.

Troy didn't tell the girls the good news as they drove to City Hospital. When they stepped into Jermel's room, they nearly passed out. Peanut, Liona, and Joyce had stepped out for a bite to eat, so the three of them momentarily had him to themselves.

"Oh, y'all was scared or something?" Jermel joked in a low, weak voice. He lost a significant amount of blood and weight. His skin was near grayish. His eyes were weary. It was obvious that he was working with very little strength.

"Chubby!" Ella stood still with both hands over her mouth. "Oh my god!" She ran to the bed and hugged him a little too tight for his condition. He grimaced and grunted, causing her to let up a little. "Don't ever do that again!" She nudged his shoulder. A tear rolled down her cheek.

"What up, Metal Mouth?" he continued with the humor, using the name he teased her with when she wore braces. "Happy Valentine's Day."

"Shut up." She had an ear-to-ear smile now. "Now my Valentine's Day is happy."

Trina walked over and gave him a kiss on the forehead. Troy stood back and just stared. They felt the love and relief with no words even being exchanged.

The girls knew that the brothers were going to want to talk alone, so they got in as much as they could before Troy asked them to excuse themselves after close to an hour. They humorously rolled their eyes and faked an attitude as they stepped out.

"Maybe the streets don't fear your pretty-boy, silky-haired ass no more," Troy jabbed. His words were light, but the anger inside of him was heavy.

Jermel's hazels turned dark and hard. His newly transfused blood rose to his pained face. Though he was physically weak, strength illuminated through his glare. "Dogg, I'm mad as shit, 'cause I keep running shit through my mind and can't get it out. On, doggs. I don't even know if it came from my end or Peanut's end."

Troy told him to break it all down to him. He sat in attentive silence as Jermel struggled to speak. He heard Peanut's account over and over but absolutely needed to hear things from Jermel. No matter what Jermel or anyone else thought, Troy knew that this attempt to kill came from Jermel's end.

As Jermel spoke, the thing that caught Troy's attention most was Arthur's name. It was the only thing out of place. "I ain't know you was still fuckin' with Arthur, dogg." His voice was accusing. "His ho ass still live in the building next ta Ella, right?"

Jermel got offended by the chastising tone. "Dogg, you knew I still been hittin' Arthur off! Don't get on that bullshit now!"

"I don't give a fuck about you getting mad, dogg. I'm tryna figure out who tried ta kill yo ass!" Troy was no-nonsense, but he tried to lighten the mood with a little humor. "Don't act tough, yo. I'll pull one of them staples out ya stomach."

Jermel calmed down and managed a chuckle. "I feel you being leery with dude, but he ain't had shit ta do with it. Trust me." He had to pause to catch his breath. "Arthur only hit me up that late 'cause I kept dodging him all day and kept telling him I was on the way. Dude ain't got the heart ta rob me, dogg. I kept spinning him ta come see yo ass dribble that ball. He don't know none of our stash spots, anyway, dogg. Them dudes was posted at the spot, waiting for one of us ta show up. They was probably posted up all night."

"What you saying? You think it's some inside shit?"

"I ain't sure, dogg, but I'mma find out…and muthafuckas is gonna die. On, doggs."

"Aight, dogg. We'll get ta the bottom of it. I gotta ask you something, though." Troy looked uncomfortable in his pause.

Jermel studied him, then asked, "What's on ya mind?"

Troy still didn't answer. He was trying to figure out how to get the question out, but before he could voice his thought, Jermel answered, "Nah, dogg!" with absolute certainty.

"You don't even know what I'm bout ta say, yo. Hold up."

"Bet a stack I know," Jermel challenged. "We go back ta diapers. I know everything you thinking."

"Hell no!" Troy laughed. "I ain't bout ta give you no free stack. You already owe me for these past couple weeks." He zoned out for a moment. "So everything's cool with them?"

"Yeah, they cool," Jermel confirmed. "Ella will ride with us before she fuck with them chumps around her way. Believe that, dogg. Peanut told me Neesie and them was 'bout ta whoop they ass in the emergency room." He gave a weak laugh that really hurt his chest. "Damn." He rubbed the spot that hurt, then disregarded it. "I'm glad you ain't let 'em get dogged." Jermel went into deep thought again, then said, "You might as well stop pitying little ole Trina and tap that pussy. You know she already in love with yo ass, and you ain't even hit it yet. Hold up, you slick-dick muthafucka, did you already hit it?"

"Nah. I ain't even on it like that with shorty. She mad cool, but like you said, I went through that shit already. I ain't tryna play grief counselor."

"You can't slick a can of oil, yo. This me. Trina's a twenty piece, and all she want is your nine iron up in her." He laughed some more.

Troy called Trina and Ella back in the room when he and Jermel were done. They all kicked it a while longer. They made plans to visit the same time the next day, then Troy led both overly sensitive girls out to his whip.

After leaving the hospital, Troy stopped down Dudley to treat the girls to a meal at the Silver Slippers restaurant. They were all hyped about Jermel and needed to sit and kick it.

As they ate and laughed together, Troy thought about Jermel's confidence in the girls, specifically Ella. He trusted Jermel on that tip. He had an even higher level of respect for them himself for how they rushed right to their side in their time of need that night.

He was definitely feeling Trina. He was tired of holding his feelings back just because she got a little emotional at times over losing her brother. He felt like it was the perfect moment to reach out to her.

"Trina…what you doing tonight?"

"Oooh, oooh, oooh! I knew ya fine ass was feelin' my girl!" Ella was hopping up and down in her chair, smiling and pointing an accusing finger.

Troy waved off her accusation and tried to remain cool. "Calm ya ass down, yo. I'm just tryna see if Trina's tryna chill later."

"Shut up, Ella!" Trina playfully punched her in the arm, then focused fully on Troy. "I'm not busy tonight. Did you have something in mind?"

"Bitch, stop frontin'," Ella taunted Trina. "It didn't matter if you was busy or not. You know damn well—"

"Shut up, Ella," Trina said. Her face was blushing.

Troy ignored Ella. "Yeah. I wanna take you out, if it's cool with you." He was uncharacteristically nervous.

"What time you picking me up?" she asked in her sweetest air, revealing a half-smile that Ella knew was ten times larger inside.

Trina was really big on Troy. Possibly love at first sight. His reluctance to go beyond a cordial relationship made her want him even more. She got to know him so well over the short span of five months. He was more than just an attraction. He was a necessity in her life. That was why when he pulled up to her building at 6:00 p.m., she did a triple take in the mirror to make sure she was on point.

Troy knocked on the door to her second-floor apartment. Though she was well aware of his presence, she waited until he knocked again so she didn't appear overly anxious. When she finally let him in, the look on his face made her feel like the cure to cancer.

She sported a formfitting dark-blue Polo skirt that sat just above her knees, exposing enough thick caramel to shame a candy factory. Her hair favored its darker color during the winter months, but its natural shades of brown complemented her eyes. Sky-blue and white seashells hung from some of her dreads, matching her Carolina Tarheels shell-toe Adidas.

Troy stared as if he'd escaped a dark cave and was suddenly blinded by the bright light. Without even realizing that the words were leaving his mouth, he said, "Yo…you beautiful, Trina." His mouth stayed open as he stared in awe.

It was the approval in his eyes and the way he said it that nearly caused her to come in her panties. She had craved this type of attention from him since day 1. She savored the moment.

Unfortunately, Trina's most sensual moment with him to date was rudely interrupted by Lady. Lady was the family's eleven-year-old black Chihuahua. She trotted into the living room, making a fuss because she didn't know Troy and she wasn't being acknowledged. She wasn't giving her intrusive growl, which made Trina feel even better about Troy.

Lady's judgment was trusted in the Goslin home. She was merely barking to make her presence felt, but Trina could already tell that she liked Troy. She was actually flirting even more than Trina.

Troy looked from Trina to Lady, then back to Trina. He thought back to the night outside the emergency room at City and said, "I thought you said you would never hurt me." He had a mockingly concerned expression on his face.

They both laughed.

He took in the scenery of her apartment. He was in enemy territory, all the way out of bounds. The inside of the building and apartment wasn't much different than OP's. He never thought he would enter a building in the A, let alone an apartment.

There was a bit more space, but it was the same one-way-in, one-way-out, cement-surrounding, compact housing. Beads, common in these types of apartments, hung from the ceiling to the floor in an empty door space. The beads played the part of the door, dividing the front and back of the place. Troy accurately envisioned the miniature bathroom and few bedrooms lined on each side of the walls in a short hallway beyond the beads.

"Lady, be quiet and stop showing off!" a voice said from behind the beads.

As Troy and Trina laughed at his joke about Lady, the dog continued to bark lightly, hop, and twirl, until Ms. Goslin stepped through the beads to shut her up. She wore a too-big West Roxbury High School football T-shirt, cutoff jean shorts and flip-flops. She was beautiful. Beautiful but pained.

She looked like Trina's older sister. And not much older.

Age added a little pudge, and instead of dreads, she wore a short-cut perm. Her thirty-eight years were worn well, but hard times and heartache were written all over her like with so many mothers in the hood.

"Mmm, hmm," she sounded and smiled with just her lips. Her arms were folded across her chest as she stared at her daughter. "I see why you been in my bathroom all day, taking up all the mirrors in the house."

When Ms. Goslin focused on him, Troy felt the same strange vibe that he felt when Trina stared at him. They both appeared to be looking through his physical body, deep into his soul.

Being the natural charmer that he was, he countered her unspoken compliment with one of his own. "Thank you, Ms. Goslin. It's nice ta finally see where Trina gets her beauty from."

Ms. Goslin blushed.

He smiled and extended his hand in a formal introduction. She took his hand into both of hers, then released an assortment of pre-planned and spontaneous questions. "Where you from, Troy?"

"I already told you, Ma," Trina whined, trying to stop the unavoidable.

Troy cut in, showing a pleasant willingness to answer her questions. "Orchard Park, ma'am."

"Mmm…Orchard Park." She repeated the name like it was her first time ever hearing it. "Do you work? I see you have a nice car outside."

He assumed the question and statement were an accusation. He dressed his answer up the best he could. "Oh," he said, playing modest, "that car's not as expensive as it looks. My uncle bought it for me for less than half its value at an auction. I work as an engineer and producer at Player Recording Studio downtown."

"I hear you're a good basketball player, even read about you in the papers a few times."

"Oh, thank you, ma'am. I try my best."

"Are ya grades good? Are you going to college?"

"I plan to go to college. I'm still undecided on which one, though."

Her expression became pleasant yet gloomy. With a proud mother's smile, she told him, "You remind me a lot of my son, Manny. Did you know him?"

She finally made Troy uncomfortable. Jermel's antagonizing voice crept in his head. He was going through the same grief-counseling relationship again. This was why he didn't want to deal with Trina. He knew this was the sorest subject for these two women. "No, ma'am. I didn't know him personally, but his reputation on the football field was well-known and respected, especially by us athletes. He was an amazing athlete and, from what I hear, an even more amazing person. I'm sorry about your loss," he finished sincerely.

"Thank you, Troy. Those were beautiful words. Don't be sorry, though, be careful. Be careful of who you choose as friends, and be careful of the places you choose to hang out. My...my baby should be in Ohio...in a class and on the field right now, but...these streets took him from me." She was choked up but holding strong. She didn't expect to go this far with Troy, but his peculiar, familiar presence made her reflect hard on her only son.

"Ma!" Trina prevented her from continuing. "Not right now, please." She gave a wide-eyed warning.

"No, no, it's cool, Trina." Troy looked at her to let her know that he was really all right, then looked back to Ms. Goslin. "Manny's reality may save my own life or others on the same path. His memory definitely helps me appreciate my opportunity."

His words were appreciated by both women. He literally felt their energy. He spoke what he genuinely felt inside. His sincerity was obvious.

Ms. Goslin appeared to be satisfied as she smiled and changed the subject. "Where y'all kids off to tonight?"

"The R. Kelly and LL Cool J concert," Troy answered coolly, as if Trina already knew.

Trina's eyes lit up like a Christmas tree. "For real? R. Kelly and LL? What? You ain't tell me that!"

He smirked. "I know. It was a surprise. Happy Valentine's Day."

"Oh no! Did I ruin the surprise?" Ms. Goslin asked.

Trina was still beaming just thinking about seeing the artists perform live for the first time. She and Ella had spoken about the concert for over a month, but she never thought she'd be going, especially not with Troy.

"Nah, Ms. Goslin, you didn't ruin nothing. I was just about ta tell her." Troy chuckled.

Ms. Goslin put a soft hand on Troy's elbow and ushered him toward the door. "Well, I don't wanna hold you kids up. Take care of my baby and have fun."

"I promise. She's in good company."

Troy kept a tight grip on the .380 in his jacket pocket as he stepped out of Trina's door. He kept it as casual as he could while they walked out of her building. He didn't want to alarm, her but he refused to get caught slipping.

The coast seemed clear as they approached his whip. He clicked his alarm and opened the passenger-side door for Trina.

She went to get in but hesitated at the sight of a small red gift bag in the seat.

Troy smiled. "Go 'head and get in. The bag's for you."

Trina looked at him curiously, picked up the bag, and got in.

He shut the door, then opened his trunk just to buy time for her to open her gift. He saw movement out of the corner of his eye and reflexively reached for his pistol.

"Be easy, dogg. We ain't on it like that," Buff said. "You would've been hit if we was."

"You out of bounds, though, so watch yaself," Steady cautioned.

Buff was a twin from the Timberwolves, up the street in Egleston, and Steady was a chubby hustler from the A-Team. Their gangs were close to one and the same, and both were strong representatives. Even in the mid of beef and just outright dislike, the A and OP had strange bonds. This was clearly one of them. Troy, Buff, and Steady had always been on decent terms, and it never completely changed at the height or low of war. They never had a real friendship, but the mutual respect they shared went a long way in the hood.

"What up with y'all?" Troy asked.

No daps or other physical contact was made. Just nods.

"Same ole shit. Getting this cream," Steady said. "What up with you?"

"Taking shorty ta the concert tonight."

"She good peoples, yo," Steady went on. "Take care of her."

"We just cool. I—"

He held up a hand. "That's y'all business, dogg. I'm just letting you know she official."

"I respect that."

Buff cut in and changed the subject. "What up with ya crazy-ass brother? He a pain in the ass, dogg, but that shit ain't come from over here. On, doggs." Buff didn't bite his tongue.

Troy had to respect it. The subject was too touchy, though, and it showed in his face. He kept his answer simple. "He came out the coma today. He'll be aight."

"Keep his ass on a leash," Steady added.

Troy just shrugged.

"Aight, dogg. We'll see you when we see you," Buff said.

After the short verbal exchange, the rival gang members walked away.

To the average person, their exchange could be taken as borderline hostile. The truth was, it was amazingly cordial and healthy. If they were on neutral turf, dap would've even been given and the conversation would've been broader.

By time he got in the car, he realized that Trina didn't notice when Buff and Steady approached him. She was so caught up in her gift that nothing else mattered around her. She was near tears.

"Troy…this is beautiful!" She pouted while holding the gold Cuban link necklace. "Why did you do this?"

"You're a special girl" was all he said as he backed out of the parking space and pulled off.

The Boston Gardens was packed. It was two perfect performers for the occasion. The atmosphere was a ten-to-one women-to-man ratio. Troy didn't care if it was ten thousand to one; he had Trina on his arm.

Hustlers and divas were heavy in attendance, which was a show in itself. Trina's elegance complemented Troy's plain yet trendy style. He thugged out in black SilverTab jeans, with a red polo button-up, black Tims, and a Portland Trailblazers cap to top it off, Trailblazing. Even among the elite, Troy and Trina shone. His ability to be the center with such humility always impressed Trina. She was sort of amazed at all the people, from all ages and areas that he knew. He dapped and hugged with nearly every step he took. She even received extra attention and courtesy that she wasn't used to.

He introduced her as his "friend," but she liked the melody in his cadence when he said it. She brushed off the envious glares from some females and focused strictly on being the best companion she could be. If only for one night, he was hers, and nobody was going to ruin that.

OP was in the house, but for the first time, she felt like she had him exclusively and everyone else had to vie for his attention. He appeared proud with her next to him, and though she didn't want to get delusional, it made her feel like she really was "special," like he told her in her parking lot.

The concert was outstanding. Troy and Trina danced together and sang along with hit song after hit song all night. Troy took her backstage with his VIP pass and took pictures with every person of importance that they came across.

Troy really made her Valentine's Day when he disappeared into a room, then reappeared and invited her in. First, he introduced her to an older white man named Ben Player, whom he said he worked with in the studio. The shocker was, R. Kelly and LL Cool J were sitting on the couch, watching a tape of their own performance that they just put on. The megastars appeared as normal as anyone else as Ben Player introduced everyone. Trina's excitement almost brought her to tears as they all took pictures together.

When the show ended, Troy and Trina went back to his crib to finish what they started on that first day of school. It was a rough five-month journey, but they arrived through all the bumps and forks in the road. They now understood their final destination.

Troy kept the concert vibe going with both R. Kelly CDs in his stereo. He skipped to "Honey Love," pretended to have a microphone in his hand, and did his best Milli Vanilli-inspired impersonation.

Trina laughed hysterically and admired him. She was caught off guard by this loose side to him.

After thoroughly and humorously entertaining her, Troy got down to the real after-party once they reached his house and made themselves comfortable in his bedroom. "We here now." He purposely put the ball in her court.

Trina refused to back down. She responded boldly, "We sure are."

"Come here" was all he had to say to release the beast in both of them.

Their first kiss was an amazing display of fireworks. It was so strong that they locked lips and bodies as if to prevent an escape. Their hearts raced at Olympic speeds but sounded as one. The purity of it went unnoticed. They squeezed, scratched, and pulled at each other's clothes with purpose, until they were gone. Her dreads filled his nostrils with sweet coconut. Her mouth had the taste of cinnamon.

Troy hadn't actually made love to a female before but physically was a natural romantic. He'd been with experienced and inexperienced females in his eighteen years. He was confident in his ability to please, and it all started with the childhood game seven minutes to heaven.

He sexed in hallways, cars, his crib, their crib, but nothing exclusive. His room was clean but boring in the intimate sense. It was more suited for his boys than it was for romance, but he made it work.

He laid Trina on top of his full-size mattress and admired her. In his mind, he had always known she would be fine naked, but the reality of it still had him in awe of her perfection. Her skin shone. Breasts spread beautifully. Pubic hairs trimmed to a V. Thigh muscles and toes flawless. Her eyes dared him.

He straddled her, gripped her breasts, and teased her nipples with his tongue while pressing his bulge between her thighs.

Trina had waited for what seemed an eternity for this. She refused to not satisfy. She was going all out, even if *all out* meant things she'd never done or didn't originally approve of.

She talked sex to him as he worked his tongue from her nipples to her stomach. She massaged his wide back with palms and fingertips, lightly pulled on his braids. She felt him stop at her navel. She uncharacteristically and prematurely whined, "Don't stop, Troy." She was very timid and prude in her limited experiences, but this night she felt loose, wild.

Her pleading excited Troy even more. He pulled at her V with his lips, teased her into a near frenzy. He pushed her thighs back and spread them wide for a close-up shot of her beautiful, dark slit, with a knuckle-size clitoris.

He sucked on her clit and, at the same time, let his tongue slide up and down her entrance. She tensed, but he tamed her body with a strong grip on her thighs. The powerlessness she felt made her hotter. She was completely under his control and made sure he knew that she was fine with it by whispering for him to take her body however he wanted to.

Troy pushed his middle finger in below his tongue. Her body quivered.

"Oh, Troy!" she cried out. "Baby…oh…right there. Right there. R-r-r-right there. Ah, ah, I'm…oooh, Troy!"

She powerfully pushed on the back of his head, as if trying to suffocate him between her thighs. She was so wet he actually felt a drowning sensation as her juices went into his nostrils.

"Oh my god…oh my god! I never…Troy…I never did that before!" She was out of breath and had a slight smile across her lips.

Before she could fully recuperate, Troy was already slipping on a Magnum condom. He climbed on top of her and began easing his meat inside.

"Oooh. Please, Troy, please be gentle," she begged.

"Damn, this pussy tight," he whispered while slow pumping himself farther inside. "You feel good, girl."

He continued a shallow pump with no hands on his shaft, while licking behind her ear and down to her neck. With no warning, he bit her shoulder, and she flinched. He pushed his full length deep inside of her.

"Ahhh! Ooooh, Troy, that hurt," she purred but gyrated her hips. She felt her own wetness between her thighs, his balls on her ass with every downstroke. And she loved it.

"You feel me, Trina?" he whispered.

"I feel you, boo," she responded, matching his tone. "I love it! Take your...oooh! This always been your pussy."

He stroked hard and soft, shallow and deep, round and round. He moved like a master of her vagina within minutes. He felt pleasure in every stroke and did his best to make sure she did as well. He put a thick thigh on his broad shoulder, turned her on her side, groped one breast, and pumped with the pleasure of the new position.

She screamed loud enough to startle him. He stopped, but she pressed into him even harder, then he picked his pace back up.

"Like that, baby girl?" He checked to see if they were on the same page.

She loved that he called her a cherished name. "Yeah, baby. Just like that. I'm ya baby girl." She was in elation. A world she never knew but instantly wanted to live in forever. "Give it ta me just like that. Like that! I love it. Oooh, I love it! I love you, Troy!"

He stopped stroking completely.

She put her hand over her mouth, eyes wide with embarrassment. "Oh my god! T-Troy, I...I...I'm sorry. I didn't mean it. I—"

"Shhh." He leaned down and kissed her mouth. She tasted her own pussy for the first time. He sucked her tongue softly, grinded inside of her as deep as he could push.

She seethed through her teeth, closed her eyes, and put her head back.

"Tell me again," Troy whispered.

Her mind asked, *What?* She was in shock of his request, but her mind and body were under his control. She was having an out-of-body experience underneath the man she already knew she truly did love.

The words left her mouth, with her lips barely moving. "I love you, Troy." A single tear followed while he continued his rhythmic motion.

"I love you too, baby girl."

His words woke her out of her trance.

"What?" This time it wasn't just her mind; the question actually came out of her mouth. "Do you, Troy? Are you just saying that 'cause we're having sex?"

"I love you, Trina." He made it clear. "You got some great pussy, but I always knew I loved you."

Trina smiled. Her heart began to beat again. She rolled flat on her back, cocked her legs wide, and tried to swallow him inside of her. He moaned loud, tried to postpone the inevitable, but she refused to let him—she was in control now.

"Come, baby! Yeah! Come!" she begged.

They both pumped hard and gripped each other for their last intense moment. Gibberish escaped their lips as they exploded together.

Troy rolled off to the side, perspiring and breathing heavily. He lay on his back, unable to move. He had to laugh at the wonderful experience.

Trina rolled the Magnum off him, cuddled under his arm, and giggled too.

Chapter 6

Jermel finally got out of the hospital a week after Troy's birthday, the week before his own. Troy turned eighteen on February 24, and Jermel on March 9. Jermel didn't start to feel comfortable with his body until around mid-April, and even then it was just barely comfortable.

His lungs were damaged. That, along with the bullet still near his heart, caused his normal breathing to be labored. He couldn't stay on his feet long and got tired at unusual times.

Peanut's wound ended up affecting his shoulder more than his back. It took several weeks for him to recover, but he felt fully stable. His slim frame allowed the bullet to cause maximum damage, whereas Jermel's bulk protected him.

Danisha and Ms. Goode waited on Peanut hand and foot. And he loved it. He played the injury all the way out when they were around.

When it came to his comrades, his defense was his humor. His ability to cap anybody down prevented them from clowning him.

Troy and Amin took care of the streets. The hunt for the stickup kids was a top priority. Peanut was back in the mix, but only hustling in the projects for the time being.

They all copped new whips mainly for show but also to demonstrate to the city how their bank was still up. Troy and Jermel stepped up to the matching 7 Series Beamers. Troy got the fully loaded triple black with Giovanni rims, and Jermel got the Blazer red with black interior, sitting on Lorenzos.

Amin stunted in a loaded black Pathfinder with gray guts. Peanut copped a maroon Q-45 Infiniti.

The first week of May brought the high school basketball all-star elite game to the Boston Gardens. Attendance was heavy. Parents and fans from all over Massachusetts filled the arena. The hood came out in numbers. The event was a chance to see the best prospects in the whole state.

Troy was among the top of that class. He was the actual city of Boston's representative, teaming up with and going against the best of the capital's surrounding cities.

Joyce grew a real liking to Trina and Ella, meeting them the night Jermel and Peanut were shot. Over the three months since, the girls were around her home more often and they got better acquainted.

She always let Troy know that Trina was a keeper.

Joyce had always argued with Troy about his female company and about having sex under her roof, but her thoughts of Trina were evident when she didn't scold him about having her in her house or about her spending the night.

Trina and Sis were two of Troy's biggest fans. They chose to enjoy the game in the company of Joyce and a few of her coworkers.

Jermel was in a corner, kickin' it with Crystal, when Arthur spotted him among the crowds of people. Arthur waved to him, then signaled for him to come over. Crystal angrily protested, but he told her to calm down and excused himself.

"Damn, dogg! I been tryna catch up with you, but ya beeper and phone numbers ain't the same," Arthur said as Jermel approached.

He had his hand out for dap, but Jermel ignored it. The disregard or disrespect made Arthur uncomfortable. He brushed it off, though. "Sorry ta hear about you getting hit up. I was fucked up about that. On, doggs. You still looking good, though."

"Yeah...I'm better now. What up with you, though?" Jermel's voice wasn't cool like Arthur was used to.

"Ain't nothing up with me," Arthur said, shaking his head in disgust. "I fell all the way off since you stopped fuckin' with me. These chumps out here don't show me no love like you." It was a true statement.

Jermel studied Arthur as they spoke. He had always been a short pudgy dude, but he put on noticeable weight. His eyes were cowardly. He was unintimidating. He always dressed fly, even if he was broke, in order to look like money. Arthur was a dependent hustler, so Jermel didn't doubt that he really was doing bad on his own. He actually liked him but knew that he couldn't deal with him at all. At least not this early. If he even tried to, he would hear it from everybody, especially Troy.

Jermel said, "I just had ta fall back for a sec and see what's really good. You hear anything about that shit?" He studied him harder.

Arthur gave nothing away. The passage of time probably helped his poise. He knew he was in the clear. Beam and Q were the only two who could link him, but they couldn't do that even if they wanted to. He hadn't even talked to them since two weeks after the robbery. They argued, then fell out with one another, because Arthur knew that they were lying to him. He really couldn't do anything about it, though. They paid him two grand to set Jermel up, then they were supposed to split everything three ways after the robbery. When the robbery went bad, Beam and Q told Arthur that they didn't get anything out of it.

"You still on?" Arthur asked Jermel. He really regretted messing up a good, well, his best connect ever, as well as the good relationship he had with Jermel just for a petty payoff. Actually, the money had nothing to do with it. If anyone else offered him even triple that, he would've turned it down. The truth was, Arthur was scared of Beam and Q. He understood that their offer was actually an ultimatum, set up Jermel or have beef with them.

"Of course I'm still on!" Jermel answered, offended by the insult. "You think some suckers getting a bird, some jewels, and a few grand is gonna stop my flow? Come on, man. Them chumps got the come-up of they life, but I'm even stronger now. They should've killed me, though, 'cause I ain't gonna stop till I find 'em. On, doggs!"

Arthur was heated. Jermel confirmed what he already knew about Beam and Q. *Muthafuckas!*

"Yo, dogg, my numbers ain't change. I need some flave, so holla when you ready. I'll keep my ear ta the streets for you too."

"Aight, yo," Jermel said, ending the conversation. He spun off to head back to Crystal.

The finicky look on Crystal's round manila face told Jermel what he was in for before he even reached her. All five three, one-fifty radiated enough anger to shoot through her baby browns and crack her glasses.

"What that snake want?" She spit the question out.

"Chump just tryna feel me out. I was doing the same."

"You better watch his ass…and that bitch you stay up under."

Jermel's scowl came instantly. "Watch ya mouth, yo. I told you she official. Respect that."

"Yeah, aight," Crystal said dismissively. "Just give me some money so I can get us some food and drinks before the show start."

Crystal was always like an older sister to Jermel and Troy. She could get away with anything with them. After Jimmy got killed, they were always there for her and Jimmy Jr. She was finally beginning to deal with life after Jimmy, but some wounds would never heal.

Jermel understood her total resentment toward the A. He felt the same way.

Before the actual basketball events started, other entertainment was put together for the audience. The almighty RSO, New Edition, and Ed OG were set to perform before the game and at halftime. Troy had Ben Player pull strings with the program directors and show promoters to get Chris a fifteen-minute slot. Chris took full advantage of it.

Troy didn't tell a complete lie to Trina's mother about working at Player Recording studio. After Chris recovered from being shot in the park, Troy really took him under his wing. He had always had love for Chris, but after watching him almost lose his life, and Jimmy actually losing his, he brought Chris all the way in. He regarded him as a little brother.

Chris was one of the best lyricists Troy had ever heard rap. It amazed him how he stuttered when he spoke yet every word was crispy clean when he rapped. His image was perfect for the limelight. He was fly, fifteen, dark brown, with deep waves. He was getting money with an official team.

He was Scarface, raw, and Tupac, poetic, with Nas and Jay Z skill. He only kicked that rugged street flow through. It was all he knew growing up, Trailblazing.

His father was totally disappointed with his direction in life, but Chris disregarded Reverend Child a long time ago. They were night and day. One preached the gospel, and the other spit hellfire.

Troy saw the promise in Chris's rap career. He saw it worthy of investing his time and money into. Chris knew he had the talent, but Troy's guidance made him see how far he could go with his talent. They spent many hours a week in Ben Player's Player Recording Studio, working on beats, singles, and mixtapes. When they weren't in the studio, they still brainstormed as they hustled in the projects or cruised the city on business.

When it was time to perform, Chris walked out to the middle of the arena under red and black lights, with a light fog. He laid down two of his rawest tracks. The first, "BMW (Boston's Most Wanted)" was already a well-known hood classic. He nearly tore the roof off with it. His second one was the shocker. He requested a moment of silence for all the fallen soldiers in the streets. After that moment was given, he proceeded to work a slow, methodical, bass-filled beat with an equally matching flow. The song was titled "Vengeance." The lyrics touched on OP's wounded and casualties of war. The message was threateningly clear. Not even Troy had ever heard the song before that day.

Chris moved the crowd, as most of the projects stood on their chairs, chanting, "Go, Blazers! Go, Blazers! Go, Blazers!"

Arthur squirmed in his seat and felt low as he heard the lyrics to the song.

Others around the arena bopped their heads to the good sound of the music, paying little attention to the message.

After the music was over, Troy went out on the court and represented. An outsider looking in would never believe that the phenomenal athlete on the floor was a high-rolling gang member. He won the dunk contest with a left-handed windmill, came in third in the three-point competition, and led all scorers in the actual game with thirty-three, but his team lost.

In a postgame interview, Troy revealed for the first time that he would be committing to the University of Massachusetts (UMass). He received a standing ovation and a round of applause. His revelation was headline sports news the following day.

The Marcus Camby-led UMass went on a great run, which included a showdown with Tim Duncan and his Wake Forest teammates. Though they were defeated, it set the stage for future UMass greatness. John, who lived on OP's border, and Monty, both standout ballplayers at Charlestown High, along with Troy and Rick, were all headed to UMass. They were the answer to the call and expected to go on the best run in UMass's history.

A few days after the all-star game, Troy suffered an athletic tragedy. While playing in a pickup game at Washington Park, he went up for a dunk but came down wrong. He landed on an opponent's foot, causing his own foot to bend awkwardly and snap loudly. He ended up with a vertical foot fracture and disappointedly ended his chances to play basketball for at least his freshman year of college.

*****

"Oh my god!" Ella screamed. She almost jumped out of her skin. She was still wet from a hot shower as she entered her room and saw Jermel sitting on her bed. She wasn't expecting him. "Stupid! You scared me!" She mean-mugged him, then called out, "Ma!"

"Well, hello to you too, Metal Mouth," he teased. "Ya mom's already bounced ta work. She let me in when she was leaving." Even after she recovered from being startled, he noticed that she still looked uneasy. "Why you look like that? You expecting someone else?"

She detected jealousy but brushed it off. She took a deep breath before she spoke. "Chubby...I don't like ta get in the middle of your shit—"

"Then don't," he interrupted.

"Shut up sometimes! You always think you know everything!" She caught her breath again. She was nervous, so she just spit it out. "You need ta be careful messing with that snake-ass Arthur."

"Why you say that?" he asked, not really caring for her opinion. She stayed paranoid about everything with him and the streets, especially after his near-death experience five months earlier.

She was reluctant to answer, but her anger at his nonchalance pushed the words out. "'Cause he might've had something ta do with you getting shot."

Jermel sat up straight and began paying attention. He also knew that females were information magnets, whether through one to the other. He took her warning seriously. Even though he trusted Ella, he never spoke in depth about the streets with her. That just wasn't his nature.

"What you mean, yo?" he asked her. His tone told her to come out with it.

She stalled, feeling his hazels burning a hole through the side of her head. She rubbed the towel over spots on her body that were clearly dry. She was trying to think. She wrapped the long yellow towel around her body, slipped into her puffy Tweety Bird slippers, then stomped over to her dresser, pretending to check her hair in the mirror.

"Did you rob Steve and them in my hallway before?" She was pouting. Unsure. Ella hated to even mention her ex-boyfriend's name around Jermel. Just the mention of it usually led to an argument.

He was annoyed about being questioned, especially about some fucking Steve. He lashed out, "What the fuck that gotta do with anything?" His scowl was menacing.

Ella was always uneasy when he got worked up to that point. He was never violent toward her, but she had witnessed his violence toward others for next to no disrespect. Just because he thought he was violated. Now she wished she never said anything, but it was too late to turn back now. Her anger brought plenty of fire to her tone. "Did you?" She was angry with him for flaring up on her yet worried about the potential threat to him in the streets.

Jermel thought back to that dreadful summer day with rage and regret. There was maximum loss for a minimal gain in all aspects. When he thought of Jimmy, he still regretted that he hadn't avenged him properly yet. He would, though. There was no doubt in his mind about that.

"Yeah, I did! They was talking shit when I left here," he lied, "so I laid they asses down. It wasn't no big deal or nothing."

His last statement made absolutely no sense to her, so she disregarded it. She said, "I was talking ta Tanyah—"

"What her loud ass got ta do with this?"

"Won't you shut up and let me finish?"

Jermel looked at her to let her know he was ready to listen. *Hurry the fuck up,* he thought to himself.

"Anyway, Tanyah be fuckin' Arthur. She told me that he ain't happy with how Beam and Q supposedly played him out of some money..."

Jermel zoned out, trapped inside of a menacing thought. Their dialogue immediately turned into Ella's blurred, irrelevant monologue. He was no longer paying her any attention. As soon as he heard Beam's and Q's names, he knew for sure that they were the culprits. *Damn!* Why weren't they on the suspect list, anyway? Ella's mouth was still making a high-pitched, blurred sound when he finally snapped out of his own thoughts.

"What you just say?" he asked, as if just being awakened from a deep sleep.

Ella didn't even notice his reaction to Beam's and Q's names. When he realized that she was too caught up in talking to catch it, he composed himself and pretended to have little interest in what she said.

She was heated. "What you mean what I say? Ain't you listening?" Here she was, relaying information that she didn't want to get involved in, for his safety, and he wasn't even listening. The only reason she went against her rule to stay out of his business was that she couldn't risk losing him. She loved him, and even though they never used the cliché phrase or even had a formal commitment, she knew he loved her too.

"Just say it over again!" he snapped.

Ella rolled her eyes, then began by reminding him that it was Tanyah who called to let her know that something was wrong when she drove up on the scene and saw his car that night. She was fortunate that Jermel put her on the cell phone plan that Troy had hooked up through his basketball coach. If she didn't have the phone, she would've missed the call, because she and Trina had stepped out of the house.

Tanyah was on her way to hook up with Arthur, but when she got there, he was nervous and uptight. They didn't even have their usual late-night sex—he was so unsettled.

A few weeks after the all-star game, Tanyah was over his crib when Arthur confronted Beam and Q over the phone. The argument was heated. She lay in his bed and listened as he made phone calls to other people about the situation. He was nervous and seeking some sort of support. When he got Steve on the phone, he seemed to finally find an ally.

It was during this conversation that Jermel's name came up. Steve and Arthur spoke about Jermel getting what he deserved for robbing Steve's dice game and that Jimmy's bullet was intended for him.

Before Ella even finished giving him Tanyah's whole spiel, Jermel's mind was already made up: all three of them would die by his hands. This new knowledge made him feel victorious. He felt good all of a sudden. Powerful.

He blocked out Ella's babble again and focused on her cleavage. He gave her a seductive smirk. "Come here with ya sexy, Almond Joy-looking ass." He knew why she was upset, and planned to make up for it immediately.

But Ella wasn't letting him off the hook that easily. Her feelings were hurt. She was upset with him for lashing out at her when she was only trying to look out for him. She crossed her arms over her chest in defiance to his request.

"I'm sorry, baby. Come sit with me," he said, mocking a beg.

He wore a huge smile, displaying an even set of pearly whites. He was equally cute to her when smiling as he was scary when scowling. She could never resist the deep dimples in his soft, peanut butter skin.

She maintained her angry stance. "I don't feel like coming over there."

"Well, I'll come ta you, then, sexy." He got up, stepped into her personal space, and wrapped his arms around her waist. "You smell good, girl."

She avoided his eyes as she rolled hers again, this time adding a little head and shoulders with it. "I always smell good."

He kissed her neck.

She resisted with about one-tenth of her strength.

Jermel removed her towel, spun her toward the twin-size bed, and laid her on her stomach. "Don't move," he ordered. He walked over to her dresser, opened the bottom drawer, and pulled out the bottle of erotic Motion Lotion. He stripped down to his silk boxers as she lay in wait. He straddled her, then rubbed, pressed, and massaged the lotion all over her body. They were freaky lovers, into toys, porn, role-playing, and adventure.

He turned off the room light, clicked on the blue light, putting her body in a dark, constellation-like glow. He kept massaging while admiring her firm backside. He parted her legs and squeezed her ass cheeks with the tips of his fingers. She loved a butt rub, and nobody knew this better than Jermel.

He rubbed down each leg, paying close attention to every muscle, then continued on both of her feet, heel to toe. Her body began to loosen while he performed his magic.

She felt his tongue stroke the palm of her foot. When his mouth covered her toes, she gave a light moan, smiled, and licked her lips.

He kissed the tops of her feet, then her ankles, all the way up her long slender legs. Ella was the only recipient of his full affection. He loved dedicating endless time to intense foreplay with her. He spread her butt and rubbed his thumbs along the insides of her cheeks.

Her body tensed.

When his tongue grazed her asshole, she breathed out a heavy, satisfying sigh. He licked over and around, causing her to arch her back and grip the fresh cotton linen while he rubbed her clit between his thumb and index finger.

"Oooh, boyyy! You know I love that shit!" she whined. "I love when you on ya freaky shit."

Jermel didn't respond verbally; instead, he kept working until she trembled with her first orgasm of the session.

They had learned and experimented on each other's bodies for nearly four years. They were experts of each other's anatomy. Jermel was able to make her come at will.

While caressing her body, he slid out of his boxers. When he reached the back of her neck, his full erection was pressing between her thighs.

She loosely pressed her thighs together, hugging his dick with them. He grinded between them for a minute, then she opened her legs back up to let him slide inside of her.

"Damn, Chubby, you know ya pussy," she complimented. Then, in a pleading tone, she said, "Is it my day, baby?" The answer was obvious, but she loved to hear him confirm it.

"Yeah…it's your day, baby," he answered while slow-stroking.

Ella flipped the script completely after getting her answer. Her voice went from sweet and pleading to deep and demanding. "If it's my day, then get off that sweet shit and fuck me like I'm your ho!" she demanded in a medium yell just loud enough for him to know she meant business.

"Hooker! Who you talking to like that?' Jermel pumped hard now. "You always my ho!"

"Ahhnnn!" she shrieked when he got aggressive.

Jermel pounded away. "Shut the fuck up!" His big body was on top of her with force so she couldn't effectively resist. He bit down into her upper back with just enough resistance to prevent the skin from breaking. She screamed and found enough strength to lift him up slightly but quickly lost her balance. Her face fell into the pillow. Instead of helping her up, he stuffed her face deeper into the pillow and switched to a hard grind. Her muffled screams meant nothing to him.

He lifted her head by her hair, and she gasped for air.

Smack! Smack! Smack! Quick, hard open hands on her ass forced out the breath she was searching for.

"I'm sorry, Chubby! I'm sorry!" she screamed, almost at the top of his lungs now.

"You damn right, you a sorry-ass ho! Ya sorry ass ain't got my money, so you gonna pay with this pussy! You think I'm playing 'bout my money? Huh?"

"No, Chubby! No, no…I know—"

He pulled out, flipped her onto her back, held her thighs back gently, and French-kissed her pussy.

"Thank you, Chubby. Thank you…" She took deep, relaxing breaths, grateful for the air. "Thank you, Chubby." She was almost delirious. Her body finally relaxed.

"Yeah, Chubby…yeah. I knew you was a weak-ass bitch! Suck this pussy! Suck th—ahh! Iye! Oh my god! Hell no!" she screamed loud enough now to make the neighbors believe she was really being raped.

Jermel had her ankles inside of his tightly clenched fists. Body bent like a pretzel. Her knees touching her ears. His dick deep in her ass.

She clawed at his neck and chest, throwing her head from side to side while losing a few microbraids in the process.

He long-dicked her ass smoothly.

"I said I'm sorry!" she cried. "Stop, muthafucka, stop!" Her voice was getting hoarse.

"Shut the fuck up!" he screamed back. "Who's a bitch now, huh, ho? Who's a bitch now?"

"I am! I am! Please, Chubby! Owe!" she begged.

He let the head pop out of her ass on an upstroke, then pushed it inside of her pussy on the same downstroke. She began to pump back and match his thrusts. They were both soaking wet, bruised and nearly exhausted.

"Oooh, Ella! You might've got lucky. This pussy so good! You a lucky-ass ho today! Damn, you got some bomb-ass pussy."

She went even deeper into her role. "I love being your ho, Chubby." Her voice was titillating now. "You pimp this pussy good, Daddy. You felt so good in my ass…oooh, oooh! That dick's in my stomach, Daddy. You sexy, ass-licking, pussy-sucking, big-dick pimp!"

She felt his nut nearing. "Chubby…put it in ya ho's mouth. I wanna taste us! Is that okay, Daddy?" She sounded sweeter now. Her words were so foul he was excited beyond control.

"Please, Daddy…let me taste it."

"Oh, shit, girl! Oooh! You…"

"Give it ta me!"

Jermel slid out of her so she could sit up.

Ella guided him to the edge of the bed while jerking him off. She got on both knees on the floor and stuffed her face between his legs. She easily took his familiar muscle in her throat.

Jermel called her name, gripped her three-hundred-dollar micros, and fucked her mouth like it was the last hole on earth.

Their mixed aroma heightened Ella's arousal. "Let me taste it… mmmm, mmwaa." She slurped, sucked, and talked.

"Shut up and suck it, ho! Ahh! I'm comin'!"

"Mmhmm, mmhmm," she hummed obediently instead of talking.

"Take all this nut, take it. Ooooh!" He exploded. His come gushed out longer than usual, but Ella handled it all. She gagged but simply let the nut and saliva dribble until he was done pumping her face. He fell back on the bed, completely drained.

"Baby…you the fuckin' best, yo."

"Anything for my Chubby," she said proudly, cleaning her chin with her towel. She leaned back down and sucked his limp dick a few more strokes. "Now ya'll cleaned up."

"Come here," he demanded. She laid her sexually battered body on top of his scarred chest.

They kissed and cuddled.

"Next time, I'm gonna be a virgin, 'cause you go hard on a ho," she joked.

They both laughed.

"Shit…you make a muthafucka go hard with that filthy mouth of yours. I'll tell you what, though? You call me a bitch again, we gonna be beefin' for real." He squeezed her tight to get his point across.

"Damn! You just beat all my holes up. Ain't nothing else left ta beef wit, Chubby." She still had humor in her. "I don't know where that came from, anyway. You had me wide-open, on some other shit."

He kissed her forehead and ran his hand through her destroyed hair. "You must've needed this mess done over. That's why you made me go off and pull on your shit," he teased while pulling more loose micros out of her head.

"That's one reason," she teased back, "but for real, I needed my body hurt today. You was right on time." She cracked up, laughing, and slapped him playfully. Then, out of nowhere, she fell silent before speaking again. "Jermel."

Oh, shit. He knew she was back on the Arthur topic. She hardly ever called him by his real name when they were alone.

"What up, Metal Mouth?" He tried to stay in the lighter mood they were already in.

"Stop playing!" She punched his arm and started examining his body. "You still gotta put back on a little more weight. My zipper's cute, though," she said while tracing the permanent scar on his stomach from surgery. Her face was serious.

"What up, baby?"

"You gotta be more careful!" Her anger was back. "Are you gonna stay away from dude?"

"You got that, baby. You say dude ain't no good, I ain't fuckin' with him no more. You and Tanyah just make sure y'all don't say shit about this ta nobody else. I don't need no unnecessary problems."

He gave her power through the answer she wanted to hear. It made her feel even more special. In her mind, she helped make a major decision in their relationship. His reality was to let her have that so he would be less suspect when the bodies started dropping.

"Yo, dogg, meet me at Play Time." Jermel called Troy as soon as he stepped out of Ella's crib.

Troy knew it was a problem. "What up? I need ta come alone?"

"Who you with?"

"Trina and Chris."

"Yeah. Drop Chris's soft ass off. He ain't built like that. He's your flunky. And definitely drop off Trina."

"Aight, dogg. I'll be there in a half. I'm leaving Ashmont right now."

"Hurry up, yo." Jermel was frustrated. He knew that the only reason Troy was all the way up in Dorchester was to pick up Chris from one of his girls' cribs.

Troy hung up and remained silent as Trina and Chris went back and forth about his newest song that was playing in the car. Trina and Chris got real close since she started coming around with Ella and even closer when she and Troy became a couple. They were tight enough for Chris to respect and value her feminine perspective on his music. She saw him as the younger brother that Troy saw him as. He gave her a thorough insight into Troy that no one else did. Chris knew she was a plus, and he felt like his older brother deserved that.

They were all headed to the studio, but Jermel's call changed everything.

When Troy pulled in front of Chris's crib, Chris thought he wanted him to run in and grab something for the six-hour session that they had scheduled. He was mad as shit when Troy told him that they had to cancel the session until later, or possibly the next day.

"D-d-damn, dogg. I th-thought we w-w-was gonna m-master these tracks up?" Chris complained.

"I gotta take care of something, dogg."

Chris was never one to do much arguing with Troy. He knew Troy always meant well, especially when it came to him. He felt fortunate to be as close to him as he was. "I-I respect that. You sure you d-d-don't need me?"

"I'm good, little bro. Good lookin', though."

"I hope you know this music's what's r-r-r-really gonna blow us up. This Blazer Town m-m-m-mixtape's g-g-gonna bump!" He tapped Trina on the shoulder, sending a silent goodbye as he hopped out, then knocked three times on the hood as he stepped off toward his building.

As Troy pulled away, Trina's eyes were glued to his head. "What's up, boo?" he asked.

They were a well-known item after nearly five months together. She represented him well daily and hardly ever gave him any problems. They, along with Ella, graduated from Madison a week earlier and were just beginning to enjoy their first summer together.

In less than a year's time, Trina learned the depths of Troy better than almost anyone. As she always put it, they were soul mates, created solely for each other. Even Joyce agreed with that. She openly rooted for Trina to be her daughter-in-law.

What Trina knew at the moment was that something had to be wrong with Jermel. She never ceased to amaze Troy by suggesting, doing, or asking the right thing at the right time.

"Is ya brother okay?"

"How you know something's wrong with him?"

"You just told me."

"Stop acting stupid. I'm talking about before I said something."

"You didn't have ta say anything. That's how you told me." The concern on her face never left.

He took note of the look. "I don't know what's up yet," he said. "So ya taking me home?" Her disappointment was obvious. He looked away from her and put his eyes back on the road.

"Take me ta the Dark Side. I don't wanna be in the house all night. I'm gonna go see Tanyah."

His temper flared up like she intended. "Listen, yo. We already on Washington. Your crib's around the corner. Let me drop you off and I'll be back ta scoop you as soon as I'm done."

"When's that, Troy?" She pouted.

"It shouldn't be too long, baby."

Trina knew that Troy preferred she be at her or Ella's crib when she wasn't with him. She completely understood why. She understood and was cool with it. She never fooled herself about who her man was in the streets just because she knew another side of him. She had no intentions of going to Tanyah's or anyone else's crib; she just threw it out there because she wanted him to know her frustration with being abandoned.

"Okay, baby. Drop me at home, but please don't forget about me. I wanna see you later. Oh yeah, me and Mommy are gonna be going over class schedules and stuff. Did you do anything with yours?"

Troy's dedication to college had nothing to do with academics. After suffering his foot fracture, he wasn't committed enough to sit out his freshman year with an NCAA medical redshirt. He backed out of his commitment to UMass. John and Monty graduated from Charlestown High and kept their UMass commitment. Rick settled on Roxbury Community College.

Without basketball, Troy actually gave up on college as a whole, but Trina wasn't hearing it. His GPA was high. He was highly intelligent. She refused to let that go to waste. She knew he would no longer go far away, but with some convincing and a lot of begging, she persuaded him to enroll part-time at Northeastern University. She enrolled full-time and was satisfied with his effort.

It was when crucial decisions like this arose that it was obvious that Troy needed Trina in his life. She was truly his better half. Nobody else put their foot down with him like she did. She instilled logic in his decision-making. She was his Gazoo to Fred and Barney.

Her vision for him, her, and them was beyond even his own comprehension.

"Nah, I ain't do nothing with my schedule yet. Y'all put it together for me. You know the classes I want, so mix and match."

She was pleased with both answers. She managed a half-smile. When he got to her lot, she kissed his lips, then hopped out.

He waited for her to get upstairs and wave out her living room window like he did since their first date, then sped off to Play Time.

Play Time—the barbershop's origin and legacy was formed by entertainers and hustlers. As it was located across the street from Dudley Station, its outside and inside were a common OP hang out. A hardware store, pizza shop, a couple of small stores, and a hole-in-the-wall club shared its fifty-meter block. Vendors set up all around the area.

Four barber chairs and a wall-length mirror lined identically on both walls. Mixtapes, hair products, and refreshments were sold from a glass counter in the front. Black market VCR tapes played in a TV built inside of a high wall. A PlayStation video game was hooked up to the TV for even more customer entertainment.

When Troy entered the shop, he stepped right up to his personal barber, Dwight, and asked if he saw Jermel.

"He in the back, dogg," Dwight told him. "He ain't looking too good either. I was just about ta call Amin or Peanut and let them know his wild ass was here."

Dwight wasn't from the projects, but he was a longtime older friend of theirs. The back of the shop was a relax spot for the barbers and close associates of the shop. Troy acknowledged the rest of the barbers and some of the customers he knew, then dipped off into the back.

When he got to the back, he came across a drunk Jermel, who was seated on a cream pleather sofa in the small living room-type area. When he saw Troy, he simply handed him the bottle.

Damn. This can't be good, Troy thought to himself.

Troy wasn't a casual drinker, but by the looks of his brother, he figured the situation called for a few swigs.

Jermel didn't speak; he just sat in deep thought, which caused Troy to do the same thing. Troy didn't press for an explanation. He was just attempting to let the situation play out. He had been racking his brain about the purpose of this summons all the way from Ashmont to OP, from OP to the A, then from the A to Play Time. What went wrong? He couldn't figure it out for the life of him.

Then, as if hit with a prophetic beam of light, he saw it. The bleary hazel gaze told the story. It was about murder. A visual was all he needed to figure it out.

Troy knocked back a few more swigs of the cognac, then spoke. "Either you got robbed again or you heard some good news."

Jermel wasn't surprised by the comment. He reached for the bottle, took a long swig, and let the story out.

Troy's eyes were balls of fire. The vein in his neck protruded from the force of his clenched jaw.

Jermel gave an A-through-Z of what Ella told him as Troy sat in deafening silence. He never interrupted or gave off any definitive vibe besides rage. *I told you so* was on his mind, but also irrelevant at this point.

When Jermel was done, Troy asked, "You sure Ella ain't hip ta your thoughts?"

"I told you, dogg. I played it like the shit wasn't even important ta me. She ain't thinking shit."

Troy thought for a moment. "You gotta make sure she don't tell Trina, dogg. Them chicks tell each other every damn thing. You can't let her tell her about this."

"How the fuck am I suppose ta stop her?"

Troy ran his tongue along the inside of his teeth as Jermel sat patiently and waited for an answer.

"Make it seem like you don't even want ta know," Troy said, as if he just figured it all out. "Make it seem like, if I find out, I might start going off and shit." He thought a little more. "She gotta keep Tanyah's ass quiet too. Call now, 'cause Trina's at the crib."

Jermel sobered up a bit and jumped to it. He had to call Ella three times in order to wake her up from their earlier wild tryst. He ran down what he needed to be done.

She happily agreed. She felt like she was helping him stay out of trouble when she actually just put him in the game.

Chapter 7

Troy had Club Quito O'Shea's, in Brockton, booked on July 21 for Trina's eighteenth birthday. He planned on doing it big for her. Over one hundred invitations went out a month in advance, and double that were expected to show up. Chris was set to perform as an opening act for Fat Joe and the Terror Squad.

Troy purposely avoided Trina for a little over a week leading up to her birthday. He did it to annoy her a bit in order for him to set up his big surprise. He used business, studio time, and the need to take advantage of his last bit of summer freedom as an excuse. To say Trina was pissed off was an understatement.

When her big day finally came, he called, waking her up at 5:00 a.m. to wish her a happy birthday, like everything was normal. "I wanted ta be the first ta wish you a happy birthday," he told her.

Trina was so mad at how he'd been treating her she was ready to get into their first serious argument.

"You been running around wherever, with whoever, avoiding me for the past two weeks. Now you call me this early with this weak-ass 'happy birthday' shit? What the fuck am I suppose ta be happy about, Troy? I don't even know if I got a man anymore."

Trina hardly ever cursed, so Troy knew she was really heated. He had never heard this side of her before. He thought her groggy-voiced feistiness was sexy. He held his mouthpiece away so she wouldn't hear him giggling. He had to compose himself so he could fake concern.

"I just been a little busy, baby. Why you acting like that?"

"Ya always busy lately! You make my world revolve around you, then kick me to the curb whenever you feel like it!" Her anger was building by the second.

He ignored her complaint and sounded enthused while doing it. "We got the bangin' party at Quito's tonight!" He was laughing harder with the phone away from him, but nothing was funny to her.

"Yeah, yeah," she said, yawning. "I appreciate that. I hope you make it. I'm surprised you even remember. Matter o' fact, when you gonna pick me up so I can take care of this last-minute stuff for tonight?"

He acted like the question was the most aggravating thing he ever heard. "Last-minute stuff? What you still gotta do? Damn!"

"I gotta—"

"Whatever, yo! I'm out here in the streets now, so I'll be there in a half. Be ready!"

"This fuckin' early, Troy?" she exploded. "Nothing's even open yet! Stop acting stupid!"

"Trina, I'll be outside in a half. Don't have me sitting in no punk-ass A-Team parking lot, waiting." He hung up without allowing her to respond. He was holding his stomach, laughing. He discovered a new side to his girl. He pictured her thick bottom lip poking out, eyes squinted and nostrils flaring, a picture worth a thousand words. What made it even funnier was that he was across the street from her parking lot the whole time.

Trina walked out of her building exactly a half-hour after they hung up. She was wearing one of his black Champion hoodies, gray sweatpants, construction Tims, and a Boston Red Sox cap over her dreads. She scanned the lot for his car.

When she didn't see his car, she started to pull out her cell phone, but a big red ribbon caught her eye. It was wrapped around the hood of a '94 Acura Vigor coupe. Her favorite cartoon character, the Tasmanian Devil, was on the front of a three-foot-long birthday card on the windshield.

She walked slowly toward the vehicle, then noticed the card said, "Happy Birthday, Baby Girl!"

Trina put both hands over her mouth, out of necessity, to prevent a wild scream. She stood frozen for a second, then reached for the card as if to see if it was real. She opened it and was lost in the fairy tale that was the reality of Troy's words.

It read, "Baby Girl, I would be a fool not to recognize my heaven on earth. In case you don't know, I'm talking about you. (Smiley face.) You are my heart. My everything! I loved you ever since I first laid eyes on you. I told you on our first date, you're a special girl, and I mean that. You're meant for me. We're meant for each other. I will always love you. I will never let you go. Happy Birthday!" It was signed, "Your humble servant," with another smiley face.

He watched her begin to melt, then honked his horn as he drove into her lot. It was a beautiful, warm morning. It appeared that only the two of them were out and about.

When he stepped out, she jumped in his arms, held him tight, and cried. He laughed as he held her like a child and squeezed her back.

"Whoa, baby! You ain't no lightweight, and you know my foot's still fucked up."

It was like she didn't even hear him. "I love you, Troy," she said, sobbing. "Why you been treating me like that? I thought you didn't love me no more."

"My fault, baby. I was just messing with you. I'll never stop loving you. Never. We soul mates, baby." He smiled. "You the only girl in this world for me." He was laughing as her tears wet the shoulder of his Terry Glenn Patriots jersey. "You gonna open ya present? You know I can't be out here too long."

She got down, wiped her eyes, and a bright smile appeared as she examined her ride. When she popped the trunk, she stepped back and gasped. It was female heaven! It was filled with gift bags and clothing bags full of designer apparel and footwear.

"Baby, you did all this for me?" She felt love from a man like she never felt before.

Before Troy, Trina had two boyfriends. Both relationships were short-lived. Her first took her virginity at fifteen. There was never really love there; he was a couple of years older, popular and cute. All the girls at West Roxbury High wanted him, but all he wanted was her. They were a couple for a little over a year, but he became aggressively possessive. Manny, along with some of the A-Team, had to step in and check the situation.

Her second relationship was a rebound that only lasted for six months. Tanyah hooked her up with a guy from Jamaica Plains, but he ended up being too childish for Trina's maturity level.

She almost jumped in Troy's arms again but opted to hug him tight and kiss him long and deep.

They sat in her coupe and kicked it a little longer, then he had to run. She thanked him for her Cuban link necklace from their first date, the concert, her cell phone, and all the other gifts he showered her with. Most importantly to her, she thanked him for loving her the way he did.

He brushed it all off as true love. Then he joked that he bought her the car so that she could run her own errands. He got no complaints about that as he kissed her mouth and hopped out of her car all smiles.

*****

As expected, Trina's party drew a large live crowd. The spacious club had two bars, three cloth pool tables, a small stage, and a packed dance floor.

While everyone partied, Troy, Jermel, Amin, and Peanut stayed visible, trying not to appear on edge.

Troy was going to make Trina's birthday a big deal no matter what, but he was fortunate to book Quito's. Besides Quito's being a popular club at that time, the city of Brockton bordered Taunton. Both cities were about fifteen miles outside of Boston.

Amin got word that Beam and Q lived with their children's mothers in Taunton and both of them would be there on this night. Bingo.

Peanut jumped onstage, grabbed the microphone, and gave the crowd twenty minutes of outstanding stand-up comedy. He picked apart the audience, caused stomach-grabbing laughter, then wished Trina a happy birthday. It was all part of his well-thought-out idea before he slid out the door of the club. The other three followed discreetly, one at a time.

Chris was the only other person on point. His job was to make sure their cover wasn't blown. He was to begin his performance once they left, then be sure that the main event started on time and ran smoothly. If anyone happened to be looking for any of them, they were in the back office with show promoters and the club owner.

Jermel and Peanut were two of the best car thieves in the projects, so they usually got the hotboxes for the missions. They completed that basic assignment the night before.

Amin and Peanut rode in a dark Dodge Stratus while Troy and Jermel trailed in a Blue Toyota Camry. Both pairs went over their assignments with each other as they rode. They all wore black flight suits, latex gloves, and had ski masks at the ready.

Taunton was an urban/suburban mix. The 10:00 p.m. movement wasn't as plentiful as it was in the Bean. Fortunately, the complex that Beam and Q lived in was on the urban side of town. They wouldn't stick out too much. The complex was a small one-way-in, one-way-out trap, but that didn't bother any of them. Each brick-and-vinyl apartment had two floors and its own front door but was all connected side by side in a row.

They parked two lots away from their mark.

Peanut stepped out of his whip. He walked to the Camry's passenger side, leaned in the window, and kicked it to Troy and Jermel.

"I'm bout ta handle my handle. Y'all muthafuckas stick ta the script. Whoever come out the crib gonna get it if they act up." He looked away from the driver's seat and directly into Troy's eyes. "Your cripple ass sure you can move fast enough? Stay in the fuckin' car if you can't."

Before Troy could respond, Peanut stepped off.

Peanut strolled casually from one lot to the other and saw a familiar car in the lot. Two spots down from where he was standing, he saw a pumpkin-orange Mitsubishi Gallant that belonged to Beam's girl.

Word!

He walked up to the Gallant, used a spark plug to break the driver's-side window with minimal noise, then squatted next to the bumper as the alarm sounded.

The alarm was cut off after about forty seconds.

A pretty, well-tanned brunette opened the door to the apartment. She resembled what a common sitcom star would look like.

Peanut was disgusted that Beam and Q would let their child's mother check on the disturbance so late at night.

She stepped out in loose-fitting jeans and a short yellow T-shirt. She scanned the lot, then seemed to be trying to figure out if her window was broken as she approached the car. When she opened the driver's-side door, Peanut approached her in a low crouch, out of sight, to just about anyone except her. He pointed his .357 long and ordered her to get in and shut up.

Brunette Sitcom saw the large barrel of the gun and would've screamed if it weren't for the voice behind the mask ordering her not to.

"Don't scream, bitch." His words were low and calm, but forceful. "I ain't got time ta play with you, so if you wanna live, do what the fuck I say. Ya hear me?"

She gave a petrified affirmative nod.

"You ever been raped?"

The question turned her summer-tan pale. The fear was obvious. "N-n-no," she answered.

"Good. Act right and tonight won't be ya first time."

Her pleading blue eyes showed a spark of relief.

"How many people in the house?"

"My two-year-old daughter and niece are in there. I don't have any money, please—"

"Bitch! That's the last mistake you gonna make! The next one's gonna get the whole house killed." He gritted through a clenched jaw.

"Now…how many people in the fuckin' house?"

She said, "Five," and tried not to even breathe hard after.

"Who?"

"My sister, the two children, and our boyfriends." Brunette Sitcom was all the way shaken up.

"Aight, this what it is. First, stop all that fuckin' shaking. You making me nervous."

She looked baffled by that statement.

"I ain't here ta harm you unless you make me. That's a promise." He stared deep into her eyes, then said, "Listen close, 'cause I ain't gonna repeat myself. It's been too long out here already. Think with ya head, 'cause ya heart will get ya whole family killed. Y'all boy-friends are gonna die tonight."

She flinched, and Peanut put his hand on her knee to calm her.

"Ain't nothing you can do ta stop it. All you can do is cooperate with me and save ya family. I got three men with me, two at ya back door and one across the lot." This time when he paused, her nod was more assuring. "How's ya crib laid out, and where Beam and Q at?"

If she wasn't totally aware of the serious situation already, hear-ing the masked man say their boyfriends' names definitely did it. She felt hopeless for them. Self-preservation immediately kicked in.

Peanut, the philosopher, was good with persuasion. The crew completely trusted whatever initial method he used to get them to their prey.

Brunette Sitcom's voice trembled as she gave a quick layout of her apartment. She even volunteered extra information, which let Peanut know he had her exactly where he wanted her. Beam had just gotten in the shower. Q was on the couch in the living room with her sister and the children. Nobody was armed, but there were guns in the house.

Peanut laughed inwardly at how comfortable the two dope-fiend robbers were. They thought they were safe just 'cause they had a honeycomb hideout in Taunton.

Peanut instructed her to walk in the house in front of him. Once he had his gun on Q, she was to open the back door, which was in his line of sight. He couldn't believe how sweet it was going down.

Troy smiled when he saw the pretty white girl leading Peanut to the front door. He was unsure of the situation at first, because Peanut was talking to the girl for over three minutes at the car.

Troy leaned against a truck in the parking lot like it was his own. He watched Amin and Jermel disappear to the back of the building and didn't see any movement through any windows in the house. He was comfortable with things so far. He was itching to get his hands on Beam and Q.

He pulled his mask over his face as Peanut neared the door and gripped the .38 snub in his pocket. If any sudden movement happened, he knew that Peanut would drop to the ground and shoot, allowing him to run up, blasting. It wasn't necessary, though; Peanut eased right in behind the girl, and Troy wasn't far behind them.

*****

"Somebody! Anybody! Everybody scream!"

The whole crowd screamed as the Terror Squad hype man got them to make noise and get even more involved with the performance onstage. Fat Joe had one of his artists, Big Pun, free-styling for the crowd. The tough Boston audience showed the new artist a lot of love.

The crowd was all the way live at Quito's.

Trina pumped her fists in the air with Troy's cousin Moe in the middle of the floor.

Ella and Tanyah danced with Buff and Steady from the A.

It was one of those weird nights when the A-Team and their affiliates were able to move in harmony with OP and theirs. Meech, from Egleston, even performed onstage with Chris. Some smaller groups within and some individuals chose not to mingle with the opposition at all, but there was no tension in the air.

The club was lined wall to ceiling with birthday wishes for Trina, a good reminder of whose night it was. True friends of hers and Manny's enjoyed seeing her happy and enjoying herself again. Manny was killed a week before her birthday just one year prior.

When Fat Joe took the stage himself, the crowd surged toward the small stage and pumped their fists even harder. Bottles were popped, and people rapped along with his hits.

*****

Peanut and Brunette Sitcom walked into the small plain apartment. He immediately saw a pretty blond female similar in looks to Brunette Sitcom sitting on the couch.

Q's puny head was in her lap.

Blond Sitcom was barefoot, with long slender legs, wearing sweat shorts and a wifebeater. She looked away from the TV to Peanut and Brunette's direction, as if she were about to ask a question, but the masked man caused her eyes to almost pop out of their sockets.

Both Peanut and Brunette Sitcom, unplanned to the other, held up a silencing finger. That startled Blond Sitcom so much it was probably the only reason Peanut reached the couch without her screaming.

The .357's stainless steel barrel poked Q's forehead. His good eye opened wide with fear. "What the—"

"Shut the fuck up, chump," Peanut cut him off in a threatening whisper.

Brunette Sitcom waited for her cue.

Peanut saw that she was truthful. He could see the back door from the living room, so he gave her the go-ahead nod to open the door.

Brunette Sitcom walked the ten paces from the old cotton sofa to the kitchen and unlocked the back door. By time she walked back into the living room, the original masked man was gone and a taller, broader one was holding Q and her sister at gunpoint.

Blond Sitcom gave her sister the bewildered look of the year when she re-entered the living room with two more masked men.

As they came in from the kitchen, Troy signaled for Jermel and Amin to handle the living room, then he limped up the steps on his tender foot to find Peanut. When he got to him, Peanut had his revolver aimed at a naked Beam in the shower.

Troy instinctively upped his .38 too.

Beam knew he had no wins. He figured he was dealing with some amateur stickup kids that would take what they found and run, so he didn't resist when the taller masked man who came up the stairs told the other one to tie him up.

Beam knew he would find out who they were, then kill them later.

Once Beam's large body was secured, Troy left him with Peanut and went back downstairs.

Amin already had Q tied up and was working on Blond Sitcom while Jermel kept his gun pointed, oblivious to the sobs from the women and children.

Brunette Sitcom didn't like the looks of things. She started crying for Peanut. "Where's the other guy? He promised he wouldn't hurt us!"

"You know these people?" her sister accused.

"No! But the first guy promised…he promised he wouldn't hurt us if I did what he told me to."

Troy hushed her with his finger. He approached her, and instead of tying her hands to the back like they had Q and her sister, he tied hers to the front. He sat her on the couch with her sister and placed her daughter and niece in between them. He signaled for Jermel to help him bring Q upstairs.

Amin gave Troy an eye that said, "Hurry up." Troy nodded his understanding.

Once upstairs, Q was thrown on a bed next to his naked most trusted comrade, Beam.

Beam showed no fear. "What you petty muthafuckas want?" he spat. "We don't keep our shit where we rest, so y'all made a bad hit."

Jermel stuffed both their mouths with socks he found on the messy bedroom floor, then they all removed their masks.

"Remember me, muthafucka?" Jermel asked with malice. Beam and Q literally saw their lives flash before their eyes. All cockiness vanished.

Fuckin' Arthur! Beam thought.

The plan was to put bullets in their heads, but Jermel wanted to change it up at the last minute. "Hold up," he said. "I'm 'bout ta go get some knives ta carve they ass up."

Troy grabbed his arm as he attempted to walk out. "We ain't got time for that."

Jermel was upset but conceded. He grabbed a pillow instead, and Peanut followed suit.

There was no action-movie, tough-guy bravado at this point. Beam and Q were nothing short of terrified. It was evident when one of them released their bowels.

Peanut and Jermel put the pillows over their victims' faces. They squeezed two shots apiece.

Troy followed up with one to each of their heads for him and Amin.

The shots were only slightly muffled, a lot louder than anticipated. It was time to get out of there in a hurry. They pulled their masks back down, walked down the stairs, and exited as if it were a normal visit.

Peanut was last to walk out. He stepped to Brunette Sitcom, stared her in the eyes. "I kept my promise. Do the right thing and keep ya mouth shut." He walked out behind his brothers.

They were in and out in less than twenty minutes and back at Quito's in a little over an hour. As they walked back in the club, one at a time, Chris gave a thumbs-up. They blended right back in.

Trina was tipsy. When Troy walked up on her, she was turned up and turned on. She pulled him to the dance floor and put all the moves on him that she held in all night.

Amin pulled Chris aside to let him know that everything was all good. Jermel hit the bar while Danisha and Ella danced with Peanut.

The whole club screamed along with the Terror Squad and Fat Joe.

"It's just another ordinary day! Drugs is the key ta success, money is the key ta sex..."

Chapter 8

❖❖❖❖❖

Since Troy was enrolled and set to start his first part-time semester at Northeastern University, he moved in to a modest brownstone on Huntington Avenue. The small building and the ones surrounding it were mostly occupied by college students. He tried to get Joyce to move in to the two-bedroom with him, but even if it weren't such a young environment, she still would've refused.

Joyce was old-fashioned, completely at home in the projects, where she spent all her forty years. Her mother and father gave birth to her on Harrison Avenue. She moved to the park side of the projects when she was nineteen, and she and her boyfriend, Macky, settled into their own Albany Street apartment. Her parents relocated to Cathedral Projects a few years later, where they still resided.

Macky eventually ran off down south with Sinclair, one of his sidepieces, when Troy was three. Joyce occasionally heard from him for a while, then he lost all contact by time Troy was seven.

She didn't speak to Troy too much about his father. She had nothing good to say and didn't simply want to bash him. She struggled with welfare and many odd jobs to support herself and Troy his whole life.

Northeastern University had facilities up and down Huntington Avenue, which ran for miles from Brookline through downtown Boston. Northeastern's main campus buildings were sprinkled around the outskirts of Mission Hill Projects, which was where Troy chose to cop his own apartment.

Amin had already moved in to a one-bedroom apartment in Madison Park Village, right outside Orchard Park, a few months before Troy moved.

Jermel copped a sizable two-bedroom in Codman Square. His Dorchester crib was built inside of what used to be a school building on Talbot Avenue.

Peanut had no intentions on moving anytime soon. He was content at home with his mother, and she was too.

Troy breezed through his first semester at Northeastern. Academics always came easy to him, and that didn't change at the college level.

He actually grew to like the college atmosphere and even made some out-of-the-ordinary friends. Without even trying, he attracted people from all walks of life. Before college, he never had an associate who wasn't black or Spanish, but between classes and the tenants in his building, his circle of friends broadened sizably.

His college enrollment was part-time, but he was still a full-time Trailblazer in the streets.

Trina stayed in his ear about doing something productive financially instead of always stashing money in shoeboxes and constantly re-upping on drugs. He spoiled her rotten, but she started to refuse a lot that he offered, mainly because she wanted him to stop being so irresponsible with money. She was never negative energy; she remained supportive but strived to guide him down an alternative path.

Troy ignored most of her lifestyle and financial advice, but that was only on the outside. In his heart, he knew she was right. He considered a lot of what she showed and told him. Her advice was equal to, if not more important than, his college education.

All he understood was getting money in the streets. College wasn't exactly providing him with a financial education. The streets gave him a raw entrepreneurial mentality, but he only understood it through guns, drugs, and cash.

"What you doing, dogg?" Jermel asked over the phone.

"Chillin'. What up with you?" Troy held the phone to his ear with his shoulder as he wrote on a piece of paper and spoke to Jermel at the same time.

"Come through and get some of this cream. It's pumpin' hard in the bricks tonight."

"Nah. I got mad work ta knock out. On, doggs. I got this marketing class tomorrow. Y'all get that paper. I'll catch up with y'all tomorrow night."

"Dogg, what the fuck's wrong with you? Why you still wasting your time with that bullshit? Ya NBA dreams is over, and all the NBA cream you need is out here!" Jermel was heated.

Troy brushed off his attitude. "I started this, yo, so you know I'm gonna finish it. I don't leave shit half-ass. I already knocked out one semester. This shit will be over in no time."

"Finish it for what?" The thing that really had Jermel heated was that he felt like school was keeping Troy away too much. He knew what to say to get under his brother's skin. "Trina got you on some bullshit."

Troy didn't feed. "She ain't got shit ta do with this. Eighteen months from now, I'll have my associate's in business management, and we gonna clean up some of this bread."

"Yeah, aight. I'll holla back." Jermel wasn't trying to hear any of that.

The phone went dead.

Troy shrugged and went back to studying. Jermel's attitude didn't bother him at all; he'd been dealing with it since they were babies. He knew what he was striving to accomplish and knew, like always, Jermel would be on board once he could actually see things play out.

Most people never understood Troy's travel until he reached his destination.

*****

Six months passed since Beam and Q were murdered. Not much was made of it throughout the Bean. The two of them had so many enemies, so the A had nobody specific to target for retaliation. Their murders even caused riffs inside of their own hood.

Not many people knew where Brunette and Blond Sitcom lived. Beam and Q scared a lot of people, and they did far too many people wrong. Most of this was in their own hood alone, so people thought it was very possible that one of their own hit them.

Arthur was the mastermind behind the robbery, and neither Troy, Peanut, Amin, nor Jermel was satisfied with just the hit men being dead. Arthur had to go too. It was all in the timing, though.

To be safe, Troy had them all agree to give it a minimum of a year before they got Arthur. He wasn't a threat to any of them, so there was no rush and it would keep the heat off them. Their team was doing good, so the last thing any of them needed was to go down for a body simply for the emotional pleasure.

After hanging up the phone in Troy's ear, Jermel was heated. He convinced himself that his brother was slipping.

Jermel's thinking was usually irrational. When it came to his mind versus his feelings, emotions usually won the bout. The reality was that Northeastern took up a lot less of Troy's time than Madison Park High and his basketball obligations did, but Jermel wasn't always into what reality had to say.

He knew how to get Troy back into the swing of things. He knew all too well.

Fuck that one-year shit.

It was a cold winter afternoon almost a year from when Peanut and Jermel were robbed and nearly murdered. Jermel used the anger he knew that Peanut still had about that day to amp him up.

Peanut was sitting on a large cement landing attached to the building on the Bumpy Roads side of the projects. He was bundled up and blacked out in a Trailblazer's Skully, Adidas hoodie, leather shearling, SilverTabs, and Tims.

He blew out a large cloud of cold breath and weed smoke as Jermel approached.

"What up, Nut?" Jermel dapped Peanut up when he walked up to him.

"Getting this extra paper, dogg. What up with you?"

"I'm fucked up, that's what's up! You know next week make a year, right?"

Peanut looked like the question insulted him. "Of course I know! Them suckers ain't here ta see it, though." He puffed hard, then passed it to Jermel.

Jermel hit it and inhaled deep. "I don't want bitch-ass Arthur here ta see it either. You ready ta get his ass yet?"

"Fuck you mean yet? You and Troy the ones on that wait-a-year shit. I wanted ta get his ass the same night we got the other ones."

Only Jermel knew the totality of why Troy got them all to agree to wait at least a year, but he disregarded that to suit his current motivation. Troy wanted to be sure that Ella and Tanyah wouldn't get any ideas that they had anything to do with the deaths. If all three bodies dropped too close together, the girls would most likely get suspicious, considering the conversations they had with each other and whoever else. Suspicion meant loose lips and loose ends; it was the innocent gossip of females that led them to their victims, but they had to be careful not to meet the same fate.

Jermel said, "Fuck a year! It's been six months since we hit they asses. That's long enough! Shit, it been a year since we got hit up!" Jermel was so mad he was crushing the blunt in his hand. "We riding tonight, if you with it. I'll be back in a couple hours." He handed Peanut the blunt, then headed back to his whip.

"You ain't said nothing but a word!" Peanut yelled to him. "Hurry yo ass up!"

Less than two hours after they agreed on getting Arthur, Jermel pulled back up in front of the building in an '88 Chevy Blazer. Peanut was in the same spot, looking like he never even moved.

He called for little Lee. His young protégé came running out of the building. Peanut gave him instructions, then hopped in with Jermel and bounced.

Jermel jumped right into his spiel on how they were going to carry out the hit. He was going to drop Peanut off on Creston Street, in the Grove Hall section of Dorchester. One of his old customers was away for a week, and he had the keys to his crib, so Peanut could lie low there. Jermel was then going to go pick up Arthur and bring him back to Creston. When they pulled up, Peanut would run up to the Blazer, pull Arthur out, shoot him, then get in. They would drive off smoothly.

When Jermel was done relaying his plan, Peanut had to refrain from smacking him upside the back of his head. He asked him,

"When the fuck you come up with all this retarded-ass, complicated-ass, goofy-ass shit?"

Jermel stared, confused. "What you mean, dogg?"

Peanut shook his head. "Man! Man, man, man! You really is retarded, huh? I thought you just be acting like that sometime. You sure know how to complicate some simple shit."

Jermel looked hot.

Peanut didn't let up. "You talking about Jimmy on Creston?" he asked in reference to the old customer's house Jermel spoke about.

"Yeah" was all Jermel answered.

"Aight, he definitely gonna be gone?"

"He gone for a week." Jermel was obviously still fuming about how Peanut came at him.

Peanut got mad at Jermel's childish attitude. "Give me the keys ta the crib, dogg! And go ta the South End. I'mma grab a hotbox, park it on Intervale, then walk through the alley ta Jimmy's crib. When you pull up, just get the fuck out, walk through the alley, and get behind the wheel."

"Fuck, I look like wrestling with some muthafucka in the middle of hot-ass Creston. It's bad enough you chose that hot-ass block! Arthur's bitch ass ain't getting out this Jeep till they pull him out."

Peanut held a firm eye with Jermel to be sure he understood that this was the plan, not a suggestion.

Jermel pulled the Chevy Blazer beside an old-school Impala in the South End.

Peanut hopped out and was in the hotbox within ninety seconds. He rolled down the window and stared at Jermel again. "Clear ya young-ass mind out, yo! I ain't got time for ya petty attitudes! Be on point! I'll be ready when you get there."

*****

Arthur was overly overjoyed that Jermel had finally stopped ignoring him and was ready to hit him off with some work. He wasn't even close to being the baller that he was before he messed everything up. As a matter of fact, he'd been on his ass for nearly a year, all because he wasn't man enough to stand up to Beam and Q.

Glad them muthafuckas are dead! he angrily thought to himself. Arthur was a braggadocious, flamboyant hustler and a real serious trick. He wasn't mentally or physically tough enough to run with the best of them in the streets, but he knew how to get in where he fit in. Knowing his position, plus the fact that he was from the A, got him by in the streets. He always found good connects, so he was usually valuable to the A-Team, but that wasn't the case as of late. Truth be told, all his good connects were one connect. Jermel. He just faked like he had multiple sources to appear more resourceful.

When Jermel called and told him that he would be coming by to scoop him in a few hours, Arthur couldn't hold in his enthusiasm. He had a sexy, exotic piece, named Jessica, from the Dark Side, at his crib. He hadn't stopped talking for two and a half hours. He broke his plans down from A to Z as she lay across his mattress in a T-shirt and panties.

He hadn't fucked her in over three months, but she still stopped by from time to time. She genuinely liked Arthur in some sense.

Jessica was all about a dollar. A *gold digger* would be an understatement in reference to her—she dug for platinum. If a man couldn't provide for her, there was no chance that she would be around long.

Arthur could no longer afford her. He was definitely on the verge of losing her completely. Losing her was something he really couldn't afford.

"Yo, Jess…Jessy, Jess! I'm bout ta blow, girl!" His excitement was written all over his face. "I told you I won't stay down long! I'm back! You gonna be happy you stuck with a playa!"

"I hear you, boo." She was happy to hear him talking money, which was her only language. Even after she had listened to him for over two hours, her nipples were still getting hard, pussy getting wet. He still ain't getting none until he showed and proved.

"I'm bout ta lock the A down! All that cream-up Eggie gonna be mine too," he said, referring to Egleston Square up the street. "Jermel don't play! Fuck the rest of them OP cats. He run them, anyway.

They all be hating on me 'cause he show me more love than them. You remember when I had all this shit on lock before?"

"Mmm, hmm." She nodded and smiled seductively. *This dude's delusional. He damn sure gonna take care of me, though,* Jessica thought.

"It was that bomb-ass flave from Jermel that put me on top then!"

A horn sounded.

Arthur looked out of his third-floor window and saw Jermel in the Chevy Blazer. He couldn't get his fatigue jacket on fast enough. "There go my muthafuckin' man!" He smiled wide and rubbed his hands together like he was trying to warm them up. He told Jessica, "Keep ya sexy ass right in that bed. You gonna give them skins up tonight! I won't be long!" He laughed, then mimicked the Notorious B.I.G. "I love it when you call me Big Poppa. What's the name of them jeans you wanted?" He laughed even harder at his own corny humor.

Jessica pretended to find it entertaining as well. "It don't matter the name of 'em, as long as you pulling them off me after you buy them." She started to smell money, so she put on a little extra. "Hurry up, big boy. You know my pussy miss you."

On that note, Arthur flew out the front door and nearly leaped down all three flights of steps.

Being the professional platinum digger that she was, Jessica already had plans to be with Arthur the next time he met up with Jermel. She wanted to meet Jermel herself because he was the real money, so he was her ultimate goal.

She peeked out of the window to size him up.

Jessica knew she was a dime and not a cent short of it. She was Asian, Puerto Rican, and black. She had hair that dropped to the small of her back and had a ballerina's body. Her looks got her everything she ever wanted in life, and she was tired of settling for less.

As she stared out the window, she was absolutely disappointed when she saw Arthur get in the old, beat-up Chevy Blazer. That definitely wasn't the picture she drew up of Jermel's whip. She got a good look at him, thought he was cute, but cute wasn't enough. Cute didn't buy the finer things in life. Cute didn't pay.

She figured Arthur was exaggerating about how big this Jermel guy was in OP and the streets. He was just trying to get some pussy.

Jessica slumped back down on the bed. She had let Arthur work her up for some mediocre bullshit.

*****

"What up, dogg?" Arthur gave Jermel an energetic pound as he got in, and didn't let his hand go for a minute. He was clearly overly excited. "You finally back at ya boy! You know how I gets down! We 'bout ta get this cream!"

"No doubt!" Jermel tried to match his enthusiasm, but it was impossible.

If Arthur weren't blinded by visions of crack, money, and pussy, he would've noticed the malice in Jermel's eyes.

Jermel continued, "I just had ta lay low for a little while."

"I know it's hard on a boss," Arthur said, trying to kiss his ass.

"We 'bout ta shoot ta Creston so I can get this half-a-bird for you. How fast can you make it fly?"

"Dogg, I'm bout ta sell twenties for dimes! I'mma kill 'em fast! On, doggs!"

Arthur was so full of energy that Jermel almost felt bad for him. His smile was from ear to ear. He rocked the Jeep side to side every time he bounced up and down with excitement.

But Jermel was stone-cold. Zero understanding. Even if he knew that Beam and Q threatened Arthur's life to set him up, Arthur would still be in a passenger seat of death.

They pulled up on Creston fifteen minutes after they left the A. Creston was about 150 yards long, with three-story brownstones on one side and triplex houses on the other. It was residential, but the block was known for getting money since '94.

T, who started Creston pumping, was from OP. His circles from the projects were welcome on his block. He went to Madison Park with Troy and Jermel and was especially tight with Troy, Jermel, Peanut, and Amin.

When Peanut stepped out of the alley between Intervale onto Creston, T spotted him and stepped to him. Peanut's first instinct was to lie, but he knew T was solid, plus he was in a terrible position, considering the number of people out on the block.

It was obvious that Jermel didn't consider the heat they were about to bring on T and his crew with this plan. Seeing T actually woke up the principles in Peanut.

"What up, Nut?" T greeted. His greeting was warm, but his eyes were still suspicious. "What got you up my way? Jimmy been gone for two days already. You know that, right?"

Peanut said, "T, I ain't even gonna bullshit you, dogg. I got some bullshit going on."

"You need somewhere ta lay low?" T asked.

Peanut was still hesitant. He really didn't know what to say or how to say it. *Fuck it.* "Dig this, dogg. Me and Jermel found out who hit us up. We 'bout ta straighten it out. I should've holla'd at you, but this hit—"

T was initially looking confused when Peanut was talking, then a light went on. "Oh, shit! Y'all found out? Me and my mans was on that, but nothing ever came up. That shit came from around here? You need me for something?"

"Nah, it ain't come from up here, but..." Peanut looked around at the block.

T understood. "Say no more, yo." He gave Peanut dap and a hug, then stepped off.

Peanut walked across the street into Jimmy's crib and watched the block from the window. He saw a few people who were posted up in front of buildings get in cars and drive off. The younger kids went inside. T was discreetly clearing the block.

Word, Peanut thought.

When Jermel pulled up on Creston Street, he took one last look at Arthur's gleeful face. He wanted to slap the smile off it, but instead, he just stepped out and stepped off.

As he walked through the alley toward Intervale, he heard a small *pop pop* from Peanut's .22. It looked like a professional hit.

T watched the hit from a brownstone's first-floor window. He had the stereo all the way up, so none of his crew heard the shots.

Peanut and Jermel were in the hotbox Impala thirty seconds after the shots and on their way back to OP as if they made a store run.

Chapter 9

◆◆◆◆◆◆◆

Jermel dropped Peanut back off in the projects after they hit Arthur, then went to dump the Impala. Once he did that, he hopped in his Beamer and went to pick up Ella right on schedule—no suspicion. He pulled back into the same lot he pulled out of an hour earlier.

Opposite of the courteous manner that Troy used when picking up Trina, Jermel had his system blaring. It filled the lot when he opened his door.

Jessica heard the loud music and looked out of Arthur's bedroom window. When she saw the big Beamer, she moaned and rubbed her titties. Jermel only had his foot out the door, so she couldn't see him, but all she could think about was riding shotgun with whoever was driving.

Jessica turned her nose up in disgust and rolled her eyes as she saw Ella walk out of her building. *This raggedy bitch is getting in there?* She always felt like the Light Side girls gave all of them a bad name.

As she hated on Ella for heading toward the Beamer, she did a double take when she noticed that it was Jermel who got out to greet her.

"Ain't that the dude Arthur just left with?" she whispered in confusion. "Damn, he is ballin'."

Jermel grabbed a bag out of Ella's hand as she got in, and threw it on the back seat.

Jessica continued to size him up and drool over the thought of getting with him. Then the obvious question popped in her head.

Where's Arthur?

She picked up the phone and dialed Arthur's beeper number as she watched Jermel pull out of the lot with Ella leaning across the center console into his seat. She assumed that Jermel was about to get some head, which made her even more jealous.

She beeped Arthur three times over the next half-hour. When he didn't call back, she figured he stopped somewhere to put his work together before getting back home. She lay back. Her spirits were lifted once again. She was no longer worried that Arthur wouldn't be able to take care of her.

And ultimately, she would get Arthur to introduce her to Jermel. She realized that Jermel was a smart baller. He only drove the ugly truck to keep a low profile while handling business.

If Ella could get him, there was no way she couldn't, she figured.

Jessica eventually dozed back off while waiting for Arthur. She was startled awake by his mother when she came storming hysterically into his bedroom. Her wide bare feet were cracked and ashy; excessive gut hung over her faded jeans from under the biggest bra Jessica had ever seen. The pink rollers in her hair all had her fit for a mental institution.

"Jessica! Jessica! Where my baby at? Where my baby?"

It took Jessica a minute to clear her head. She was disoriented from being jolted awake. "He went out with his friend," she managed. "Why? What's up, Ms. Howard?"

"Turn on the TV, girl!" She pointed at the television. Jessica grabbed the remote and clicked on the box.

Ms. Howard had her turn to the news, then she sat on the bed next to Jessica as they waited. She explained that a man was killed in the Grove Hall area. A resident on the street was being interviewed and said that she recognized the victim as a guy named Arthur from Academy Homes.

After about twenty minutes, the story appeared again.

Jessica had to fight for air before a word was even said by the reporter.

Ms. Howard's heart nearly stopped. Her eyes widened at Jessica's reaction. Something was wrong. "What? Jessica! What's wrong, child?"

"Oh, shit." Jessica's eyes were far off, her voice distant from her own body, and her head began to spin. She felt nauseous. "That's the truck Arthur got in with Jermel." She could not believe that the reporter was reporting that the victim was found in the Chevy Blazer.

Ms. Howard lost her mind. "Ohhh, Jeeesusss!"

Jessica was momentarily frozen in a zone of her own. When she snapped out of it, she dialed Arthur's beeper number over and over.

Ms. Howard had already run out of the room.

Jessica got up, put on some clothes, and went to find her. She sat with her, calming her down and instilling hope.

A few hours into Jessica's consoling of Ms. Howard, the phone rang.

Ms. Howard ran to the kitchen and snatched the phone off the wall, praying that it was her son or at least someone who could change her fate. But instead of her fate being changed, it was sealed.

She was asked to identify herself then was asked to come down to the morgue at the end of Albany Street to identify a body.

*****

After killing Arthur, Peanut went by Amin's crib and enthusiastically gave him and Troy the details. He conveniently left out the part about being spotted creeping by T.

Troy listened with tight fists and thoughts of snapping his neck. Amin knew things were about to get heated with every detail Peanut expressed.

Troy went off as soon as Peanut finished.

Peanut shrugged him off and stressed that it was already done. The three of them sat and watched the news together.

"I hope y'all dumb muthafuckas ain't bring more heat, yo," Amin said.

Troy unleashed. "We already hot e-fuckin'-nuff! I hope fuckin' Ella, Tanyah, and the rest of them broads don't start tryna put all types of shit together. Shit!" He saw the lack of understanding in their eyes. "That's how we got word on the whole damn situation!" He shook his head.

"Yo, Nut," Amin interjected, "you don't think the boys know who we are?"

"Yo, we got big whips, money. We flossin' in the projects and all over the fuckin' hood. What was the rush?" Troy said. "I spoke ta Jermel's ass earlier. He ain't say nothing about doing no dumb shit like that!"

"Man, bruh pulled me up. I figured y'all was hip." Peanut looked at Troy. "I definitely thought you was hip. You know bruh's crazy ass, though. If I ain't go with him, he might've tried ta do it on his own." Peanut was trying to get Troy to see a broader picture. Then, out of frustration, he said, "Fuck that sucka, anyway! He tried ta get us killed."

Troy felt his point, so he let the situation die with Peanut.

His real beef was with Jermel. Jermel had been reckless since they were snot noses. But they were grown now. He wasn't maturing with the rest of them.

Overall, Troy was relieved that the whole situation was dealt with, but was concerned about the girls and if the hit actually went clean or not.

As soon as Troy saw Jermel the next day, he went at him.

"Dogg, what type of crash-dummy shit you on?"

"Ain't nobody crashing! You just been lost in the sauce, dogg. I handled what needed ta be handled."

"Lost in the sauce? Muthafucka, we getting money, living good, and ain't took a short since we was short! You the stupid muthafucka lost in the sauce!"

The two of them stood in a corner behind the building they were born and raised in. The chill factor and light snow on the ground had just about everyone besides them on the move or in a hallway. It was obvious that they were in a heated conversation, so nobody bothered to interrupt.

"Don't come at me with this bullshit today! I ain't tryna hear this shit! On, doggs! You stay laid up in the crib with Trina and going ta them bullshit-ass classes. Man, we ain't even hit a bank in over a year! When's the last time you did an all-nighter with us?"

Troy looked disgusted. It was more disappointment than anger. He stuffed his hands inside his leather Avirex coat pockets, shook his head, and traced the inside of his teeth with his tongue.

"First of all," Troy started, "lower ya fuckin' voice, yo. You tryna tell the whole projects what we on?" He spoke slow and calm. "Fuck an all-nighter! I got paper. I hustle when I wanna hustle. You one of the stupidest muthafuckas I know. I put you on ta the banks so we could come up. We came up, dogg! What we need ta hit another one for?" Troy wasn't looking for a response. He didn't let Jermel even think of giving one. "You just like doing unnecessary shit. Play with ya own life! Stop jeopardizing ours!"

The more shallow Jermel's attention span appeared to get, the deeper Troy continued to cut.

"All the dumb shit you do come back ta haunt you. Most times it fucks up everyone around you! How much dumb shit you do that got both of us in DYS? Or in stupid-ass beefs? Ya dumb-ass stick-ups got us in a hundred shoot-outs, and one got Jimmy killed! And fuckin' with Arthur got you and Peanut hit up. I been told ya ass he was gonna cross you! When you gonna smarten up? Muthafuckas love you, but you make it hard for even me ta wanna be around ya ass sometimes. And I hope you covered ya tracks. Creston? Dogg, Creston? Of all places, you chose Creston? You tryna make T and them hot up there? I already know. You ain't even think about that. You don't think."

Jermel had it with Troy's tirade. "I ain't tryna hear none of that shit you talking, yo! Get ya nose out them books and that pussy and put it back in the streets, where it belongs! Shit ain't all sweet like you think! And for the record, I always held my own. So fuck you and whoever else got a problem with me!" Jermel turned and made his way through the snow. He never looked back.

Troy let him go. It wasn't their first argument and wouldn't be their last. He didn't sweat it.

Fuck Jimmy Jr. too? That was what Troy wanted to ask Jermel since Jimmy Jr.'s father, Jimmy, died trying to defend and protect all of them. He never even had a real chance to "hold his own" against his killers.

*****

Two days after Ms. Howard confirmed her son's death, homicide detectives showed up at her house to do their routine follow-up questioning. They had no expectations except to hear the usual sob story of a single black mother and how sweet her child was and how he either wasn't involved in crime or was on the verge of changing his life. Blah, blah, blah! Same old bullshit.

Detective Daniel Teeler was a longtime veteran in the homicide division. His partner was only on board for two years, but it didn't take long for the legendary homicide detective Teeler's unruly influence to rub off on him. Both of them were tired of hearing the "good black boy" sob stories over and over, and they actually made fun of some of the grieving parents as soon as they left their houses. They were nasty men, in thought and duty.

They could tell that Ms. Howard would provide lots of comedy for them. She began her weeping as soon as they stepped in. Typical crackhead, Detective Teeler thought.

The detectives sat with disrespectful impatience as Ms. Howard spoke. Their interest was only piqued when she got past the story of her son's life and began telling them the things Jessica told her.

Detective Teeler leaned forward in the chair and began to drill away with questions about this Jessica and her story. Finally, he asked if Ms. Howard could get in touch with this Jessica.

Ms. Howard told Teeler that she had Jessica's number in her bedroom, then she got up to get it.

Teeler and his partner gave each other approving looks at the potential in this Jessica.

When Ms. Howard returned, she volunteered to make the call for them. Teeler nodded, and she began to dial.

"Jessica?" she said after the third ring.

"Hi, Ms. Howard." She still sounded extremely sorry for the woman.

"Jessica, I got some detectives over here that wanna talk ta you about my baby."

"Detectives?" It was obvious Jessica didn't like the sound of that. "Ms. Howard…I-I don't wanna talk ta no detectives."

"Why not, child? They're tryna solve my son's case. Don't you wanna help my baby?"

There was so much hurt in Ms. Howard's voice that it hurt Jessica too.

"Yes, I wanna help, but…but I don't know about talking ta no cops."

Both of the experienced detectives knew exactly what was going on. Teeler thought about snatching the phone and threatening this Jessica with jailtime if she didn't tell him everything she knew. Instead, he opted to allow Ms. Howard's pity-party tactic to play out first.

Teeler's outlook on ethics was exactly that, his outlook. He didn't think twice about bending or even breaking the rules in order to get the job done. Loads of young minority men convicted of murder were behind bars, doing life sentences, because he brought them to his justice. Doing things his way.

If DNA evidence or all the forensic crap didn't lean in his favor, then Detective Teeler did his best to completely tip the scale. It was nothing for evidence to come up missing, accidentally or on purpose. Breaking in an evidence room, redirecting witness testimony—that was all part of good detective work.

Beyond a reasonable doubt? What the fuck was *reason*? Teeler knew a murderer when he saw one. He knew an individual who deserved to spend their life in a cage just by talking to them one time.

He thought the entire legal system was too damn soft. *Liberals!* It allowed no-good, going-nowhere criminals to remain in the streets, committing crime after crime, for far too long. The system needed men like him. So what if he had to adjust the law to get justice served on a lawless scumbag? If that was the price for justice, then homicide detective Teeler would front the bill.

All a crackhead junkie, sex-craved maniac, or ignorant thug could do was produce more of the same to further diminish the value of this great country. Teeler knew that and couldn't have that. He wished that the drug and gang task forces would get their heads out of their asses and get with the program. They dealt with the filth a lot more than he did.

Teeler's moto was, "A man has to do what a man has to do," and he was the man for the job. That was why his superiors gave him the power to move as freely as he wanted to. *Stay the fuck out of my way!*

"Jessica," Ms. Howard continued to plead on the phone, "baby, please don't let my son, your friend, die like that…with no friends in his corner. You already told me, but they wanna talk ta you. Come over, baby. I'm waiting."

The finality in Ms. Howard's statement caused Jessica to give in. "Okay, I'll be there in about twenty minutes."

When Ms. Howard hung up, she wore a wide but sad smile. "She'll be by shortly," she told the detectives.

Teeler faked a smile back. "That's great news. We'll be able ta pursue the animal who did this ta ya boy immediately. You've been very helpful."

Detective Teeler couldn't care less about Arthur Howard. Arthur Howard was just one less waste to worry about. His enthusiasm came from the possibility of locking up another thug for the too-often-senseless act. Kill two thugs with one stone.

When Jessica arrived, the sight of Detective Teeler and his partner scared her. She was reluctant to speak.

Teeler's murky blue eyes had no good in them. They hid beneath a long flat forehead and thin curly hair on his head. His tall narrow body was upright in the cotton chair, left leg crossed over right, with skeletal fingers folded across his lap.

Neither detective made an attempt to stand to greet her. They arrogantly waited for her to take a seat.

Jessica's beauty instantly had Teeler hope that she opted for witness protection at some point during this case. Witness protection usually meant a few weeks, maybe a couple of months in a motel. Women sometimes became vulnerable in those types of situations. Teeler got lucky a few times in his years and seriously hoped he could luck up again with this one. He would pay a pretty penny for Jessica.

His partner, Detective Nee, was a short, pudgy, balding man. He had pasty white skin that revealed green veins, and an easily disliked face. He sat with the fidgety demeanor of one who despised sitting in a ghetto apartment, and wanted to get the interrogation over with as quick as possible.

"Jessica," Teeler began, getting right down to business, "this isn't the first time I'm hearing Jermel Gilliard's name in connection with a homicide. He's a very dangerous boy. Tell me what happened."

As soon as Ms. Howard mentioned that Arthur's friend was Jermel from Orchard Park, Teeler knew exactly whom she was referring to, but hearing his full name confused Jessica at first. She gathered herself, then began by describing Arthur's enthusiasm when Jermel called and why. She broke it all down to the point when she peeked out the window and saw Jermel and Arthur pull off in the Chevy Blazer.

When she mentioned Jermel showing back up an hour later in a different vehicle to pick up Ella, Teeler was sure he had his man. He was sure that Jermel was the cold-blooded killer that he often heard he was. To kill then continue his day like nothing ever happened was the sure sign of a heartless thug.

Teeler made his mind up at that moment: he would nail Jermel Gilliard for this homicide, no matter what. He thought back to Shawn, Jeffery, Donell, and others that he fixed evidence against. He knew that Jermel would be added to that list if the actual evidence wasn't strong enough to hold up.

He nodded and jotted down notes as Jessica spoke. Things were shaping up extremely well extremely fast. Too many similar, simple cases were dragged out in the ghetto because a bunch of going-nowhere, soulless slime wanted to all of a sudden act self-righteous and not cooperate with law enforcement. He couldn't stand that. Or them.

Fuck their worthless morals! This epidemic couldn't be allowed to spread outside of the ghetto.

Detective Teeler rose from his chair, out of dominance, not respect, and shook Jessica's hand. He fantasized again about having sex with her but appeared professional. He made sure that she knew he would be back in contact with her.

Jessica was still uncomfortable with the whole detective situation, but she assured Teeler that she would be available if they needed her.

For three weeks following his interview with Jessica, homicide detective Teeler worked day and night digging up all he could on Jermel Gilliard. He knew he had his man, but all the evidence was circumstantial. He needed hard proof. He was fortunate to find one eyewitness, but the account he was given was shaky at best and needed his professional tweaking.

He needed Jermel Gilliard off the streets. A locked-up Jermel Gilliard would be a lot less intimidating when it came to gathering witnesses and evidence.

Teeler had many informants, but of them, three were his prized informants. Ones he was proud to break and that provided top-of-the-line, reliable information. All three of his prized informants confirmed that Jermel Gilliard was the real deal. More importantly, one confirmed that he was Arthur Howard's main source of drugs.

And most importantly, all of them said that they wouldn't be surprised if he killed Arthur Howard.

Chapter 10

✦✦✦✦✦✦

The evidence against Jermel wasn't solid, but because of Detective Teller's reputation, and the judges he had in his pockets, it was solid enough to secure a warrant for his arrest. Teeler and a SWAT team executed the warrant at 4:23 a.m.

Jermel was in a drunken sleep with a female he met at a club the night before when his door was kicked in. He was arrested and initially only charged with first-degree murder. A large amount of cocaine, three handguns, and over one hundred grand were recovered from various areas of his apartment. These things were the subject of more charges added onto his indictment for murder. He was taken down to Dorchester Police Station, booked, then tossed into a freezing holding cell.

The next morning, he was given a cold egg-and-cheese bagel and an eight-ounce carton of orange juice. He left it untouched when the officer came to take him to Dorchester court for arraignment.

The pale old man in the black robe behind the high bench looked down on Jermel through expensive wire-rimmed glasses. He turned his nose up and denied him bail. Seemingly without even considering a word Jermel's court-appointed attorney had to say.

Jermel was hauled off in cuffs and shackles. He was taken from the courthouse to downtown Boston, the Nashua Street Jail.

"Damn, yo. This shit's bugged the fuck out," Troy said. Troy looked miserable and worried, two attributes Jermel rarely saw in him.

Troy sat, shaking his head, on a metal stool in a three-by-three-foot booth, with two-inch-thick glass between him and his best friend in the world, his brother.

Jermel said, "I can't call it, dogg. The chump they assigned me for arraignment said something about getting some discovery papers. I told his ass, don't even bother, 'cause I ain't fuckin' with him."

Jermel sat in an identical booth, dressed in a red top and bottom that resembled something a nurse would wear. He looked dejected. His first few nights in jail already had him stressed out. How did this happen? Who said what? *Damn!* Jermel slept for a mere three hours a night at best.

"This ain't DYS no more." Troy stated the obvious, but Jermel knew there was more to it. Troy went on, "Ain't no more of that court-appointed-lawyer shit like we had growing up. I ain't hearing that! We eatin', so we gonna get the best."

"Good lookin', dogg." Jermel's shoulders were slumped forward.

"I got this older dude that did a few lectures at Northeastern. He was diggin' me. He a cool muthafucka. We even went ta lunch twice. He a top-notch lawyer and told me ta holla if I ever needed him. You wanna fuck with him?"

"You know I trust ya judgment." Jermel's eyes looked away. "You always been smarter than me. You called it when you got in my shit last month. I be on some dumb shit."

The heat that ran through Troy's body could've set the room on fire. "You think I give a fuck about that bullshit right now? All I care about is getting you the fuck out of here! I can't believe that punk-ass judge ain't give you no bail. No matter what this punk ass came up with, we would've came up with more ta get you out of here! On, doggs!"

Jermel knew he meant every word. His hazels began to beam. Confidence started to come back. Ever since they were children, Troy had given him an extra sense of strength. He felt like he could take on the world with his brother by his side.

"Hurry up and work ya magic, then, dogg. In the meantime, try ta get me right up in this piece." He finally managed a smile.

"Who you playing with?" Troy playfully challenged. "You act like you forgot my name or something. I'm already on top of that. On, doggs! Soon as I stepped up in here, I bumped into someone who can be real helpful. I gotta get her on the team."

"Her?" Jermel was clapping his hands and doing half-spins on the stool. "You always stay with one in the chamber! I knew you ain't lose a step. By the way," he said, his voice saddening, "happy birthday. This the second year in a row I missed it."

"Ain't nothing. We got plenty more ta enjoy. I need ta see if I can get you ta enjoy yours in here."

When the visit was over, they both stood and put a fist to the thick glass. It was one of the most awkward moments they'd ever had between them—so close yet so far.

As soon as Troy stepped into Nashua Street Jail's lobby, he saw Tanika. She was a very pretty Cape Verdean he often saw in passing at Northeastern University. The eye contact she usually gave him spoke volumes. They never spoke beyond an occasional simple greeting, but all that was about to change now.

Tanika was a lieutenant at Nashua Street. Troy didn't tell Jermel, because he didn't trust the booths, plus he wanted to surprise him once he got her on deck. There was no better way to take care of him than paying a jail employee. Yes!

When Tanika spotted him in the lobby, she made no secret that she was looking for and waiting to see him. The conversation between them was welcoming and casual. She inquired about whom he was there to see. They kicked it for a little bit longer and exchanged numbers. She convinced him to let her cook him a birthday dinner later on that night.

After Troy left Nashua Street, he drove deeper into town to meet with Attorney Hemenway at his eleventh-floor State Street office.

Attorney Herbie Hemenway had more salt than pepper hair along the sides and back of his head and was shiny bald in the middle. His thick mustache matched his hair. His deep, dark skin belonged with the ancestors on the walls of his office. He had a sturdy five-eleven frame with an energy that reduced his actual sixty-two years to about forty-eight. He radiated confidence, not cockiness, and possessed a distinguished humility.

His office told many chapters of his life's story. There were reflections of 1960s civil rights demonstrations and images of Hemenway standing side by side with prominent leaders of those times, along with his college and law credentials. A black leather Bible and green hardcover Quran lay open on his large organized wooden desk. The office layout was more tasteful than most homes Troy had ever been inside of in the hood. There was leather and marble furniture, a microwave, a small refrigerator, and wall-to-wall carpeting.

Hemenway gestured toward a sofa.

Troy sat and sunk into the soft forest-green seat. He was a little uneasy, which was obvious to Hemenway, so he broke through the tension with nonlegal small talk. He began by walking him through the posters and photos on his walls in order to paint a clearer picture of who he was and what he stood for. He took an immediate interest in the young man the first time they spoke at Northeastern University. This was an opportunity for Hemenway to truly see his worth.

He walked Troy through the many nonviolent marches that he participated in in the South, orchestrated by Dr. Martin Luther King Jr. and others under the Southern Christian Leadership Conference. He explained how, after experiencing the constant assaults, he realized that those weren't his type of movements. He didn't agree with marching nonviolently into the clutches of the most violent oppressor he'd ever known, ones who beat, raped, and lynched since the inception of this nation. He wasn't okay with trying to force himself and his people into a society so savage, a society that didn't want to accept them in it anyway.

He personally edged more toward segregation, even total separation from a society of such evil. Go for self. Do for self.

Some of the same nonviolent marchers that he marched beside readily went to war overseas and committed the ultimate acts of violence, side by side with the same oppressor who beat, hosed, and lynched them. These nonviolent marchers committed these acts of violence against people who never committed a single act of violence against them. Hemenway saw this as absurd and cowardly. Some nonviolent marchers, after being spat on, beaten up, and attacked by dogs went back to their own communities and committed acts of violence against their wives, children, and people they considered neighbors. It was absurd and cowardly.

Hemenway aligned himself with organizations focused on self-consciousness and strength. He formed personal relationships with powerful, self-dependent leaders and teachers. He developed a deep love for his people during the struggles of the fifties through the seventies, then dedicated his life in the eighties and nineties to making sure that the victories of those days bore fruit. He assured this through his law practice, teaching black history at Roxbury Community College, lecturing at schools and forums and interacting one-on-one with prodigies like Troy Newton.

Troy was captivated throughout the entire ninety-minute journey that Hemenway walked him through. He didn't interrupt, nor did he desire to. It was one of the most personal and powerful history lessons he'd ever had in his life. It instantly affected how he saw different aspects of his own life.

He respected the lecture and understood that he was privileged to get the uncut version. Hemenway opened the door for a professional and personal truth to be shared between them. This was extremely important for what Troy was in his office for.

After their acquaintances were complete, they got down to the business at hand. Hemenway was shocked that Troy was seeking his services for a homicide. From the few discussions they had had before this one, he sensed that Troy was straddling the fence between the streets and academia. He expected this to be a meeting about retaining him for a gun possession or drug case.

Attorney Hemenway had a stellar record when it came to homicide cases. He was respected in every courtroom he stepped in. He wondered if Troy was out of his league and whether or not he could afford his high, five-figure fee.

He sat, right leg over left, fingers rubbing his chin, listening as Troy explained Jermel's situation. He quickly recognized his ignorance of law and politics. He was glad that Troy chose to come to him instead of a hotshot, slick-talking attorney with all the commercials and radio ads.

His financial worries were answered as soon as the subject came up. He stated his usual fee, but Troy disregarded it and gave his own offer. He pulled out five ten-thousand-dollar stacks from his jacket and pants pockets and laid them on the desk. He told Hemenway that he would pay two thousand a month until his brother was released.

Hemenway let him know that homicide cases usually took at least two years before going to trial and that he could never guarantee Jermel's freedom. He promised to do his best and even hoped there were some judicial loopholes to jump through to get him acquitted on legal technicalities through pretrial hearings.

Troy was satisfied with his choice of Hemenway. They stood, shook hands, then he stepped out of the office.

Hemenway went to work on Jermel's case as soon as Troy shut the door.

*****

Everyone knew that Troy's mind was preoccupied with Jermel's dilemma, so they just had to accept that he turned off his phone and disappeared for his birthday. That was his intentions regardless, but his encounter with Tanika gave him even more incentive to do it.

Trina was pissed. This was her first birthday with him as her man, and she couldn't even spend it with him. She understood, though. She kept her anger to herself and was prepared to console or support her man however he needed her when his mind was clear and he came back around.

After driving aimlessly on the highway, in deep thought for a while, he drove back to the Bury and stopped by Tanika's house in the Warren Gardens apartment complex. It was a nice escape for him. Nobody would ever know to look for him there. Plus, he could make a business proposal on Jermel's behalf.

He had a long three days. He was ready to kick back, eat, and relax.

When she opened the door to let him in, Tanika had on spandex pants, with hot-pink panties showing through them, and a wifebeater with no bra.

Troy unconsciously grabbed his dick, thinking, *I guess this is gonna be the business proposal and the deal sealer.*

Her hair was pulled back into a tight ponytail. Her pretty, bare feet held a gold anklet on the left side. She swayed her dainty, toned body across the wooden floor, letting her ass jiggle for him to lust after.

She was a short five two, even by five-two standards. A well-proportioned 115 pounds. Her nose, chin, lips, and eyes were round as buttons on top of smooth mahogany skin.

Tanika had a sophisticated beauty that assisted in her line of work, the way a slutty beauty assisted an exotic dancer.

Troy had never been involved with a female more than three years older than him. Tanika was plus eight. She was an all-around new challenge, from occupation to sophistication.

On top of Tanika being too close for comfort at Northeastern University, Troy loved Trina like he never loved before. Those factors made him never even give her the time of day. He hadn't been with another female since his third month of officially being Trina's man.

Not only was Trina his girl, but she was also one of his best friends.

Tanika's small but classy crib had an elegance to it that Troy really took to—two commendable environments in one day. Her furniture was tan and cream. Dark-colored tribal art lived inside of black vinyl frames on white walls. And to top it off, the place smelled like a five-star restaurant.

"What you cooking?" Troy was sniffing the air like an animal using its sense of smell.

"Steak, mashed potatoes, green beans, and corn. Oh, and a fifth of Rémy. Is that okay with you?" She turned to see if he approved, then laughed at his exaggerated sniffs.

"Hell yeah! That's more than okay!" He rubbed his stomach.

"You don't have to stand in the doorway all night. Kick off those boots and get comfortable."

Tanika knew that she froze him with her assets. And it made her feel even sexier. She walked back to him, removed his Perry Ellis leather jacket, and hung it on a coat rack near the door. She guided him to the love seat and gave him a remote.

"I need a few more minutes," she told him. "Get comfortable."

Troy did just that. He kicked back, fiddled with the channels, but mostly paid attention to Tanika. He just happened to have a great view of the kitchen from where she sat him down. He watched her stretch and bend all around the kitchen. *Whoa!*

"The food is delicious!" Troy commented once they sat down to eat.

As they ate, they spoke about school, her job, the hood, sports, goals. Troy needed to be strategic about sliding in the conversation about needing her to help him keep Jermel straight while he was at Nashua Street.

The conversation had its deep points, but it was mostly easy-going and full of laughs. When Tanika was comfortable with where they were with each other, she got down to her business. "So why your handsome young ass never even gave me a second look?"

"'Cause you beautiful. Why else?"

His savvy retort caused her to blush. Though there was humor in it, she understood the significance of what wasn't said.

She nodded with genuine approval and respect. "That's good… really. I respect that. Why now?"

He played slow. "Why now what?"

"Why I get a second look now?"

"Oh…you mean why we see each other twice in one day?"

She gave a slight laugh with his continued humor. "Why I get ta have you tonight, Troy? On your birthday and all?" She rolled her eyes and looked sexy doing it.

"Who said you get ta have me now? I'm having a friendly birthday dinner with a schoolmate." He wore a sly smirk.

"If you think for one minute that you had me in that kitchen all afternoon and I'm letting you out that door without getting some, you really lost your mind."

He laughed at her forwardness. He liked it. Her nipples were hard, looking like dessert through her tight wifebeater. The Rémy had them both feeling nice.

"Is that right?" he asked in response to her forwardness.

"Hell yeah, that's right! I fed you, and I'm gonna work them extra pounds off you too."

Her promise made his dick hard.

"Troy, I want you to know you ain't dealing with no little girl. I don't play games," she said soberly. "You have a beautiful, very nice young girlfriend. I'll never do anything to try to come between y'all."

He gave a sarcastic, mocking look. They were in her living room, talking about sex.

She sucked her teeth.

He laughed at her recognition.

"Whatever." She brushed off his sarcasm. "If you let great sex catch you up, then that's on you, honey." She got serious after that comment. "I have a man too." She saw the surprise in his eyes. It almost offended her. "What? I ain't good enough to have a man?"

"Nah, I—"

"Whatever. You're so cute with your young ass over there, fumbling over your words." She giggled. "As long as we know our boundaries, we'll be okay."

Tanika went from touching on the guidelines and getting everything understood to being ready to play. "One thing I know is, I been waiting to taste you for the longest."

"Oh yeah?" He backed his chair away from the table and pulled his dick out. "Come taste me, then."

"Troy! Don't play me like I'm some type of ho or something! I don't suck and fuck just anybody!" She was offended. She didn't want him getting the wrong impression of her character.

"Whoa, whoa, whoa! You got it twisted, OG!" Troy spoke slow and thoughtful. "I ain't just *anybody*! If I was, you wouldn't have me here right now. I'm me! That's why I'm here. I see exactly who you are, and I respect who you are. I never had a woman come at me as real as you just did. That shit turned me on!" He held her eyes with every word. "I ain't got you being no ho. I got you knowing exactly what you want and not being afraid ta go for it. You want me. I want you. We both right here. Ain't no sense in bullshittin'. We both checking out, so let's go all out."

The concern in her eyes was replaced by captivation and admiration. She clung to his every word. She swallowed them like she was thirsty. They were the raw truth. She was digging his whole style and delivery. Her man was a corporate square. He was a great man, and she loved him deeply, but she craved some thug loving.

Troy sensed her understanding, then demanded this time, "Now, come taste me." His dick went a little limp as he spoke, but he had no shame.

"Mmhmm," she muttered, still trying to sound defiant. She stood up obediently and stepped over to him slowly. The demand in his voice confirmed that he was the answer to her sexual call. She stood between his legs. Her presence alone caused him to grow back to full length and width. She stared from his dick to his eyes, then back to his dick. "I'm impressed," she said as she stared approvingly at it. Her nipples were now large pebbles underneath the cotton. "And who you calling OG? I'mma teach your young ass about a woman tonight," she vowed while squatting and sticking out her long pink tongue.

She traced her tongue from the bottom of his shaft to the head. She kept her eyes on his for a moment and wrapped her lips around his mushroom while pulling down his jeans and boxers. He slid farther down in the chair, and she took him even deeper into her throat.

"You like that, young boy?" she asked while taking a quick breath from a very professional deep throat, the best he ever felt.

"Hell yeah! I like that." His answer came in a whisper through clenched teeth.

Tanika squeezed his shaft with both hands and sucked on the head like it was a large pacifier. He neared a nut two times, but she teased his climax by pulling up and smiling.

"Follow me." She stood up and headed toward the back. She peeled off her wifebeater and let it drop to the floor.

Troy stroked his erection while watching her tight ass shake in her spandex.

When they reached her bedroom, he took it all in briefly. He admired her renaissance art, paintings, and especially the African warrior sculptures that sat in the corner and on the bureau. After silently admiring her style, he refocused on the live work of art in front of him.

"You a sexy muthafucka, Tanika. No bullshit."

She blushed, then proceeded to peel her spandex and panties to the ground.

He slid on a Magnum, then picked her petite body up like a child. Her breasts were deceptively large. They hung firm, with light long nipples.

She wrapped her legs around his waist and her arms around his neck as he placed her back against the wall and drove inside of her. Her pussy was wet, tight, and shallow. He felt her like he never felt a pussy before. He couldn't believe that such a small body possessed so much pleasure inside of it.

The feeling didn't get better than this.

He took Tanika, or rather, they took each other, from the wall to the floor, to the bed, and to the shower. They wore each other out. When they finally called it quits, she lay across his chest and admired him.

"Thank you, Troy. I needed that more than words can describe."

He smiled, appreciating the approval. *Thank you? That's a new one.* A confidence booster. She cuddled up, and he rubbed her narrow back.

His mind drifted to Jermel. There was a list of things he needed to do to be sure he was straight. He was on the job. Hemenway was on board. Tanika was too; she just didn't know yet.

He had a silent conversation with her three-foot warrior sculptures. They seemed to be able to travel where his mind went to and give him positive feedback. He related to them and made a mental note to find out where she got them from. He did all this right before he passed out in her bed.

Within two weeks and four more passionate sexcapades, Tanika was bagged and Jermel was living good in Nashua Street. He called Troy, going ballistic after Lieutenant Lopes called him into her office, hit him off with an ounce of hydro, and told him to come see her if he needed her for anything.

Troy laughed and assured him that he was on top of everything that needed to be done.

Tanika was perfect. She had her own life and presented no type of drama for Troy. They both felt a little guilty at times, but their passion was powerful and the ventures became emotionally easier with each one.

Chapter 11

‹ ✦ ✦ ✦ ✦ ›

"Hey, Chubby!" Ella's voice was full of enthusiasm as well as pain when Jermel entered his side of the booth.

Jermel wore a toddler's smile at the sight of her. "What up, Metal Mouth?" He was really excited. It had been more than six months since he last saw her in person. She had to clear up some minor court issues before the jail cleared her for visits.

"Chubby, I miss you!" She pouted and folded her arms across her chest.

"I know, I know, Metal Mouth. I miss you too." They both laughed together. "What's up out there?"

Once he asked the question, she began to vent. "That witness they been keeping from you and ya lawyer is this stank bitch Jessica, from the Dark Side! Her ho ass always tryna sell her raggedy pussy ta somebody! I just found out the other day, 'cause Arthur's mother was crying on the phone ta my mother about the whole situation! Best believe I already told Troy! And this creepy-looking detective named Teeler came by my crib, asking questions about you, and I told his ass that you was with me and I'm gonna testify for you—"

"Whoa, baby, slow down. Slow down. I hear you, boo, and I'm feelin' ya concern, but you not 'bout ta get involved in this shit. You—"

"I ain't tryna hear that shit, Chubby! They tryna take you away from me and…and…" She couldn't finish before getting choked up. The tears came gushing.

He had to speak calmly. Sensitively. He had to do something he hardly ever did, choose his words wisely. "Ella, baby, calm down and listen ta me. All you gotta do is keep ya eyes and ears open. Don't do nothing. Just let my brother know whatever you know. You know he ain't gonna let them play me. He gonna go all out."

She had faith in Troy, just like Jermel did. The mention of his name also made her feel confident. She was out there, watching how hard he was going for Jermel. He turned over every stone and searched high and low to find ways to help her man.

Jermel continued, "Now, check it. This lawyer Troy got me, Hemenway, is a beast! He on everything! Once he hear about this Jessica broad, he gonna get on her. Some old lady on Creston supposedly picked me out in a lineup, but all she said was she saw me get out the truck Arthur got killed in. Hemenway said the shooter could've been tryna hit me up too."

Ella had a deep concern in her eyes. It had been eating at her ever since the details to the murder started surfacing. The unidentified man had to be Troy. He was the first person she thought of, but Peanut or Amin weren't far behind him.

She knew the two brothers were bad but didn't think they could just kill someone that easily. Stories about them were popping up all over the hood since Jermel got arrested. Most sounded too gruesome for her to believe. Some sounded within their capability.

The Troy and Jermel Ella knew were ruthless at times but were mostly fun and sensitive. To hear that they had actually killed as early as fourteen was unrealistic to her. She wanted badly to ask if the things she was hearing were true but knew to mind her business. The stories scared her, not because of the content, but because if they were heard by the police, they could get both of them into even more trouble.

"Chubby...I wish I never said nothing ta you that day." She wiped away some of her tears. A new pain was in her face.

"Ella!" His hazels burned now. "Don't start that shit! You ain't got nothing ta do with nothing, and I don't neither!"

"I know. I know. Okay, I'm aight." She seemed to calm down a bit, like a realization just came over her. "I'm just worried about you. I don't know what I'll do if you never come home ta me. You're my heartbeat. I love you."

Her words landed on him like an elephant. His stomach felt empty. His heart hurt when he breathed. He was afraid to blink, for fear of a weakness being exposed through teardrops. He fought the inner fight of his life to keep his composure.

His mind reflected on all their years together. How loyal she was to him. How he never appreciated what he had in her. From their very beginning, he had to trust that she would never set him up or cross him in any way. And she held up her end to the fullest.

Her ex-boyfriend, Steve, lived two buildings over from her. He and Steve had always disliked each other—an A and OP thing—but it wasn't until he charmed Ella away from him that Steve forged their never-ending war. They fought three times, had many other controversial run-ins and a few shoot-outs, one resulting in Jimmy's death.

The fourteen-year-old girl with the braces was whom he fell in love with. Yes, there was no question in his mind that he loved her. He just didn't actually realize it until he was at his bottom, facing the rest of his life in prison.

Ella changed him and helped shape him in ways that nobody besides the two of them knew. He never openly spoke of his love for her. He didn't know how to, but he hoped she knew how he truly felt right now. She stuck with him through a lot, but he never really showed his appreciation. He couldn't try to make up for it all right now, so he just left it alone. He didn't want to come across as being fake.

"You know you my heart too," he told her. "I won't be in here forever. I told Troy ta give you my keys today. I want you ta keep my crib warm for me, yo!" he snapped to wake her out of a dream like slump. "You hear me?"

"Huh? Oh, yeah, I hear you, Chubby. I got you. You know I'm gonna hold you down."

An officer tapped on the door, letting her know that her time was up.

"Oh yeah, Peanut and Amin both gave me a G ta put on ya account. I'mma drop it off on my way out. You need me ta do anything else?"

"Nah. I'm cool. Don't have nobody at my crib besides Trina and Tanyah!"

"Aight, Chubby." She kissed her two fingers and touched the glass before she walked out of the booth.

*****

"Man, what y'all tryna do about this Jessica broad?" Peanut was ready to blow her head off. "She been out there somewhere in the Bean for eighteen months now, waiting ta tell on bruh!" Peanut was aggravated and trying to pick a fight with Amin or Troy if they didn't agree with him at the moment.

They were in the studio with Chris while he put the finishing touches on his latest mixtape. Chris was in the booth, spittin' murder music over a bass-filled track. The whole vibe was fueling the rage Peanut was already in.

Amin took a deep puff on a Backwoods before he answered, "We gotta leave the ho alone like we been doing, dogg. You heard what Hemenway told Troy. Po-po waiting for someone ta knock her head off so they can really run down on us." He was laid back on a leather couch, trying to feel the new music being created. He really didn't feel like dealing with Peanut's hot head. Amin looked at Peanut's face and knew he had to go in a little deeper. "The case ain't even that strong, dogg. Think about it. Nobody can even ID you. We just gotta trust Attorney Hemenway. He been thorough so far. His strategy is to present to a jury that Jermel and Arthur were both targets of a hit. We gotta roll with that. If anyone gets knocked off, it needs ta be that Skeletor-looking homicide detective Teeler."

"Dogg, if you don't feel that," Troy jumped in, "I don't know what ta tell you. I can't explain it no better."

"I feel y'all, but damn! Bruh been locked up eighteen months now! We knew this broad was gonna be a witness for a year now! The courts is just dragging bruh!" Peanut was extra upset that Jermel was denied bail on three occasions.

"Be easy," Troy tried to assure him. "Hemenway got the judge ta throw out the drugs and gun charges against him, so let him focus on beating the body too. He made it clear that it wouldn't look good if this girl ended up dead. If he's good enough ta prove that po-po only had a body warrant for Jermel's arrest when they raided, let him show that Jermel ain't have shit ta do with Arthur getting hit up."

Amin studied Peanut as Troy spoke. He got frustrated with his impatient body language. Peanut had irrational tendencies like Jermel did when things weren't going his way. They couldn't afford to even let him ponder any other course of action.

"Listen, dogg! We falling back! Y'all muthafuckas already did enough damage by being impatient! Hemenway said it would be about two years till trial, so shit's still on schedule."

Peanut wasn't feeling the conclusion, but irrational or not, he was a thinker. He knew Amin and Troy were right. He acted as if he didn't care for their opinions as he bopped his head to the music, but he gave his word that he would roll with the decision. On, doggs.

Chapter 12

––––– ✦✦✦✦✦ –––––

"All rise!"

Everybody in the packed Suffolk County Superior courtroom stood up when the court officer gave the order.

Judge Patrick Ball emerged from his chambers. His black robe overwhelmed the tiny frame beneath it like a tidal wave does a surfer. He wore thin-rimmed glasses with thick lenses in the middle of his long pointy nose. His face was completely bare. Thin gray hair sat on top of his head, and deep almost-pink wrinkles were under his eyes. He walked with humility, yet his aura was of absolute authority over his courtroom.

When Judge Brady took his position behind his high bench, the court officer gave his next order in the form of a suggestion.

"You may all be seated."

The twenty-five months from Jermel's arrest to the start of his trial were too long and too short, depending on who was asked. OP and the A were heavily in attendance. The tension in the courtroom was sky-high.

Jermel Gilliard's trial had court officers getting good overtime money. Security was bulked inside the courtroom as well as the courthouse on a whole. Even the court officers who secured other courtrooms throughout the building were alert and on standby.

Troy had cut off his braids a few months prior to the trial. The deep waves in his head resembled a jet-black whirlpool.

He bought sharp two-piece suits from his Latino spot downtown for each of the predicted seven days of trial. He advised everyone that he knew was going to attend the trial to dress casually presentable.

Chris and Draymon sat with him. They were also sharp as nails. They chose to blend in in the third row, while Peanut, Curt, Rasaun, and some of the rowdier ones manned the front.

Trina and Ella sat with Joyce and Liona. They ignored the disapproving glares they got from some of their own peoples from Academy Homes.

Jermel was behind the defendant's table, still with a little too much slouch for the occasion, but definitely more attention than usual. He wore tan ENYCE khakis, a light-brown button-down, with a sharp edge up on his short curly fro.

Hemenway had Troy bring Jermel casual, light-colored outfits to prevent him from resembling danger in as many ways possible. It was also Hemenway's advice for Troy to make sure that Jermel's supporters didn't appear to be thugs and henchmen in the courtroom. Hemenway, on the other hand, looked like a million bucks.

The prosecutor, Masai Pawn, came right out, attacking Jermel in his opening statements. He was a chubby-faced, light-brown young man on a mission to make a name for himself in Suffolk County. And he thought this was the case to put him on the map. It wasn't a walk in the park, but it was winnable, and he was going to win. To add to the triumph of this victory, he would be defeating one of the most respected minds and established defense attorneys in the state. Masai Pawn didn't respect Hemenway's mind. He thought most defense attorneys were unethical scum, but the judicial world respected the mind of Herbie Hemenway and they would respect his when he came out on top.

Masai Pawn painted a picture of a high school dropout and an ignorant thug from the ghetto who murdered Arthur Howard in cold blood. He based his claim on the long-standing feud between their neighborhoods, jealousy, and an owed drug debt. He painted a violent picture of war, from the eighties to the present, and placed Jermel Gilliard in the center of the portrait.

For the most part, for those in the know, DA Masai Pawn's opening was exaggerated, but not too far off from the truth. Masai Pawn really underestimated Herbie Hemenway's cunning. The way the older attorney sat, watched, walked, and talked showed that he belonged in a courtroom. The courtroom was his comfort zone, his basketball court to Michael Jordan. When Masai Pawn finished his opening statement to the jury, Hemenway stood up, in his thousand-dollar suit, and graced his way to the jury box.

Fourteen jurors were seated, twelve to reach a verdict and two alternatives. There were five black women and two white, along with two black men and five white. The average age was approximately forty. Hemenway stood so close to the jury box he could've been mistaken as the fifteenth juror.

The language of his body was certainty and sincerity. He appeared a lot younger than his sixty-four years.

"Ladies and gentleman," he called poetically, "contrary to the quite-nefarious, inaccurate accusations made by my brother District Attorney Masai Pawn to describe my client, Jermel Gilliard, you will not learn about an animal throughout this trial. In fact, you will learn about an influential, intelligent human being. What you will hear throughout the testimony in this trial is evidence of two longtime friends who were able to maintain their friendship despite an ongoing feud between their respective neighborhoods. You will hear an extensive history of Jermel Gilliard and Arthur Howard working to bring peace between their respective neighborhoods."

Hemenway placed both hands on the front of the jury box. He made eye contact with all fourteen jurors before making his next statement. "And yes, ladies and gentlemen, you will also hear about the very tragic murder of Arthur Howard on January 21, in the year 1998, on Creston Street, in Dorchester." He paused again, allowing the sentiment to build in his eyes. "A murder in which my client"—he pointed—"Jermel Gilliard, just narrowly escaped with his own life, A tragedy that will forever haunt this young man."

He walked from the jury box back to the defendant's table, stood behind Jermel, and placed a fatherly hand on his shoulder. "A tragedy that has been compounded by false charges, witnesses with ill motives, and ambitious law enforcement eager to quickly close a case."

His final words came with absolute conviction. "When you, ladies and gentlemen of the jury, have heard all the evidence, you will feel compelled to find this fine young man not guilty of the murder of his longtime friend!" Hemenway looked from the jury to Judge Ball, to the prosecutor's table, then popped his collar and sat back down next to Jermel.

Old-school playa. How you like that?

For the next week following both attorneys opening statements, they conflicted back and forth, winning some battles and losing some. Detective Teeler, Ms. Howard, a sixty-something woman from Creston Street, and Jessica were the government's star witnesses.

Ms. Howard lied, convincingly, with the pain and wrath of a grieving mother. She took what she learned from Jessica and reiterated it as if it were firsthand knowledge. To worsen matters for Jermel, she added lies, such as overheard conversations between him and her son, a recent argument, and the fact that Jermel influenced Arthur to sell drugs.

The sixty-something eyewitness from Creston Street initially told the police that she saw Jermel pull up in the Chevy Blazer and exit it. Then she saw another man walk up and shoot inside of it. Detective Teeler, with his knowledge of the Chevy Blazer being stolen and who Jermel Gilliard was, coached and coaxed her in the weeks approaching the trial.

When the older lady took the stand, her once-basic statements became a motion picture.

On the stand, she said that Jermel pulled up in the Chevy Blazer, exited it, and walked into a nearby alley. Within thirty seconds, a masked man fitting Jermel's description emerged from the same alley and shot three times into the Blazer.

Ouch!

Hemenway stood and emphatically objected to her speculative and, obviously to him, coached testimony. Though Judge Ball instructed the jury to disregard the woman's speculating, the damage was already done once it was said and heard.

Hemenway was heated. He knew he would have to dig deep into his bag of tricks also. Allowing a witness to utter incriminating statements was a ploy often used by the prosecution. Its purpose was to taint a trial with their own theories. Even after an objection was sustained by a judge, the jury was undoubtedly influenced by the clever maneuver.

Jessica was the most damaging witness against Jermel. Though she never chose to go into witness protection like Detective Teeler encouraged, he was able to work with her on her appearance and testimony points extensively. He wanted the pretty, innocent nineteen-year-old girl who lost her boyfriend. He wanted to use her to depict Jermel Gilliard as a longtime menacing enforcer.

Instead of simply telling the truth, which was incriminating in its own right, she went into a horror tale of how Arthur was frightened when Jermel called him. Jermel was upset with Arthur for being short on a payment and threatened him. When Jermel told Arthur that he was coming by to pick him up, Arthur told Jessica to keep paging him if he wasn't back in an hour. Arthur needed an excuse to get away from Jermel.

In perfect accord with the horror tale she told the jury, the police found Arthur's pager inside of his jean pocket with fifteen beeps from his home phone in it.

Hemenway thoroughly cross-examined every witness. He did his legal best to mix up Masai Pawn's theories and put in his own. He attacked the old lady like she was the criminal. She was visibly shaken up. He threatened her with jail time for committing perjury.

Masai Pawn angrily objected.

Hemenway really shook up Jessica and Ms. Howard. He poked holes in their stories but couldn't completely discredit them because their tales were founded in truth also.

The prosecution and defense rested their cases after Jessica's testimony. Jermel's fate was in the hands of the jury.

Hemenway spoke with Jermel in his cell in the back of the courthouse. He gave him his honest legal opinion on how the trial went. He was still upset about some of the shenanigans that Masai Pawn pulled. He all but guaranteed Jermel that if the verdict didn't go in their favor, he would win his case in the court of appeals based mostly on the blatant prosecutorial misconduct conducted by Masai Pawn.

The problem with appeal was, Jermel would be stuck far out in the Department of Corrections (DOC) rather than right downtown at Nashua Street Jail. Plus, it would be at least another two-year process.

When Hemenway shared this possible appeal process with Troy, he took it worse than Jermel did. Jermel was already in a state of mind to accept the good or bad. After two years of being fed up, he grew to understand how possible it was that prison could be his home for a long time.

Troy felt like he would personally be letting his brother down with anything less than an immediate victory. Hemenway explained all the technical and legal ramifications of the situation and reminded Troy to stay positive. From their first meeting in his office, he told Troy that positive energy activates constant elevation. Troy had been applying that to his daily life ever since.

The trial was hard-fought. Evidence was condemning. However, the jury decided that there was at least reasonable doubt to acquit Jermel Gilliard of killing or acting in accessory to Arthur Howard's murder.

Not guilty was the verdict!

Jermel's supporters erupted in the courtroom, while Arthur's mourners stormed out. There were tears and scowls among the residents from Academy Homes, but the A-Team didn't care about the verdict one way or another. They planned on dealing with their own justice in the streets or behind the wall. Wherever and whenever they saw Jermel, it was on.

Ms. Howard was hysterical. She screamed at all the happy supporters and damned them to hell while her child was resting in heaven. Most of them laughed at her and taunted her with no remorse. Orchard Park parents intervened, telling the young crowd to be happy for Jermel but not disrespectful to Ms. Howard. Peanut sneaked in a wink and made a simulation of a gun with his thumb and pointy finger. The gesture almost caused Ms. Howard's heart to stop.

Homicide detective Teeler gave Troy a look meant to intimidate. But Troy just smiled and jacked his slacks. The homicide detective got up and left the courtroom with his pudgy partner in tow.

Troy knew not to take Teeler lightly. He was happy that the man couldn't completely conceal his emotions. The look let him know that he was on his radar and alerted him of the danger that the dirty veteran presented.

Hemenway schooled Troy on many different levels over their years together. After the many lectures about J. Edgar Hoover's intelligence programs infiltration tactics disguised as intelligence gathering, Troy knew not to take any aspect of government or law enforcement lightly. Over the course of several days, upon Hemenway's instruction, Troy read and became familiar with the United States Constitution. He acquired a limited understanding of corruption at many levels, how certain power structures went to great lengths of treachery to have the majority of the population see life from a very influential minority's viewpoint.

Jermel had to be taken back to Nashua Street Jail with the sheriffs to be officially processed out of the system. He sat in the back of the dark sheriff's van. There were two skinny wood benches separated by a rusty cage, which left hardly any room to move his legs, but he had a smile on his face. Two sheriffs were in front—one driver, one riding shotgun, with a 12-gauge shotgun between them and revolvers on their hips. They were separated by another smaller cage and sliding glass window.

He usually couldn't stand the stale, cramped vans, but it didn't bother him at all on this day. Before his trial began, he had been back and forth to court in the sardine-can vans for unsuccessful bail hearings and legal motions seven times. The seven-day trial was even worse on his body, but it was finally over. None of it mattered anymore.

The worries, the nightmares, the headaches—it was all over! The child-size beds, the tiny, claustrophobic cells, the tasteless food—it was all over! Jermel could smell freedom. And it sure smelled good.

Nashua Street Jail was finally finished discharging Jermel at 7:00 p.m. Troy and Ella were waiting in the lobby for him. They all embraced him in a bear hug.

When they walked out the front door, Jermel stopped in his tracks when he saw the black stretched Cadillac fit for President Bush.

They hopped in the limo and cruised the town and highway for an hour. There was small talk and catching up a little, just what

Jermel needed. When they finally pulled into Jermel's lot, he was taken aback.

"A, dogg!" Jermel complained. "I'm cool with the welcome-home shit, but why all these whips at my crib?" He stared at Troy, then Ella. "Didn't I tell you only Trina and Tanyah at my spot?"

Troy and Ella laughed, but Jermel found no humor in the situation.

"We don't live here no more, Chubby," Ella teased, then kissed his cheek before getting out.

Before Troy could get out, Jermel grabbed his arm.

"Troy, I love you, dogg. Thanks for everything. On, doggs." They dapped each other, and Jermel smiled. "You wild as shit, yo!"

Troy's smirk remained. "This ain't shit, dogg. You would've done it even better for me."

When they entered the nearly unfurnished apartment, Jermel got rushed with daps, hugs, and kisses. Ella fell back with a tinge of jealousy but knew that he was hers after two years of holding him down.

"Uncle Jermel! Uncle Jermel!" Jimmy Jr. came running full speed at him. He jumped off his feet with no regard for his own safety. He looked more and more like his father as he got older.

Jermel caught him and smiled from ear to ear. "Whoa! Look at you! You got big!"

Jermel was genuinely surprised at how much he grew. Crystal brought him on a few visits, but not for the last seven months or so.

Jimmy Jr. smiled. "I know I got big! I'm six. I can fight!" He proved that by punching Jermel in the chest with a nice blow for his size.

"Oh yeah?" Jermel challenged. "Me and you gonna have ta go a few rounds later, then." He put him down, and Jimmy Jr. was off and running again.

"Damn, boy! Look at you!" Crystal hollered over the music. "You got all slim and built. And ya skin look so fresh!" She reached up and rubbed his face. "Oooh, I missed you!" She wrapped her arms around him, almost as if to see if he was real.

Everyone complimented his 190-pound frame. He had started working out and eating healthier at Nashua Street, and he hoped to carry both new habits back into the free world with him.

Trina, Tanyah, and Danisha had the smell of fresh seafood coming from the kitchen. The speakers pumped Chris's music, Wise Guys and Ruff Ryders. Jermel couldn't stand still for more than two minutes without being pulled to the side to kick it with one of his people.

When the homecoming celebration ended, Troy, Jermel, Trina, and Ella hopped in the stretched Cadi and headed downtown. They toasted glasses of cognac, and Jermel and Ella sparked a blunt.

"Aight," Jermel said on one of his inhales, "y'all dun got rid of the crib, so what alley we sleeping in tonight?" He looked out of the window. "Damn, yo! What, y'all taking me back ta Nash?"

They all laughed.

Ironically, they were back in the vicinity of Nashua Street Jail. Just as Jermel asked the question, the Cadi pulled into an underground garage of a high-maintenance high-rise on Newbury Street and parked next to a '99 cherry-red Chevy Tahoe. They got out, and Troy thanked and tipped the driver before he pulled off.

"Dogg, this a pretty muthafucka!" Jermel said while circling the Tahoe and mentally speculating. When he got to the other side and saw a matching black one, his speculation was confirmed.

Troy laughed as he tossed Jermel the keys to the truck.

"This look like me! I'm feelin' this shit, dogg!"

After Jermel finished examining and playing with his new set of wheels, they got on the elevator to the seventh floor. Both of their pads were along the same thin-carpeted hallway. Troy was in suite 707, and Jermel in 701.

Joyce, Liona, Peanut, and Amin were in his living room, kicking it, when they all walked in. Ella had the crib furnished with red and black reclining chairs and sofas, black ultrafine cotton window shades, and a Bose-everything entertainment center—and that was just the living room.

"My baby!" Liona leaped off the sofa and ran to Jermel as soon as he walked in.

His eyes watered, but he didn't let anything fall. He had never seen his mother look so beautiful in his life. He spoke to her, heard about when she started cleaning herself up, and even glanced at her in the courtroom, but never did he expect this. She wasn't able to visit him at Nashua Street Jail due to her own extensive criminal record.

Shortly after Jermel got locked up, Liona fell to her lowest point of existence. Rock bottom. At her lowest, she literally came crawling to her big sister, Joyce, for help. Joyce picked her off the Blue Hill Avenue corner and drove her home. Liona had been beaten badly. Her face looked like a Halloween mask. Liona stayed with Joyce for a week, recovering. It was in those days that a light shone on her. Joyce advised, lectured, cried, and prayed with her little sister. It was a life-changing experience for Liona, one she would forever be grateful for, so she agreed to try to clean herself up. Troy put her in an in-house drug treatment program for six months. She went through extensive mental and physical pain during her first thirty days, and she attempted to leave the program three times. But she ultimately endured. When she successfully completed the program, Troy had a crib waiting for her with Joyce in the Hyde Park section of Boston.

Joyce and Liona had been living together for a year at this point. Liona was beautiful, drug-free, attending the Kingdom Hall, and working.

"I missed you so much, baby! Look at me!" Liona spun around, showing off her shape. A person who didn't know her past would never know that she was an addict. At thirty-six, she could stand out in a crowd of divas in their twenties.

Jermel pulled his mother into a strong embrace. He looked at all the faces in his new crib. He was scared to speak, for fear of getting choked up. But he let the words go, anyway. "Thank y'all, yo. It don't get no better than y'all." He took another look at his mother. "You look great, Ma." He felt great saying it.

They all kicked it until after 2:00 a.m., then decided to leave so that Jermel and Ella could be alone.

"I was wondering when y'all planned on rolling out." Ella faked an attitude, rolling her eyes and neck. She was loving the family reunion but itching to be with her man.

The guys planned to meet up the next afternoon, and the mothers said they'd be by after they got off work. As soon as the last person was out of the door, Ella smiled mischievously. "I got a CO uniform in the closet. Guess who I wanna be tonight?"

Chapter 13

While Jermel was locked up, Troy earned his associate's degree in business management from Northeastern University. Trina was still in the process of earning her bachelor's degree.

Hemenway, a few college friends, and Trina's influence helped Troy make a few productive moves to legitimize himself. He first found an ideal location in Dorchester and opened a corner store. That business proved to be a lot more profitable than he anticipated. Next, he acquired an A-1 car auction license, which first led to him dibbling and dabbling in the buy-low, sell-high business. The vehicle-flipping formula reminded him of the drug game. He caught on fast and actually enjoyed it.

His first baby was New Edition. New Edition was a clothing store he opened in Mattapan. Even before he had thoughts of doing any type of legal hustle, he had always wanted to open his own clothing store.

He, Peanut, and Amin had a good portion of the streets on lock. The game was going good, but a lot of Troy's focus was on his businesses and Chris's music career, which was starting to really take off. Troy and Amin were promoting shows and parties all around the state. Chris opened shows for Ruff Ryders, KRS-One, MOP, and other A-list artists. It was only a matter of time before acts would be opening up for him.

When it came to Jermel, Troy knew his mentality. Running the streets was Jermel's number one priority ever since he could walk. If Jermel chose not to be a part of his business ventures, Troy was ready to take an even farther step back from the day-to-day operations in the streets to let Jermel handle all that he desired. Troy still loved the streets and had no intentions of relinquishing that type of power, but the expansive entrepreneurial world was his new excitement. He loved to conquer new challenges.

Troy moved out of his Huntington Avenue apartment, into his Newbury Street spot, in the summer of '99. After he completed his college obligation, he needed a change of scenery to complement his new lifestyle.

Trina moved in with him on his twenty-first birthday and officially made his house their home. He never thought for one minute about Jermel losing at trial. All his preparations were based on his brother's release, so after a week of Trina living there, Troy was already in the process of getting Jermel and Ella a spot down the hall.

"Hell no! I ain't selling no damn clothes and cars!" Jermel yelled after Troy presented him with the idea. He didn't entertain Troy's fifty-fifty business offer at all. "Pass out flyers ad push shows for that little bastard? Who I look like, Dame Dash, Russel Simmons, or something? Troy, I'm a hustler, dogg! I drop muthafuckas! Hos love me. I'm Trailblazing for life! You already know that! All that other complicated, educated shit's for you!"

Troy knew that there was a good chance that he would get this type of reaction from Jermel. No matter how hard he tried to broaden his perspective on life, Jermel repelled it.

"Whatever, dogg."

In a weird way, he didn't even know if he wanted Jermel to change how he was. He loved him for exactly who he was. Troy told him, "Get ready ta pump then, dogg, 'cause the game stepped all the way up! On, doggs! We got enough flave ta flood the streets like the days of Noah." They dapped and hugged.

Jermel had no hesitation or caution in him. He jumped head-first back into the streets with more aggression than ever. He felt untouchable! His name rang bells for years, but beating a body that everyone knew he was responsible for had him feeling superior. He had lost two years of his life behind bars.

His mentality rubbed a lot of people the wrong way. Jermel and Chris never really got along. This wasn't evident to the outsiders, but the inner circle saw that it was an ingredient for trouble. Chris was now eighteen and a lot more outspoken. Jermel couldn't stand it.

Jermel saw Chris as a nobody with too big of a say in their maters as a crew. Troy was wasting too much time focusing on his bullshit rap career. It angered him even more, knowing that his own actions caused Troy to pull Chris in even closer.

After Chris got shot, Troy basically adopted his worthless ass. If something happened for the wrong so-called reason or to the wrong so-called person, Troy's stupid conscience always ate at him. Jermel, on the other hand, couldn't care less about right or wrong, right or left, up or down.

What Jermel did love, though, was the fact that Troy made Liona the sole manager of his clothing store. The store's name, New Edition, represented both Orchard Park and the R&B group New Edition. They, too, were from OP.

Jermel drove up to Mattapan at least four days out of the week just to stop in and kick it with his mother. He was happy to get to know her and her story from her own mouth.

Joyce always spoke to him about her good points. She told stories of how Liona was as a child and how she was one of the smartest and prettiest girl in the projects. She told Jermel how much she really loved him, but all seemed like a myth to Jermel. Jermel's only reality of his mother was the crackhead hooker he ran into a few times a week either in the house or in the streets.

He even learned about his father from Joyce. Sometimes he wished that the man stayed alive longer so that he could've been the one to kill him, not a train.

It was Joyce who gave him his family history. Gave him a sense of worth. He appreciated her for all that she did for him, but his life felt so much more complete when he heard things through the eyes and truth of his mother.

They were finally able to catch up on a lifetime of lost time. He was blessed to learn to love and respect the biological mother he never had.

"Joyce and ya brother helped me so much, baby," Liona told Jermel while they sat in New Edition and talked. She was happy as a child on Christmas whenever he was in the store with her. She could never stop talking. "All of them helped, really. They all love you, baby. And you better do right by my Ella."

Jermel chuckled.

Liona giggled with him. Then her eyes drifted sadly. "It was hard for me. I ain't ever looking back, though. It's still hard, but I won't let you down like that again. I promise. I ain't perfect, but I'm taking it one day at a time." She wandered off in thought again but this time came back with a smile. "You see how much Troy trusts me? I been running this store ever since he opened it eight months ago! Joyce runs it with me. She taught me the ropes, but I'm here every day. It's my baby!" She looked like a happy teenaged girl.

"Don't worry about letting none of us down. It's all about you, Ma. We all love you. I see it in ya pretty hazels, you serious about never messing with them drugs again. I'm proud of you."

The approval from her only child meant the world to her and made her tear up, but she felt much better when Jermel pulled her in for a comforting embrace.

*****

It didn't take long for Jermel's recklessness to resurface. By the time that summer rolled around, he had already been the cause of a few problems. Most of his drama was tolerable, but some went way too far. If trouble didn't come his way, it was like Jermel had to go looking for it.

Jermel knew that he needed to stay as far away from the A as possible. With Ella living with him now, he had no reason to be around there. He drove past the Dark Side in late July, but instead of continuing on, he saw Tanyah sitting in her car on Columbus Avenue. He used that as an excuse to pull over.

"What up, Light Skin?" he called to Tanyah through his passenger-side window.

"Hey, Jermel! How you been?" she asked with a genuine smile. Her face almost instantly grew concerned. "Why you double-parked? You know you ain't suppose ta be around here!"

He stepped out of his Tahoe and walked over to her Honda Accord. Her driver's-side window was open as she cleaned her car out. He said, "I can go anywhere I want! This ain't private property."

Tanyah was a couple of years older than him, pretty and cool as a fan. They always got along, so conversation came easy.

Jermel noticed that her skin and lips were pale and dark bags were under her eyes. He inquired, "How's ya health?"

Her health was always a touchy subject. She had diabetes or sickle cell—he wasn't sure which one—but at times it seemed to affect her mood. She was usually loud and energetic. When she was down, like she seemed at the moment, he always figured she wasn't feeling well.

Him inquiring about her health darkened her mood even more.

"I'm cool!" she snapped. "Look, you need ta get from around here. Them dudes is right around the corner."

Her revelation was old news to him. He spotted them as soon as he neared the area. That was the main reason he pulled over. He wanted to have a little fun. "Fuck them suckers!"

"Jermel! It was nice seeing you. Now, get out of here before you get some bullshit started!"

Too late.

"I know that ain't that bitch ass!" Steve couldn't believe his eyes. "I know that ain't. That's that muthafucka Jermel!"

D was by his side, squinting to see if it actually was Jermel.

"I'm 'bout ta kill his ass right now, dogg. On, doggs!" Steve said, then got up from the stoop he sat on. He had no idea that Jermel already had an eye on them and a finger on the trigger of the .45 in the pouch of his hoodie.

It was well-known around the Bean that Steve killed Jimmy in the park, so tension between his specific circle and OP was even higher than the rest of the beef. To compound that, he and Jermel's beef behind Ella had two of the hottest heads in the city in a standoff.

Steve was thorough, respected by his peers and foes. He rarely slipped. He was a lot harder to hit than Beam, Q, and Arthur. He rarely even left the A, so he was usually playing with home field advantage. He was an ordinary five ten, one-seventy, but had the heart of a lion.

"Yo, duke! Yo bitch ass must be tryna see Jimmy!" Steve snarled as he approached Jermel. His hand was gripping a pistol in his waist-line, ready to pull it out.

Jermel whipped out an already-cocked .45 from his hoodie. Steve put his hands up in almost-mock surrender.

"You tryna see Arthur, chump?" he shot back. His hazels smiled, but his mouth scowled. "I see I ain't welcome here, so I'll bounce," Jermel said sarcastically. "You be easy, Tanyah," he said without taking his eye off Steve.

Tanyah was already laid across her center console, protecting herself from the bullets she expected to fly.

Jermel told Steve, "I'll catch ya bitch ass on a better day," as he backed away.

"I'mma kill you and ya mans! On, doggs! Ya crash dummy ass, playing a game you ain't built for, duke!" Steve was heated and meant every word he spoke.

Jermel laughed, jumped in his truck, and peeled off.

Boom! Boom! Boom!

Jermel saw the fire from D's gun before he ducked his head down. D had ran up on the side of the truck out of nowhere. His front and back passenger-side windows were blown out. He skidded and sideswiped two cars before gaining control of the wheel. He sped away, shaken up a little but unharmed.

"I'mma kill them suckers!" Jermel vowed.

*****

Tanyah called Ella and cussed her out. Steve slapped her for having Jermel around the A. Ella couldn't get Jermel on his phone, so she called Troy to find out what happened.

Troy had to fight to compose himself so that he didn't explode on the phone. It was the first he was hearing of the incident. He was beyond heated. He pretended to have it all under control, told Ella to apologize to Tanyah for them, and hung up. He almost crushed his phone in his hand.

Later on in the night, Amin, Peanut, and Troy were kickin' it in the park when Jermel pulled up in the projects in a rental car. Troy wasted no time getting in his shit. His vein was bulging out of his neck, and his jaw clenched in anger.

"Dogg, it's been quiet for damn near a year. Now you come right home and start some bullshit ta fuck up our money!"

"Don't come at me with this bullshit! Why I always gotta be the one starting shit? Them suckers stepped ta me!"

"Come on, dogg! Why the fuck you even go over there?" Amin jumped in. He was really fed up with the foolishness also.

"That's bugged out how soft y'all got! I—"

Before Jermel could finish talking, he felt the blow and tasted his own blood. Troy caught him with a hard jab and was headed to the nearest hallway, signaling for him to follow him.

Five years before this, Jermel almost got Troy killed when he did a robbery on Columbia Road and didn't tell him about it. The dudes he robbed caught Troy off point a week later. That was the last time they had a fight. He was fed up with Jermel being selfish and putting everyone in danger.

"Damn!" Peanut yelled. "Here we go with this shit!"

The only fair fight they ever gave was with each other. All four of them respected one another's hands. Any outsider, even in the projects, didn't have a chance at a fair one, and it really got ugly when they jumped somebody.

As soon as Jermel walked into the hallway, Troy came at him with a four-punch flurry, connecting with two of them to actually wake him back up from the first jab outside.

They squared up and began exchanging blows. Jermel was back to about his normal 210-pound frame, so Troy's 220 didn't overpower him. Regardless of his weight, Jermel hit with the power of a sledgehammer. A three-punch combination nearly lifted Troy off his feet. Every blow each brother threw looked like the one that would knock the other off his feet.

They both kept standing. Both kept swinging.

After a full two and a half minutes of calculated blows, they finally locked horns and began beating up the walls with each other's bodies. When they started sucking wind and had no effort left, Peanut and Amin intervened. Jermel and Troy got an extra dose of false strength and courage once they realized that the older two weren't going to let them back at each other.

"Yo!" Amin yelled. "On, doggs. The next one of y'all that swings is gonna have ta come at me! I ain't bout ta play with y'all little muthafuckas!"

"Man, get the fuck off me!" Jermel said while pushing away from Peanut. "I'm tired of y'all acting like these streets is sweet! That muthafucka Steve killed Jimmy, and he still alive! If Tanyah wasn't there, I would've killed his ass today! Fuck that! They my enemies for life! I don't know about y'all!" He pushed his way through all three of them, out the hallway, and bounced in his rental.

"Yo, dogg," Peanut said to Troy. "You know bruh's my heart, but you the only one he listen to. You gotta calm his ass down, not be out here fighting with him! He be on some bullshit, some death-wish shit for real!"

"That muthafucka don't listen ta nobody, dogg. That's why I made him listen ta these." He held up his fists. "He been hard-headed his whole dumb-ass life!"

"Yo, dogg, just go home and take it down for the night," Amin said. "I'mma pull up on little bro when he cool down."

That night, Troy couldn't sleep. He was up late night, clicking through the channels. His home phone rang. He answered it on the first ring to avoid waking Trina.

"Yo," he said into the phone.

"Open the door," Jermel said on the other end of the line.

Troy got up, massaging his sore neck. Jermel caught him with a blow right below his left ear that he knew was going to hurt for at least a week. He opened the door.

Jermel walked in with a large ninety-nine-cent corner store bag of ice over his eye. "Where Trina at?" he asked.

"In the bed."

"Good, 'cause I need ta holla at you. My fault earlier. I…I know I be on some bullshit sometimes." He slumped down on the couch.

Troy took a seat next to him.

Jermel's face was strained as he continued, "I hated them kids forever! On, doggs! I know y'all do too. Y'all just know how ta control shit better. I know y'all ridin' with me no matter what. I gotta stop taking advantage of that."

"What you been smoking, dogg?" Troy had an eyebrow raised.

"See! I'm tryna man up and apologize, but you playing and shit!" He started to get up.

Troy reached out and grabbed his arm. "Aight, aight!" He laughed. "I'm done bullshittin'. Go 'head!"

"I knew that I shouldn't've come down this muthafucka to holla at you!" Jermel gritted his teeth. He was really agitated with Troy taking his apology for a joke.

"Shut up, dogg! You ain't bout ta get all sensitive now 'cause I made a joke! Keep apologizing!" Troy still had a playful glitter in his eyes. He was enjoying his brother being uncomfortable.

"Nah, just listen, yo. You got better focus than me. I ain't gonna front. Sometimes I get mad at that shit. I mean, I don't get mad at you. I get mad at myself. I'm happy that the only muthafucka smarter than me is my brother."

"What about Peanut and Amin?" Troy was still taking advantage of the moment.

"Yeah, Amin and Nut might be a little smarter than me too. All y'all is fam, though, so I'm cool with that. But I'm gonna calm down with all that shit."

"I hope so, dogg, 'cause we all love you. Just tighten up and get this money, yo. On Jimmy."

They dapped and hugged, then put on Eddie Murphy's Raw.

They laughed for a few hours while Eddie performed skit after skit on the stage, showing why the eighties comedy scene was so special. Troy reveled in the moment.

Jermel was sincere in telling Troy that he was going to calm down, but he put out so much negative energy before his promise that it all started coming back to haunt him.

Two weeks after his conversation with Troy, D and three young A-Team gunners ambushed him in a downtown hat store. They didn't see little Rise sitting in a rental car across the street, waiting for Jermel to come out.

Rise jumped out the whip, bussing. Midafternoon meant nothing to him. He hit two of the ambushers, but D and the other one got away. He called for Jermel, who came running out when he realized he was on the winning end of the bullets. They took off and made it back to the projects safely.

The two Rise hit were injured badly. The incident set off a series of violent events. The projects were back in an all-out war with the A. For four months, both Hoods were flooded with police. The hustle was slower. Day-to-day life was tense.

In the mid of all the chaos, Troy and Jermel fell out again, but this time they fell out like never before. It wasn't the actual chaos that caused their fallout, but they fell hard.

The whole projects began to fall out with Jermel, all at the same time, for one reason or another. Everyone was beginning to call him for the bad apple he was and always had been.

After Troy and Jermel didn't communicate for a full two months, Ella and Trina tried to get them in the same space, to no avail.

What brought Troy to completely cut Jermel off was deeply rooted in their bond. It could literally only be understood by the two of them. Jermel knew in his heart that he was dead wrong for the things he said to cause their fallout. He felt like Troy needed a wake-up call back to reality again. Still, if he could take his words back, he would, but he refused to be the one to patch things up this time.

Jermel went all the way out of control, and it was the result of not having Troy in his corner. Just about everyone, Joyce and Liona included, tried to get Troy to talk to him, but Troy wouldn't even entertain their pleas. He needed some serious time away from his brother, for both of their sakes. A line was crossed that never should've been under any circumstances.

Jermel was getting overly rowdy in clubs. He blew money like never before. He dived deeper into his secret new habit that developed while he was in Nashua Street Jail. The stress of possibly spending the rest of his life in prison got to him. He ended up experimenting with sniffing some of the cocaine he got from some of his associates. The experiment quickly turned into something he enjoyed a bit too much.

His recklessness caused him to blow his own money, as well as too much money from their collective pot. Peanut helped him out once with replacing the pot money, but he knew he couldn't ask him a second time.

He had to find a way to replace it. Actually, he had no way to replace it in the streets. This dilemma caused him to cross another line that was never supposed to be crossed.

Jermel knew, after the numerous jobs he and Troy did, that he had the bank game down pat. Peanut was family. He was in on the other family business that ran a lot deeper than robbing banks, so Jermel saw no harm in bringing him on a job.

The banks weren't "circle" business. They were a secret, strictly between brothers. Jermel knew he was violating, but he didn't care. He and Troy had quite a few sacred oaths that were supposed to go to their graves with them, but Troy forced his hand on this one. Jermel was in too deep. He needed a quick fix.

Jermel broke down the bank game to Peanut as if it were something he learned from a Charlestown friend in Nashua Street Jail. It sounded good and adventurous, so Peanut was all for it. He actually commended Jermel for bringing such a clever idea to the table.

The bank job went smooth, in and out without a scare.

Peanut was in awe of how easy it actually was when they were finished. The money wasn't what Jermel exaggerated it to be, but he didn't sweat that. He had his hand just inches from his waist the whole time that Jermel was at the window with the teller.

There was only one problem with the seemingly flawless heist. It was a major problem. Jermel forgot one extremely crucial detail that Troy always did.

The teller never gave Jermel the note back. The FBI's bank task force lifted his latent fingerprint off it. After positively identifying Jermel Gilliard from the fingerprints, the FBI ran his name through their system and saw that he was a high target on the DEA, ATP, and BPD lists. Instead of running down on him for a simple unarmed bank robbery, they shared their information with the other three agencies and held the bank as their trump card. A full-scale investigation was launched on Jermel Gilliard. Operation Cease Problems.

Chapter 14

+ ✦ ✦ ✦ +

"What's up, young boy?" Tanika said over the phone. "Come through here tonight. I need to see you about something."

Troy said, "It ain't a good night, OG. I got some shit ta handle." Trina was in the bedroom, with the music playing, and he was in the kitchen, talking low.

"I said I need to see you, not want to see you."

Troy could hear the anger in her tone.

"Don't act brand-new, 'cause you don't need me to take care of your brother no more. It might be like that with you, but ain't nothing fake about me! I see you as a friend, but I guess I'm just a fuck to get what you want!" She felt like he was trying to dismiss her like a groupie.

"Damn! Slow down, OG! I ain't mean it like that! My brother been out almost a year now, and I ain't switch up. I'll be there in an hour. You always worth my time, friend." He hung up, walked to his bedroom, and put on some clothes.

"Where you going, babe? I thought you was in for the night." Trina's intuition was telling her that something was wrong.

He kissed her forehead. "I'll be back in a few. I got some business ta handle."

Trina never questioned him about his business in the streets. He never gave her any reason to suspect that he was being unfaithful, but her senses were running wild anyway.

"Hurry up back and be careful." Both requests had more than one meaning.

"Okay, Joyce," he joked as he headed for the door.

*****

Troy knew that something was wrong as soon as he stepped inside Tanika's door. She looked frightened. He didn't know what to think of it.

"What up, OG?"

"Troy, I swear I didn't call you over for this, but now that you're here, can you get me off before we talk? I can't resist you sometimes," she pleaded embarrassingly.

"You serious?" He looked puzzled. He wasn't repelled, just humorously shocked at how she asked.

She smiled shyly. "Yes. I'm serious."

He took her into his arms and kissed her softly. He squeezed her petite body just tight enough to relieve her of control as his tongue moved in light circles with hers. She relaxed. Submitted.

He placed her in the love seat, slid off her jeans and panties, then fucked her, intensely, for ten minutes. She cherished all six hundred seconds of pounding. She got exactly what she needed.

"Damn! Thank you, young boy." She didn't bother to get up.

She stayed slouched in the love seat, in her T-shirt, admiring her young lover. The way he blew her mind was something she couldn't describe in the English language, or her native Creole.

"Troy, something is going on around you, and it's not good."

She saw she had his undivided attention. She went on to explain that the FBI requested all the records that Nashua Street Jail had on Jermel Gilliard. She was the active-duty officer who received the request, so the assignment was hers. She personally faxed them the file. The request worried her, so she phoned in a favor from a friend who worked in the ATF office. The matter was highly classified. Her friend was reluctant to reveal even the little that he found out. A bit of flirtatious begging opened him up. He told her that Jermel Gilliard was a suspect in a December 3, 2000, bank robbery.

Troy's knees wanted to give out on him, but he kept his cool.

"Shit, they must've got their signals crossed somewhere, 'cause he don't even know what an ATM machine is, never mind how a bank operates. We project kids, OG."

She read him as he spoke. She wanted to see his immediate reaction before she continued. "My ATF source also said that the bank discovery led to another type of investigation that is 'project kids' related," she said slickly. "Be careful, Troy." She went from informative to protective. "You're a real special person. Plus, you have a real special dick. I don't wanna have to sneak in a cell to get it," she tried to joke, but her face was unsmiling.

He acknowledged her only with a nod, then walked to the bathroom mad as fuck. He hopped in the shower, washing with the same Dial soap that he used at home. He tried to make sense of the mess as he went out to his truck and sat with his head on the steering wheel.

Tanika peeked out of her window and watched his actions. She knew that things were bad, and knew that he knew it too. She felt bad but did her part. She hoped he would do his part in staying safe.

What Tanika revealed was like a death sentence. December 3? It was January 23, but Troy was hot enough to melt the winter. He hadn't spoken to Jermel since October but dialed his number as he drove away from Tanika's crib.

"Yo," Jermel answered. There was a lot of background noise.

"Where you at, yo?" Troy's voice was calm, but Jermel felt the coming storm.

"Amin's crib. Why? What up?"

"I'll be there in a half." He hung up before anything else could be said.

He called Trina to let her know that he was headed to Amin's and that he was okay. She told him she was going to bed. He promised to be next to her shortly.

Amin had moved in to a high-rise on Staniford Street, across from the Boston Gardens. He was right down the street from Troy and Jermel's pads. When he opened his door, he was apprehensive.

Troy felt Amin's mind searching him for answers.

"What up, dogg?" It was a question rather than a greeting from Amin. He knew that something was all the way wrong for Troy to want to see Jermel immediately. They hadn't spoken in three months.

"I don't know yet" was Troy's answer to Amin's inquiry as he walked right past him. Troy saw Jermel in the kitchen with Peanut and signaled for him to follow him. He didn't even acknowledge Peanut's presence.

Jermel caught up with Troy in Amin's bedroom and shut the door behind him.

"You hit a bank, yo?" A simple question filled with complexity. Jermel obviously wasn't prepared for Troy's straightforward question. He was momentarily stunned. He was undecided on whether to lie or not. He wanted to punch Peanut in the mouth. They gave their word that the heist was between them. Why the fuck did he tell Troy? he wondered.

As the number of troubling thoughts invaded his mind, Jermel realized he was busted. It put him on the defensive. It angered him. He felt like he had to answer to Troy like answering to a father. He never had a father. He rubbed his nose and gave a hard, throaty sniff. "Yeah, I did! Why?" His response could've just as easily been the end of that, but he added, "Peanut don't know how ta keep his fuckin' mouth shut."

"Peanut?" Troy was thrown off when Jermel said Peanut's name.

Jermel sniffed. "Yeah. Peanut told yo ass, right?" Jermel's arrogant stance said that he didn't care that Troy knew or that Peanut told him about it.

Amin sat on the living room couch while Peanut sat in one of the high chairs at the kitchen counter. Troy and Jermel were only in the bedroom for a few minutes, but it felt like an eternity. They speculated about what could be being discussed behind the closed door, but neither had a clue. It was like this their whole lives, with them always into their own shit. Amin and Peanut had to just sit and wait.

The bank job wasn't even a thought that Peanut ran through his mind. He wondered if Jermel messed up some more money and Troy found out this time. Really, he hoped that it was some type of beef in the streets that would force all of them to have to go handle it together. Anything to get those two back together.

Jermel being reckless was the story of his life, so Amin just figured he was at it again. Amin, like Troy, just accepted Jermel for who he was.

Troy turned his back on Jermel in the bedroom. He opened the door and walked back into the living room.

Jermel was stuck for a moment, then walked out behind him. "You got a big fuckin' mouth, dogg!" He verbally assaulted Peanut as soon as he got back to the kitchen.

While Peanut and Jermel went back and forth, Troy asked Amin, "You know about the banks too, dogg?"

The question jerked Peanut and Jermel out of their spat. They both looked toward Amin to hear his response.

"What you mean banks?" Amin asked through a scrunched-up, confused face.

Instead of answering his question, Troy turned from Amin to Peanut. "Listen real good, dogg, 'cause I don't know how much this piece of shit did or didn't tell you." He turned back to Amin. "I'm just gonna let y'all hear it all so you know what time it is."

All eyes were on Troy as he told how he and Jermel hit seven banks between '96 and '97. The confusion, interest, and curiosity in their eyes told him that neither Amin nor Peanut knew about this part of their past.

Jermel sat, in his total arrogance, until Troy brought the story up to the present.

"This clown thinks you told me that y'all hit a bank last month," Troy told Peanut while pointing at Jermel.

Peanut looked at Jermel and shrugged his shoulders, indicating that he didn't say anything.

Jermel was nervously curious at this point. "How you know, then?" He sniffed again.

Troy continued his story, now up-to-date, and revealed the information that Tanika had just laid on him.

As he spoke, Jermel's eyes burned. Amin's face crinkled.

Peanut's mouth couldn't shut.

They were all speechless.

"Once again, we all in danger 'cause of…" Troy didn't even want to say Jermel's name or look in his direction again. He never took a seat, so it was easy for him to just turn and walk out.

Chapter 15

"Manny, I miss all the little things we use ta do together." Trina pouted in the middle of their conversation. "Remember when—"

Her words were cut short as Manny began to back up and seemed to fade away.

He spoke with a chuckle. "You aight, yo. Trust me, you good."

"No! Wait!" Trina was hysterical. "Don't go!"

It was too late. Manny was gone.

Trina was sitting upright in her bed in a shallow sweat. Her heart raced for a moment, then she lay back down, hoping to close her eyes and see Manny again, even if it was just a dream.

Something was terribly wrong in Trina's bedroom. What was wrong wasn't inside of her home, though; it was housed in the mind of her man. He didn't even budge when she jolted from her dream. She wanted badly to know what was wrong but knew that finding out would be next to impossible. Troy wasn't exactly secretive when it came to her, but he unapologetically protected her from information and situations he felt could be disheartening or harmful. She truly appreciated his guard but often felt overprotected.

The entire apartment was still. The only prominent sound was the ventilation system's soft purr pushing out a comfortable, warm current. Trina hardly made additional noise when she rolled over in the soft king-size bed and rested her head on Troy's chest. The off-white satin sheets titillated the hairs on her nakedness, allowing a discreet appreciation for the self-gratifying pleasure. The familiar musk of Dial soap, along with the natural masculine scent of his body, was both pleasing and suspect but placed her in a state of complacent security.

His chest moved up and down with an even thump and rhythm that interrupted the ventilation system's purr. It drew her attention completely to her man. He was awake, his hard brown eyes burning a hole in a single spot on the ceiling. Both hands were clasped behind his head. The steam emitting from his nose and ears was merely a figment of her imagination, but his mood was evident.

She peeked over at the black marble nightstand. The large red numbers read 6:33 a.m. on the digital clock.

Troy never liked to be up in the mornings.

Instead of immediately voicing her concern, she lay in silence, consumed in her own thoughts.

She adored the diverse array of memorabilia around the room. Some reflected the times they shared together. Most illustrated who Troy, the person, was.

Two large framed pictures of his favorite Rap and R&B artists, R. Kelly and Scarface, dominated one wall. The Boston Celtics All-Star Paul Pierce had nearly a wall of his own. Troy's most personal wall was filled with strong, influential leaders from the past and present.

Trina smiled at the picture that Troy took of her with R. Kelly and LL Cool J on their first date. It was a day she would never forget.

She found his recent love of African art and warrior sculptures, like the ones that sat on his bureau and in the corners of the room, very tasteful. Had she known that his love for these forms of art was inspired by Tanika, she would probably detest it all.

The large spider plant that he had had since it was a baby was now full-grown and crawled along the white walls and ceiling, enclosing the entire room in its web, as did Troy's presence wherever he was.

"What's wrong, baby?"

After four years of their being together and eleven months under the same roof, there wasn't much Troy could hide from her, and he knew it.

"Ain't nothing," he lied. "I just woke up and couldn't get back ta sleep." His mind was running wild about this new problem Jermel had caused. His mind couldn't rest ever since he walked out of Amin's apartment.

Trina was a master of his mind and body. She went to work on momentarily easing his problems. She sucked and sexed him crazy, gave him some encouraging words about him and Jermel's ongoing feud, then they were back to sleep by 7:00 a.m.

*****

The circle was on edge for the next few weeks following the bomb Troy dropped on them. They cut back on business and outside communication. They even fell back from each other a little. They wanted to see if and how the law exposed their hand before they made any more major moves.

Disregarding their collective agreement, Jermel was out and about after about a week of lying low. He was moving as if nothing ever happened. His "on edge" wasn't the same as the rest of the circle. His was more so anger, not paranoia.

He argued and lashed out at Ella for small things that they usually laughed off together. He had two scuffles in the projects and got even worse with his nose candy.

Amin and Peanut weren't cool with how he was moving and felt the need to say something about it. They sat in his garage and waited to catch him. A serious talk was necessary.

When Jermel finally pulled in the garage, his Tahoe looked pink from being covered in salt from the snow-filled streets. It didn't look like he washed his truck in weeks. When he stepped out, his usually smooth peanut butter face was scruffy. His jeans were wrinkled. Eyes bloodshot and tired.

"What y'all doing here? Y'all come ta whack me like the mob?" Jermel joked bitterly.

Amin ignored his sarcasm. "We need ta kick it."

"Let's go upstairs, then," he said as he headed toward the elevator.

No dap or hugs were extended; Peanut and Amin just followed. When they entered Jermel's apartment, they were all still in the silence of their own thoughts.

Ella didn't hear them come in, but they could hear her on the phone in her bedroom. She was complaining to someone on the other end of the call, "I don't know what's wrong with him anymore! I don't even know his ass no more. He act like he's on drugs for real." She paused to listen. Then she said, "No, but he's really starting ta scare me. I hope he don't know nothing about us."

All three heads in the room jerked, and they froze in place when they heard her last statement.

She kept talking. "Why else would he be treating me so foul? You sure that ain't why y'all been beefin' with each other?" She paused. "Well, I don't know what else ta do. You need ta be the one ta talk ta him."

Amin's and Peanut's eyes nearly popped out like a cartoon. Jermel's hazels might have really turned devil red.

Amin was seated on the couch but popped up and grabbed Jermel's arm before he got his senses back. "Come on, walk back out-side with me, dogg," he whispered in Jermel's ear. It sounded almost like an order. He looked at Peanut for assistance.

Peanut snapped out of his trance and helped Amin escort Jermel out the door. They rode the elevator back down to the garage in a different silence than they did on the ride up. There was no eye contact.

When they got off in the garage, Jermel looked the two of them in the eyes. He sniffed. "I'm out, yo. I need ta be alone."

They understood where his mind was. Their current problems were already bad. This new development could possibly compound things times ten. They had to give him space to clear his mind, but they also couldn't put off their original conversation too long.

Peanut spoke up. "Don't jump ta no conclusions, bruh. You need ta holla at Troy and see what's up."

"Fuck a Troy! I'll holla at y'all later!"

Peanut grabbed Jermel's arm as he tried to storm off. "Hold up, dogg. Give me ya word you'll holla at me in a few hours when ya mind's clear. We got a lot of shit we need ta kick it about."

Jermel wanted to rip his arm away but knew it wasn't going to work like that. Not with Peanut. "On, doggs," he said.

Peanut released him then he got in his truck.

Amin called to him, "We gonna holla at Troy ta see what up, dogg."

"Do what y'all want!" Jermel backed out and pulled off. Amin and Peanut stood in the garage, baffled.

Amin dialed Troy's cell phone. "Where you at, dogg?"

"Mom's crib. What up?"

"Stay there. Me and Peanut's coming through."

Forty-five minutes after Amin called Troy, the three of them were in Joyce and Liona's living room in Hyde Park.

Troy read their faces and knew it was another serious problem on top of the rest. "What up?" he asked.

Peanut explained Ella's conversation they overheard when they stepped into Jermel's crib.

Troy looked ashamed and embarrassed. He dropped his head toward his lap. One of his darkest secrets had come to light.

He silently reflected on that night in April '99 while Peanut and Amin waited for his answer.

Over a dozen of them from OP were at the Dublin House that night. It was a hole-in-the-wall not far from the projects. Chris was performing. The spot was packed. Ella was there with a group of her girls from the A. Trina was nearing the end of her semester, swamped with work, so she stayed home that night.

Ella and her girls sat in two booths, drinking and enjoying the night. A group of guys bought them more rounds and did their best to bag the whole group for themselves. Ella actually let one of the guys get a little too loose with her, which didn't sit well with most of the crowd from the projects.

Peanut found Troy, pointed out the situation, and told him to get Ella. Troy was so caught up getting the equipment ready for Chris that he wasn't paying attention to much going on around the club. Peanut heard the whispers about Ella from people, and it embarrassed him.

Troy was heated when Peanut broke down what was going on. Especially since this was the second time he heard some shit about Ella getting too loose since Jermel was locked up. There was no way he was going to allow her to embarrass his brother in front of the whole city. She was living at his crib; he was still supporting her, and she was representing his name. *Hell no!*

Troy approached the booth that Ella, some of her crew, and now some of the guys were in. He greeted everyone, then asked Ella to come talk to him.

With no warning, the guy who was working on getting Ella jumped up in Troy's face. Reflexes caused Troy's right fist to connect with the guy's nose and graze the left side of his face, but his kicks to the guy's head and body were calculated once he hit the ground.

As soon as Troy dropped the first blow, the whole project was on the rest of his team. They tore the club up, then, after smashing the other clique, they stood outside the club, hoping for more drama.

Neesie, Penny, and Nadia were trying to get at Ella again after already roughing her and her girls up inside. Chuck and Ace kept them separated.

Troy manhandled Ella to his Beamer and threw her into the passenger seat. He blacked out on her the whole way to Jermel's crib. She did her best to put up a defense, but he wasn't hearing it.

"I wasn't doing nothing, Troy! People just hating on me!" she whined.

When they got to Jermel's crib, he walked her inside. They were still going back and forth.

"Ella! Ella! Listen…" He lightened up a little after cursing her out for forty minutes already. "I believe you. On, doggs. You say you ain't fuckin' around. I don't doubt you, aight? You gotta be even more careful, though. I don't want Jermel hearing no extra bullshit in there."

She suddenly got emotional. Tears started flowing. "It's hard, Troy! It's fuckin' hard! I only been with two dudes since I met Chubby. And only two before him! He was out here fuckin' and doing whatever else, with whoever else, but I was still by his side, and I still am! Some of my girls be clowning me for keeping it tight for him now, and he might never come home. Shit, he was with another bitch when he got locked up!" She shook her head with the painful thought. "Do you know how humiliating that is? No! You don't even think about that, 'cause it's always about Jermel! He never even made me his girl! I don't even know if he loves me!" She sounded defeated. "I ain't fucked nobody since he been down, and I ain't even his last piece of pussy!" She got angry again. "I get offers all the time, Troy. I ain't gonna lie, I'm starting ta get weak." She cried a little harder. "I'm still young, Troy! I got needs too!"

She opened his eyes to her side of things, to the whole picture. He was always caught up in his biased perspective from a sibling point of view, but he understood her pain a little better. He felt sympathy. But he still wasn't changing his thought process. She couldn't be out their making his brother look bad.

"I know it gotta be tough, yo, but you gotta stay strong."

"Be strong, huh?" She rolled her eyes, with her hands on her hips. Her posture was defiant. "Troy, do you even care about me?" The question was a condemning indictment.

"Of course! You my sister, yo."

"And you're my brother," she quickly countered. "So help me right now. Help me. I'm begging you."

"What up? I got you."

"I'm hurting, Troy!" She wiped away her tears. Her voice shifted from pleading to stern. "Mentally, emotionally, and sexually, Troy. I'm hurting. I need you ta fuck me." She saw what she expected in his face. Astonishment. She went on without allowing him to think.

"Troy, if you fuck me, it'll ease my pain, then I know I can still make it with Chubby. Just this one time, Troy. You're my best friend's man. My man's brother! I know I can't have you, Troy. It can work. Just tonight. Please!"

His face became unrecognizable to her. She wasn't sure if he looked at her in disgust or disappointment. Either one was just as painful.

"Ella, go clean yaself up and get ya head together real quick, yo. That liquor or one of them fists upside ya head got you talking stupid." His voice was a low growl. "I'mma act like this conversation never happened." He turned and walked toward the door.

"Oh, you really fuckin' care about me! I see! You just gonna leave me like this, Troy? I just played myself telling you the fuckin' truth about everything. Now you just gonna leave me here looking stupid? Huh? You can act like this conversation never happened all you want, but it did, and now only you know how I feel!"

"Get ya fuckin' self together, Ella." He let the door shut behind him without even looking back at her.

Troy walked through the dark parking lot in an even darker mood. Ella watched him from her window, not knowing what to think or feel. When he sat in his Beamer, he leaned his seat back and held both hands over his head. He didn't even put the key in the ignition. He was fucked up.

Ella knew that she put him in a terrible situation. She messed his head up. Would they ever even be able to be around each other again? Did she mess everything up? She walked out to the parking lot and tapped on his passenger-side window. She noticed that she startled him, and felt bad.

He popped the lock and let her in.

"Listen, Troy, I-I'm sorry for what I just did. That was stupid. I—"

"You ain't gotta apologize." He spoke in an exhausted breath. "Just get focused and don't—"

Before he could finish, Ella nearly crawled across the center console, grabbed a handful of his dick, and stuck her tongue in his mouth. Her tongue circled with no immediate response, then he followed suit. She hit the button on the side and reclined his seat farther, climbed all the way over, and straddled him. Her shirt was over her head and bra unfastened faster than it was ever done before.

She stared into his unsure eyes. "Just this time." She pulled his head into her breasts.

Troy cupped the midsize beauties in his hands. He sucked them one by one, then together, as she licked her lips and moaned. She aggressively grinded on top of him, finally living a secret fantasy of her own for years.

"You got a condom?" she asked, cautious not to lose momentum and risk the moment.

"Mmmmmm." He shook his head from left to right.

"We'll be careful," she said, leaving no choice as she unbuttoned his pants.

He moved her to the side, pulled his jeans and boxers down, leaving them wrapped around his ankle.

Ella removed her panties and was butt naked. She grabbed his dick in her hand and smiled her approval. "I'mma ride this dick like I always wanted to." She revealed her secret yearning. *Fuck!*

She leaned down to take him in her mouth, but he grabbed her head. She looked up at him, confused.

"Uhn, uhn" was all he said while shaking his head.

She climbed back on top of him, grabbed his dick, and rubbed it on her pussy. She smiled at the expression on his face. His lips didn't smile, but his eyes danced to her beat.

When she slid him into her overly tender slit, her ass and legs tightened. Her pussy tried to resist him against her own will. He held her waist tight, helped her relax, then her love muscles expanded and accepted him.

"Oooh, oooh...ooooh!" she cried out every time she came down on him. "I knew this dick was the bomb!" After less than two minutes, she yelled, "Oh, Troy! Troy! I'm c-comin', oh shit! I'm comin' already! Ohhh!"

He held her tighter and helped her bounce into her orgasm. She shook lightly and tightened up, then laid her face in his shoulder, continuing a hard grind. He wrapped his arms behind her back and held the back of her shoulders while grinding back with her.

The realization of whom she was sexing with awoke the freak in her. It took her out of her relaxing slump. She sat back up and rode him like a madman. She was fuckin' his brains out! She never asked if he enjoyed it; she knew he loved it. She understood that he was trying to get her off with no emotional attachment. She tried to focus on just getting off, too, but knew that she could fall in love with the penetration she was feeling.

When he took control, he lifted her off him and put her on her back in the passenger seat, her fantasy fully come to life. She had him open. He was feeling her. And she knew it felt good to him.

She seized the moment as he spread her legs back and pumped in and out of her. "Take it, Troy! It's yours tonight! Take it!" she yelled and pumped back as emotions overwhelmed her.

"Damn, your fine chocolate ass feel good!"

She rocked his Beamer back and forth with him. Her juices flowed down his shaft onto his plush leather seat. She screamed with pleasure through multiple orgasms.

He stiffened.

She anticipated his final strokes. Her gyrating got even harder, moans louder. She envisioned his chocolate dick in her mouth but knew he wouldn't go there.

"Mmmmh!" he grunted and slammed into her. "Who you fuckin, Troy? Whose pussy you in?"

"I'm in your bomb-ass pussy, Ella. Believe me, I know. You got some good pussy, girl."

Her experience was complete. She loved her girl and her man, but she always knew she would love to have Troy's dick at least one time.

"Oooh, Ella, I'm 'bout ta buss!"

"Buss, baby, buss!" she talked back. "Look at me. Please look at me. Ahh! Ahh, oooh! Remember this pussy, boy!" She threw her ass off the seat, squeezed his ass cheeks, and challenged his thrusts to prevent him from pulling out.

She wanted the full experience. "Ahh! Damn, girl!" He bussed hard.

She felt his semen shoot inside of her. She couldn't care less about any consequences while in the moment. She wanted to please him to the fullest. Yes! He damn sure gave her all that she needed physically. She only hoped that she could refrain from an emotional attachment.

Troy rolled back over to the driver's seat and lay back to catch his breath. "Get out, Ella," he said without looking at her.

The sudden, empty dismissal was enough to damage a girl's self-esteem for life, but in a weird way, it gave Ella even more satisfaction. She understood exactly why he reacted that way. One of the reasons was that he enjoyed it so much.

She smiled while getting dressed, then leaned over while his eyes were still closed and sneaked a quick mouthful of his now semierect dick just to let him know the offer still stood.

He jumped up from his slump, but Ella was already climbing out of his car, smiling. She held the door open and caught his eye again.

"Thank you, Troy. This will never happen again. I promise." She shut his door and swayed to her door, floating on air.

Troy enjoyed the scent in his car and finished catching his breath. He wondered if he was dreaming as he pulled off.

Troy snapped out of his reminiscent thoughts and came back to the present, which was his mother's living room. The reality of being confronted. The reality of being exposed. The reality of having to explain. It was all overwhelming. He sucked it all up and explained the situation to Peanut and Amin, sparing them the erotic details of his and Ella's affair. They clearly remembered the night but were blown away by the revelation. Troy's word wasn't in question, so the act was weighed on a moral scale.

"Dogg, I can't call this one," Amin said while shaking his head. "That's a tough call. For real! Shit! That's a hard call. I can't say I would be cool if it was me, but if the shit stopped her from acting up, I don't know, dogg…"

Peanut added, "That's definitely some bugged-out shit, dogg. We all know you ain't no foul dude. You made a helluva decision, though. Now you just gotta see how it plays out. I ain't bout ta dwell on that shit, but bruh…" He shook his head. His eyes widened, and his forehead wrinkled. "Trina ain't gonna have understanding! She might try ta kill both of y'all!"

Peanut waved his hand, got Troy's attention, and motioned for him to lift his head. Troy had been staring at the ground the whole time and listened to their immediate comments after without ever looking up. Peanut, the philosopher, wanted Troy's undivided attention as he broke down how he saw the situation. "This ain't gonna soothe ya conscience, 'cause I know you feel fucked up, but I gotta put it out there for you, 'cause it's real. Those two wasn't a couple like you and Trina. We all know how they were, and that's good and all, but I'm just manifesting this truth to the situation. It's like me and Nish. She got my daughter. I love her. But I never officially made her mine. Somebody gonna tap them skins from time to time, but I can't beef 'cause it's me who's leaving an emotional void by not committing. We gotta be accountable for our own shit! If it's any type of voids, our broads ain't gonna be secure enough ta ride no bid, yo. Listen to the things you said Ella said ta you that night? Bruh's lucky she ain't bounce soon as she heard he got knocked with another chick in his bed! It's only natural. The commitment and security gotta start out here. If we wait till some bullshit go down then try ta forge the bond, it ain't gonna be strong enough. I know for sure Trina won't be emotionally confused like Ella or Nish if you got locked up. She would know her role and play her position. You got her emotionally secure out here, so she know exactly what it is with you."

Troy was nodding, not in agreement, but in attentiveness. Amin cut in. "You still gotta ask yaself if you would be able ta deal with that, dogg."

Troy finally found his voice again. "Yo, on, doggs. I never felt good about this shit. It just happened, so I let it be. I ain't acting like it was a bad experience with her. I just wish the shit never even went down like that. After that night, Ella was back ta being Ella, though. I liked that. She never fucked the game up coming at me again or nothing. She started visiting Jermel every week again, stayed out of the streets, and all that. She only mentioned the shit twice, once when she thanked me after one of their visits, and today, 'cause she's worried about how he's acting." He paused, then, as an after-thought, said, "She think he on coke."

The last four months of drama ran through Troy's mind, especially the last three weeks. He went from feeling guilty to offensive. "Man, y'all might not feel me on this, and I ain't tryna make excuses, but he brought all this shit on himself! And he still doing it!"

Peanut said, "I told bruh's ass ta hit me in a few hours. I'mma kick it to him about a lot of shit!" He was still on edge about the bank job. He changed the conversation to the investigation.

"Tanika ain't hear nothing else yet. Trust, though, I'll let y'all know as soon as I hear something new. I was thinking over the past week. We should bounce for a couple of weeks."

"Y'all will work all this shit out," Amin said with a shrug. To him, this was the same old story. He said, "Fuck it. Let's hit Miami or something. Get the fuck away from here so we can relax and think."

"Sounds good ta me," Peanut said. "As soon as bruh call, I'll holla at him about it."

When Amin and Peanut left, Troy called Ella. "He knows." She didn't ask any questions. The statement was clear. She dropped the phone and screamed at the top of her lungs. Troy called her name through the phone until she picked it back up.

She couldn't believe what she was hearing. She tried to tell him that she was right about Jermel knowing, but to learn that he found out from her own mouth was too much to bear. She had no idea that anyone had ever been in the house.

He tried to calm her and assure her that he, Peanut, and Amin were going to do their best to deal with Jermel, but she wasn't impressed. She knew that her world was turned upside down.

Troy was honest in telling her that he knew Jermel would eventually get over it with him but he couldn't call it with her.

"Just sit tight and don't panic, yo. After we all kick it, I'll let you know what's up. It ain't open and shut, so don't make no crazy decisions yet."

Ella was dumbfounded. She knew that she was about to lose the love of her life and best friend both in one day. She curled up in the living room recliner and cried a river.

Chapter 16

Nobody heard from Jermel for two weeks after the phone incident with Ella and Troy. He turned off his cell phone, bought a new one, and holed up in the Ramada, deep in Dorchester, away from the hood. Ky, one of his girls from Heath Street Projects, stayed with him. Her younger brother, Martin, did the majority of Jermel's moving and hustling for him while he lay low.

Jermel and Ky were on and off since '95. He had Martin working for him since he got home from Nashua Street Jail. Martin was only fifteen when Jermel fell for killing Arthur but was trying to make his way in the streets. He used to beg Jermel to put him on back then, but Ky knew that her little brother wasn't built for the streets and forbade Jermel to deal with him.

Jermel honored Ky's pleas with fifteen-year-old Martin, but when he came home after his trial, Martin had matured in his eyes. He was already petty hustling, so Jermel just helped him step his game up. And Martin had been a good worker ever since. Ky was just being overprotective, Jermel always thought to himself.

What neither Jermel nor anyone else knew was that Martin got pulled over a couple of months back, in December, and arrested. It was immediately after he left one of Jermel's stash houses. He had 250 grams of crack, eleven thousand cash, and a gun on him.

A task force had surveillance on Jermel for only two weeks after the bank heist when they struck snitch gold with Martin. Instead of going to jail, Martin agreed to cooperate with the investigation as a confidential informant, CI#617-1.

Martin was the master key that opened the door to the federal investigation that was Operation Cease Problems. He wore wires at times, made controlled buys with government-marked money, and reported to agents many times a week under the code name Steve. He was instrumental in building a case against Jermel, and now was an opportune time to get it over with. Jermel was uncharacteristically revealing stash houses, clientele, and other usually personal knowledge. Martin planned to capitalize on it.

He was tired of feeling like a snitch and a coward. He wasn't a snitch; he just wasn't going to jail if he didn't have to. He wanted the feds off his back, so he made the call that would finally end his obligation. He informed the agents that Jermel would have at least two and a half kilos with him at the Ramada and three more in a stash house on Blue Hill Avenue. To boost his story up, he told them that Troy would also be at the Ramada. His final move was to make sure that Ky wasn't in the room at the Ramada when the raid went down.

When the Ramada door was smashed in and Jermel heard all the screaming, his brain and body froze. The dark windbreakers and vests with the large yellow letters caused a lump to form in his throat and emptiness in his belly. He stared down the barrel of their weapons in defeat.

Jermel had a kilo on the bed and was in the process of cooking half of another one. His gun was under his mattress, his phone ringing off the hook with waiting customers. The Blue Hill Avenue stash spot was raided at the same time, compounding the many charges that he already had against him.

He was taken to the DEA barracks in South Boston, thrown in a cage, and left in cuffs for four hours. He was livid. Livid and lost. He strained his brain trying to figure out what happened. What went wrong? All he could think about was Troy's warning. He couldn't believe he got caught slipping again.

Not even a full year out of jail yet. How'd he fucked up? He had no answers. He started to focus on Troy. Jermel couldn't believe they were betraying him like that.

Wild thoughts tugged his brain in many directions. Troy hadn't even acknowledged him in four months. Trina changed his whole attitude. Her presence alone messed with Troy's conscience.

It made him want to say, "Fuck the world!"

Jermel never, ever understood how Troy could be so cold and ruthless, then warm and caring. What the hell was that? he thought.

Fuck Trina! Jermel wanted Troy to accept that shit happens in the streets and everything ain't his mess to clean up.

Sitting in his cell, Jermel knew that he shouldn't have threatened Troy with talking about their past life in the streets to Trina. He was only bullshitting, anyway, but Troy was too sensitive about her to see it.

Troy had let too much come between them over the years. He wasn't the same brother Jermel grew up with.

On the ride from the Ramada to the DEA barracks, the agents advised Jermel to help himself by helping them. He told them to suck his dick.

One agent replied that he would be asking a lot of men to do that for him for the next thirty years.

Jermel stood his ground against the agents' verbal chastisements, but he was bitter to the core. The obvious was on his face. Martin set him up, but he couldn't see it through his anger. His anger made him entertain the more improbable thought: Troy might have crossed him.

Sniff. Sniff.

Everybody had more love and respect for Troy. Troy was the smart one. Troy was the athlete. Troy was the leader. Liona, his own mother, even loved Troy more than him. If he fell for thirty years, he would have nothing. Troy would turn his back on him, because he'd always been a fuck-up, and everybody else would follow his lead.

Fuck it. Fuck it and fuck everybody!

"Jermel." Agent Story broke his name down, just as he intended to do the young man's whole character. "I don't play assistance. I'm going to give your ass one chance to save yourself. If you don't want this chance, let me know and you can go back to that holding cell."

Agent Story wore a short blond spiked fade. He had strong military features in his face and body. Jermel figured him to be anywhere from thirty to forty and well-seasoned. His eyes were thin slits with hard emeralds in the center. His lips were hardly there.

Jermel looked him up and down. "What the fuck can yo ass do for me?" He was vexed that this man had his life in his hands.

Agent Story shrugged. "It depends on what you can do for me."

"I been in the streets my whole life. I know the game, but it ain't about that. You got a little coke and a burner. That ain't shit!"

Agent Story unnecessarily adjusted his body in his chair. He saw that his prey was falsely confident. He was going to have to knock him off his sense of pride. Story dealt with a thousand Jermel Gilliards in his working life, but he knew that Jermel Gilliard never ran into even one of him.

He kept his small office at the barracks dimly lit and cluttered. His military and agency credentials were usually recognized by the scum he interrogated in there. They were meant to intimidate.

"A little coke and a gun, huh?" He mocked Jermel. "You been in the streets your whole life? That's an unfortunate fact, but you definitely don't seem to know everything," he continued. "You know what? It wasn't hard to catch up with you at all."

Agent Story watched the cockiness begin to dwindle from Jermel's face. A trace of embarrassment crept in. This pleased him. "We hit your Blue Hill Avenue stash house too. And oh," he added, as if he just remembered, "I got your prints off that note you gave the bank teller too. You're in a lot deeper than you think, kid." The agent wore a victorious smirk.

Jermel was busted. He couldn't maintain even a modest poker face after Story mentioned the note. He was giving himself a mental ass-kicking that was reflecting through every aspect of his demeanor.

That's how all this shit started? It dawned on him, and he felt like an idiot. Troy warned him to always get the note back when they hit the banks. Shit!

The bank he hit with Peanut was his first time actually approaching the teller. Getting the note back slipped his mind in the anxiety of the moment. He wanted to strangle the scrawny, big-headed lady for turning the note over to the authorities.

Jermel now saw that he was in a lot deeper shit than he thought. He made his mind up. It was a decision that would rival the very essence of his being. He couldn't half-step if he wanted to get out of the mess he was in. He had to go all the way.

Agent Story enjoyed watching him squirm, then pressed on. For the next three hours, Jermel played rat-and-cat, then eventually laid his trump card on the table. Agent Story was noticeably impressed— no poker face for him either. He couldn't believe how easy it was to break the Jermel Gilliard. Especially to the degree that he did.

The cherry on top was that the rest of his circle would surely fall with him.

Agent Story had a very long arm in the United States Attorney's Office, as well as many political circles. When he made a call, things got done. He was sure that Jermel Gilliard's rats' cooperation would be well worth his and the other departments' time. He was so sure he granted Jermel a request that he never thought he would ever even entertain. Jermel Gilliard was immediately released.

Jermel thoroughly convinced Agent Story that even one full night behind bars would jeopardize his ability to carry out all phases of his cooperation. Nobody could know about his arrest, or everything would be compromised.

When he left the barracks, Jermel checked in to a Holiday Inn across from the Ramada he was raided in. He snorted more raw coke in his three days of misery than he ever had in any other full month.

He was dejected. Confused. But he had a complicated job to do.

Two days after setting Jermel up, Martin uneasily explained to Ky what he had to do in order to save himself from prison. He knew that she had strong feelings for Jermel and would look down on him for ratting him out. But overall, she would have to be happy that her little brother wasn't going to rot in prison.

Ky's disdain was far worse than he imagined. She showed no signs of being relieved that he wasn't the one in jail. She looked at him as if he literally were a rodent. She cursed him for being weak and playing a game she always told him he wasn't built for.

She was pissed with Jermel too. She told him over and over that her brother was weak. She cursed Martin even more for putting all their lives in danger.

Martin really felt like shit when he saw how much that he did hurt his sister. She cried hard and vowed to never forgive him. Jermel took care of her, emotionally, physically, and financially. Even though she accepted that Ella was his true love, she was always grateful to have him.

After she got over her initial anger and emotional meltdown, her mind went into damage control for her and Martin. Martin simply told her that he set Jermel up, but she had no clue how deep it went. She figured he got busted with a little bit of drugs and maybe a gun at the Ramada. His money was long enough to have him out on bail in no time.

Ky needed to check to see how he was thinking and feeling about getting busted.

Ky and Danisha were cool since their middle school days. She called her the next day to feel the situation out. When Danisha told her that she had no idea that Jermel even got arrested, Ky was puzzled. She explained the situation about the Ramada, then told Danisha to tell Jermel to call as soon as he got out.

When Danisha hung up with Ky, she immediately called Peanut to find out what happened with Jermel. She wondered why he didn't mention anything about him getting arrested to her. She was thrown all the way off when he didn't know anything.

As she explained to him, he was upset, but not shocked at all. He wondered out loud why Jermel hadn't at least called him. He brushed it off and planned on calling him. If he still didn't answer, he was going to have to check Nashua Street Jail to see if Jermel was there, trying to make bail without alarming them. He had been doing so much fuckin' up he probably didn't feel like hearing all their mouths.

After they went back and forth about Jermel and his situation, they started talking about their daughter. Peanut had to cut into their conversation. "Nish, we'll holla about this later. That's bruh hittin' me on the other line now." He clicked over, disconnecting her. "Damn, dogg! What the fuck's up? That's how you do me?"

Jermel figured that Peanut's dramatics came from him disappearing for the past couple of weeks. He didn't pay it any mind.

"Ain't shit, dogg," he answered coolly. "What up with you? I just had ta get away for a second. I'm good now, though. Just running around, handling business. I'm 'bout ta stop by the crib."

Peanut was confused by Jermel's calm and lack of information. His analytical antennae went up. Something was definitely wrong. "Where the fuck yo been?" He checked his temperature.

"At Lynn's crib on Intervale," Jermel answered with no hesitation. Lynn was their homegirl. but Jermel couldn't have been there all this time. Peanut's mind started calculating numerous scenarios at once, and not one of them was good. "When you coming down the projects?"

Jermel told him, "I'll be through in a few hours."

"Aight, bruh. Hit me when you on ya way."

Jermel parked his truck around the corner from his building. He entered through the garage to make sure that Ella's car was gone. He saw Troy's truck and Trina's Beamer, but Ella's Infinity was gone, like he expected. She was usually at her mother's crib, doing hair at this time.

He crept up to his crib, packed some clothes, and cleaned out his safe. He knew that he would have to lie low for a while, let people get over the speculating when shit went down. He called Peanut just to check the temperature. Everything sounded normal. When he figured out what the rest of his plan would be, he could come back around and clear his name.

People close to him might suspect that he told, but they would have a hard time believing that he was a snitch, and an even harder time confronting him. Jermel, a snitch? When he came back around, his money would be all the way up and he could spread enough love to silence the whispers.

Bottom line was, doing thirty years was out of the question. *Fuck how anybody felt!*

While Jermel was in his crib, packing and mentally going through his distorted version of the truth and traitorous game plan, Troy's phone was ringing down the hallway.

"Yo," he answered.

"What up, dogg?" Peanut said with an edge. "I got Amin on three-way, and you need ta really listen up. I ain't tryna repeat this shit over and over."

After Peanut finished running everything down, there was an uncomfortable silence, then Troy spoke. "What the fuck you tryna say?" He was pacing his room, heated at the whole situation.

"Dogg, I ain't saying nothing! I'm just telling y'all so you know what the fuck's going on!"

First, Amin came at him aggressively, then Troy did the same thing. He wasn't feeling it. All he was doing was putting them up on game. They wanted to kill the messenger.

"Nish probably got the story fucked up" was all Troy could think of to say.

Peanut got offended. "Dogg, stop tryna play my girl out."

"I'mma call Ky and see what up myself," Amin said. "I ain't spoke ta her in a minute, but she always keep it official wit me." Amin had a relationship with Ky before Jermel did. Ky caught Amin with one of her friends and paid him back by fucking one of his.

Troy was already putting on some clothes to go check the situation out. "You said he's headed ta the crib, right?"

"Yeah," Peanut answered.

"I'll holla back at y'all. I'm 'bout ta shoot down the hall." Troy hung up and finished putting on his clothes.

*****

When Jermel stepped out of the door to his apartment, he was momentarily paralyzed. Life began to move in slow motion, as if the world were a big screen and he were an intoxicated viewer. He could not believe his eyes. He wasn't prepared to come face-to-face with this reality. His large travel bag almost fell from his grip. He fought the urge to take off running.

He had no idea that DEA agent Story and his team would move so fast. Agent Story and another guy, who Jermel knew had to be an undercover agent, were knocking on Troy's door, posing as maintenance workers. Six officers were lined up against the wall, in full riot gear, ready for action.

Then he spotted a face that angered him, that hurt his heart and really made him regret everything he did. *Homicide detective*

Teeler. He hated Teeler with all his soul. He couldn't come to terms with knowing that Detective Teeler would be the beneficiary of his cooperation.

He never even stopped to think about Detective Teeler. Jermel snapped back, then turned and hit the stairwell instead of waiting for the elevator. As he descended the second flight of stairs, he heard a loud bang, and screams followed.

"Get on the ground! Now!"

When Trina saw maintenance workers, she cracked the door.

Agent Story and his team kicked the door in, breaking the safety chain and knocking her to the ground. They rushed the home like wild bandits, guns drawn and screaming orders.

Troy came running into the living room. When he saw the SWAT team, he skidded on his heels and did a double take. Five guns were aimed at him. He surrendered and dropped to his knees with both hands on top of his head.

Two officers approached him and roughly cuffed his hands behind his back. He didn't care how they treated him, but a fire rose inside when they cuffed Trina. The raid didn't worry him at all. He never kept drugs or excessive money in his crib. The only gun in the home was legally registered to Trina.

It had been over five years since he was in handcuffs, but sadly, the feeling still seemed sort of natural. He was a lot more careful since the age of seventeen. He had no idea why a SWAT team chose to storm his home, but they were fishing in the wrong water.

Trina's eyes were worried. He knew it was him, not her. He gave her a reassuring half-grin. "Don't worry about them, baby. They just bored. We aight."

"We aight?" Homicide detective Teeler mocked.

Troy's face turned hard when he saw the corrupt homicide detective. He was parading around in his living room, and he didn't like it.

"Yeah right," Teeler continued. "You wish you were all right."

He had victory written across his wrinkled, skeletal face. He slid his body between Troy and Trina so that their full focus was on him. "Troy Newton..." His name slithered off his tongue as if an actual live serpent were speaking.

Troy was unfazed by his attempt to intimidate.

Teeler held eye contact with the subject of his own division's investigation and chuckled. He hissed his name again. "Troy Newton, you, young man, are under arrest for the July 14, 1996, murder of…" He watched with a child's joy as the date set in inside of Troy's head. He held the torturous breath as long as cruelly possible before letting the victim's name slither out. "Manny Goslin."

Troy closed his eyes. His chin hit the top of his chest. His entire body tried to give, but he refused to give Detective Teeler the full pleasure of his triumph. He dared a look in Trina's direction. He saw complete confusion. She was trying to make sense of what the detective said.

Before Troy could figure out if she caught on yet, she fainted.

The officers on each side of him lifted him up as Teeler finished reading him his rights and charges. The other ones tore his apartment apart. He was dragged out of his home onto the elevator and stuffed in the back of an unmarked police cruiser.

Detective Teeler and Agent Story sat on both sides of him. Teeler's pie-faced partner sat behind the wheel.

Meanwhile, Jermel climbed into one of his many coming-home presents that Troy gave him and drove away from the building in silence. At a red light, he sniffed a hefty line off a dollar bill and began to reminisce.

He remembered their early years, when he and Troy used to spend a quarter out of a food stamp just so they could get seventy-five cents back in change to play games at Penny's Arcade in downtown Boston. He remembered how they used to push a shopping cart all around Tropical's Market, pretending to shop, while opening boxes of cereal, cakes, and cold cuts, eating their only meal of the day at times. Sometimes, after they left Tropical's Market, they stole the shopping cart and pushed it around the neighborhood, collecting empty cans and bottles to turn in for five cents apiece at a liquor store.

The highway was clear as Jermel pulled onto it. He laughed while thinking about the time that Joyce whooped both of them with an extension chord in front of the whole projects. They had royally embarrassed her in front of her coworkers. They were caught stealing out of Filenes clothing store and were only let off easily because Troy was her son. They wore sweatpants into the store, grabbed a pair of jeans off the rack, and put them on under the sweats in a dressing room. They got away with this about six times, but a nosy security worker was onto them that day.

He thought of the many good times, then wondered how it got to where it was now. He controlled the steering wheel with his knee as he rolled up a blunt. How the hell did it come to this? He definitely wasn't going to do no thirty years. Troy never did a day of his adult life in a cell. Maybe a taste of it would knock him off his high horse. If Troy weren't acting all crazy lately, none of this would've happened.

He really wanted to get back at Trina too. She and Troy would feel the same pain they put him through. She turned his brother against him. He would deal with Ella eventually. She was another level of betrayal.

There was no sweet feeling in what he did, but it had to be done. This was what it came down to. Agent Story meant business. Jermel justified his actions by understanding that one of them had to go.

The reminiscing was still impossible to avoid after Jermel had driven for over an hour. He reflected on that dreadfully sweet day. That day they went Trailblazing. After he robbed Steve's dice game and the A retaliated as strong as they did, he and Troy vowed to each other to strike back with nothing less than a body in return.

It took three weeks after the shooting, but they finally caught the A-Team slipping. They saw a group of them in a Light Side parking lot, looking like they were in a dice game.

They jumped out of a hotbox, a black Ford Escort, blazing. Jermel dropped Troy off in front of their building when they were done while he went to dump the car and guns. Just in case they ever needed the guns again, he put them in a plastic garbage bag and buried them in a field behind Madison Park High School on the Ruggles Projects side. When Troy asked about the guns later on, Jermel lied that he threw them in the Charles River. He hated to throw any gun away, no matter how dirty they were.

Jermel was nearly legally untouchable. DEA agent Story got the United States Attorney and Suffolk County District Attorney's Offices to grant his star informant immunity for any prior crime he helped solve. Jermel was on board as code name Bury.

Both agencies were ready to take back the agreement when Jermel revealed his involvement in the high-profile cold case of Manny Goslin. They had to swallow their detest and recognize his overall value. When Agent Story and the United States Attorney contacted Detective Teeler and Suffolk County District Attorney Paul McDonald, they nearly crawled through the phone to hear from Jermel Gilliard.

Meetings were set up, and Jermel told them all they needed to know to convict Troy of the Manny Goslin murder, plus some. The authorities didn't even care that he appeared to be high when he spoke to them at times.

Jermel took them to the field behind Madison Park High School and dug up the bag. An eager Detective Teeler had the contents of the bag in a lab within hours. Jermel's partial prints were on both firearms. A different partial thumbprint on the handle and an index fingerprint on the trigger of the .357 had enough points for a lab specialist to determine that they matched Troy Newton.

Teeler reviewed his files from 1996 and was more enthused by his initial police report. A few witnesses, including Trina Goslin, described the height and build of Manny Goslin's shooter. Trina Goslin's description specifically matched Troy Newton.

With the physical evidence, Jermel's cooperation, eyewitness testimony, specifically Trina Goslin's account, Detective Teeler had a slam-dunk homicide conviction on his hands.

Gotcha!

Teeler refused to take another loss with this OP Trailblazers gang! He actually no longer saw Jermel Gilliard's trial as a loss. Jermel Gilliard was now his informant, his bitch. He hated Jermel Gilliard and everybody like him. Once he got Troy, Teeler would find a way to get Jermel Gilliard too.

Jermel Gilliard seemed to think he had the upper hand, but Teeler knew all the tricks. The dirty detective had no problem letting Jermel Gilliard's informant status accidentally leak into the streets. He wouldn't think he was so smart then.

Chapter 17

❖ ❖ ❖ ❖ ❖

Trina woke up in Boston City Hospital with IVs in her arms. Her vision was blurry. Her head was pounding. It took her a moment to figure out where she was. The equipment on the walls and plastic gates on the bed gave her a good idea. As her nose began to clear, she knew for sure where she was. She hated the medicinal smell, and that was undoubtedly the scent in her nostrils.

"She's up, y'all!"

Trina heard the familiar voice first, then saw Ella.

Her mother ran to her side and squeezed her hand.

"Hey, baby!" Relief was on her face with a wide smile. "You gave everyone a scare. How you feeling?"

Trina's focus got clearer. She noticed Peanut, Amin, and Joyce were in the room also. With no warning, she burst into tears.

They all expected her to still be emotional from the day's events, but her unexpected outburst still caught them all off guard.

Trina zoned out in memory of her loving, talented, handsome brother. People called her and Manny twins, handsome twin and pretty twin, but he was fifteen months older.

Like with too many children of the ghetto, their father wasn't around. Manny found his father figure in football coaches and willing schoolteachers. He easily excelled in academics and was never tempted by the allure of the street life. Trina never even met one person who would speak negatively of him.

Since Trina was eight years old, she loved watching him on the football field. He was amazing. It always seemed as if he was moving at a different speed, faster than everyone else around him. He separated himself from defenders with simplistic moves and caught any ball that was thrown in his direction. Coaches described him as a quarterback's dream and a defensive back's nightmare. Whenever he scored a touchdown, which was often, he pointed to her and their mother wherever they were seated in the stadium. Neither of them ever missed a game. Manny promised to perform the same ritual when he made it to the NFL and they were rich.

E and Flave were brothers who lived on Dimock Street, across the street from Trina and Ella's parking lot. Flave ran harder with the Timberwolves in Egleston than his associates from the A-Team. They were all clique regardless. E and Flave gave some of the best cookouts in the A, which was what they were doing on July 14, 1996.

It was a sunny, beautiful, family-oriented day. Initially, Trina thought that somebody was letting off leftover fireworks from the Fourth of July when she heard the explosions. She quickly learned that she was dead wrong.

People were running, falling, and screaming all around her. She saw some actually getting hit by bullets, but none of it mattered when she saw Manny frozen in place. *Get down! Run!* Her mouth wouldn't move. She tried to will him with her mind. Her world moved in an agonizingly slow motion.

The masked gunman was dark, not just in apparel, but in aura. He moved as smooth as a professional, with total disregard for the chaos all around him. He was dead set on his target. Manny.

He didn't run up to her brother. His motion was a patient, determined trot. His arm raised as he approached. Then it happened.

Boom!

Trina's heart ached. Her voice cried from deep within.

The dark gunman retreated with the same calm in his escape that he had to kill.

The middle of Manny's forehead had a wide, deep hole in it. The back of his head was partially melted into the ground. Trina was too afraid to touch him. She just knelt and cried. Her handsome twin was dead. There was no doubt about that. His eyes were wide yet peaceful. His mouth slightly open. Death wasn't as ugly as she imagined, but it sure was sad.

Manny's death nearly destroyed their mother's life. Tina Goslin was beautiful. Physically, she betrayed her age by a decade. Upon meeting Tina, teachers and coaches were rattled when finding out that she was Manny and Trina's mother. She was a main attraction at his football games with her provocative outfits. She enjoyed every bit of the teenage male attention she received. She thought it was cute.

After Manny's death, Tina rarely left the house. When she did, it was usually from point A to point B. She cared less about her appearance, lost her upbeat spirit, and often dwelled in a state of depression. The loss of a child was nearly too much to bear.

Trina lost two of her best friends with one horrible, untimely death. Her brother and mother. She was on the same path as her mother. Manny was her strength. She couldn't imagine having to live life without him.

Most of his so-called friends pursued her sexually instead of comforting her, which hurt even more. Depression, mixed with those unsympathetic mentalities, was the force behind her neighborhood disdain and transfer from West Roxbury High to Madison Park High.

Fortunately, she had Ella. Ella and Tanyah were the only true friends who walked with her through her mourning storm.

Then there was Troy.

When Trina first looked into Troy's eyes, she saw that special glow that she only saw in Manny's. She actually saw Manny but wasn't aware of it at that time. She felt like she knew him for a lifetime.

She tried so hard to befriend him, but he continuously repelled her. At times, she had to admit, his rejection made her feel insecure. He was so wide-open yet still a mystery. Everyone loved him just like they loved Manny. Who was he? She knew but didn't know. She had to find out. It was a must. Ella knew him for years and described him accurately, yet she still missed the depth of him.

When he finally accepted her, she felt whole again. He didn't replace Manny, but he adequately filled a major void. He was heaven-sent. She knew that she loved him as soon as she laid eyes on him. Even though he showed no feelings toward her, deep down she knew he felt the same way. They were soul mates.

It all made sense now. She completely understood it, and it was crushing. She understood why he never wanted to get close to her and, once he did, why he committed his entire being to her, to them.

She understood now why he never forgave Jermel. Jermel threatened him to reveal their dark secret. Troy never knew, but she overheard them arguing the last day that they spoke to each other, the day he cut his brother off for good. She replayed the verbal spat in her mind.

"Dogg, you still on the same bullshit! Money's fucked up, the Hood's hot, and we bussin' and ducking 'cause of you again!" Troy complained.

"Whatever, dogg. You just on ya goody-goody shit. You been tap dancing for Trina all these years instead of being who you really are. I should tell her who you really are! I bet her ass be out that door and yo black ass be in the joint. You better recognize who's who and get ya face out her ass."

Troy's face looked disgusted. "You a selfish muthafucka, yo. I can't believe the bullshit that come out ya mouth sometimes. Damn near all the drama I had ta finish in my life, you started. Me recognizing who's who ain't never in question. You forced my hand, out of love, since we was babies, dogg. Get the fuck out my crib. Don't ever holla at me again either."

Trina understood it all now. At first, she thought that Troy might have been cheating on her or, even worse, living a completely secret life with another woman and family. No evidence pointed to that theory, though. And she trusted her man anyway.

After thinking deeply for weeks, and keeping a sharper eye out, she figured Jermel was just upset about Troy's more positive path and making a baseless threat that finally got Troy fed up.

Jermel really didn't know how much she already knew about her man. He sheltered her, but they communicated profoundly. She advised him on things and listened even more. Jermel probably thought that Troy hid everything from her. She was well aware of the bad Troy did, but it was about his core with her, and his core was good.

That argument between Troy and Jermel was more profound than Trina had ever imagined. It was a casual dispute between brothers about the demise of her brother.

When Trina returned to the present from her mental travel, she calmly asked all the women to step out of her room for a moment. They figured that she needed to deliver a personal message from Troy, so they exited without protesting.

"What up, sis? How you feeling?" Amin spoke first.

Trina's eyes shot daggers at them. "How could y'all look me and my mother in the face all these years like nothing ever happened?" Her voice was low and hoarse, but the anger was evident.

Peanut was thrown off by her hostility. "What you talking about, yo?"

"I thought y'all was my friends. I thought y'all was m-my brothers," she said, beginning to tear up again. "I can't believe I was so blind. I hate y'all!" She started crying again.

Both of them, genuinely concerned and hoping she wasn't having a meltdown over Troy, stepped closer.

Amin rubbed her shoulder. "We are your brothers, Trina. And we here for you no matter what. Why would you doubt that?"

Through her tears, she gave an evil glare that made her resemble an angry Troy. "Y'all ain't my brothers. Y'all killed my brother!" She tried to yell, but the tears choked her.

Peanut and Amin were all the way thrown off.

Peanut said, "Trina, what the fuck is you talking about?"

Even though she was angry and hurt beyond control, Trina was able to recognize their genuine confusion. She reflected back to when Manny was killed again. Two gunmen, Troy and Jermel. Now that she knew them all so well, she knew that her brother's murder was a secret between brothers, not all four. It could've easily been Peanut and Amin involved, so it didn't lessen her anger that they weren't there. If they were asked to be there, they would've been there.

Without even waiting for an answer, she continued, "Do y'all know why Troy got arrested?"

"Nah. Nobody do. Not the whole scoop," Peanut answered.

"Joyce said they bagged him for a body. We figured you was the only one who know what's really up."

Trina closed her eyes, like she was instructed as a child, sighed, and counted to ten. "Troy got arrested for killing my brother."

At first, they appeared not to speak the same language as her. When the realization set in, Peanut and Amin were almost knocked over, like her words were a well-put-together combination of punches.

"Who?" Peanut almost shouted. "Where you hear that shit?"

"That homicide detective…Teeler. The one who was after Jermel. He read the charges against Troy in my face. Please…just leave. And I never wanna see y'all again. Take Ma—"

She caught her words.

"Take Joyce with y'all."

"Trina," Amin said with compassion, "I'm sorry as shit ta hear this, but I haven't heard no crazy shit like this before. They tryna set my peoples up. You ever think about that?"

"Yes," she said calmly, "I actually just thought about it real hard. The police ain't set him up. Jermel did. Y'all never heard about it 'cause they never told y'all or anyone else. Now, please leave!"

The truth in her analysis seemed all the way on point. It had the details of a well-put-together thought by Peanut. It added up and got an A+.

They both walked out of her room in a daze. Peanut stepped to the women in the lobby. He addressed Ms. Goslin and Ella.

"Listen, y'all. I'm very sorry about all this, but I don't believe it's true either." His eyes went back and forth between both women. "Me and Amin is gonna get ta the bottom of this. If y'all never speak ta us again, that's understandable. Know this, though: we truly love y'all."

All three women looked at him like he was strange, then Ella spoke up. "Peanut, what's wrong with your overanalyzing self? We all family. I know y'all gonna get Troy out just like y'all got Chubby. When Chubby hear Troy's locked up, he'll be back around and on his job."

Peanut was deflated. He had no more energy to expound. He couldn't even look into their eyes anymore, especially not Ms. Goslin. "Just go holla at Trina," he said.

Amin put a hand on Joyce's arm and began to escort her toward the exit door, but she protested. "I wanna see Trina! Is she okay? What's wrong with y'all?"

Amin looked at her as if he were the parent. "Not now, Joyce." Maternal instincts kicked in and frightened her. Something was wrong, terribly wrong! She played a part in raising Amin and Peanut. She understood them like her own. She reluctantly allowed Amin to usher her away with no further resistance.

They exited the hospital in silence and walked her to her car. Peanut told her that they were going to follow her to her crib so they could sit and talk.

Joyce didn't attempt to ask any more questions. She was terrified.

Fortunately, Liona wasn't home when they got to her and Joyce's house. Jermel was in question, and they didn't want to have to discuss that issue in front of her if it came up. Their Hyde Park home was cozy, far more generous than the congested apartments of Orchard Park.

The projects were definitely still in Joyce. The home's vibe was still OP. There were furniture updates, but most of the scene was the same that Peanut and Amin knew since they were children.

Peanut plopped in the same wooden rocking chair that he rocked in since the 808.

"You know why Troy's locked up?" Joyce asked. She filled her lungs with a roomful of air, then released it slow and hard. "They said my baby took another person's life. He been working so hard lately I don't know why they think he's out there tryna kill people." The statement was naive and stupid, but she wasn't thinking clear. "I know y'all gonna get my baby out of there." She tried to find confidence in the labyrinth of sorrow and defeat.

"Of course we gonna get him out! Even if we gotta break him out! But, Joyce, you need ta know something." Peanut was almost lost for words. He realized he had to just say it. "They saying he killed Trina's brother."

Joyce put both hands to her mouth. Her eyes opened wide as windows. "Oh, Jehovah! No! Please no! Manny? He died five years ago. How…how could that be? I was just preparing with Tina and Trina for Manny's fifth-year memorial service. Troy was helping us."

Peanut and Amin explained the things that Trina told them. After they finished, Joyce sat in complete silence. Her body didn't even move. She understood that Tina and Trina would need some space to think. She would give that to them. She wasn't exactly sure when, but she would reach out to them at a more appropriate time. She accepted that her son was a product of the streets, but being a murderer never crossed her mind, at least not for serious consideration. Even though Troy never really took to the Word, she still instilled it in his being. She didn't want the accusation to be true. Normally, she wouldn't ask any questions either, but her relationship with Tina and Trina couldn't continue if she was in the blind.

Joyce had to ask, "Did he do it?"

The two were caught off guard by the question. Denying crimes and wrongdoings was second nature to them, so Peanut easily blurted out, "Nah! He ain't do it!"

"Listen ta me." She spoke soft and strict. "Y'all are my children. I know y'all are bad in them streets, but I also know that y'all are good young men. Y'all love each other. I know that. I wouldn't ask this if I didn't need ta know. It's important that I know, so I don't make a mistake when dealing with Tina and Trina." Joyce closed her eyes lightly. Her large body rocked a little in her armchair. Her words weighed heavily on Peanut and Amin. They looked at each other. Peanut gave a nod for Amin to speak.

"Joyce, this is the truth: me and Peanut's just now hearing about this."

She stared at him. Insulted. "Amin, I'm asking you ta be honest with me. I don't care if you heard it from five minutes ago! You know my son. Did he do it?"

Amin couldn't even hold eye contact with Joyce. He shook his head in defeat. He didn't know how he felt. "Most likely," he said to Joyce.

Peanut looked just as uncomfortable as Amin. He was glad he wasn't the one put under the gun by Joyce.

"Thank you," Joyce said, choked up.

*****

Ella and Ms. Goslin entered Trina's hospital room with extreme caution and curiosity after Peanut and Amin apologized and forced Joyce to leave with them. The whole sequence put a major scare in them. They had no idea what to think of the situation. At first, they seemed to be overreacting about something, but when they literally forced Joyce out of the building, it was evident that the problem was on a greater scale.

Ms. Goslin fainted as Trina sobbed the reality out to them.

Ella was scared, speechless. Her body was frozen so stiffly she had no chance to pass out.

As nurses attended to her mother, Trina explained what she understood to Ella in full detail. Ella mechanically shook her head. Tears filled her eyes the whole time. All the rumors were true. She clearly remembered that day. She was inside of her hallway when the shots rang out. She never saw the shooters. She would've recognized Jermel no matter what disguise he wore, probably Troy too. Jermel even consoled her the next day. She took a cab to his crib and cried on his shoulder for hours. How could he be so cold? She was sad. Angry. Life as she knew it was over. Things would never be the same.

Chapter 18

Troy paced back and forth in his six-by-ten cell, his tongue tracing the inside of his teeth. The totality of his environment for the past week was a one-piece metal toilet and sink, baby-size bed, and a metal-barred, two-inch-thick-glassed window.

When he arrived at Nashua Street Jail, he was put in the hole and had no contact with anyone. He argued to no avail. A short light-skinned, curly-haired lieutenant with a thick beard told him that his case was considered high profile, so he had to be cleared before being released to general population.

After a week, a tall heavyset white CO told him that he was getting released to general population. As the CO slid him a lunch tray through the metal door's slot he gave Troy the news. That was music to his ears.

Troy took his tray and sat on his poor excuse for a bed. He was no longer enraged, but more disappointed than anything. After he had run everything through his clouded mind over and over all week, every conclusion he came up with sucked. Maybe someone recognized him and Jermel that day and decided to come forward now for some reason. Maybe somehow some evidence surfaced from back then. But the most likely and most obvious conclusion really sucked. He tried to deny it, but he couldn't realistically exclude Jermel ratting on him. No other conclusion was logical. Troy went through the whys and came up with disturbing answers to all of them. Why him? Because Jermel was angry, envious, jealous, and rightfully hurt. He got busted again for his own stupidity and put the blame on someone else, like he always did. Why rat him out about this murder? The answer was clear. It was because Jermel grew disdain for Trina and knew this will hurt her also.

A half-hour after Troy barely touched his small plastic lunch tray of slop, the CO cracked Troy's cell door open. The CO was the only person who said any words to him all week. He was cool. It was obvious that he didn't necessarily approve of how Troy was being treated. While escorting him to the elevator, he gave Troy a few words of encouragement.

"Good lookin' out, Lydon." Troy thanked him and stepped off the elevator onto the fifth floor.

He walked into a small lobby area with a reception desk and ten metal chairs bolted to the ground. Six of the chairs were occupied by inmates. A blank-faced white lady behind the desk handed him some papers to fill out, then he was taken to a nurse's office, where he received a mandatory tuberculosis shot. He was told to wait in the lobby after, so he took a seat on the edge of one of the metal chairs.

"Newton!" He heard his name called a few minutes later.

He approached the CO who called his name. The man just pointed in the direction of an office door. When he entered the office, he smiled for the first time all week.

The office was in disarray, messy, but not dirty, with papers scattered everywhere. The cabinets were pulled all the way open. It was only a little bigger than the hard, claustrophobic cell he just left, but the soft, friendly face behind the desk made his day.

"What up, OG? I was wondering if you still had love for me." Troy's face was beaming, even though it was scruffy and restless.

"I didn't even know you were here until this morning. I been busy all week. Damn, boo, look at you." She was obviously worried. "How did you get yourself caught up like this? Murder?"

Troy plopped in a stiff wooden chair. He explained as much as he could to Tanika. She leaned forward. Her head was inside of her hands, propped up on both elbows on top of her desk. She took the news as hard as he did.

After he finished revealing all that he was willing to, he asked if she was going to remain by his side. She gave an insulted, affirmative nod and fought back the tears that were forming.

"Not now, Lieutenant Lopes," he warned with a little humor. He rubbed her eyes and smiled against her hurting will. His addressing her formally was awkward. He told her some things that he needed and some things that he needed her to do. She took notes.

As a runner, he could get around the jail easier than the typical prisoner, so she immediately put him on hallway duty.

"Young boy, I'm putting my job and freedom on the line. Don't fuck up!"

Troy smiled. "Am I worth it?"

"You're worth everything."

Her answer was a lot stronger than he expected. His question was lighthearted humor that received a heartfelt, sincere answer. For the first time, he realized that Tanika might be in love with him. The feeling was awkward and different from his feelings for Trina. He might have loved her too.

"I got you, OG," he said, ignoring the comfortable moment. "I won't put you in no danger."

When Troy left the infirmary, he was placed on Unit 6-2. The sixty-by-thirty-foot unit had a high ceiling with dim nearly yellow lights. Thirty-two cells were split between two tiers, sixteen on each one. One TV for sixty prisoners, four showers, and eight phones—a recipe for trouble.

All prisoner activity was done on the unit. The only reason a prisoner left the unit was to go to the infirmary, religious service, or occasional inconsistent hour that the jail gave inmates to go to the gym once a week. Daily recreation was considered time spent outside the cell and on the twenty-by-thirty-foot recreation deck attached to the unit.

When Troy stepped through the unit's sliding sally port door, he was greeted by many associates. His arrival was anticipated due to the news coverage that his arrest generated. The media was doing a good job of making sure that Troy was found guilty in the court of public opinion before he even stepped foot in a court of law.

Basketball star accused of shooting rival football star to death. Headlines like these were run for three days straight.

Troy kicked it with his people for a while, trying to get an initial feel for his first adult jail experience. A lot of his people, and the people he peeped around the unit, were in DYS with him at different times. After a couple of hours of kicking it, he excused himself and headed to the pay phones.

Joyce broke down into tears when she heard his voice. This really concerned him. Tears were uncharacteristic from his mother. His ability to stay strong under any circumstance came from her endless examples. He didn't understand the tears until she told him that she spoke to Peanut and Amin about some things. He knew then that her tears weren't for his current condition but her knowledge of his actual act.

They switched to a lighter conversation when he reminded her how hard they would be on his calls. When they wrapped up, Joyce told him to keep a visit open for her on the weekend. She knew he would have to see other people to secure his assets and fight for freedom on his first few visits.

Troy hung up and called Amin. He told him to send his sister up to see him the next day. Neither Amin nor Peanut would be able to visit him, so certain messages would have to be relayed through trusted family and friends.

The next day, a CO tapped on Troy's door at 8:00 a.m. and told him he had a visit. He was already up and anticipating it. Pooh, Amin's sister, was very reliable. He brushed his teeth and headed up the metal stairs to the visiting booths on the top tier.

Most people slept in until after the first count cleared at 10:30 a.m. The unit was quiet. He entered the first of three booths and waited for Pooh. He sat on the metal stool and looked around the tiny booth in disbelief. How did he end up on this side of the glass? The reality of betrayal set in again.

He thought back to how hard he fought to get Jermel from the side of the glass he was now on. Jermel was disrespectful, reckless, selfish, but never did Troy think he could be a rat.

After about five minutes of Troy waiting, instead of Pooh, Trina walked in on the other side of the booth. A strange feeling of fear came over him. He popped off the stool and put both hands on the glass. He wished he could walk through the glass and hold his woman.

Troy thought about Trina all week, damn near every hour, and wondered when he would see her again. What he would say. How she would receive him. How she was doing. He obviously never wanted her to find out that he killed Manny. Especially not like this. At times he toyed with the thought of telling her, being forgiven, and living happily ever after. Maybe that would've brought closure. But those were just thoughts. He knew he couldn't bring closure. Realistically, he could never admit to it, but he could do his part. He could look out for Trina and Ms. Goslin. Bring happiness to their lives. He strived to do this for the past four and a half years. He knew that they saw Manny in him; it was evident through their words and actions. He did his best to always show them his better side, which was where he knew Manny lived.

All week he hoped that Trina would weigh the situation out and see things for the way they were. What was done was done. It was time to move forward. He couldn't bring Manny back, but he loved her and was truly sorry. Did she believe he did it? Of course she did. Trina knew him like no other human being did.

He looked in her eyes and saw the tears from the past eight days. They were puffy. Her skin was flushed. She looked scared, just like he felt, but she was calm as she sat down on the stool. It took him a second longer, then he followed her lead and sat too.

They stared at each other. It was the most awkward silence both of them ever felt while in each other's presence. They were completely different beings than the ones who woke up next to each other a week prior.

He took the initiative. "Baby...how you doing?" He kicked himself in the ass. He wanted to take back the stupid question as soon as it left his mouth.

"I'm doing bad. How 'bout yaself?" Her retort was venomously sarcastic.

Troy never heard her sound like this before. He sighed. "I'm doing terrible too, Trina."

"Troy—"

"Baby! I don't trust these booths." He lowered his voice.

"If you wanna discuss some personal things, wait a few days." He told Tanika to get him a cell phone and planned to do all his talking on that.

Trina gave a nod of understanding, then looked into his soul with her mind and eyes.

He felt the question being asked. He looked away from her eyes, then regretted the action instantly.

A tear slid down her cheek, into her mouth. She stood and began to leave.

Troy stood and yelled, "Trina! Baby, wait!"

She turned back to face him.

His face was pleading. "It's a lot ta this. We need ta talk."

"Troy, we never need ta talk again." Her words were controlled and cool. "You had many chances ta talk, but you never chose to." Her anger went to another level. "And my baby will never have an uncle or daddy now!" She gave him no chance to respond before turning and walking out.

Pregnant? Troy sat in the booth with his head against the glass. He came close to breaking down. After what seemed like forever, he heard the CO announce lockdown for count. He pried himself from the stool, stepped out of the booth, and dragged himself back to his cell.

His man Rick from Heath Street was on the phone and saw him come out of the booth. "Keep ya head up, dogg. Some's gonna be good, some's gonna be bad."

Troy needed the words of encouragement. He took them in stride.

After count cleared and lunch was finished, Troy went to his hallway runner's job and to see Tanika. She had the cell phone earlier than he expected, as well as a plate of home cooking. The plate wasn't one of his requests; it was her love. He appreciated it.

He tidied up her office while she brought him up to speed on things. Her ATP plug told her about Jermel's fingerprint on the note and the raid at the Ramada.

Troy shook his head in disgust. He was happy that, like Trina, Tanika didn't ask many questions. He thanked her, then left.

As soon as Troy got back to the unit, he went to his cell, powered up his cell phone, and called Amin.

"Yo," Amin answered. "What up, dogg?"

"Aight, then!"

Amin was relieved to hear his voice straight through with no operator.

"Shorty came through on the cell, so we can kick it now."

"That's what's up. I brought Pooh up there about an hour ago, but they told her you had a visitor already. You know sis wanted ta see you anyway. She was mad as shit."

"Yeah, Trina came through."

Amin could hear in his tone that it was a tough one. "That bad, huh?"

He told Amin that she straight up let him know that she was going to testify against him. To hear that angered Amin to the point of wanting to kill her, but he kept it cool. He told Troy how she lashed out at him and Peanut at the hospital.

On instinct, he disarmed Amin. He understood where his mind went when signs of danger were pointed in their direction. Troy told him not to sweat Trina's attitude right now. He tried to sound sure in convincing him that Trina was just momentarily upset. If it were anyone else, she would surely be dead within a week.

Her being pregnant was another touchy subject. His seed meant the world to him. The circumstances made it mean even more. They discussed ways to assist her, even though she was now technically the enemy.

Amin didn't agree with aspects of how Troy wanted to deal with her, but he respected his wishes because he knew that Troy would do the same for him.

They knew that Joyce would be crushed when Trina and Ms. Goslin shut her out. Joyce didn't see the look in Trina's eyes or hear her position. She was still hoping for civility where none existed. It could never work. Joyce would feel deeply for their loss but never go for them attempting to keep her son in prison.

Jermel was the sourest subject of all. Troy explained as much as he could.

Amin listened with no interruption. The act didn't surprise him at all. The irony, however, was the shocking part. He was well aware that Troy and Jermel had countless secrets, but how this one played out was straight up weird.

Amin thought of how Trina always told him that she and Troy were soul mates, brought together by divine intervention. One murder led to another, which sent her from one school to the other, which led her into Troy's life. That was divine intervention, all right. He was blown away by all of it.

While Troy broke certain things down, it was clear to Amin that Jermel ratted on him. He let Troy know that Jermel disappeared and that they were looking for him to "talk" to him.

That news brought no reaction out of him. He didn't even know how to feel about it.

Amin told Troy how he met up with Ky the day after he got arrested. Ky explained to him that she was staying at the Ramada with Jermel nearly every day. Amin didn't know, but she sensed his hostility and was nervous. She thought it was aimed at her and her brother. She figured he might be trying to find out if Martin had anything to do with Jermel's arrest.

Her nerves were calmed when Martin happened to walk in the house and Amin gave him a warm welcome.

"Martin! What up, dogg?" Amin hadn't seen Martin in a while, since he wasn't dealing with K.

"W-w-what up, Amin?"

Amin dismissed the boy being nervous as expecting him to be there to collect money that he might have owed Jermel. "I ain't here about you and Jermel's business, so don't sweat nothing you owe him. I'm here ta find out what really happened with his ass."

Martin's and Ky's faces showed concern for his tone. They still couldn't figure out where it was aimed.

"Listen, yo," Amin told Martin. "I knew Ky since we was young and you was a baby. What, you seventeen now?"

Martin nervously nodded. "Yeah."

Amin continued, "I know she can keep her mouth shut. You better be cut from the same cloth, 'cause this conversation stays here."

Martin gave another nervous nod of understanding.

"I need ta know everything y'all know about how that raid went down, 'cause Jermel's ratting now."

Martin looked like he choked on a canary. Ky was blown away. Sister and brother stared at each other, speechless, until Ky told Martin to speak up. Martin explained the runs he was making for Jermel and how weird he had been acting. To Amin's and Ky's surprise, he also told them that he saw Jermel sniffing coke. He added that the day of the raid, he and Ky found out about it from the receptionist when they got back to the motel. This part of the story was rehearsed together with Ky. Martin delivered his spiel convincingly. He saw that Amin believed his story, and danced inwardly. If Amin didn't suspect him, his name would remain good in the streets.

Troy listened disgustedly on the other end of the phone. The coke use wasn't surprising, since Ella already suspected it, but he was fed up with Jermel's problems always becoming his.

Amin was more all-around responsible than Peanut.

Troy ran down a list of things he needed him to do to keep things running as smooth as possible. He anticipated Trina moving back in with her mother. He wanted Chris to move in and maintain his crib. Trina would reject direct support, so he wanted a twenty-five-hundred-dollar money order mailed to her on the first of every month.

He gave him his coke connect's information and stressed the importance of pushing Chris's music career. Keeping his business running was one of his top priorities. He didn't bother to mention Joyce and Liona; things like that were understood since their youth.

*****

Attorney Hemenway showed up at Nashua Street Jail two days after Troy got out of the hole and let him know that he was already on the job. This put Troy at ease.

The attorney visiting room was a small office on each unit.

It had a beat-up, half-centimeter-thin carpet, dim lighting, and a lone metal desk. The jail provided attorney and client privacy, so no glass separated them.

Hemenway dressed down in faded blue jeans, leather dress boots, and a Sean Jean sweater. Troy was used to the sharp suits; the switch knocked another ten years off his legal representative/mentor/friend. Yes, Herbie Hemenway was all those things to Troy.

Troy explained the little he knew about the conditions of his agreement. He expressed his displeasure with the betrayal along with the facts all in one breath, then never mentioned it again.

Hemenway had favors owed in the DA's office and was able to solicit the critical information earlier than the opposition wanted him to have it.

Troy couldn't disguise the defeat he felt when Hemenway told him about the gun. He had always figured that that gun was at the bottom of the Charles River with a lot of other dirty weapons he and Jermel got rid of. They agreed that the river was safer than the sewer when burying weapons.

Fuckin' Jermel!

Troy still knew where dirty weapons were buried around the city. He hadn't thought about them for years until that moment. He even remembered exactly where he buried the 007 foldout knife that Jermel stabbed an older man with when they were twelve.

They were trying to rob the man after he made an ATM withdrawal, but the man wasn't giving it up without a fight. That cost the man his life. Troy punched him in the jaw, Jermel plunged the six-inch blade in his chest, and they watched their first victim die.

They took the sixty-four dollars that the man had in his pocket, then ran off.

Hemenway promised to give his all. He was brutally honest in letting Troy know that the physical evidence was as concrete as it got. The potential eyewitness accounts were overwhelming also. The only thing that they had on their side so far was the passage of time, which was over five years, but still wasn't much at all. Troy respected Hemenway's honesty, but it still hurt.

Chapter 19

Fall River, Massachusetts, was a city of roughly sixty to seventy thousand people. It was known for its textile factories and mills in the early 1900s. By the end of the twentieth century, the city was filled with poverty-stricken, drug-infested ghettos.

The city sat forty miles west of Boston. It was an attraction for hustlers, hood runaways, retired couples, and partiers from Boston and surrounding cities.

Jermel copped a two-bedroom apartment in the Maple Gardens apartment complex. He traded in his flamboyant cherry-red Tahoe for a modest '98 Toyota 4Runner and assumed a lower profile than he was used to. He gained back the weight he worked off in jail and added a little more on top of that. He let his silky black hair grow into short corn braids and kept a light shadow beard and mustache.

He easily got business moving with the superior coke he initially showed up to Fall River with. Within a couple of months, he assembled a small team to move at his command. Within three months, he was actually enjoying his life in the smaller city.

He occasionally ran into people from the Bean, some he knew, some he didn't. None were aware that he was just a shell of the man he was known to be. Those who knew him or knew of him respected him as Jermel the hustler and killer. They assumed that he chose Fall River for the easy money.

From time to time, his conscience ate at him, but he convinced himself that his whole circle did him wrong. After some time passed and he got to explain himself, get the truth of things out there, then people would see the situation his way. He would be able to get his normal life back together. Troy wouldn't be there to undermine him and turn everyone against him.

Fall River was good for the time being. The hustle was good, the club scene was cool, and he tricked with a new chick on the regular. Getting used to Fall River was easy.

*****

The summer night was hot. Chris was in the middle of Lenox Street Projects, battle-rapping against everyone that came at him. Lenox resembled Orchard Park in many ways and was only a short distance away. It was still against the norm to see a well-known OP Blazer in the middle of Lenox alone. The whole Bean was anticipating his debut album, so Chris was an exception in most hoods.

His local rap stardom allowed him to travel from hood to hood with less problems than most gang members did. He featured artists from many hoods on his mixtapes. That gave them good exposure and generated a lot of hood love for him.

After he finished battling Jesus and C-Black, he sat back and kicked it with his homegirl, Nina, in front of her building. Nina was a pretty, slim, brown-skinned tomboy whom he met at Estelle's, the popular Lenox and Mission Hill hangout, and kicked it for the past two years.

Nina's homegirls, Missy and Monica, came over to them to give Chris his props for the battle and let him know that they had his newest mixtape. They began talking excitedly about a battle that went on at club Froggies, in Fall River, a couple of weeks prior, which drew Chris's interest. He was always interested in a new battle scene.

Missy was dark-skinned, with pretty, beady eyes and a wide smile that showed off her pearly whites with pink gums. Monica was tall, five foot seven or eight, vanilla complexion, with Asian genes blended with black.

As they described the battle at Froggies, Monica asked Chris, "Why wasn't you there with Jermel? You would've dogged them other dudes in the cipher. On, doggs."

Chris flinched at the mention of Jermel's name. His face betrayed his calm act. Fortunately, none of the females picked up on his sudden mood shift. Not many people outside of OP knew Jermel's status. Chris engaged more into the Froggies battle talk with more interest in order to get a better idea of the environment. He learned exactly where it was and what nights it was live.

Saturday nights were the best hip-hop nights. Neither Missy, Monica, nor Jermel ever missed it.

Chris played it off like it was common knowledge to him that Jermel was always at Froggies. He told the girls that he would pop up and rock the battle scene soon, one weekend.

When Chris and Nina were in her crib, putting product together and counting money, he was unusually quiet. She was used to his fun-loving energy when they were alone, so his mood concerned her.

"What up, C?" she asked. "Why you so quiet?"

"Ain't sh-shit. I j-j-just got a lot on m-m-my mind."

She wanted badly to pry further, but she always did her best to show him the difference between a lady and a girl. She had five years on him and prided herself on how he saw her. He didn't even look in her direction as he spoke. She didn't like it. "I'm here for you if you need me, C. You know that."

No response.

Chris just kept putting coke on the scale and into baggies. He usually sexed her before or after they handled business, but he rose to leave when they were done.

She pouted. "I guess I ain't getting none today, huh?"

"I'll b-be back th-through tomorrow, boo." No smile. No emotion. He kissed her lips and headed to the door.

"Be careful, C," she called behind him before the door shut.

*****

It was the Saturday following his conversation with Missy and Monica in Lenox Street Projects. He was sitting low in a hotbox black '93 GTI across the street from the club Froggies in Fall River. It was a diverse scene, an obvious good time. At the moment, though, he wasn't on any of that. He was on a mission.

During the couple of hours of him watching the parking lot and entrance to the club, he began to think about his father, Reverend Childs. Even Chris addressed his father formally at times. Reverend Childs had come around a bit. He began to show a genuine interest in Chris's life, no longer just meddling, and he actually supported his music career. He didn't necessarily encourage it, but he no longer despised it. His newfound understanding eased a lot of tension between them and allowed a good father-to-son relationship and friendship.

It all started a year prior, when Chris walked into his crib and saw his pops in his room, on his bed, listening to one of his mixtapes. He thought another heated argument was on the way, but Reverend Childs simply asked Chris to sit next to him.

He asked about the lyrics to many of his songs. About the nineteen pairs of Adidas in his closet and the numerous Portland Trailblazers hats. There was no chastisement in his inquiry, just genuine interest.

He let Chris know that he had been listening to his music and studying his room for a few months at that time. Instead of feeling violated, Chris was okay with the curious invasion. It seemed to open up his father's one-tracked Christian mind.

Chris was surprised at how thoroughly Reverend Childs understood his lyrics. He was able to build with him on his overall view of life simply by deciphering his songs. He gave opinions and advice, but most importantly to Chris, he gave his approval. Though their relationship was strained as he was growing up, inside Chris had always wanted his father's approval. The bond they forged from that day on brought peace to both of their worlds. Chris reminisced about that day as he rapped his song "Chosen" in his head. "Chosen" was one of Reverend Childs's favorite songs.

Just when he thought things wouldn't go according to plan, Chris saw Jermel step out of a maroon 4Runner Jeep. His heart raced. He was stuck between jumping out or waiting. Everything seemed to be moving too fast.

He noted Jermel's change of appearance. That was smart. He had long braids, a full beard, and thirty extra pounds. A person who wasn't close to him could easily miss him at first and second glance, but plastic surgery couldn't throw Chris off his mark.

He got over the initial shock of the situation and was able to relax now that he saw Jermel with his own eyes. He didn't tell one person about his knowledge of where Jermel frequented on Saturdays. Jermel crossing Troy was more than enough schooling for him to move alone.

Chris had never killed before, but for Troy he would do anything.

He looked up to Troy all his life. Troy was his big brother, teacher, and friend. Most of what he knew in the streets, he learned from Troy. He never liked Jermel, so killing him wasn't a tough emotional decision to make. Peanut and Amin would knock him off, too, no doubt, but their love for him ran deep. Relieving them of the burden was also a pleasure for Chris. He loved those two too.

One thing was for certain: Jermel wasn't making it to court now that he had a say in it.

Little did Chris know that killing Jermel was easier said than done. Froggies started pouring out drunken partygoers at 2:00 a.m.

Chris parked the GTI on a side street to avoid as much foot traffic as possible. He left the engine running and walked the two blocks back to the parking lot. He stood a few cars away from Jermel's 4Runner.

The parking lot wasn't too big, a fifty- to sixty-car capacity, but the lighting was bad, which was good for his purpose. Everyone besides him seemed to be intoxicated, searching for whom they wanted to spend the rest of their night with. No extra focus was on him.

Jermel came slightly staggering out of the club with two attractive girls on his arms. One was tall, slim, and blond. She wore a shiny silver top that resembled a strapless sports bra, a matching skirt that sat just below her crotch, and spiked, peep-toe heels. If she bent over, she could easily pass for being naked.

The babe on his other arm wore an overflow of makeup and a one-piece, formfitting skirt. It was pink and hugged her curves nicely. She almost broke a heel while stepping off the curb into the street, but Jermel braced her. They shared a laugh as he saved her from her tumble.

Ever since Missy and Monica had mentioned Jermel's name, Chris had movie visions of looking him in the eyes and saying something memorable before he shot him. Now that the time was here, those thoughts were long gone.

Jermel had his beige Kangol tilted to the left, and black leather ENYCE jacket over his shoulder. Troy taught Chris to wear his jacket the same way in a crowd so that he could keep his gun in hand, so he knew Jermel was locked and loaded.

The August night was humid and still. The only action in all of downtown Fall River was right in the Froggies parking lot. A patrol car was visible, but across the street, so Chris disregarded it.

He took a deep breath, then made his move. When he stepped out of his hiding spot, an already-broken bottle crushed loudly beneath his boot. The sound startled him as well as Jermel.

Chris saw the ENYCE jacket lift up quick. *Shit!*
Boom! Boom!

*****

A sudden chill came over Reverend Childs as he sat at his desk in his bedroom. He was working on the last bit of notes necessary for his morning service. He glanced over at his clock, 2:13 a.m. Saturday nights had been long and pressure-filled for all twenty-five years of him heading the congregation. This Saturday night was overexcessive, though. Regardless of the laborious Saturday nights, Reverend Childs never missed a service, which was just one of his many blessings from the Lord. This Saturday night felt different, though. There was something in the air. Something he couldn't quite grasp. Divine intervention entered his life through the spirit of his late wife. What a beautiful woman. Her spirit lived daily through their only child. He saw it and was thankful for it. She inspired a message of peace, which he would deliver in the morning.

The diabetic seizure that put her in a coma she would never wake from seemed so unfair at that time, but he put his trust in God and allowed faith to guide him through. He wished that Chris could've experienced her presence on this earth for more than just five short years. She was the compassion and understanding that he, as a father, wasn't. She was whom Chris needed more of while growing up.

Reverend Childs vowed to be the best parent he could be, and though it was tough alone, he stuck to his word the best he could.

Chris even began attending a good chunk of his services over the past year. He usually shied away from the actual church but spent an hour with him at home after the services.

Reverend Childs was looking forward to his afternoon service with his son in less than twelve hours. He smiled at the thought of it.

*****

The first shot that was fired went through the back of Jermel's skull before he could fully extend his arm to get off a shot.

Boom!

The second one entered his back as he fell.

Boom!

A third went through the side of his face and made his whole body jump.

Boom!

When the slaughter was over, Chris didn't look at anyone. He tucked the .38 in his pocket, kept his head low, and scurried away with the panicking crowd. A sense of calm came over him as the anxiety faded.

The two females with Jermel seemed to be the only two who weren't running frantically. They froze and screamed at the top of their lungs as they watched Jermel's Kangol and matching Tims turn crimson.

His face lay on the pavement, surrounded by a riddled puddle. Chris dropped the .38 in a drain, hopped in the GTI, and eased off.

He felt great. Better than great and realer than ever. He was certified. Loyal to the game. Loyal to Troy.

Red, white, and blue lights lit up about twenty yards behind him. The illumination darkened his glory. He wished he hadn't dumped the pistol. Damn! He could've used the three bullets now.

The bullhorn sounded as the patrol car rode his bumper, signaling for him to pull over. Chris figured his chances of escape were better on foot anyway.

As he pulled over to the curb, he steadied his breathing and tried to appear normal. Before he could even completely pull over, the police car flew right past him. It was signaling for him to get out of the way.

He sighed in relief, then pulled back onto the road. His mental elation came back as he reached Route 24. He let the window down and breathed in the polluted night air. It was oddly refreshing. The old mills of Fall River faded in his rearview mirror as he left that page behind him and continued on to the next chapter in his life.

Chris parked the GTI in a Store 24 parking lot about a half-mile from Troy's building, then walked the rest of the way. Troy's apartment was his home for the past five and a half months. It helped with his maturity and sense of business on a whole. He couldn't believe it at first when Troy had Amin give him the keys.

He spoke to Troy often and was playing his position. Peanut and Amin treated him like the adult he had become, making him strive even harder to always pull his own weight.

He didn't sleep when he got home; his adrenaline was still on one thousand. Getting some rest wasn't even a thought. He turned on the TV and listened to music at the same time. By 6:00 a.m., he still didn't see any reports on the shooting but knew that the hood wire would have word traveling through the Bean by the afternoon.

*****

Liona opened New Edition at 5:00 a.m. Sunday through Thursday ever since the business got off the ground. Chris had three places that were mandatory that he be on this Sunday. The first was with Liona when the news of Jermel reached her. He figured it would be perfect to be there to comfort her and to avoid any possible suspicion, if any existed.

He did occasional all-nighters in the streets, so it was sort of ritual for him to pop up at New Edition early Sunday mornings. He always needed new white T-shirts and fitted caps to go with his wardrobe, plus he wanted to see Liona.

"What's up, M-Ms. Liona?" he greeted her.

"Hey, Chris!" she said with a bright smile.

It used to be very hard for Liona to face Chris and lots of other young guys that she used to trick with to get high. After more than two years of her being sober, it became easier as she grew comfortable in her own skin.

She was aware of Chris's secret crush on her but acted like she wasn't. She thought it was cute.

"What you want, boy? Some white tees and jeans?" she asked, knowing his style.

Chris used to enjoy Liona begging to give him a blow job for a few rocks, mainly because she was the first to ever give him a blow job and she was the best at it. He also enjoyed it because he couldn't stand her son. When Troy took him all the way in the circle, his perception started to change as he saw her through Troy's eyes.

Troy treated Liana like his own mother, which made Chris feel a little ashamed.

What really changed the way he viewed her was seeing Troy and Joyce put so much effort into helping her clean herself up. When she actually did it and stuck with it, he had a newfound respect. The lewd visions of pleasure he had with her were tough to block out, but he did his best to treat her as if those days never existed.

He bought two fitted caps, three oversize white T-shirts, and a pair of Antonio Ansaldi jeans. They kicked it about the Patriots needing to have a better season as he searched the shelves and racks, then they sat and continued with small talk.

They laughed and joked for over an hour as customers came and went, then the store phone rang.

"New Edition," Liona answered in her sweet, professional voice. She sat in silence, then her face turned into a horror show.

Chris knew it was the inevitable call. It was either going to be him or her receiving the call while they were in the store together, just like he planned it. He was genuine in wanting to console her when the painful news came.

Liona dropped the phone, clutched her stomach, and screamed. Chris faked surprise as he took her into his arms and let her tears stain his chest. "W-w-what's wrong, M-Ms. Liona?"

"Oh no! My b-bay! No, no, no!"

Chris sat with her for another hour as she wept, then Joyce walked in. He used her entrance as his excuse to exit. He told them that he had to attend Bible study with his father, then he was going to find out about Jermel. He added that he would say a prayer for Jermel, then kissed and hugged both women before walking out.

Joyce and Liona closed New Edition and drove out to Fall River to identify their son. They teared as they viewed what used to be a beautiful human being lying on a metal slab, disfigured. His face looked burnt on one side. The other side was actually missing a chunk. The once-soft peanut butter skin looked like rugged ground beef. His silky braids were matted into a stiffness of dried blood. Even though it was the most grotesque sight they'd ever seen, they squeezed Jermel's lifeless hand, found a clear spot on his face, and kissed it.

Then they drove back to Boston in silence.

Chapter 20

"Newton! Visit!" the CO yelled.

Troy had just finished eating lunch and was playing bid whist with DB, Grit, and Mike from OP.

"Yeah!" Grit shouted at Troy. "Yo ass better run ta that V-I, 'cause I was bout ta take them soups and fish out ya cell with this hand."

"You wasn't bout ta do shit!" Mike shot back, flashing his hand so DB and Grit could see that he had seven hearts, the king and queen of spades, and four boss clubs.

Troy and Mike were always gambling partners. Each player had to put up two bags of ramen noodles and one pack of mackerel each game. They all grew up together and were only a few years apart.

Grit was a dark-skinned, skinny, beady-eyed stickup kid. He stayed in Nashua Street Jail nearly as much as he did OP.

DB was a stocky light-brown hustler with a coconut head. He was fighting a double homicide.

Mike and Troy were cousins, him his father's brother's son. He was a short, chubby-cheeked thoroughbred in on a drug case.

"Tell 'em something, Mike!" Troy yelled while showing Grit and DB his hand, which complemented everything in Mike's.

Troy got up and went to his cell, laughing at the heckling still coming from their card game. He put on a fresh white T-shirt and pulled his visiting uniform from under his mattress. He kept it there so it stayed pressed and fresh.

He took two metal steps at a time to the top tier and peeked in the booths. He was totally surprised when he saw Chris sitting in the last booth, waiting for him. They spoke a lot over the past six months, but this was the first time he showed up in a visit.

Chris had an open drug case plus was on probation, so Troy never expected to see him. The fact that the visit was unannounced was what told Troy that something was either really wrong or really right, most likely the former.

Troy studied his protégé. He saw a fierceness that he never saw before. Maybe it was the passage of time. Chris stopped growing when he was a five-eight, hundred-sixty-pound sixteen-year-old. He was never physically imposing, yet he somehow seemed to take up the entire booth. His usually smiling eyes were murky and distant. Though he sported white and light-blue gear, his aura was dark.

Chris left Joyce and Liona at New Edition, went to his Bible study with Reverend Childs, offering no prayer for Jermel, and this was the third mandatory stop of his Sunday. He saw the question in Troy's eyes.

"I-I used Lee's ID," he said. "What up, b-b-big bro?"

"What up with you, little bro?"

Chris's opening was a greeting. Troy's was a question.

"I-I always kn-knew, dogg." Chris held strong eye contact to be sure he was understood.

Troy's short nod told him that he was indeed understood.

Chris continued, "I knew when I g-got out th-the hospital that—"

Troy cut in. "I see an oak in yours now."

"You must ain't watch n-no TV today, huh?"

"Nah, I been playing cards with these crazy muthafuckas since the doors opened."

Troy was interrupted by a knock on the booth door. He swung around on the stool but didn't see anyone. Jail courtesy was to knock, then stand away from the door, if one prisoner needed to interrupt the next man in a visit.

Troy pushed the door open and saw DB standing on the railing, looking fidgety. He turned back to Chris, put up a finger, signaling for him to give him a minute, then stepped out of the booth.

"What up, dogg?" he asked DB.

"I just spoke ta Giz, yo," he said, referring to his younger brother. His eyes were alert. "He just told me Jermel got bodied last night."

Troy stood in a daze for a few seconds. His brotherly instincts allowed pain to pierce his heart like an arrow. He almost forgot how to breathe. He used the railing to keep from collapsing. Jermel, little chubby Jermel flashed through his mind. He wanted to hold him. To protect him. Little Jermel that slept in the same bed with him. Shared the same clothes with him. Jermel that hid in the closet when Troy brought girls up to his crib and watched and vice versa. Little Jermel and little Troy. Brothers.

After the initial pain and shock, Jermel's betrayal surfaced and washed the pain away. Troy regained his focus and told DB he would holla at him after his visit. He made no comment on the news at all.

Troy scanned the unit before turning back to the booth. He saw Grit and Mike on the phones. Their body language said they were getting the same news.

When Troy re-entered the booth, he understood that he was face-to-face with the man who killed his brother.

"W-was th-that my m-man DB?" Chris asked in his usually light tone.

"Yeah," Troy answered, semi-spaced-out. "He told me what you came ta tell me."

The mention of the real topic put Chris back in his dark place. In coded language, he let Troy know that he knew that Troy had avenged him and Jimmy and how much he always appreciated it.

After he finished his praise, he explained as much as he could about Jermel. He wanted to be sure that Troy knew that it was all about honor and justice, two principles that Troy always stressed to him. Chris saw the pain that the subject brought, so he spared the long version.

Troy thanked him for the justice he served and for always being loyal. Now that Chris took a life, a tough life to take at that, Troy knew that he could do it again. That fact, along with his loyalty, made his camaraderie even more valuable.

"You and Rev still aight?" Troy changed the subject to Chris's father.

"Yeah. W-w-we just finished one of h-h-his famous Bible studies." Chris chuckled out.

"Well, stay in the studio and push them singles. Don't ever lose focus on that. You always said that's our way out, so get us out. I'mma holla at Hemenway about everything."

"N-no question! I got you, d-dogg. You kn-know I'mma stay on p-point. Oh yeah." Then he continued in a different lane, "I s-saw b-big sis the other d-day. She b-big as a b-beachball, and p-pretty as ever." Chris knew it was killing Troy, but he had to tell him. Trina hadn't allowed anyone, including Joyce, to even talk to her. He continued, "I-I p-pulled next ta her whip in South Bay P-P-Plaza. I asked if sh-she would let me help with anything, b-but she just ignored me and kept p-putting her b-bags in the trunk. Sh-She only s-stopped ta stare at me, but it was s-spooky, like she was looking through me."

Troy had a perfect picture of the scene Chris described. He knew the stare well and understood it. Unconsciously, he gave Chris the same stare. "I'm glad she at least kept the whip."

"Dogg, y-y'all kinda look alike. I'm g-gonna try t-ta holla at h-her. You know she got a s-soft spot f-for me." He smiled, back to his upbeat self.

"Normally, I would tell you don't waste ya time, but she do got a soft spot for you. She love you for real, but don't waste ya time if she on her bullshit." He took a deep breath, still in deep thought. "She got a wild ability ta cogitate and analyze situations. I hope she ain't associate you getting hit up with her brother getting hit up."

"I-I-I told you about using them l-long-ass c-c-college words, dogg."

"Whatever, dogg." Troy laughed. "It means ta think deep."

"Oh, I like th-that shit! I'mma m-make a song c-called cogi-gi-tate. On, doggs!"

"Go for what you know, dogg."

When the visit was over, Troy and Chris pounded the glass, then Troy went downstairs to kick it with his people. There was a bunch of mixed feelings about Jermel's murder. They all knew that it had to be done, but no one was happy.

It was a lose-lose situation. Jermel was Orchard Park Projects family. He was loved by most, but was also a traitor who was despised.

Speculation ran wild about who could've gotten him. Could they even retaliate if it was the A or any of their other enemies? It was a tough situation.

Chris walked out of the jail doors and sat in his triple-black 740i. He just thought for a moment, cogitated. He focused on who he was and where he was in life. He was in a decent place. His music was going to be the key. But until then, he had to move safely in the streets. He had to do all that he could to get his big brother out of those prison garbs and back into some Adidas jumpsuits. Amin and Peanut were working hard, but Trina was the key. She had to make a choice. She couldn't be allowed to work against him; that wasn't tolerable.

*****

On October 26, Trina lay in the bed at Beth Israel Hospital, squeezing Ella's hand and silently cursing Troy's. It felt like she was trying to shit out a bowling ball. The pain was unbelievable.

It took seven hours of agonizing labor before Taj was finally out and crying. He didn't have to be spanked or washed for everyone in the room to see that he was his father's son.

Two days after giving birth, Trina was free to leave the hospital. Ms. Goslin, Ella, and Tanyah were always by her side, assuring her that she didn't spend much time alone. Between the four women, Taj hardly ever touched a flat surface for more than ten minutes. They fought over their time with him as if he were being courted for a royal marriage.

When alone with Taj, both Trina and Ms. Goslin held him and cried for hours at times. He represented so many worlds.

Love, Manny, Troy. He brought a sense of comfort to their lives that once existed then left. Then came back. Then left again. An immaculate conception in his own right.

Taj was only four months when Ella went all the way out on a limb to return a major favor. Trina was back at work for a month as a nurse's assistant at Brigham and Women's Hospital in Boston. It was Ella's turn to babysit Taj. That's what friends are for.

*****

"Boston, muthafucka!" DB yelled as he and Grit made every book in the hand.

Troy and Mike just sat on their stools, looking stupid, while Grit and DB grabbed all their ramen noodles and mackerels off the table.

"Yeah!" Grit heckled. "Y'all muthafuckas gonna starve tonight!"

A barrel-chested CO with a small head walked over and tapped Troy on his shoulder. "You better hurry up and get upstairs ta your visit before you don't have no more food."

Grit and DB laughed as the CO spun off from the table.

"I'll see y'all on the court after count," Troy threatened as he walked away. He hurried up and changed into his visiting uniform, then strolled up the stairs to see Joyce or Liona, or they both had a habit of popping up unannounced.

He nearly stumbled when he saw Ella and a child who was obviously his.

The sparkle in Troy's eyes brought instant tears to Ella's. Flashbacks, all the way to their freshman year of high school, flooded her mind. She was overwhelmed. All doubts she had about taking this risk were washed away with her tears.

"You know you can't tell nobody about this," she said between sobs.

Troy's mouth was wide-open, oblivious to her existence for the moment. She watched as Taj's baby browns focused on his father. It almost seemed as if he recognized him. It was magical.

"His name's Taj," she managed to get out between tears.

Troy kneeled with both knees on the stool and continued to stare in awe. "Thank you, Ella."

Hearing his voice brought her tears back full force. "I miss you! How did all this happen? Why it gotta be like this?" she cried out.

"You in jail, Chubby's gone, my Chubby's gone, Troy! Trina's not even Trina no more!" She dropped her head and squeezed Taj, as if trying to gain strength through him. "Troy...they locked you up for killing Manny." Her voice was strong, but low and confused. "I was out there that day. I—"

"Ella! I love you, yo! I love all y'all! You know that! I been in the streets all my life! A lot of shit happened I ain't happy about, but shit happens! None of us can change the past, but we control our present and future! What they got me in here for is bullshit!" He stared hard, telling her that he wasn't insulting her but also wasn't slipping in the booth. "The way shit's going down is fucked up! I'm sitting in jail, waiting for the people I love ta bury me alive in court!"

"Everybody's hurt, Troy! I'm hurt!"

"You don't think I fuckin' know that, Ella? You think I ain't hurt? I'm fuckin' dying inside, but this shit ain't right! This might be the only time I ever see my son!" He shook his head in frustration.

"I ain't the only one who cares, Troy, you know that."

"You the only one who cares even a little about me!"

Instead of their going back and forth, he asked for an update on things over the past year. The majority of the news was depressing, but he was never one to duck reality. Ella always gave it to him exactly how it was.

After an hour of mostly misery, they lightened the mood by reminiscing. Amazingly, they got a few good laughs out of each other.

When it was time for her to go, he stood up and looked back and forth from her to his sleeping son. Their friendship was real, built on a solid foundation. She was risking everything and was allowing a glimpse of light into a dark place. "Thank you, yo. For real, Ella. It don't get no realer than this. You didn't owe me shit. You did this 'cause we been family forever. I know you can't tell them straight up, but take my love and condolences ta them."

"I will...and happy birthday. Taj was a good present, huh?"

She smiled bright.

"The best. Thanks for remembering." He smiled back weakly. "I been spending too many of them in these booths." Troy would be twenty-three in two days.

*****

By late June, Troy had over fifteen months in at Nashua Street Jail and was in a routine. He worked out early in the morning, watched a few programs, then played dominoes or cards with his people.

He read all throughout the day regardless of whatever else he was doing. He initially read a lot of novels and biographies, but once he stumbled upon *Rich Dad Poor Dad* by Robert Kiyosaki, his selection broadened immensely. Autobiographies of the rich and lessons written by the rich became his primary interest.

After lunch, he went to his hallway detail like usual, as well as after lunch and dinner. By this time, most of the COs knew him and were fond of him. He wasn't overly sociable but was good-natured and able to hold conversation on multiple levels.

It was evident to some that Lieutenant Lopes was fond of him also, but the extent of their relationship was never in question. Troy protected their existence with his life. The advantages he had due to her were never flaunted. He even feigned hard times once in a while.

He finally needed to relieve over a year of backup and stress. It was good that he and Tanika weren't on a hot list.

She was on the phone, with her office door open, so he tapped lightly before entering. She really went all out in sticking by him, even acting as a liaison between him and Hemenway.

When she hung up the phone, Troy began to ask questions concerning Hemenway that he already knew the answers to.

She decided to take the pressure off her young lover and thought it was cute that he was lost for words. He stood in front of her desk with a noticeable hard-on, babbling like an eighth grader trying to find the words to ask her to the school dance.

"Who's working the hallways, Newton?" she asked in a superior, professional manner.

"Kenny's out there. Why?"

Kenny was married to one of Troy's cousins. He always played fair with him too. Besides that, he was one of the all-around coolest COs in the jail.

"That's perfect." She paused for a second to think. "You finally got horny enough to come get some, huh?" She gave a short knowing smile.

His demeanor showed that he was busted. He smiled back, shyly averted his eyes. "I mean…yeah."

She was enjoying his discomfort. "I was beginning to wonder…"

"Wonder what?" he shot back in a no-nonsense tone. "You better stop playing with me."

She blew off his anger with a laugh. "Damn, young boy. You need to lighten up. You know I'm just joking."

She had been addressing him by his last name for so long it made him feel great to hear her say her nickname for him.

Tanika watched as his defenses went down. "I don't have any condoms, so you better be careful," she warned as she raised her petite body out of the chair and unfastened her belt.

The simple motion of her beginning to remove her clothing rocked his dick all the way up.

She smirked, understanding how anxious he had to be. She was really loving the fact that she was the only woman available to him. He could've taken her anytime he wanted to, but she needed him to come to her. She masturbated, sexed her plain man, and even went through intense exercises before getting to work at times. She had to maintain control of herself around him. All to avoid being the aggressor, breaking down and straight up asking for the dick. She had to have some type of control in their relationship.

He caught her all the way off guard this day. Two weeks prior, she read the situation wrong when he told her he needed to see her. She thought it was on then, but he only needed her to get some information to Peanut for him. After he gave her the information and left, she sat behind her office desk and screamed as she rubbed her thighs together in heat.

"Close the door," she said, rolling her eyes, enjoying his gawk. Once he closed the door, she approached him, fell into his arms, and stuck her tongue in his mouth. His touch drove her wilder than ever. It was still familiar. She spun around, stepped back to her desk, and let her uniform slacks drop to her ankles. Both hands were placed on top of the desk; her bare ass was stuck out as far as she could get it.

Troy stepped up, rubbed two fingers through her soft bush and wet pussy. Tanika pumped in heavy anticipation.

With no time to waste, he dropped his pants, gripped his shaft, and pumped it in and out until he was comfortably all the way in. *Mmmmmm!*

She bit down on her lip and gripped the side of her desk hard enough to turn her knuckles white. Her brace fueled his aggression. He took it as a challenge and pushed even deeper.

She did her best but couldn't stay completely silent. Instead of letting out the loud moans that were fighting to escape, she sucked in deep breaths and pushed them out with the limited muscle control she had left in her abdomen. Even when she thought she had the technique down, a grunt still managed to escape.

Troy was working powerful thrusts that started in his thighs and ended with the tightening of his ass muscles. He avoided slapping up against her. He pulled slowly out and then slowly slid back in. The harder she breathed, grunted, and squeezed, the more his excitement drove him.

It was less than five minutes of the same rhythmic pleasure when her ass cheeks tightened and left leg began to tremble. She received him even deeper and lathered his dick with clear cream.

Her creaming controlled the brain in his smaller head and caused it to react accordingly. He obliged with her whispers.

"Come with me, baby. Come, come with me…ooh, ooh, let it go."

He came so hard his dick felt like a high-powered water hose with enough pressure in its blast to propel him into the wall behind him. As it neared the end, he pulled her by the waist and pushed in as far as he could. His strength finally left. He went limp inside. When he let loose, his soft dick involuntarily fell out of her, polished and still partially hard, but not ready for more work.

"Damn, OG!" he said with ultimate satisfaction.

"Whew, boy. I missed that big ole young ding-a-ling," she said seriously. Then, in a lighter tone, she added, "And let me know when you want some ahead of time next time, so I can be prepared."

"Who said it's gonna be a next time, Lieutenant?" he joked.

She gave him a sinister glare.

"Calm down, sexy!" he said with his arms outstretched to protect himself. "You know well and good I'm just bullshittin'. You better come in prepared tomorrow."

She felt great after he said that but played it cool. "I hear you. Now get out my office before I hit my body alarm and get you put in the hole for engaging in sexual activity."

Chapter 21

—— ·◆·◆◆◆·◆· ——

On July 13, Chris knocked on Trina's door. It was the day before the sixth anniversary of Manny's death. Regardless of the date, it was time for him and Trina to have a talk. She had to hear him out about the position she was taking in Troy's fight for his life.

When Ms. Goslin opened the door, Chris saw that she appeared to age a lot in seventeen months. When Troy was home, Chris was the only one who came around alone. He had a good personal relationship with Ms. Goslin too. If Trina wasn't with Troy, Ella, or Tanyah, she was probably with Chris, going over music or just kicking it.

Ms. Goslin knew how fond Trina was of the young man in her doorway. How fond she used to be of him. She stared at him, nothing but sorrow in her eyes, with no words for thirty seconds, then she stepped aside for him to enter.

Trina walked into the living room and jumped back when she saw Chris. "What...what you doing here?"

Her outburst didn't faze him one bit. He was determined. Both women recognized his powerful presence.

"F-first, I w-wanna offer my s-s-sincere cond-d-dolence for Manny, on m-me and my brother b-b-behalf." He looked both of them in the eyes. "Second, T-Trina, can I talk t-ta you for a m-m-minute?"

Lady howled and barked from behind a door to make her presence known. Ms. Goslin yelled for her to stop showing off as she walked out of the living room and left them to talk.

Chris didn't waste any time getting to the point. Neither of them sat down, and she didn't offer, but he understood. He let her know that he shared her pain of losing a loved one but pointed out that pushing him and others who loved her away was causing more loss and pain on herself and everyone else.

He never acknowledged or denied Troy's involvement in Manny's murder but reminded her that Troy supported her and did so every year following the tragedy. Troy even mourned with her.

Chris made it clear that he was disappointed in her for assisting the law in deciding Troy's fate rather than dealing with the situation on other terms. Even though it might have been insensitive, he let her know that if Troy were worthy of spending the rest of his life in jail, she wouldn't be alive. It was possibly cruel to say yet necessary to open her eyes back up. Chris felt like Trina lost focus on the true Troy. The Troy she always told him about.

Chris wasn't a deep analyzer like Peanut, nor could he speak from the heart on his behalf, but he did reiterate the love that Troy had for her, her mother, their son, and yes, her brother. He asked that she see things for what they truly were, not what they appeared to be.

Trina really listened to Chris. She sometimes stared off in deep thought. He was really hitting home with some of his points. She truly loved Chris. He was her little brother and admired how much he had matured from the fifteen-year-old boy she met at Troy's first basketball game to the twenty-year-old young man in front of her.

She knew that he was sincere, and commended his dedication to Troy. None of that was relevant, though. Trina refused to betray Manny, even in memory, by associating with any of the people responsible for his death.

"Chris," she said, distant and cold, "I gave you the respect I feel you deserve and heard you out. I believe a lot of what you said, but my family comes first. I don't wanna have this conversation anymore. I don't want you ta come back over here again either. If you really respect me, you'll do that. I honestly wish the best for you in life, but I can't allow y'all ta be a part of me and my son's life."

Chris was dejected. Her conclusion hurt. He couldn't understand it at all. He kept his composure. "Can I at l-l-least see m-my nephew th-this one t-time? I'll respect ya wish even th-though I th-think ya making a b-bad decision for everybody."

She obliged.

Trina turned, and Chris followed. Lady met them in the short hallway, jumping up and down on his leg, demanding his attention. He bent down to rub her head and belly as she sneaked in a few doggy kisses. It drew a sad smile to Trina's lips. Lady still flirted with and took to Chris. It was obvious that even she missed his jovial presence.

Chris looked the part of a proud uncle when Trina handed a wide-eyed Taj to him. She stepped back and watched. The scene forced a single teardrop. Taj was dominated by women around him, so he took to Chris with curious excitement.

Trina couldn't help but think about how Troy and the rest of his people would spoil Taj. She really wished it didn't have to be like it was, but it was, and it wasn't his fault in any way. Every time a sympathetic thought crossed her mind, she thought about Manny, then hurt or anger replaced the thought.

Chris laughed and kicked it with Taj like the child was a grown man already. There was no "Goo, gaa gaa" from uncle Chris. When he laid his nephew back on the bed, he placed seventy rubber band-wrapped hundred-dollar bills in his blanket. He had the money ready to give to Trina or Ms. Goslin in case he wasn't even let in the house.

He kissed Taj on the forehead, then hugged Trina's confused body against her will. She didn't want to show or allow herself to receive affection, but her brain wouldn't register to resist the natural brotherly love.

Chris told Trina to call him for anything, then he patted Lady on the head, yelled goodbye to Ms. Goslin, and walked out.

Lady whined, jumped wildly, and scratched at the door as it closed behind him.

Chris walked slowly down Trina's steps, in deep thought, with Troy and Taj on his mind. He had to find a way to convince Trina to at least let him be a part of his nephew's life. He looked just like Troy. Chris couldn't wait to brag to Troy about seeing and holding his son first.

The thoughts were bittersweet, but he was confident that Trina would snap back to her senses and that there was room for reconciliation. He was still mentally connecting the dots with the complicated situation when he sat in his Beamer; that was why he didn't notice the dark-blue Buick Skylark until it pulled in back of him, blocking his ability to back out.

Minutes before they spotted Chris, Steve was putting the final touches on their plan.

"Yo, Ty, as soon as that sucker get in his whip, block his bitch ass off," Steve spat from the back seat of the hotbox Buick Skylark. He had homicidal holes beneath his eyelashes, and they were dead set on Chris. "D," he said, looking over at his other man in the back seat with him, "you ready?"

"No doubt," D shot back while gripping a MAC-11.

"Good, 'cause we 'bout ta air this rapping-ass coward out," Steve finished.

Steve saw Chris when he first pulled up to Trina's building and had a hawk's eye on him ever since. He gathered up Ty and D and got them ready to ride with him. Steve didn't give Chris a pass based on hip-hop, like a lot of others did. To him, Chris was simply a Trailblazer, and a Trailblazer was always his enemy.

When the Buick's tires screeched behind him, it snapped Chris out of his thoughts. He reached for the .44 on his waist, but he heard and felt bullets piercing his car and flesh. It seemed like bullets were coming from everywhere as he coughed blood and glass out of his lungs.

He managed to stagger out of his car door and look his assailants in the eyes as they continued to fire rounds into him. It felt like rocks and razor blades were ripping his body apart.

Chris lifted his .44 as D yelled for Ty to take off. As Ty screeched off, Chris squeezed the .44's trigger twice, shooting aimlessly.

Strictly muscle reflexes must've allowed Chris to even get off a single shot, because he was paralyzed before his body hit the pavement. He had seven bullets lodged inside of him, and three more tore clean through his small frame. He fell to the ground like a wet blanket full of holes and lay in the middle of the Academy Homes parking lot.

Trina heard the thunderous gunfire outside and ran to her living room window to check on Chris. By the time she got there, she saw him slumped against his open car door. She bolted out of her front door, dashed down her stairs, barefoot and frantic, with Lady right behind her.

As she neared Chris, she heard a gargle coming from him. She had a terrifying flashback of Manny lying dead just a hundred feet away from where Chris lay. But Chris wasn't dead. She couldn't let him die too.

She sat down on the ground and lifted his head onto her lap to stop him from choking. "Chris!" She called his name to let him know that she was with him. "Just calm down, Chris. The ambulance is coming! Just calm down and stay with me."

His eyes were opened wide with fear. His lips trembled as he tried to form a word, but nothing came out.

"Don't try ta talk…just relax." Her voice and body betrayed her own advice.

Through all the blood and torn tissue in his face, a tear was recognizable as it left his frightened eye. He'd been here before, six years ago. It wasn't the same this time, though. It was a higher degree of pain, of pulling away from the world he knew into a world of the unknown. He wanted to tell Trina to tell Troy that he loved him. That he was sorry for letting him down. He wanted to have at least one more Bible study with Reverend Childs, his daddy. Chris wanted a lot of things at that moment, but the unknown wanted him more.

His back lifted off the ground, high into the air. A loud moan came through bloody, clenched teeth. "Errrr!"

"No, Chris! Please! Calm down, please!" Trina panicked.

His chest and back rose two more times. A quick, violent shake overcame him. His eyes rolled back in his head. His body seemed to become lighter in her arms.

It was over as fast as it started.

"Chris…please," Trina whispered, begged, to no avail.

She cradled his head and broke down. It was all too much to bear. Too much loss. Too much pain.

Lady whined and licked Chris's lifeless face. She knew there was trouble waiting for him but couldn't communicate it properly.

Twenty minutes after the shooting, the ambulance arrived and loaded Chris in one truck and a hysterical Trina in the other.

By the time Ty made two quick left turns then a right down the back streets to flee the scene, he looked in the rearview mirror and saw D panicking. He was holding Steve across his lap, trying to cover his neck so that blood would stop gushing out.

One of Chris's wild shots landed right below Steve's ear and had the young enforcer fighting for his life. D was using his own shirt to slow down the bleeding, but it wasn't helping much.

"Oh shit!" Ty yelled when he noticed the tragedy. "We gotta get ta the fuckin' hospital!"

"I know, dogg," D said nervously. "We gotta get out this hotbox and dump these burners."

"Toss them burners, dogg! They dirty, anyway! Y'all aired his bitch ass out! We gotta get my dogg ta the hospital! Now! Don't let him slip, D!"

Ty was frantic and giving an order that none of them had control over. He sped through red lights and stop signs. Drove the wrong way on one-way streets. It was all for nothing.

Steve stopped breathing and died in D's arms.

All Ty had to do was look through the rearview mirror at D's expression.

"Fuck!" Ty banged the steering wheel with his fist. He continued on. When they got to Boston City Hospital's emergency entrance, he made a tough decision. All he could hope for was a miracle revival.

Ty hopped out and opened the back door. D was still sitting in a daze with his dead friend in his lap.

"Come on. Let's get him out," Ty told D.

D looked confused. "What?"

"Dogg, ain't nothing else we can do. We gotta leave him and hope they can pump him back ta life or something. We can't go down for no body, though."

They slid Steve's body out of the car and laid him on the ground in front of the electric sliding doors. Through the glass doors, Ty caught the eye of an old lady sitting behind the reception desk and flagged her. Without waiting, they jumped back in the hotbox and sped away.

*****

Troy finally broke down. The weight of his world was finally getting too heavy for his shoulders. He held it up and held strong through crisis after crisis, but now it was an overload.

He sat on the bunk in his cell and let the tears flow. They flowed for Jimmy. They flowed for Manny. They flowed for Jermel. They flowed for Chris. They flowed for Trina. They flowed for Taj. They flowed for himself. It was overwhelming.

He told the COs on every shift, for two days, to leave his door locked. He refused to report to Lieutenant Lopes's office upon request and didn't even respond when threatened by other lieutenants to lose his hallway runner's detail.

He went through phases of guilt, sorrow, and vengeance. He tried hard for Chris. Damn. *Why Chris?* He loved him. His death broke him. Guilt dominated his being. He failed him. He wasn't there with him to continue to guide him.

Even more so, his guilt came from knowing that Chris died for showing his continuous loyalty to him. For trying to look out for him. He knew that Chris was only in the A to try to talk some sense into Trina.

Suddenly, he hated Trina. She wasn't worthy of living. She didn't care about his or Chris's life, so he no longer cared about hers. If she weren't snitching and kidnapping his son, Chris never would've been over there to be an easy target.

He wrestled with guilt and hate. Would he allow Trina to live if she didn't have his son? Taj was a reality, though, and the what-ifs didn't matter. Eventually, if not already, another man would be raising his son. This thought was unbearable.

If Trina got killed, he wouldn't stand a chance at getting away with it. Plus, the truth was, he couldn't kill her under any circumstances. He was a man. As a man, he had to be able to look himself in the face for the rest of his life, even if that life was behind bars.

He had to calm his emotions and think rationally. It took him a couple of days to do it. Hemenway taught him to think three times before acting, so that was exactly what he did.

In the early morning of his second day holed up in his cell, Grit slid a kite under his door. He opened it later in the afternoon and appreciated the news. Steve was killed by Chris's gun.

Chris took Steve with him. That warmed Troy in a way that the average person could never understand; only a killer could. Steve was a dogg; there was no denying that. So was Jermel. His young protégé, his little brother, banged with and took out two of the best he ever knew. Through different types of tears now, he laughed out loud at the thought. He was momentarily in a psychotic state of bliss.

After his days of mourning at his own pity party, he got himself together and called Peanut. Peanut brought him up to speed on everything that was going on in the hood. Peanut's jaw dropped when Troy told him that Chris killed Jermel almost a year ago. Troy told him to keep that information close to the chest until he was able to really build with Liona.

Peanut and Amin were doing their best to make sure that things were as straight as possible for when the time came for Troy's trial. They were paying Hemenway, tying up loose ends, intimidating and eliminating potential threats. The only thing lingering was the big pink elephant in the corner of the small room. Trina.

"Fuck it, dogg," Peanut said in the middle of their conversation. Troy could tell that something was bothering him. "What up, dogg?"

"Man, you and Amin ain't tryna bring this shit up, but it's real as a muthafucka, so ain't no ducking it."

"I feel you. I ain't gonna front. I been thinking about it a lot. On, doggs." Just saying anything about Trina out loud drained him emotionally. "We just gotta let it play out, dogg," Troy concluded.

*****

JB Johnson Funeral home resembled a small white house with a large uninviting parking lot. Unfortunately, or fortunately, its services were used often. It had about fifteen rows of long wooden benches on each side of an aisle and held a capacity of about three hundred. It sat on Warren Street, a short distance from Dudley Square, and was a regular home-going house for Orchard Parks' deceased.

For Chris's home-going service, JB Johnson Funeral Home had triple its capacity. People packed the inside, stood in long lines outside, and waited in vehicles just to view his casket.

His casket had to remain closed. Even the excellent work of the funeral parlor wasn't enough to make Chris presentable. Reverend Childs wanted his son to be remembered as the beautiful young man that he was, not a damaged body inside of a casket.

His casket was black marble with red trimming. A forty-eight-by-twenty-four-inch photo of him performing onstage sat on top of it. On the side of the casket was a large chest.

Whoever wanted to put memorabilia in the chest was welcome to. The chest got filled with pictures, money, clothing, jewelry, and even strands of hair.

Several people spoke in Chris's memory. Big Will, a former Trailblazer turned minister, moved the crowd with a heartfelt ode to the celebration of his life, not the mourning of his death. He lifted spirits and brought life into the building.

Will was respected by the projects and throughout the Bean. He did time for his part in a homicide as a juvenile. He was wild in his days, but his change in life was real and respected.

Reverend Childs cried for three days after his son was taken from him, then, as if instructed by Chris's spirit, he never cried for him again. He was at peace with the twenty years that his son spent on this earth. He wished it could've been longer, but he honored his allotted time.

The last two years were their most enjoyable as father and son. He found out who his boy actually was while he was here, which allowed him to understand where he was now that he was gone. Once again, his faith would see him through and give him the strength to stand strong.

Everyone in the funeral parlor was shocked at Reverend Childs's choice of words and intimate knowledge of his son. It wasn't expected for the megapopular, straitlaced, strict reverend to speak such strong words, in a language other than the scriptural dialogue he usually stuck to. He spoke from the mouth of a clergyman, historian, and revolutionary. Most notably, Reverend Childs quoted his son's words, recognized by many in the crowd through his lyrics.

He thanked all of Chris's supporters for paying respects, then invited them down to his church on Sunday to hear the New Testament that he would be preaching with the help of Big Will. A testament aimed at the youth of the inner city, their struggles and real solutions. He labeled this seven-week series of ministry as a call to the people. Chris was his angel, his savior. The one who showed him his true path.

People wept, laughed, and reminisced throughout the funeral home. A large screen showed clips from his last performance, and everyone bopped their heads and rapped along. Outside, Chris's music blared from vehicles. It felt like an outside of a concert. Chris would forever be remembered.

Chapter 22

The ongoing violence between Orchard Park and Academy Homes had homicide detective Teeler and District Attorney Kelly Richmond nervous. They figured it would be wise to stop prolonging Troy Newton's trial before they lost the last of their witnesses. Only one victim of the shooting and Trina were left as eyewitnesses.

DA Kelly Richmond took a deep pull on a Camel cigarette and let the smoke ease out of her nose and mouth as she strolled. It was a short distance from her office to Attorney Hemenway's, so she strolled slow, still planning her approach.

Kelly Richmond was no slouch. In fact, she was a veteran of the judicial system also, so Hemenway had his hands full.

She was an impassioned orator who knew more Constitution and case law than most of even the longest-tenured judges who presided over her cases.

At forty-nine, she was a fairly attractive woman, no grays in her short blond hair, very pale skin, and disciplined blue eyes. She never dressed overly provocative, but a trained eye could see that she had a nice body beneath her too-long, too-thick skirts and pant suits.

She soaked up the needed sun, contemplating deeply with every step she took. She didn't want to take this case to trial if she didn't absolutely have to. It was nearly a slam dunk at trial, but the six-plus-year gap from the murder to the present didn't sit well with her.

The purpose of this meeting that she was about to initiate with Attorney Hemenway was to avoid a trial. She mentally juggled the lowest numbers she would entertain on a plea offer and hoped that Hemenway could be swayed slightly above it.

She stomped out her cigarette in front of his building, then stepped through the doors into the main lobby. She smiled and nodded at a few familiar faces as she moved toward the elevator. When she stepped off the elevator, onto the eleventh floor, she was startled as Hemenway was about to step on.

From years of interrogating, Hemenway recognized that he knocked a thought out of DA Kelly Richmond's head when he bumped into her on the elevator. It made him smile. For Richmond to be in his building, on his floor, he knew that it was time to play the plea bargain game. He decided to play the fool first.

"Kelly," he said, exaggerating his surprise, "how are you doing? What brings you to this side of town?" He gestured with his hand around the lobby.

"Actually, Herbie, I was here to have a moment with you. Are you on your way out?" She didn't miss the sarcasm in his tone and gestures. If anything, it angered her. She couldn't have this game start off in his favor, but she was already playing defense.

He faked frustration, checking his watch before he spoke. She tried to ambush him, but it got reversed on her. "Well, I was on my way out. I guess I can hold off a minute. Would you like to step in my office?" He turned on his heels as an answer to his own question. "I would've been better prepared if you called first." He made his last statement strictly as bait.

Kelly Richmond was one of the most organized and tactical DAs he'd ever known, so for her to pop up at his office unannounced made him sense desperation.

She bit. "Oh…well, actually, I was in the building and thought I'd stop by since I was in the neighborhood." *Shit!* She hated her response immediately. *Busted!*

She confirmed his suspicion. *Let's play chess.* He held the door to his office open for her, then closed it as they both entered.

"Glass of water?" he offered, knowing she would decline it. It was an antidote that attorneys offered nervous witnesses.

"No, thank you," she declined sweetly.

"Well, have a seat, then."

Richmond sat down. Her posture was no-nonsense.

Hemenway studied her usual, plain style, mentally redressed her, then saw a younger, more attractive woman. The knee-length brown wool skirt suit did nothing for her.

He hadn't faced Kelly Richmond in a courtroom in over seven years and was simply sizing up what the jurors would see. He did this with all his competition, then figured out his own dress code, mannerism, and all-around courtroom presence.

"Let me hear it, Kelly," Hemenway said while taking a seat across from her.

As soon as she began her plea offer spiel, he cut in, almost guaranteed that his client would not entertain any plea. She boasted her two eyewitnesses and damning physical evidence, along with public furor over Manny Goslin's senseless, brutal murder. He countered by reminding her that she started with six eyewitnesses; now two were dead, and two recanted, and that the public furor over Manny Goslin's murder was in 1996, not the present, 2002.

Richmond put a life sentence with the possibility of parole after twenty years on the table. Hemenway emphatically rejected it.

They sparred back and forth for about an hour, then agreed on an offer of fifteen years to life, where Troy would be parole-eligible after the fifteen-year minimum sentence.

DA Richmond was content but far from satisfied. The agreement they came to was within her limits, but it was her absolute bottom. She hoped that Troy Newton accepted the generous offer and avoided a time-consuming, expensive trial.

*****

The day after his meeting with District Attorney Richmond, Hemenway went up to Nashua Street Jail to visit Troy. He explained to him that, as an officer of the court, it was his duty to inform him of any plea offers by the prosecution. With all the formalities out of the way, he laid out the terms of the plea offer that DA Richmond reluctantly left on the table.

Troy stared, blank-faced, the entire time that Hemenway spoke. When the veteran attorney was finished, Troy spoke through gritted teeth. "If you ain't wanna fight with me, you should've told me when I first got locked up!"

"No, no, no!" Hemenway defended himself. "Don't get me wrong, Troy! I'm more than ready to fight to the death. I just have an obligation, by law, to let you know certain things—"

"Well, don't let me know shit unless it's my trial date or these damn charges get dropped!"

Hemenway was so used to the cordial Troy Newton, but this Troy had him on his heels. For the first time, he was face-to-face with Manny's and possibly Arthur Howard's killer. The man who had a powerful grip on the streets, powerful enough to nearly clear the witness list against him.

"What, I look like taking fifteen damn years?" Troy continued to vent. "You still with me or what?"

"Troy," Hemenway said, leaning forward in his chair, hoping to calm him, "I'm sixty-six years old. I've been practicing law for over forty of them." He began to regain his composure and take back over the situation like he was used to. "I've seen just about everything these people have to offer. I'm not intimidated by none of it. This system isn't fair! It's set against you in every way. To deceive the masses. The masses don't see behind-the-scenes or the under-the-table deals! There's the privileged rules versus the rules for the poverty-stricken and downtrodden. They don't have a clue about the political agendas involved in judicial decisions or who owes who what favor! They don't know these things. That's why I'm here to help!"

Hemenway's temper was on blast. It stunned Troy and forced him to back off a bit. He always respected Hemenway and felt foolish for questioning his character and loyalty.

Troy said, "My fault. I—"

Hemenway held up a hand to silence him. "I'm all the way with you and pleased that you're not willing to accept a plea. My duty to inform you of the plea is fulfilled, so now we can get past this and focus on our trial."

"We'll be ready for whatever they come at us with," he said with more confidence than he actually had. "Don't ever forget all that we've been through, and don't ever forget where we come from and what we stand for."

The conviction of Hemenway's final statements was the assurance that Troy needed. Over the years, Hemenway had been his father. Troy was grateful for his intervention in his life. He knew that he was with him.

Attorney Hemenway called DA Richmond as soon as he stepped out of Nashua Street Jail to inform her that his client was not interested in her offer.

She promised him that Troy Newton would literally regret that decision for the rest of his natural life.

Three days later, both attorneys were in front of a judge. A trial date was set for September 2.

Hemenway sent word of the trial date to Troy through Tanika. Troy was more than ready for it to arrive.

*****

At 7:45 a.m. on Monday, September 9, 2002, Trina, Ella, and Tanyah sat on a bench outside of the courtroom in Suffolk County Superior Courthouse. A large crowd filed into the building, and media and supporters filled the courtroom for the start of Troy Newton's trial. Technicalities pushed the date back a week.

Once again, security was beefed up, but even more so at this time, because besides the hood's ongoing war, the country was also at war. It was only two days until the first anniversary of the attack on the World Trade Center in New York and the Pentagon in Virginia. Both marks were struck by American airliners, the former being struck by planes that flew out of Logan Airport, in East Boston. Another plane was taken down over a field in Pennsylvania. The president of the United States declared war against Islamic extremist.

When Joyce and Liona entered the courthouse, they walked past Trina, Ella, and Tanyah without even a glance in their direction. Joyce always felt that "hate" was too strong of a feeling to harbor, but when it came to Tina and Trina, that was exactly what she felt. None of the women considered their feelings or opinion in their common astronomical dilemma. She had reached out to them but was snubbed every time.

She was a single mother of a single male child. She never even saw her grandson's face. She felt their pain, but for over four years, they were family and dealt with many tough times together. She prepared two memorial services for Manny with them. They should've at least had one discussion about this situation.

The majority of Troy's supporters were formally and casually dressed and on their most humble behavior. They ranged from young and old project tenants to Northeastern University graduates and bank managers. The natural diversity was a potential plus in Peanut's eyes.

When Troy was escorted by three court officers from a holding tank in the back of the courthouse into the courtroom, he flashed a wide smile at the many familiar faces. He was shocked to see some of his college friends and business associates but definitely appreciated their support.

Once he was behind the defendant's table, the court officers removed his cuffs and shackles. By law, the jurors were not allowed to see a defendant in chains, as it could draw up a criminal element in the minds of the impartial fact finders.

Six blacks, eight whites, mostly middle-aged, made up Troy's jury. It was a majority of women, which Hemenway found favorable. He preferred women in homicide trials for their compassion, outlook on justice for both families, and reluctance to punish with such finality.

Hemenway still looked like an Oscar nominee with his sharp shave and suit, but he toned down his flamboyance so that he didn't appear so Hollywood. He didn't want to send the wrong message compared to Richmond's main street look.

DA Kelly Richmond was her usual boring self, with a tan cotton pant suit, nonexpensive flats, hair in a neat bun.

Troy was Catholic school casual, in relaxed fit khakis and a yellow satin dress shirt.

District Attorney Kelly Richmond was only boring in appearance and little in physique. When she spoke, as she did in her preamble to the jury, her raspy voice boomed and filled the entire courtroom.

She began her opening statements by praising Manny Goslin and highlighting his short yet accomplished life. The jurors were obviously receptive to her, displaying many emotions as she took them to the highs and lows of her truths. Richmond painted a perfect picture.

She transitioned smoothly from praise to defamation as she introduced Troy Newton to the jury. She pointed and scowled at him as she described the vengeful, homicidal animal that he was. His motive for murdering Manny Goslin was revenge for his fallen comrades three weeks earlier.

The looks of sorrow from the jurors during her endearing buildup of Manny Goslin was replaced with curious concern as she slandered Troy Newton.

Richmond skillfully used the entire floor. It was obvious to Troy that she was far more dangerous to him than DA Masai Pawn was to Jermel. He didn't like it.

By the time her allotted thirty minutes were up, the jury knew Manny Goslin as an honor roll student, all-scholastic football star, and beloved son and brother who was mercilessly murdered by the cold-blooded thug sitting at the defendant's table.

Troy was vexed after DA Richmond convincingly delivered her opening. He was jittery inside but cool as ice on the outside. He had to pick and choose when to show certain emotions. Right from the beginning wasn't a good time. Hemenway taught him better than that.

Hemenway, never one to be upstaged, put on quite a performance as well. Instead of staying within the courtroom boundaries, against Richmond's objections and the judge's instructions, he used more than just the attorney's floor. He ventured off into the courtroom's aisles. He walked among Troy Newton's supporters to be sure that the melting pot of loved ones didn't go unnoticed.

He described his client with all the praise that Richmond gave to her victim, plus some. He approached the jury box, the judge's bench, Richmond's table, and stood by Troy's side throughout his opening. He spoke to individuals. He spoke to the entirety. He delivered with all that he had.

Hemenway brought it all home by promising the jury that Troy Newton was not a murderer. That when the trial was over and all the evidence was presented, they would see that he made bad choices as a teenager, as everyone did, but murder was not one of those choices. Just as Manny Goslin was a wonderful young man, so was Troy Newton, who was still alive and deserving of his freedom but set up by a desperate friend-turned-traitor. A close friend who Troy Newton considered his brother, who was now deceased but, when alive, was always into trouble. Who got himself into yet another jam at a time when he was on bad terms with Troy Newton. Who manipulated a past situation to bring Troy Newton to this day at the mercy of the court.

Testimony was brutal from the outset—twelve days of verbal combat. There was no sparing the eyes or ears; the exhibits were gruesome, and no rock was left unturned.

Richmond called ten character witnesses on Manny Goslin's behalf whose testimony had no relevance to the facts of the case but worked well to make the jurors more sympathetic.

Hemenway countered with only half that number for Troy, but they were extremely effective.

Nine officers were used by the prosecution for what they labeled as expert testimony. Their expertise ranged from the history of the feud between Orchard Park and Academy Homes to crime scenes, ballistics, and forensic evidence.

Hemenway was a master at cross-examining the prosecution's witnesses. He mentally and emotionally rattled civilians and law enforcement when they dared to take the stand. He brought out the lies of any conflicting statements. If testimony seemed too truthful and damaging, he manipulated it to sound contradictory.

Richmond couldn't suppress her anger at times. Hemenway walked such a fine line. At one point he seemed to be in total violation. Then before she could call him on it, he would be back within bounds of the legal playing field. She popped up from her seat to object to his tactics so many times she could've been mistaken for a jack-in-the-box.

The most damaging and anticipated testimony would come from Trina Goslin, so when she entered the courtroom and took the stand, there was an awkward silence.

She wore an elegant two-piece checkered blue skirt with matching suit jacket. It was formal enough for the occasion yet sexy enough for the eye. An anklet was above her tan pumps, and to Troy's surprise, the Cuban link necklace that he gave her on their first date was her casual choice of jewelry. Never one for makeup, she sat on the witness stand in her natural beauty, her dreads wrapped in a neat bun on top of her head.

Trina never looked at Troy but felt the heat coming from his direction.

Hemenway had to nudge Troy's leg under the table to make him aware of the menacing look he was wearing. Troy quickly snapped back and put the docile mask back on that he had been wearing for most of the trial.

Richmond had Trina Goslin introduce herself to the courtroom, went through some necessary formalities, then got right to the heart of the matter. Richmond prepared her to overemphasize even the smallest emotions. Trina understood that Richmond would ask her delicate questions in an insensitive manner to invoke certain emotions. It was all part of the courtroom strategy.

"Ms. Goslin," Richmond said, addressing her, "tell the court about the day that you witnessed your brother get savagely gunned down and left to die on a sidewalk."

Even though Trina was well prepared for the question, it still seemed to catch her off guard and stagger her. She took a second to take a deep breath, shifted in her seat, then began to walk the court through her memories of that dreadful day. The worst day of her life. She didn't dare one look at Troy as she recounted it. The jurors stared, studied, and dissected her every word and motion as if she were a laboratory project.

When she actually got down to the crucial details of the crime, Trina's credibility came into question for the first time. At the time of the shooting, she told the police that the shooters were driving a black Ford Escort, but in court, she said that the car was midsize and gray.

The police located the abandoned black Ford Escort near the Ruggles Projects within an hour of Trina giving them the description. Three shell casings from a TEC-9 were found on the floor of the stolen vehicle.

Trina also told the police, with certainty, that two people attacked the crowd, but now she remembered a third one. The description of the one who shot her brother was no longer a perfect match to the defendant. Now he was shorter and rounder.

DA Richmond dealt with plenty of witnesses who drew blanks on the stand. Whenever Trina's testimony was inconsistent with her prior statements, Richmond calmly and professionally placed police reports and other documents in front of her to refresh her memory. Only then did Trina claim to recall certain information, but even in the face of documentation, she still refuted some of the things written.

The extra emotion that she and Richmond worked on together wasn't there either. Her overall testimony was far less promising than anticipated by the prosecution. Though Richmond did her best to clean up the actual facts of Trina's testimony, she wondered how the jury received it.

Four and a half hours after Trina Goslin took the witness stand, she was finally finished and dismissed. Hemenway didn't attack her much in his cross-examination, because basically there was no need to.

Troy watched Trina walk off and wondered why she purposely messed up her testimony.

Trina still couldn't find the strength to confront Troy with her eyes, but she wore the necklace from their first date, his first gift to her, and hoped he read into it correctly. She played her part; now the rest was on him, Attorney Hemenway, and a higher power.

She thought back to just hours before her 9:00 a.m. testimony and thanked Manny again. It was Manny who touched her heart, who moved her to try to help free Troy, to help free herself. She walked out of the courtroom, sat on the bench in the hallway, and replayed the dream in her mind.

"Manny!" Trina was ecstatic when he showed up. "Stop playing so much! Where you been? Me and Mommy been missing you. We been hurting!" She sulked.

Manny flashed his rich smile. "Calm down, sis. I never went nowhere. You and Mommy jus' be buggin' sometimes. You see me upset?"

He walked up to her and gave her a long, loving bear hug. She could almost smell his favorite Egyptian Musk oil. His embrace made her feel secure again. After a moment, she stepped back to examine and admire him. He still looked good. He stood six four and totted a chiseled 215-pound frame. He kept a low-cut, neatly groomed goatee on his hazelnut complexion and had a fine face. He wore a green-and-white Adidas sweat suit, which was West Roxbury High School colors, and size 15 Adidas Forum sneakers. Sweat suits were his favorite. He had a closet full of them by choice. He wasn't overly stylish, just content in his own skin.

"You like what you see, sis?" he joked as she stared at him.

She laid her head back on his chest and hugged him again. She was still confused but smiling bright. "What you doing here?"

"I told you, you closed ya mind and couldn't see me no more, so I had ta pop up. You been worried about me too much, so I figured I gotta come check you out." His sparkling grin never left, but his eyes were as serious as the subject at hand. "I ain't got a lot of time, sis, so listen for a second." He paused for a long time. "When I left...I saw it destroying you and Mommy. It was my time ta change form, but y'all couldn't understand that. Y'all couldn't accept it, so I sent someone ta look after my two favorite girls." He smiled brightly again with the statement.

"Who?"

"Who you think, silly? Troy!"

Her confusion was compounded tremendously. "But—"

"I know, I know." He waved off her obvious thought. "But stop sweating the small stuff and see the bigger picture. It was my time ta go. How I went really ain't that important. Once you and Mommy found out all those unnecessary details about Troy, I knew y'all ain't fully recognize my work no more, so I sent y'all another sign. I forgot how hardheaded y'all could be, though." He saw more confusion on his sister's face and laughed some more. "So what I mean, sis, is, I love you. And always remember to…"

"Remember to what? Remember to what?"

Trina woke up with her heart racing. She was sweating like she just ran a marathon. She heard her own voice but couldn't make out the words.

She rolled out of bed, feeling exhausted, like she just did twelve rounds of boxing. She peeked in Taj's crib, then dragged herself to the shower. When she got out, she took a long look at herself in the mirror and saw a strong resemblance of her mother staring back at her. She was young and pretty, but the stress was becoming physically evident. She was going through a long and trying eleven days dealing with Manny's trial, and today was her day.

She didn't realize how early it was until she walked back into her bedroom and looked at the nightstand: 3:33 a.m. She still had five hours before she had to be back at the courthouse.

She couldn't go back to sleep, so she fluffed the pillow on her wooden desk chair, sat down, and got back into the novel she was reading. It was as she turned through the pages of the book that the realization of her dream popped back into her head.

Manny being in her dream felt so real. She began to recall the things that he said. No, it wasn't what he said; it was how he said it. What did he mean he sent another sign? And remember to what? As she replayed the dream in her mind, Taj began to cry.

Taj, like his father, almost always slept straight through the night and wasn't much of a morning person. His waking up at that hour concerned Trina.

She put down her book, went to his crib, and scooped him up. She checked his diaper, then she held him against her chest and rocked him to calm his nerves. As she rocked, it suddenly hit her.

"Y'all ain't fully recognize my work no more, so I sent y'all another sign…"

Taj. Taj! The name was only screaming in her mind at first, then she screamed it out loud. "Taj! My baby!" She squeezed him and cried.

Ms. Goslin heard the cries from Trina's room and dashed in. She was wide-eyed and alert in her robe. Ever since Chris's murder, Trina had experienced random panic attacks, so Ms. Goslin kept a close eye on her. Her daughter was experiencing way too much tragedy at such a young age.

Trina only had the desk light on. Ms. Goslin turned on the room light and asked what was wrong. Trina didn't respond, so she walked over and took Taj out of her arms to check on him. Trina was still unresponsive. She rocked back and forth in the chair.

After an uncomfortable space of silence, Trina closed her eyes and began to recount her dream. Ms. Goslin sat at the foot of her bed, with a now-calm Taj, and listened. Trina was extremely shaken up but began to calm down as she spoke. She was beginning to understand the intervention herself as she explained it.

When she was finished explaining, a slight, knowing smile appeared on her mother's face, but her eyes were sad. She rubbed her daughter's leg and assured her that things would be all right.

Ms. Goslin had been through similar dreams of her own.

Chapter 23

Troy and Hemenway were positive that Trina purposely messed up her testimony, but even with all her legal experience, Kelly Richmond seemed to be genuinely deceived. If she was, she might have been convinced that Trina's pain, combined with the pressure of the trial, weighed too heavily on her.

Whatever Richmond's state of mind was didn't matter to Hemenway; he was just pleased that Trina Goslin's testimony was watered down. Hemenway's satisfaction, however, was short-lived. The raw reality of Troy's fingerprints on the murder weapon was impossible to get around. The fact that they even existed forced Hemenway into a legal strategy that he rarely used in all his years. Troy would have to testify.

Attorneys advise their clients against taking the witness stand in nearly all criminal cases. It's possibly never advised and only used if absolutely necessary. Even when absolutely necessary, attorneys still try to find other means to prove reasonable doubt.

Contrary to popular belief, the negatives of a defendant taking the witness stand far outweigh the positives. If a defendant does not take the stand in their own defense, which is the defendant's right, the jury is only allowed to decide the case based on the evidence presented during the trial.

Once a defendant gets on the stand, they give up their right to remain silent and against self-incrimination. A floodgate of evidence can be introduced at that point, which most times is damaging to the defense, a defendant's prior criminal history, and even unproven prior accusations. For those reasons, as well as most defendant's inability to match wits with savvy prosecutors, defense attorneys kept clients away from the witness stand.

In Troy's case, it seemed suicidal to leave the jury wondering why his fingerprints were on the murder weapon. It had to be explained to them. The only person who could explain it was the man whose life was on the line for the life taken by that weapon.

This was the reason Troy and Herbie Hemenway worked hard to put together the best story possible. It took many months of practice. Now was the time to see if it was perfected.

Hemenway was always an extremely ethical attorney. For over four decades, he fought some of the toughest battles that the judicial system had to offer. His decision to coach Troy at what he knew was a lie was a difficult one to make. He weighed the pros and cons. In his moral mind, it wasn't even close and the positives far outweighed the negatives. He noted the time in Troy's life when Manny Goslin was murdered and compared it to where he was in the present. He weighed his works. Hemenway saw a then-young hurting victim of his circumstances emerge as a mature, loving, responsible adult. No way was rotting in prison for the rest of his life justice for Troy Newton or Manny Goslin.

Hemenway's mind and heart told him that Troy Newton would be a better man, great father, and productive citizen if acquitted of this homicide. Guilt or innocence wasn't a reflection of justice in this case.

The judicial system was unfair in too many ways. It was only geared toward punishment, not rehabilitation, so Attorney Herbie Hemenway took justice into his own hands.

Herbie Hemenway had been an advocate and an activist for impoverished people since the late sixties. He understood all too well about oppression in America. He understood that in the late twentieth and early twenty-first century, most Americans were still unconscious that a machine existed to carry out this oppression and that the judicial system was a major part of it.

The fact that J. Edgar Hoover was still praised and his counterintelligence programs still in effect was confirmation enough for Hemenway of a dysfunctional system.

The 100-to-1 ratio sentencing disparity of crack cocaine to powder cocaine, implemented into the federal sentencing guidelines in the late eighties, was a declaration of war against minorities all over the country. One gram of crack will get a defendant the same sentence as one hundred grams of powder. How much more blatantly racist could one get?

The so-called justice system was engulfed in injustices aimed at minorities, so Hemenway balanced his practice based on sympathizer or apologist. He was tough on minority youth. He taught them to stop pointing fingers. To hold themselves accountable for themselves in order to bring about change and equality.

He now lived in the rich white suburb of Brookline, where it was nearly impossible for the youth to find drugs or buy alcoholic beverages. In every ghetto he ever lived in or visited in America, liquor stores were on far too many corners, drugs were dumped in by the truckloads, schools were run-down, and poverty was second nature. The average person allowed these details to miss them, or they outright ignored their reality, but Hemenway was far from average. He knew that it was by design, not accident or coincidence.

He knew that if you weren't part of the solution, you were a major part of the problem. Troy Newton was part of the solution. He felt it was his duty to do everything within his power to protect such an important piece to the overall puzzle. He saw Troy as a prototype to be shaped after by his peers and the impoverished all over the country.

Sure, Troy had his faults, but Hemenway knew that the worst of Troy Newton had already been displayed to the world. His best display was ahead of him, and that couldn't be accomplished if his future was behind bars.

Troy's future rested on Hemenway's ability to convince this jury that he had no role in the murder of Manny Goslin. It was a tall order, but one he was up for.

Troy Newton represented more than an individual. When Troy Newton took the witness stand, he was scrutinized ten times harder than Trina Goslin was. If Trina Goslin represented a lab project to the jury, Troy Newton was either a terminal disease or the potential cure for it. He was fortunate to be as naturally warm as he could be cold. The tenderness in his eyes came out as easily as the callous.

The opinions in the jury box ran wild before one word was even spoken. Hemenway had Troy well prepared. He sat upright, both hands in his lap, sporting a cream two-piece wool suit and light-brown button-up with three buttons open at the top. By no means was the style and manner in which he sported it without purpose. Hemenway advised him to show off his physique to the middle-aged women in the jury. It was also in sync with the young entrepreneur that he was going to introduce to the jury.

DA Richmond tasted victory. Troy taking the stand was the main ingredient for his own disaster. In her twenty-four years of trying criminals, not one ever walked free when testifying on their own behalf. She was expert at digging up all the dirt from their past, making the jury lose focus of the facts of the case and zone in on the mess she made of the defendant.

Troy had a criminal past and reputation in the streets that she was going to love exposing, even though most of it wasn't even legally admissible. He hadn't been arrested in years, but he had been suspected on many occasions. She planned to slide objections in that she hoped would be accepted by Judge Brady.

Hemenway, as usual, was a few steps ahead of his opponent. When he began questioning Troy Newton, he took him through the formalities, then methodically walked with him through his childhood to the present.

The jury heard of poverty, hard times, and hunger. He openly spoke about robberies that he committed, scuffles and petty drug dealing. He also touched on his loving mother, outstanding academic and athletic résumé, and the businesses he started all by the age of twenty.

Hemenway gave the jury the criminal they sought, then replaced him with the reformed, refined adult in front of them. Hemenway chose to bring out all the bad himself so, to the jury, Troy would appear as an honest, open book with nothing to hide. In fact, all the information would've been brought out anyway. But if it were brought out by Kelly Richmond, she would've shaped it as Troy

Newton's secret, dark past that ran parallel with the homicide that he was sitting in front of them accused of.

Richmond was furious with Hemenway's maneuver. Her face was devil red to prove it. He was playing on the jury's ignorance of judicial procedure, and she wanted to punch him in the face for it. *Asshole!*

She contemplated objecting against what she saw as borderline criminal manipulation of law practice but knew that her objections would be overruled, worthless, and actually stupid.

She crossed her slender legs, right over left, then left over right repeatedly, and idled with her pen. She sat helplessly, watching Hemenway make Newton look like a modern-day success story who had his beginnings in hell.

When Attorney Hemenway got to the part where he had to ask Troy Newton why his fingerprints were on the gun that killed Manny Goslin, the strategy got tough. This was where all their practice counted the most. One slip could cost Troy his life.

Hemenway trained Troy's eye to understand the language of his body. He had been doing very well up to this point, but it counted even more at this stage of the trial. Hemenway's right or left foot forward, arms folded right over left, or left over right, all told Troy what he wanted out of him from a mental, physical, and emotional standpoint. Some signs even called for a specific answer to a question.

Throughout the entire trial, Hemenway demonized Jermel Gilliard as the bad influence, violent, criminal-minded friend whom Troy Newton grew up with. He made Jermel Gilliard out to be the cause of Troy Newton's unlawful behavior in their youth. He spoke of Jermel Gilliard's bank robbery, suspected homicides, and numerous arrests for drugs and violence. Jermel Gilliard was the villain with the dark, secret life that neither Troy Newton nor most of their associates in Orchard Park were aware of.

Based on his character assassination throughout the trial, no accusation against Jermel Gilliard seemed far-fetched. Hemenway's bottom line was that Jermel Gilliard was involved in Manny Goslin's murder, and when he got in trouble with the law years later, he framed Troy Newton for it.

Hemenway pointed out that kids from the neighborhood used to buy guns from addicts trying to get high and how they sometimes just found guns around the neighborhood. Troy told the jury didn't know where most of the guns came from or where they ended up after they left his possession. It was mostly for sport and play. They would go to nearby fields, shoot at bottles, abandoned cars, and other harmless targets.

When showed an evidence bag that contained the .357 that killed Manny Goslin, Troy told Hemenway and the court that he remembered it because it was the only one like it that he ever touched. He remembered the day that he actually fired the gun.

He took the court through the day when he, Jermel, and another friend went to a field to shoot at a run-down, abandoned school bus. On this day, around the first week of his senior year of high school, Jermel provided the three guns out of his book bag, which included the .357. He remembered having to remove six empty shell casings from the .357 and replacing them with the extra bullets in the book bag. They shot at the bus and other targets, reloaded a few times, before having to run off when they heard police sirens.

Troy recounted that Jermel kept the guns in his book bag and he never knew what happened to them after that day. Troy didn't fail to admit that there were days when he provided the guns, but it was key to this trial that Jermel provided the guns on that particular day. Jermel's death made the trial for Troy's life a lot more manageable. As flawed and fictitious as his story might have sounded to some, it would've been impossible if Jermel were alive to testify.

It was important that Troy mention having to remove the empty shell casings from the .357 and reload it before he shot it and also the fact that this happened around the first week of his senior year in high school. Both elements were crucial for creating reasonable doubt in the mind of the jurors. Manny Goslin was murdered in July of 1996, and Troy's senior year didn't begin until September of 1996. By his having to remove the empty shell casings, it showed that the gun was used before he ever possessed it.

Sighs and moans came from the Academy Homes side of the courtroom, but Troy ignored them. He stayed focused on the jury, judge, and Hemenway, just like he was taught to do. Judge Brady pounded her gavel and called for order whenever the antsy audience became too loud or inappropriate.

Attorney Hemenway knew that his strategy was far from fool-proof, but he also knew that the jury needed to hear something to be able to deliberate once the case was taken to the jury room for them to decide Troy Newton's fate.

District Attorney Kelly Richmond might have been deceived by Trina's testimony, but she was 100 percent sure that every word Troy Newton spoke was bullshit. She was pissed off at how believable he came across and the sympathetic looks he got from some of the jurors. She came right out of her chair, firing shots at him.

The beginning of her cross-examination was difficult question after difficult question. She attempted to trip him up with every step she took him through and was successful too many times for Hemenway's liking. Her aim was to convince the jury that not only was Troy Newton a murderer, but he was also the leader of the entire Orchard Park Trailblazers gang. Give the jury an extreme accusation and hope that they rule favorably on the less extreme one. Murder. That was her sound legal strategy.

Richmond did a good job with her strategy. She also mocked Attorney Hemenway's shenanigans from his opening statements by accusing Troy's supporters in the courtroom of being his underlings and henchmen. The gloves were off.

One of DA Richmond's most damning accusations against Troy was that he was intelligent enough to take the stand and deceive the jury by admitting the things he couldn't deny and denying the things he couldn't admit.

Hemenway cringed at the brilliance of her statement.

A dirtbag like Troy Newton was not going to walk free against Kelly Richmond's will.

The predicted nine-day trial turned into fourteen. Everyone was exhausted. The jury deliberated all through Thursday, then finally reached a verdict Friday night, September 27. There was both relief and anxiety from everyone involved.

The anxiety level increased when the jury was ordered from their private chamber into the courtroom to read the verdict. They filed in, one behind the other, and stood behind their assigned chairs.

The entire courtroom remained standing as Judge Patricia Brady entered. When the court officer told them to be seated, whispers were hard from all around.

Troy and Hemenway sat in a similar upright fashion, with hands folded on the table. In a different environment, they would resemble grandfather and grandson.

DA Kelly Richmond and her superior, Paul McDonald, sat stone-faced and dignified.

Judge Brady instructed Troy to stand as the foreperson of the jury stood to read the verdict. The focal point of the trial was the murder of Manny Goslin, but in addition to that, Troy was charged with three counts of attempted murder and one count of possession of a firearm.

"As for count number 1," the tall frail white man said from the jury booth, "charging possession of a firearm, we find the defendant, Troy Newton, guilty as charged."

Loud sighs and low whispers were heard throughout the courtroom. People began to shuffle around and consult with one another. Judge Brady banged her gavel and called for order until she regained control. When it was quiet, she told the foreperson to continue.

He nervously shifted from one foot to the other. He had no idea how big of an impact what he said next would have on this hostile crowd. Troy and Hemenway sat calmly, while Richmond's eyes bore hungrily into him. The crowd looked ready to erupt regardless of what came out of his mouth. Suddenly, he wished he were just a regular juror and left the foreperson spot to someone else.

"As f-for counts numbers 2 through 4, charging attempted murder, we find the defendant, Troy Newton, not guilty as charged."

More commotion came from the audience. More approval than disapproval. And once again, Judge Brady had to bang and scream to get order. Court officers instructed people to stay seated while the rest of the verdicts were read.

Beads of sweat formed from the foreperson's balding head. He uneasily shuffled through the papers in his hand to find and read the final verdict. He knew that it was going to cause a major uproar and wondered if the court officers were plenty enough to protect him and the rest of the jurors if the crowd chose to attack him. He actually wanted to consult with Judge Brady before reading it but sucked it up and carried out the final part of his jury duty.

"As for count number 5…" He looked toward Judge Brady. She gave him a nod of confidence. He continued, "Charging first-degree murder, we find the defendant, Troy Newton, guilty—"

"What?"

"Hell no!"

"What the fuck!"

Shouts came from all throughout the audience. Judge Brady's banging gavel became irrelevant.

Nearly the entire courtroom was on their feet. Violence looked inevitable. Court officers stood between both groups, got on their radios, and called for backup. A mob environment began to form. Order was just about lost.

Hemenway faced the angry crowd, trying to find familiar faces to bring calm.

Troy seemed to be the only person seated in the whole court-room. The melee around him didn't even matter. He remained poised but distraught and squeezed his eyes tight with pain and disbelief. He knew that this outcome was a strong possibility, but the reality of it was unbearable.

Joyce—the thought of his mother's pain hurt more than his own. He didn't know how she would handle this. And Trina, what was going to happen with them? Did Trina try to help? If she did, it would make him feel a lot better. But his son would never have him in his life. His heart ached.

Peanut and Amin. His brothers. The thought of them hurt like crazy. They loved him. They stood by him every step of the way, and he knew they would never abandon him. Loyalty. His thoughts turned to Jermel. Thoughts of Jermel were indescribable, polar extremes. Resentment for Hemenway shot through his mind, but he let it go. The old man tried.

He had no heroic urges to try to break for the exit door like he fantasized about throughout the trial. He just sat and accepted his fate. This was reality. He had no time for fantasies. A life in prison was the worst life he could imagine, but he had to take it like the lives he took—Manny's life. His only hope now was that Hemenway could present a strong appeal and have him out of there within the next five or so years.

Through the fracas in the courtroom, people began to notice the tall foreperson jumping up and down. He looked like he was trying to hail a taxi on a Friday night. His dramatics, coupled with Judge Brady's standing and waving as if she were directing an airplane runway, finally got the crowd to calm for a second to listen.

"I'm terribly sorry. I-I'm incredibly nervous. I...I had count number 1 and count number 5's verdict slip mixed up in the shuffle." He paused and swallowed. "I been trying ta get your attention, b-but...I meant ta say that, as for count number 5, charging first-degree murder, we find the defendant, Troy Newton, not guilty."

Troy's head dropped again...this time in an impossible relief. He could not believe it! The court erupted, loud enough for one to think that he just hit the winning shot at one of his games. Orchard Park and the rest of Troy's supporters outnumbered the opposition, so the bliss overpowered the anger.

Judge Brady instructed the court officers to remove all unruly attendants. The court officers felt the dangerous vibe from this crowd only moments ago and really didn't want any problems. They went row to row, requesting, not ordering, people to sit down so that the court could proceed. Little by little, the crowd began to comply with the courts' orders; some sat, some stormed out.

Judge Brady quickly excused the jury and scheduled a sentencing hearing date for the following week. Based on the amount of time he had already spent in jail, it was possible that he would get a sentence of "time served" for his gun conviction. However, Judge Brady wanted a week to sort through the facts and thoroughly review the case. The crowd showed their disapproval with her decision, but she dismissed the court right after she made it.

As the court officers cuffed and shackled him, Troy turned and gave a victorious smile to his supporters. No words were spoken, but a million silent messages were communicated.

The day after Troy's trial ended, a CO unlocked his cell door and told him that Lieutenant Lopes wanted to see him. As soon as he stepped into her office, he joked that he would be a free man soon, so she didn't have to risk her job anymore. After their first booty call in her office, they had had a number of better-planned, amusing trysts over the months.

He noticed that her mood was dispirited when she waved off his humor. He recognized that they were about to have an uncomfortably serious conversation. As he lay in his cell and enjoyed his victory the night before, he also anticipated the complex moment that he was facing now.

She began by congratulating him on his victory. Then they began to go over some of the plans he had that they discussed throughout his time. She wanted to know if he was still serious about leaving the streets alone. He assured her that he was, and she was satisfied.

Tanika got noticeably nervous. It was time to touch the most sensitive topic in her life. She didn't know if it was sensitive to him at all.

They had become extremely close. It was real for both of them. She was one of his most trusted companions. They even confessed their love for each other.

Troy knew the discussion was inevitable, so he jumped right to it to take the pressure off her. He answered her unspoken questions. Did he still love Trina? Yes. Though the chance was next to none, he planned to make an attempt at reconciling and seeing if a relationship could still exist between them. He owed Tanika complete honesty, so he gave it to her.

Surprisingly, hearing the hard truth brought her out of her slump. She loved Troy, loved him with all her being, and though she loved her man, he would always be a distant second to her "young boy." She made it clear that his decision hurt but she was satisfied knowing where things stood, so she could deal with their reality accordingly.

She reiterated what she told him their first night together. That she would never come between him and Trina. She had to suck it up and stand firm on that promise now. She didn't make a fuss.

Troy felt guilty. There was no way for him not to. He felt like he was betraying Tanika. She proved to be the best woman for him. She stuck by him when Trina abandoned him. Tanika Lopes showed him that she could stand the rain. But Trina showed him what love was.

Before Trina came into his life, Troy never knew love for a female. She was his everything when they were together. And now she brought his life into this world. The betrayal was painful, but he couldn't deny what his heart felt.

He went through a period where he hated her. But all that changed when she took the witness stand. She lied. And he needed to know why.

Tanika couldn't attend his trial, for obvious reasons, so he gave her a daily update when he got back to the jail each day. The joy in his voice when he spoke about Trina the day she took the stand was unmeasurable. The love he had for Trina was still strong, just hidden beneath all the anger. That meant that the stability they built was now shaky.

Tanika relieved the uncomfortable air by letting him know that she would always love him and be there for him, then changed the subject. She playfully removed the box of Magnum condoms from her stash spot and tossed them inside of the trash bag he was holding.

They both got a laugh out of that.

He thanked her for everything, then they made small talk for a while longer.

When it was time for him to get back to his unit, he stood her up, squeezed her in a loving embrace, and kissed her full lips passionately. She stared up into his eyes, never wanting him to let her go. He smacked her on the ass and complimented how juicy it was. She smiled and shoved him out of her office.

As soon as she shut the door behind him, she walked back to her desk, sat in her chair, and cried her heart out. Pins and needles seemed to prick every nerve in her chest, causing her to clutch the left side. She cried silently, but the pain screamed as loud as a bullhorn.

Chapter 24

◆◆◆◆◆

Attorney Hemenway alerted Troy three days before his originally scheduled sentencing hearing date that Judge Brady had
rescheduled. Troy only told Joyce and Liona about his new date, so
they were the only people in the courtroom when he showed up.

Judge Brady made a good-natured joke about her courtroom
being empty and safer. Her humor got a good chuckle out of everyone. Her mood was light, which seemed to put everyone around her
at ease.

DA Kelly Richmond went right off into a violent rant as soon as
Judge Brady gave her the floor to speak. She went on about Troy being
an overly influential threat to society who deserved the maximum
five-year sentence for unlawfully possessing a firearm. She all but still
accused him of killing Manny Goslin and assured the court that he
would be in front of a jury again down the line for another offense.

Amazingly, Judge Brady waved her tirade off as baseless
and gave the floor to Attorney Hemenway with a judicial silver
spoon. Seeing that she wasn't out for a retaliatory sentence, as was
Richmond, Hemenway suggested that Troy receive time served for
his firearm conviction. This was Troy's first adult conviction. Under
the Massachusetts statute, there was a mandatory minimum of one
year for unlawful possession of a firearm, which was what Hemenway
asserted was fair.

Judge Brady partially accepted Hemenway's suggestion of the
one-year mandatory minimum and emphatically denied Richmond's
cry for a half-decade revenge sentence. She gave Troy Newton a short
lecture about how fortunate he was and advised that he steer clear
of the mistakes he made as a teenager. After that, she officially sen-

tenced him to eighteen months and gave him time served for the twenty months of jail credit he had in since his arrest.

Troy thanked Judge Brady, assured her and Kelly Richmond that they would never see him behind a defendant's table again, then turned and hugged Hemenway. It was a long-overdue hug that the old mentor understood and appreciated.

Kelly Richmond gathered her papers, in frustration, to avoid looking at the celebration that equaled her failure.

Joyce and Liona went to the defendant's table, thanked Hemenway, and smothered Troy with hugs and kisses.

Troy strutted out of Suffolk County Superior Courthouse and jumped in the back seat of his mother's modest '97 Nissan Pathfinder. As they all headed to their Hyde Park home, Joyce and Liona made him promise to stay with them his first few days out.

He agreed with no problem.

Troy didn't want any homecoming celebration; he just wanted to see Amin and Peanut. He was as focused as he'd ever been and eager to start putting his ideas into effect. He immediately called Tanika but got no answer. He discussed his plans with all of them while he was locked up, and they all agreed to be ready if he was fortunate enough to see this day that was now his reality.

Before he called Peanut and Amin, Troy sat his two mothers down and gave them limited yet strong details of his and Jermel's lives and Jermel's death. There were so many intense ups and downs that it brought tears and smiles from both women. It made him feel good to clear the air and unveil certain truths.

Seeing that Troy still loved his brother made Liona feel good through all the pain. She never fooled herself into believing that Jermel would be okay after his betrayal. She ran the streets before Jermel and Troy were even thoughts. Unlike Joyce, Liona knew exactly who their children were. She saw and heard things involving them that they never had a clue about.

She was always a proud addict in the streets when it came to her sons. She sold her body more out of habit than necessity. It was something she was taught so early in life; it was just in her. The loads of drugs that hit the streets due to her sons found their way to her in nice amounts through their lower-level associates. She was Jermel's mother, so she wasn't denied much of anything.

She also respected the life in the streets on a whole. Even though it pained her to the core to know that her son's life was in danger, she never went up to Nashua Street Jail to plead with Troy for his life. She actually never spoke in depth about it at all with him. Jermel's violation was irreconcilable. All she could do was pray for him and accept whatever Jehovah had planned.

By the time Peanut and Amin showed up, Joyce and Liona had pots of collard greens, fried chicken, yellow rice, stuffing, and corn bread ready to serve. They all sat down and grubbed like they were in mid-808 Orchard Park projects. Conversation was easy and all over the place. After a few hours, it felt like they never missed a beat.

Troy got right down to business. Everyone listened carefully. He didn't want to waste another second of his life. The world he returned to was a very different one than he was taken away from.

Jermel was such a sore spot, a stain. A world without Jermel was a world he never imagined. It tore him apart how dishonorably his brother went out. His whole reputation was void. Their legacy was permanently stained. Chris was one of them. His death still hurt Troy as much as it did when he first got killed. It was a crushing letdown. Some of his biggest plans in life involved Chris. Amin handled the masters to all his music with care. Troy vowed to do all that he could to allow his little brother to live through his art.

Taj was another game changer. In a week, his son would be a year old. That was one full year he'd already missed out on. He wondered if Trina would allow him into his life or if he would have to force his way in. Not being in his life wasn't an option. It was still hard to believe that he was a father. Unfortunately, he didn't have the feeling of a proud father at that.

He felt terrible for Joyce, but knew he would fix everything. She had never laid an eye on her grandson. He planned to make sure she saw so much of him she would have to beg him to take him.

The court thing was out of the window on the custody tip. If Trina thought for one second that she would go against him in court again and survive, she was sadly mistaken.

While the women cleaned up, Peanut and Amin brought Troy up to speed on everything he needed to know. They revealed a lot to him now that they didn't bother to trouble him with while he was locked up. Even though he planned to pull himself and his people completely out of the streets, it was still necessary that he be on point to what was happening in them.

He had big plans and was willing to let bygones be bygones, but that didn't mean that the streets would willingly allow it. A lot of blood was shed, and bad blood built throughout his run. Some people would never let things go. To totally relax would be to welcome a bullet to the head. He had to always stay on point to a degree.

His circle kept business intact. His stores and car lots were doing well.

Peanut finally committed to Danisha. She jumped on board and took over the daily operations of both car lots. Her touch had an amazingly positive impact. Even their daughter, Angel, assisted every day after school.

Just like he was in their circle their whole lives, Amin was an overall overseer. He kept the streets and the businesses intact. Joyce was the informal accountant. New Edition grew under her and Liona's management. Because of this competence and consistency, Troy was able to lay out his plans for expansion.

Peanut and Amin weren't close-minded. It wasn't hard for them to see the realities that Troy kicked it with them about. They couldn't win the drug game; only the government could.

They couldn't continue to go to war with their own people and calling one another enemies. It was totally self-destructive. They couldn't continue to be the problem. They needed to be the solution. To reach their twenties, after all they'd been through, and still be able to sit and kick it with one another was a blessing not missed by any of them.

It was no secret that Troy's acquittal angered some in the law enforcement circle. They would be under heavy surveillance as well as prime candidates to be set up. They kept Attorney Hemenway and a strong team on retainer for that purpose. Troy's philosophy was, if they put the same effort into their legal hustle that they put into the streets, they would climb to heights far beyond what the streets limited them to. They would be legitimate and not have to worry about losing it all at any minute. They were all convicted felons, but being their own bosses would lessen its relevancy. It wasn't a stretch of the imagination. It came down to being the most logical choice of survival. They'd all been behind and in front of bullets literally and figuratively, so it was this choice or choose to die by a bullet or behind bars.

After three days of only stepping outside in Joyce and Liona's backyard, Troy was ready to move. He needed the time to himself before he did anything. He hopped in Joyce's Pathfinder instead of the mint-conditioned, 7 Series BMW that Peanut dropped off, and headed to the A. It was dangerous to be over there, but it was early morning and he had to see the Goslins. He told himself that he would never make a consciously bad decision like the one he was making again but felt it was necessary this one time.

When he pulled in front of Trina's building, he sat for a moment. He envisioned Chris being ambushed in the same spot. The thought made him squeeze the thirty-six-shot MAC-II in his lap even harder. Picturing his little brother being gunned down as brutally as he was hurt and angered him, but there was still room for a smile. Chris went out like a dogg. He took Steve with him and weakened the A-Team by doing so. In Troy's current state of mind, it wasn't the ideal death, but when in the streets, like he was, it was a blaze of glory.

He climbed out the Pathfinder with his Boston Red Sox fitted cap sitting low as he surveyed the area. His black leather Antonio Ansaldi jacket was draped over his right shoulder. The machine in his right hand was off safety, with one in the chamber. He gripped it tight as he made the short distance from the lot to Trina's building.

He didn't click the safety back on until he was up the stairs and knocking on the door. He heard Ms. Goslin ask who it was. Her heart skipped a beat when she saw Troy through the metal door's peephole.

"Troy!" She opened the door and immediately stepped to the side so he could enter.

Instead of walking right in, he stood there. Stuck. Chills went up his spine as she stared at him. What was she thinking? He noticed the aging and felt directly responsible for it. But she was still beautiful.

Lady came from the back, jumping around and barking, break-ing their thirty seconds of silence. She brought an unexpected smile to his face. He stepped in, knelt, and acknowledged her with a left-handed belly rub like he always used to.

He stood, turned, and faced Ms. Goslin. "How you doing?" His eyes were sensitive, but still hard. It was a question, not the everyday greeting.

She was dressed in a green sweat shirt, loose blue jeans, and boots. She was either just getting in or just about to head out. Her jacket was thrown across the arm of the couch along with a Skully and purse.

"She always growled whenever that Steve was around," she said as she watched Lady flirt with him. She was distant. She completely ignored his question. "Trina should be back any minute. I just spoke ta her before I got in. She ran out ta get some things for Taj. What took you so long?"

She purposely ignored his question, but he didn't know how to answer her simple one. It was simple but mysterious. He didn't want to read too deep into it, and he definitely didn't want to say the wrong thing.

"Ta be honest, I just needed a little time ta think. I just got out a few days ago."

"I know. The district attorney's office called ta let us know."

"Oh…plus, I was nervous. I don't know what ta expect from all of y'all." He let his statement linger.

"Sit down, Troy." She motioned him to the love seat as she sat on the couch. "What are your plans?"

He nodded and traced the inside of his teeth with his tongue. Good question. He lifted his eyes to meet hers, then started running down his list of goals and the steps he was taking to achieve them. Ms. Goslin leaned forward, staring and listening.

What's she thinking? He could tell that she believed in his ability to accomplish all that he spoke of, but he couldn't get a read on how she felt about him.

He didn't dare bring up the subject of Manny yet. He wondered if she knew the truth, and dreaded the thought of her asking him about it while they were alone. The living room became as small as the jail cell he'd just spent too long of his life in.

Just as he was beginning to feel suffocated, a key sounded in the door. It creaked open. Trina stepped in with Taj on her hip. The sight of Troy on the love seat froze her. It looked as if she were going to pass out.

In light of her anxiety attacks and frequent fainting spells since Chris died in her arms, Ms. Goslin jumped up, grabbed the two grocery bags from Trina and put a hand on her shoulder to be sure she was steady. When she saw that her daughter was steady, Ms. Goslin locked the door and grabbed her belongings off the couch. She gave Troy another look, then disappeared to the back of the apartment.

Troy, unaware that Chris died in Trina's arms and the trauma that it caused, didn't fully understand what just went on in front of him. He was in his own state of shock. He sat his jacket with the MAC-11 wrapped in it down and rose up slowly. Breathless.

Her skin was beaming like polished oak. Her dreads hung over her shoulders, down the middle of her back. Her eyes were soft and uncertain. Beneath her quarter-cut the North Face snorkel coat her ass and thighs were thicker than ever in her jeans.

The anger he had built up for months vanished. He fell in love with her all over again, this time even more so than the first time. He approached her with a peculiar caution and guided her to the couch. He sat her down and took a seat next to her, never taking his undivided attention off her and his son. His family.

She stared in his direction, but he knew that his physical was transparent to her and she was seeing much deeper.

"Y'all are beautiful," he instinctively said from his heart. The first words he spoke to her in twenty long months.

She stretched out her trembling arms. "Here…hold him. He looks just like you." She acted and spoke with seemingly no communication from her brain.

Troy was steady and proud as he accepted Taj into his arms. Electricity shot through his veins. Taj met the awe in his father's eyes with a smile and a twinkle in his own. Troy examined his skin, his bone structure, every detail that he could see in his face and feel in his tiny body. He never felt the urge to be so gentle before. He rubbed his curly dark hair. It made him think of Jermel.

Ms. Goslin and Lady eavesdropped from the back, eager to see where Trina and Troy would go with this long-awaited face-to-face meeting.

It was the most uneasy feeling ever between Troy and Trina and the exact opposite of Troy's reunion with Peanut and Amin.

They started out by touching on the basics of the past twenty months. They stayed away from sensitive and too personal issues. She did fill him in on her pregnancy and about Taj's first year in this world. There were no laughs or smiles.

After nearly an hour of walking on eggshells, Troy knew that he was going to have to see if the shells cracked under the weight of a pressure-filled conversation, so he shifted in his seat and went there. "Why you testify like that?"

Ms. Goslin tensed up behind the wall. Lady tilted her head and let out a curious whine.

Trina loosely shut her eyes, wrapped her arms around herself as if she suddenly got cold. She began to rock a little. Her eyes opened after a moment, and she found a spot on the floor to focus on, then began explaining the dream she had the morning she was set to testify.

Troy's jaw almost hit the floor a few times as he listened to the details of Trina's dream. *This is some wild shit!* he thought. At some points, her dream literally scared him. It sounded like verses from a scriptural text. In a weird way, it made him understand his own actions better and why Trina and Ms. Goslin seemed to always see through to his soul since he first met them. It was because of Manny.

Troy's head was inside of his hands by the time Trina finished recalling her dream. He wasn't ashamed; he was astounded. He silently thanked the young man whose life he took for saving his. He couldn't believe that a dream was the cause of Trina's change of heart.

Hemenway always talked to him about divine intervention. Troy was sure that he just experienced it in his life. So it was time.

"Call ya moms in here, yo." His face was still in his hands. "Mommy!" Trina called.

Ms. Goslin waited until her daughter called her a second time, but Trina knew that she and Lady were snooping right behind the wall. She walked back into the living room as nonchalantly as she could pretend.

Troy motioned for her to take his seat as he stood up with Taj in his arms. Taj pulled at his chin and drooled on his shirt while laughing.

Troy began by assuring them that all the lies told in court were for the judicial system and not intended to disrespect or insult them. Then he did the most difficult thing in his life as he explained, in the least painful manner possible, the events that led up to Manny's death.

He touched on his personal beef with the A since preteen years, how Jermel set off the chain of events by robbing Steve's dice game, Chris's near death, Jimmy's death, and his and Jermel's retaliation.

Both women stared up at him and Taj with pain and interest. They weren't crying, but the hurt was evident. They needed closure. He did too. They were all finally assembled for it, in the appropriate setting.

Troy took a long moment to contemplate as the actual occurrence was imminent. It took him back to that day. It was as if Manny had spoken to him right before he pulled the trigger.

When they saw the crowd in the parking lot that day, he and Jermel jumped out of the hotbox Ford Escort in ambush. The group they shot at ducked and crawled for cover as Jermel sprayed endless rounds from a TEC-9 and Troy squeezed off calculated shots from a .357.

One of the teen's survival instincts failed him. Instead of finding cover, he froze.

Troy ran up to the teen who froze in place. He actually saw the welcoming of death in his victim's eyes. It was as if his body froze against his own will but in compliance with the will of his soul. A spiritual communication occurred from him to Troy, but it was beyond Troy's comprehension at that time. It was actually beyond his comprehension until he just heard about Trina's dream.

Troy raised his arm, put the last .357 bullet he had in the boy's head, and watched him collapse to the pavement.

He heard a loud scream from a female, breaking his unusual communication with his victim. "Nooo! My brother! No!"

He looked in the direction of the voice. The girl's face was a blur in his murderous rage. She seemed to be fearlessly charging at him. Instead of waiting to see her next move, he turned and got back to the Escort.

As Jermel pulled off, Troy looked over and saw the girl kneeled over the boy, crying.

"I had no idea that Manny was just an innocent bystander," Troy told Trina and Ms. Goslin. "All that was on my mind was that the A killed Jimmy and nearly killed Chris."

Trina cringed at the mention of Chris's name. It nearly brought on another panic attack, but she breathed deeply and controlled herself.

"I was a seventeen-year-old Trailblazer. When it came to the A-Team, all I saw was beef." His demeanor changed. His shoulders slumped. Taj seemed to get heavier in his arm. His thoughts and conscience were battling him. "When I saw the news, I-I couldn't believe it. He was who was I supposed ta be. I-I felt like I killed myself." His first tear fell strictly for Manny as he finished his confession.

It broke the women also. Their tears were caused by the sincerity in his admittance that Manny was a mistake and that it hurt him from the moment he learned of his error. He didn't stop when they started to cry. The tears were necessary. If they had any chance of moving forward in life together, he had to hit them with at least this onetime dose of reality.

The room was tensely silent for a moment. Only the women's sniffles could be heard. Then, Troy continued on about meeting Trina, trying to avoid her and feeling shame every time he looked at her.

Trina closed her eyes at times and nodded in agreement, remembering those times.

He made sure that there was no mistaking his motive for finally getting involved with Trina for true love. As much as he tried to avoid it, a universal order called them together. His complete recount mentally and physically drained him. He cradled Taj to his chest and flopped down on the love seat.

Ms. Goslin felt it more appropriate for Trina to speak. She looked at her daughter and nodded.

"I...I loved you from the first time I saw you," Trina said in between sobs. "Then I loved you for every day that followed it. Then I hated you. You went from being my everything to you taking everything away from me." She was tearing but not sobbing now.

"Manny told me that you and Taj are our...well, me and Mommy's, angels and...and I believe him." She couldn't help but burst out in tears now.

Ms. Goslin squeezed her shoulder and hugged her tight. She refused to give an opinion on the overall situation until she knew where her daughter stood. Now that she knew, and Trina couldn't continue, she added on.

"Troy, you took my baby from us." Her voice was accusing. A mother's heartache was on display. "But Manny sent you to us...ta help with our healing. Manny lives through, you just like he lives through us. He's actually working through you, Troy."

Troy was slumped in the love seat but obviously attentive to what Ms. Goslin was saying.

She continued, "We accept your apology and your sincerity. And we accept you as our family. I asked about your plans because I wanna know that your mind is made up. Manny believes in you, and we do too. This won't be easy, but I believe we can walk through it together."

When Ms. Goslin concluded, Troy saw the same exhaustion in her that he felt when he finished talking. He got up, held Taj in his left arm, walked to the couch, and embraced both women as they stood to receive him. They hugged him tight with love.

There would be plenty of growing pains, but they had a good start in the Goslin living room.

Chapter 25

$\diamond\diamond\diamond\diamond\diamond\diamond$

February 25, 2003, Tanika and her man, Michael, sat in the maternity ward of Brigham and Women's hospital with Tinina, their one-day-old daughter. They played checkers as Tinina lay asleep on her chest. Michael was the proudest father in the world. Tinina had smooth light-chocolate skin that looked, by the darkness of her ears, like she would get even darker. She was the prettiest baby he ever saw.

Tanika Lopes was undoubtedly the love of his life. He admired her from afar, for months, before he was even able to build up the courage to speak. She was the reason that he signed up for a membership at the Dorchester YMCA instead of at a location closer to home. He stopped through to work out a couple of times but ended up watching her work out more than he exercised.

Before he left the building after his second visit, he asked the young clerk if she was a member. The answer was in the affirmative, so he filled out the necessary paperwork on the spot.

Even after Michael had his membership and began attending regularly, he still couldn't work up the courage to approach her. He was very confident in his looks, but his experiences with meeting women were limited. Most of the women that he had in his life approached him. He was handsome and successful, but when a woman that he was interested in didn't make the first move, like the one he watched at the YMCA, he was clueless.

Michael didn't spend much of his leisure time in Boston. He was from Cambridge, and though it was right across the bridge, the cities were very much different.

He grew up a couple of miles from Harvard University's main campus, to upper-middle-class parents, and was a successful investor himself at twenty-seven.

He stood in front of the full-body mirror on the wall, checking out his toned biceps as he curled some dumbbells. His whole body was nicely sculpted on a five-ten, 160-pound frame. He was often compared with the actor Morris Chestnut and didn't mind the comparison one bit.

When he placed the dumbbells back on the rack and turned around, he saw the petite beauty that often crept into his dreams. She was just finishing up her medium-paced, hour-long jog on the treadmill and would be doing some light dumbbell work next.

He timed his move perfectly.

"Ya getting a good workout in?" Michael asked her as she approached.

She smiled. "Yes, I am." Then she picked up the five-pound dumbbells and began to curl.

Michael stood there feeling foolish. He had no idea what to say or do next. This woman had his tongue tied. He figured by asking her a question, combined with his good looks, a conversation would naturally start. *Damn!*

As she worked out, she peeped him staring and smiled inwardly, knowing that he was shy. Tanika thought that it was cute. It was a major turn-on. She watched him watching her over the past couple of months and always gave him a little extra to see. Since he finally made an attempt, she figured she'd stop being a tease and find out who this extrafine gentleman was.

She put the dumbbell back and made her introduction. "How you doing? My name's Tanika," she said while stretching herself out, not giving him her full attention.

Michael was surprised by the sudden forwardness. It caused him to get nervous. "Ah, oh. My name's Michael…Michael Herbert. Nice ta meet you."

His proper tongue made her giggle. She was well versed in formal conversations, but she didn't expect this to be one. She spoke very proper also but was hood raised and recognized instantly that he wasn't.

"Where you from, handsome?" She was enjoying herself now.

"Oh…who, me? I'm from Cambridge."

"You mean to tell me you come all the way over the bridge just to see me?" she joked but knew that there was truth to it. "I see you watching me, Michael Herbert."

Michael blushed. His eyes went from side to side when she looked up to lock into them.

"Nah…I-I'm not a stalker or nothing like that…" He couldn't believe how stupid he sounded.

Tanika kept on with her game. "Oh," she said, faking disappointment. "I thought it was nice to have such a handsome stalker."

They both laughed. Her attitude lightened the mood, and they slid into conversation.

After that day, they went on many dates, then went on to start a steady relationship. They were a beautiful couple in every way. Now, seven years later, Michael was ready to tie the knot.

He smiled as he reminisced about their beginning and where they were now. He stared at Tanika and Tinina in the hospital bed. The most precious girls in the world to him.

Though she and Michael were in the same hospital room, Tanika was off in her own world as they moved and jumped pieces on the checkerboard. While he reminisced about their beginning, all she could think about was Troy. She thought about the first time he took her body in her office. It might have been the best sexual experience she'd ever had. She had been anticipating it so much.

As soon as he shot his heavy, backed-up load of semen inside of her, she knew she was pregnant. It felt too "on time."

She promised him that she would never do anything to come between him and his woman, and she meant it. She thought about telling him but ultimately decided against it. He was already dealing with too much with his trial, being locked up, and betrayal from every angle. She refused to be an added concern.

She contemplated getting an abortion for everyone's sake but couldn't bring herself to do it. She loved him and his seed too much to destroy it. Troy didn't want her, so she made the decision to keep her secret. She was his secret lover. Trina was the love of his life. It hurt, but she chose the role and had to wear it.

If she told him while he was facing life in prison and at odds with Trina, it wouldn't have been fair for anyone. She didn't want him to choose her under those conditions. She wanted what Trina had, his whole heart.

She knew that he felt deeply for her also, but she never pressed him to express those feelings beyond his norm. She did her best to never cross that line, but if he ever came to her and wanted to cross that line, she would accept him and never let go.

Her plan was to tell him that she was nearly four months pregnant when she called him to her office the day after he won his trial. She figured he would have a clear, realistic mind, so it would no longer be unfair to lay it on him and see where he stood. Before she was able to get to it, he was honest in professing his love and commitment to Trina.

After she cried her heart out that day, she made up her mind. She would stop her relationship with him and ride out her pregnancy and life with Michael.

She didn't want Troy to think that she was bitter, so she finally answered his call, after a week, when he came home and allowed him over. Even though she gained thirteen pounds, her stomach wasn't protruding yet. Troy didn't know the signs of a pregnant woman. He just constantly complimented her on how thick she was getting.

He was a romantic. Tanika knew that he would want to make love to her after nearly two years locked up and four months of quickies. She played the aggressor to keep him off her large melons, then lay uncharacteristically in a T-shirt when they were done. She explained her position to him. She let him know that she was getting married to Michael and that they had to stop seeing each other.

To her surprise, Troy became jealous. He tried to play it cool and act unfazed, but she saw straight through the act. His ego wouldn't accept her absolute rejection. He told her that she just needed a little time and that was how he really saw it.

The day after she was with Troy, she packed up and moved to Cambridge with Michael. Troy called her phones and even checked her job but could not get in touch with her. She went on maternity leave from work and eventually transferred to Middlesex County Jail in Cambridge. She avoided all possible places she would run into Troy.

Tanika stared across the checkerboard at her fiancé as she continued to reminisce. After Troy left her house that day, she told Michael that she needed a couple of hours alone. She needed that time to shed her last tears, then her decision was final. Michael rushed to her house and cuddled the rest of the night away with her. Three days later, he proposed.

She loved him, there was no question about that, but it wasn't even close. Troy owned her heart. She could live happily with Michael, though. Yeah, she would be a good wife to him. She kissed Tinina on the head and smiled sincerely at Michael. He smiled back at his two girls and felt like a champion.

*****

Troy and Trina sat at a restaurant around the corner from Brighams and Women's Hospital. He picked her up from the hospital on her lunch break to show some extra appreciation for the birthday party she threw for him. It was off the hook.

As they ordered, laughed, and kicked it, Troy saw a flash of terror in her eyes. She froze in midconversation.

He turned his head and saw Powder, Leon, and Tai approaching fast and aggressively. All three of them were from the A-Team.

Powder reached in the waistline of his jeans, then a loud clack was heard.

"I'mma tear ya muthafuckin' head off if you keep reachin'," King snarled. He pointed a .45 in the A-Team members' direction.

Ham stood next to him with a .40-caliber Glock out.

"Fuck y'all thought, we was slippin' or something?"

Powder took his hands from his waist. The other two stood down.

Troy smirked as he watched his younger homies control the situation. Since he had come home, the projects were a bit protective of him. They recognized his change and new direction, respected it, but some thought he was too relaxed and off point. Some, like King and Ham, chose to personally make sure he was on point. They didn't mind rolling with him when he was casually out and about.

The two of them were laying low in a rental car outside of the restaurant when they spotted Powder and Leon walk in. They hopped out and crept in right behind them.

Tai was already in a booth eating. He jumped up when he saw his partners moving with a purpose.

"Whoa, whoa, whoa," Buff yelled as he emerged from the bathroom and witnessed the chaos.

"Oh shit!" Steady yelped in shock.

They both walked into the scene, coming back from a bathroom trip.

Troy and Steady locked eyes. It was a silent communication. They had always been cool. Troy was not about to dishonor that now. He caught Buff's eye too. The vibe was the same as Steady's. Their awkward camaraderie was still intact.

Steady and Buff could've killed Troy on many occasions, including when he picked up Trina on their first date.

Troy turned to Leon. "Lee, tell Powder don't pull the burner out." It was a stern warning.

Leon gritted but complied. "Chill out, Powder."

Leon and Troy always had a decent relationship through Tanyah. They were siblings, and Tanyah always spoke highly of Troy.

The restaurant they were in was only a half mile from the hood, but there was zero urban vibe there. The bystanders were in all out panic mode. What was being witnessed was far from their norm.

Troy looked at his homies. "Chill out, dogg."

King stood down, but Ham looked uncertain.

Troy gave an assuring nod, and he lowered his .40.

"Stop her," Troy said, pointing at a woman behind the counter. She was reaching for a phone.

"Don't do that, bitch," King barked. "Matter fact, all you muthafuckas keep ya hands where I can see 'em!"

Everyone obliged.

Steady asked Powder, "What up wit ya'll?"

"Man, you know what's up!" Powder spat at his man. "This muthafucka think shit sweet!" He pointed at Troy.

Trina sat frozen. Neither she nor Troy expected to run into anyone from Academy Homes in this part of town.

"Yo," Buff began, but Troy stood up and cut in.

"Dig this, Powder. I ain't on that kid shit no more. On doggs." He pointed at Steady and Buff's direction, "Those are my mans." He touched Trina's shoulder. "And this is my wife. I ain't got no beef with you, dogg." He looked at the other two. "I ain't got beef wit none of y'all."

"My man is dead," Tai jumped in. "Shit ain't easy as that."

Troy remained calm. "All of our mans is dead, yo." He was calm, but not passive. He clearly had the upper hand. "We been bodying each other forever, yo. This shit's corny. I ain't ya enemy. I—"

Buff cut in. "Listen y'all, this ain't the place for this. These people tryna call the police and shit. We gotta bounce. Trust me though…we spoke ta Troy a few times since he touched down. We all need ta kick it." He looked at Troy. "Ya wanna meet at the park tomorrow?"

Troy knew he meant Washington Park. Even though Washington Park was basically the A, it was symbolically a neutral site in Boston. He had to trust his instincts. "That's cool," he told Buff.

It was that simple. Troy guided a still-shaken Trina to her feet, nodded to his opposition, and stepped off with his crew. He simply told King and Ham that he would explain more when he saw them in OP. They pulled off in their rental, and he pulled off with Trina.

The A-Team bounced in their whips in the opposite direction.

"You aight, baby?" Troy asked Trina on the way back to her job.

"No. Okay?" She wasn't concerned with herself at all.

He sighed. "We knew this shit was gonna be tough." He paused to think. "I'mma grab my peoples, and we gonna go see what up tomorrow."

"I hope y'all can squash that shit."

"Me too." He leaned over and kissed her cheek. "Go get back ta them crazy-ass patients of yours."

She laughed and punched his shoulder. "Stop talking about my patients. I don't work with crazy people." She opened the door and stepped out. When she closed the door, she leaned in the window. "I love you, Troy."

He smirked. "I know you do. You better."

She smiled, too, then walked back into work.

As Tanika and Michael were leaving the hospital with Tinina, Trina was walking into the lobby, returning from her lunch break. The two women never spoke beyond a simple greeting at Northeastern University, but Trina recognized the friendly face and spoke.

"Hey! How you been?" Trina asked excitedly as she approached.

Tanika fought to remain calm.

"Sorry," Trina continued. "I can't remember ya name, but I never forget a face."

Tanika literally forced a smile. "It's Tanika," she said. Then she followed up with, "Trina, right?"

"Yeah! What brings you ta my j-o-b?" she joked.

"Oh." Tanika's forced smile remained as she got even more uncomfortable. "Me and my fiancé just had a baby." She placed a proud hand on Michael's shoulder. "This is Michael."

"Nice ta meet you, Michael," Trina said.

He smiled and extended his hand. "Nice to meet you too, Trina."

"Boy or girl?" she asked, figuring they would have a beautiful child.

"Baby girl! Two days old," Michael answered proudly. "Her mother stole all the looks. They have identical eyes. She's my little princess. She gave us quite a scare, though." He nodded as he thought about it but never stopped smiling. "She's almost a month early."

"Wow! I just threw a big party for my boyfriend two days ago! While we was partying, you was pushing," Trina joked. "You remember my boyfriend, Troy? He was only part-time but stayed two years."

The mention of Troy's name from Trina in front of Michael made Tanika more uncomfortable than a goldfish among sharks. She tried to keep her composure. "N-no...I never knew you had a boyfriend at school."

"Yeah, he just came and went. Not many people noticed him. Hey!" Trina said as an afterthought. "Can I take a peek at ya little princess?"

Oh no! Tanika thought. As Michael proudly went to remove the blanket from Tinina's carriage, chills shot through Tanika and goose bumps filled her body.

Trina bent down to see the baby, and Tanika felt like her knees were going to give out. *No! Please! Please! Please!*

Michael was so happy to show off his daughter he completely missed Trina's head jerk back and do a triple take when she saw Tinina's face. Tanika didn't miss it. It stopped her heartbeat. Trina looked up into Michael's face, but he was too busy smiling and admiring his little princess to notice. Tanika knew that Trina was studying his features. Her fear turned to terror.

"Congratulations! S-she's...she's," Trina said, unable to snap out of her shock. She thought she was losing her mind. She thought her anxiety medication was messing with her. Their little princess was Taj's twin. She squatted down on both knees and looked at the little girl like they were long-lost friends. "What's her name?" she asked without looking up.

"Tinina Francesca Herbert!" Michael gloated.

It felt like Tinina was communicating with her, like they were somehow connected. Trina shook off the effect, knowing that black people were deeply rooted, and really just admired Tinina's beauty.

"You got a beautiful daughter," she repeated to Tanika as she rose up.

"T-thank you." Tanika's lip trembled with the forced smile now. Tanika couldn't look Trina in the eyes for longer than a few seconds at a time. Her mind was playing tricks on her.

She knows.

No, she doesn't know that Tinina is Troy's daughter, but she knows that she isn't Michael's daughter.

But nothing added up with her and Troy, so how could Trina know? Troy was only home for four months. Trina had no idea that they even knew each other. Most importantly, Trina didn't know where she worked. If Trina knew even one of the factors that Tanika was thinking about, she would've been suspicious about their little princess, who, to a woman's eye, obviously wasn't Michael's biological daughter. Tinina's resemblance to Taj and her being Troy's daughter shouldn't cross Trina's mind.

They all shared a few more minutes in the lobby. Trina wished them the best, then they went their separate ways.

Tanika's heart was racing at Olympic sprint speeds. Beads of sweat had already formed above her brow.

Michael was still beaming.

Trina shook her head as she walked toward the elevator. The experience was strange.

Chapter 26

◆◆◆◆◆

Troy, Peanut, and Amin stuck to the game plan. The day after Troy had the confrontation with the A in the restaurant, about twenty Trailblazers met up with the same number of A-Team affiliates at Washington Park. The meeting was heated at times, but after a few hours of back-and-forth, one of the sincerest peace treaties was formed between the two hoods.

Kendrick and Draymon copped the last load of coke from Peanut, then they were introduced to the connect themselves. The streets were their bread and butter, and they had no intentions of relinquishing them. Kendrick grew up in the same building with Troy. Draymon lived on the other side of the park.

Hemenway encouraged Troy to purchase a house in Brighton, near his own Brookline home. "A new life calls for a new environment," he told him. It was a family and a business move.

He took things slow with Trina, but their bond was so natural that the pieces to their puzzle still fit perfectly. The closure that came to him, her, and Ms. Goslin as a result of the truth coming out relieved all of them of tremendous pain. They were actually able to move forward in life like never before. After Troy's being home for five months, Trina and Taj moved in with him and once again made his house their home. Their spirits were finally free. Their beings at peace with one another.

Amin had gotten into a serious relationship with Ky, but they didn't go as far as moving in with each other. She was a pretty bronze number who loved to drink and party. She would've never slowed down without Amin's strength. He was always her first choice. His cheating felt like such a betrayal in their past it sent her on a whirlwind. She was two months pregnant, about to make him the final father from his circle.

Amin kept her brother, Martin, all the way away from him. Martin was getting big money in the streets but was moving recklessly. Amin allowed no room to get caught up in a conspiracy with him. Ky didn't associate with him either, which made keeping a safe distance a lot easier.

The streets never found out the truth of who or what Martin was. He was accepted in many circles with open arms and mistakenly respected as being a "stand-up" dude. He still fed DEA agent Story information from time to time and received favors in return.

Peanut and Danisha were tighter than ever. Angel was growing up fast and a lot more stable under the union of her parents. They also copped a home in Brighton, and he wasted no time putting a large diamond on her finger as a housewarming present.

They all learned their new avenues of business together, on the fly, and enjoyed every step of it. They didn't duck out when difficulties arose in the streets, so they refused to duck anything in their new field of operation.

Troy opened two more New Edition locations, one in downtown Boston and one in Fall River. They were a huge success. Ella managed the downtown location, and Troy had his homegirl, Sol, run the one in Fall River. The women around him ran everything when it came to the New Edition chain.

It was still a work in progress for the women to heal their wounds among one another, but they were working it out.

Ella was very much still family. She finally moved on and stopped holding on to Jermel, her Chubby. She got into a healthy relationship with Mustafa, from Egleston. He was the strength in a man that she needed. They moved in to an apartment in the same Hyde Park neighborhood as Joyce and Liona. She hung out with them daily.

Trina loved working at Brigham and Women's Hospital and continued to do so. She cut her hours significantly in order to spend more time with Taj and assist in what became the family business.

She dedicated everything to the two males in her life and rediscovered the joy that was missing in Troy's absence.

Troy's first year out had more ups than downs, but it was definitely a rubber band. He was so mentally prepared for the challenge that true change brings that nothing could stop his forward progress. He continued to study and work hard and led by example.

He went by Hemenway's home often. That was his place of solace. He went by to get advice and just to kick it. Mrs. Hemenway treated him like one of her own grandchildren. She was always ready to cook and lay out the red carpet when he came around. The Hemenways were one of his main sources of information, morality, and drive.

Hemenway retired from the courtroom and chose to strictly teach at the UMass Boston campus. He had been teaching there for over twenty years and found real joy rather than work in teaching. When he retired, he was satisfied with his career, especially after winning Troy's case. Troy Newton was his family. He knew that he made the right decision in getting him acquitted of Manny Goslin's murder. That was true justice. Justice for Troy. Justice for Manny. Justice for both families. Justice for this world. He loved being Troy's mentor. Troy listened, which was why he learned so fast. Hemenway hardly ever had to repeat himself with him, but Troy asked him to at times because he loved hearing so many of his lessons and stories. Yes, the world was a better place with Troy Newton in it.

*****

Even though Jermel crossed a line that he could never return from, Troy couldn't deny the love that still existed in his heart for him. They had stood side by side from the womb. That type of love wasn't easy to erase. He would never forgive him, though. It was probably easier to feel for him in death, because if Jermel were alive, Troy had no doubt that he would kill him in a worse way than Chris did. Through it all, he had to recognize his own faults also. He strived not to make excuses, only amends.

Jermel, Chris, Manny, and Jimmy were all buried at the same Mattapan cemetery. Troy had made the tough trip to visit them once a month the entire year he was home. He kicked it with their spirit and welcomed their nearness. It was a unique vibe at each one of their grave sites, even though they were all within two hundred yards of each other. He had a deep understanding of the fact that each headstone represented a man who had a divine impact on his own life. Each one symbolized the essence of an individual who seemed to be sent to this earth partially to assist in his protection, path, and perfection. He loved them all. He owed his living life to their death.

Neither Troy, Amin, nor Peanut took their success for granted. They escaped the concrete jungle with their lives and freedom. That alone was an amazing accomplishment. The hood was still at war. People that they knew and knew of were dying and going to prison at a rapid rate. A plus was that the A and OP still moved relatively in peace.

The fact that an early grave could've easily been theirs never slipped their minds. Troy was especially grateful that his escape included two of his best friends, his brothers. Amin and Peanut. He was with the woman of his dreams, his soul mate, whom he would soon marry. His son adored him. His life was great.

Tanika's absence left a void. He loved her but had to respect her decision and hoped that she was happy. He was happy, but not satisfied. He knew that there was a lot more to his story. This was merely the beginning.

About the Author

Tee is a lifelong resident of Boston, Massachusetts. He attended Delaware State University from 1997 to 2001.

Raised in the streets, he spent a very large portion of his life incarcerated in the state and federal system.

He is currently an advocate for restorative justice practices in the legal and school systems throughout the country, as well as a mentor inside of his communities.

He teaches four principles that he feels are a must for any individual or community to properly grow and prosper:

Knowledge of self

Spirituality

Unity

Financial literacy

It is his hope that you enjoy his readings as well as learn from them.

CPSIA information can be obtained
at www.ICGtesting.com
Printed in the USA
LVHW091552010521
686193LV00004B/102

9 781646 543960